Advance Praise for S

"In *State of Lies*, Siri Mitchell has penned a page turner that I literally couldn't put down. I confess I kept reading when I should've been writing my own novel. My heart breaks with Georgia Brennan as she suffers blow after blow when a past she didn't even know she had catches up with her. Readers will applaud her resilience and determination to solve the mystery and save the lives of the people she loves—even when the face of the boogeyman turns out to be someone she never expected. Don't miss this thrilling ride!"

—KELLY IRVIN, BESTSELLING AUTHOR OF
TELL HER NO LIES AND *OVER THE LINE*

"In *State of Lies*, Siri Mitchell has created a story that will suck you in and not let go. With twists and turns, international intrigue, and danger galore, this book reads like a psychological thriller mixed with healthy doses of suspense. It's also wonderfully written with an attention to detail that had me seeing my former haunts in Arlington, Virginia."

—CARA PUTMAN, AUTHOR OF
THE HIDDEN JUSTICE SERIES

Praise for Siri Mitchell

"Stunning . . . this story is sure to impress."
—*PUBLISHERS WEEKLY* ON *RUINS OF LACE*

"A fascinating story not only about lace, but about obsession, corruption, and self-worth. The ending is tantalizingly ambiguous."
—HISTORICAL NOVEL SOCIETY ON *RUINS OF LACE*

"A well-paced and interwoven story . . . Anthony [Siri Mitchell] creates a narrative that subtly educates, poses stimulating questions and entertains."

—*KIRKUS* ON *THE MIRACLE THIEF*

"Fast-paced and engrossing . . . The book's wealth of historic detail will transport you back in time, and Anthony's plucky heroines will have you alternately biting your nails over their plights and cheering over their triumphs. Hope, faith, courage, inspiration, love—this book has it all. Highly recommended!"

—SHERRY JONES, AUTHOR OF *THE SHARP HOOK OF LOVE*, ON *THE MIRACLE THIEF*

"Christy-nominated Mitchell's latest flawlessly crafted novel is a quietly powerful tale of love, faith, and hope set in Puritan New England. With its brilliantly formed characters and vividly detailed setting, this tale combines the best elements of inspirational and historical fiction into a richly emotional, unforgettable story."

—*BOOKLIST* ON *LOVE'S PURSUIT*

"Christy Award winner Mitchell makes a successful historical debut, immersing readers in the rich historical detail of Queen Elizabeth's court."

—*RT BOOK REVIEWS* ON *A CONSTANT HEART*

"A skillful mix of tense family drama, historical romance, and memorable characters that will stay with readers."

—*LIBRARY JOURNAL* ON *A HEART MOST WORTHY*

"A well-written, enthralling historical novel, *The Messenger* will not disappoint."

—*PORTLAND BOOK REVIEW*

STATE

OF

LIES

OTHER BOOKS BY SIRI MITCHELL

STATE

OF

LIES

SIRI MITCHELL

THOMAS NELSON
Since 1798

Published in Nashville, Tennessee, by Thomas Nelson. Thomas Nelson is a registered trademark of HarperCollins Christian Publishing, Inc.

Interior design by Lori Lynch

Thomas Nelson titles may be purchased in bulk for educational, business, fund-raising, or sales promotional use. For information, please email SpecialMarkets@ThomasNelson.com.

Publisher's Note: This novel is a work of fiction. Names, characters, places, and incidents are either products of the author's imagination or used fictitiously. All characters are fictional, and any similarity to people living or dead is purely coincidental.

Library of Congress Cataloging-in-Publication Data

Names: Mitchell, Siri L., 1969- author.
Title: State of lies / Siri Mitchell.
Description: Nashville, Tennessee : Thomas Nelson, [2019]
Identifiers: LCCN 2019007287 | ISBN 9780785228615 (paperback)
Subjects: LCSH: Murder--Investigation--Fiction. | Man-woman relationships--Fiction. | GSAFD: Mystery fiction. | Suspense fiction.
Classification: LCC PS3613.I866 S73 2019 | DDC 813/.6--dc23 LC record available at https://lccn.loc.gov/2019007287

Printed in the United States of America

19 20 21 22 23 LSC 5 4 3 2 1

For Milt and Joyce
and for Tony, always.

Since quantum physics allows for multiple possibilities
simultaneously, these possibilities should then
keep existing, even after a measurement is made.
But they don't. Every possibility but one vanishes.
We do not see any of the others around us.

—Christophe Galfard, *The Universe in Your Hand: A Journey
Through Space, Time, and Beyond*

1

FEBRUARY

Sean was already pulling his shirt off over his head as he came into the bedroom.

I held up a corner of the comforter as an invitation. But not too far. The damp of a drizzly week had seeped into the house.

He stepped out of his jeans and then slid in beside me.

I nestled against him. Felt him cringe as my cold feet brushed up against him.

"Sorry."

He pulled me into his embrace. "One of these days they're going to fall off." He nuzzled my neck.

I wrapped my arms around him. "They already did. These are the replacements."

I felt his lips curl into a smile as he kissed me again.

Sean was doing that thing he does—the one that made my toes curl—when my phone twanged out the beginning notes of "Sweet Home Alabama."

My mother.

I gripped his shoulder and tried my best to ignore the phone because married sex was my personal holy grail. Always elusively tantalizing, just out of reach. I'd even put it on Sean's weekend to-do list, just after "sharpen the knives" and right before "fix the sink." It was okay because our son, Sam, was still in preschool; he didn't know how to read. That afternoon, however, our window of opportunity was about to come sliding down right on top of our fingers. Sam was down for the count due to a cold, though I expected him to wake up soon.

But the phone kept ringing.

The drums started thumping and the cymbals clashed.

I must have wavered because Sean folded me within his arms. "Georgie. Don't." He nibbled at my neck. "If you want me to, I'll throw the phone across the room for you."

"No! Shh. You'll wake up Sam—"

He rolled, switching our positions, leaving me on top.

"—and he needs the sleep to get over that cold he's been fighting."

When I put a hand to his chest and stretched for the phone, he captured my reaching arm and planted a kiss on the inside of my wrist. "She doesn't know we hear her. We could be at the mall. We could be having drinks with friends. We could be at the movies." He kissed me on the lips. "We could be doing this."

His hypnotic brown eyes began to sway me, and then mercifully, the phone stopped twanging.

He relaxed; I relaxed. Things were just getting interesting again when the phone erupted with a drum cadence that quickly segued into a marching version of "You're a Grand Old Flag."

My father.

Both of them were calling me? That wasn't a good sign. I shifted beneath Sean. "Just give me a minute, then—"

"We're in the middle of something here."

"I know." I sat up, trying to pull the sheet with me. "I know. I'm sorry." I stretched for the phone.

Sean gave up and rolled toward his side of the bed.

I swept my hair from my face with one hand as I answered. "Dad. Hi."

"Peach? Your mother wants to talk to you."

"I know. I heard. But I couldn't—"

"Do me a favor. You know how she is. Call her." He hung up before I could say anything else.

Couldn't he have just passed her his phone? Or told me what she wanted?

Sean was right. I shouldn't have answered.

But in the interest of forestalling another interruption, I returned my mother's call.

"Georgia Ann?" Her Southern accent hadn't mellowed with age. Come to think of it, nothing about her had mellowed with age.

"Hi. Sorry, I just—"

"Did you get that picture I texted you from the magazine? The one of that hairstyle? That model has the same long nose you do, and I've been telling you for practically forever that . . ."

I sent a glance over my shoulder in Sean's direction as she continued to speak.

He lifted one of his black brows and then settled on his back, folding his arms behind his head.

"Well? Did you?"

"Sorry. What?"

"The hairstyle. The one I sent you."

"It kind of looked more like a wig."

Sean sighed and closed his eyes.

"Extensions, I think. But that wouldn't be so bad, would it? You're so busy with Sam. A few extensions would give it some body. And you wouldn't have to mess with it. Besides, if you find someone who can match colors, how could anyone ever guess?"

I cupped my hand around my mouth when I answered, trying to keep Sean from hearing what I'd given up sex for. "I am not getting extensions." And my nose wasn't *that* big. "And I'm kind of in a hurry. Can I call you back later?"

"I just wanted you to be the first to hear the good news. Your father heard it straight from Scott Edwards."

"Scott Edwards?"

"From *Scottie*. The secretary of defense?"

"Right." *That* Scottie Edwards.

"He's resigning. Might not even hold out to the end of the year and . . ." She chattered on.

I'd given up sex for military gossip? I hated myself. I really did. And I wouldn't have blamed Sean for hating me too.

"And guess what?"

"Mom, I really don't have time right now."

"I'll just tell you: the president has taken Scottie's suggestion of nominating your father as his replacement—"

"Great! That's great. Dad must be really—"

"—so we'll be moving to DC."

"DC? Wow!" DC? No! I was a big girl, all grown up with a family of my own until my parents appeared. And then? I might as well be ten years old again. At least in my mother's view.

Sean's brows had collapsed.

I answered his unasked question with a look of horror as I replied to my mother. "I don't know what to say."

"I know! It's all so exciting. I knew you'd be happy for your father. Speaking of, he'd like to talk to Sean sometime."

"I'll let Sean know, okay? But really, I need to go."

"Say no more." Punctuality was one of the virtues my mother held sacred. Right up there with Respect for Your Elders, Patriotism, and Really Good Hair Dye. "We can talk tomorrow."

I was just about to sign off when her words registered. "Tomorrow?"

"When we get there."

"There *where*?"

"To DC. We fly in around three."

"You're coming *here*? *Tomorrow*?"

"We'll let you know when we land. Can't wait to see you!"

I switched my phone to silent, then burrowed back under the covers and scooted over to Sean's side of the bed. I told myself not to worry about their visit. I would deal with them when they showed up.

"They're not going to call again, are they?" Sean shifted to face me and ran his hands up my arms.

"They . . . uh . . . they might."

"Hmm?" He was nuzzling my ear again.

"They might call back. Mom said Dad wanted to talk to you." I nipped at his neck. Pressed closer.

"Me? Why?"

"I don't know." I pulled his face toward mine and kissed him. "They'll be here tomorrow, though; he'll probably tell you then. Sounds like he's going to be the next secretary of defense."

Sean kissed me back. "Sorry. What?"

I traced the tattoo that ran around his bicep. "Secretary of defense. Scott Edwards is going to resign. The president's going to nominate my father to take his place."

"Mommy?" Sam's plaintive cry filtered through the door.

We froze and then sprang apart as if we were teenagers about to be caught by our parents.

By the time Sam emerged from the cozy burrow of his bed, Sean was already at the front door, sliding his feet into his old hiking boots.

Sam ran over to him. Somewhere between his room and the front hall, one of his socks had come off. His honey-colored hair stuck up in back where it had been pressed against the pillow. "Where are you going? Can I go?"

Sean held something up, then shoved it into his pocket. "Have to fix the sink." He glanced up as I approached. "Isn't that what comes next?"

I'd put it on the list to jog his memory. He'd told me back when we first moved in that he would fix it. I was trying my best not to nag.

"If I'm going to do it, I need to find the right parts."

Sam was hopping up and down. "Can I go?"

"Not today. Too cold out. Stay with Mom and keep warm."

Sam gave me the side-eye. The look said, in no uncertain terms, that staying home with Mom was not a very good consolation prize.

I cleared my throat. "Um . . ."

Sean turned toward me as he zipped up his coat.

"Can we circle back to the things on the list that we didn't quite get to finish?" I felt so sneaky, talking in code.

The corner of his mouth quirked. "We could just push them back to next weekend. Make a new list."

"No. We can't."

He wanted to laugh. I could tell. But he laid a hand on Sam's head. "Let's play Legos when I get back, Super Sam." He sent me a glance. "And maybe we can check a few more things off your mom's list too."

He leaned over Sam to kiss me and then walked out the door.

Two hours later, Sean still hadn't returned.

I tried his phone.

It went to voice mail.

Again.

Hey. It's Sean. Let me know where to reach you so I can give you a call back.

<beep>

2

I wandered into the kitchen and eyed the faucet, wondering if whatever Sean had taken with him would keep it from running. A careful turn of the handles showed it hadn't made any difference.

Rain was pummeling the window above the sink. At least I wasn't out in it the way Sean was. But even so, our old 1920s bungalow came with a built-in draft that circulated about two inches above the floor. It also came with twelve-foot ceilings. Draft; high ceilings. Life was a trade-off.

Sam was hungry and I couldn't delay dinner forever, so I dished us up our servings and we ate together in front of the TV exactly the way I swore to my mother that I never did.

When I tried to steer him toward bed later, he balked. "Dad said we'd play Legos."

"And you will. But it's your bedtime soon and you can't play if you're asleep."

"Daddy said!"

I put a hand on his head to calm him. "I know he did. He'll kiss you when he comes back. And I'm sure he'd love to play with you tomorrow."

As Sam finished up the episode of his TV show, I called Sean's phone again. He didn't pick up.

Eventually I shooed Sam down the hall to his room. Once prayers were said and one . . . two . . . *three* stories read, I kissed him good night and then curled up on the couch in the living room, pulling a blanket over me. Our dog lifted her head, eyeing me as if wondering whether it would be worth the effort to join me.

Apparently not.

Shifting, I parted the curtains and stared out past the front porch into the night. Raindrops glittered like tracer bullets as they fell through the streetlight's diameter, but the light's glow didn't illuminate the ground. It just left silvery smudges on the asphalt.

I let the curtains settle back into place. Tried to talk myself out of the uneasiness that was starting to flutter around in my gut.

Finding a part for an old faucet at one of those home warehouse stores couldn't be easy. But calling me wouldn't have been hard.

I wished it would stop raining.

Drivers in the DC area were notorious. "Powdered Idiots," Sean called them. "Just add water."

Our dog, Alice, huffed a sigh.

"Amen."

She flicked an ear. I wouldn't have called a 150-pound mastiff Alice, but she'd already had the name when we got her.

I'd just started reading a well-thumbed copy of my favorite Asimov novel when I heard footsteps on the stairs outside.

My apprehension lifted away like a helium-filled balloon. Throwing off the blanket, I vaulted toward the door, ready to shush Sean. Sam didn't usually wake up after he'd fallen asleep, but wouldn't it have been just our luck for him to do it that night?

I yanked the door open. "Shh! You're going to—"

It wasn't Sean.

Two men dressed in identical blue uniforms, each holding a rain-flecked hat, stood in front of me. Their faces were sallow in the porch light. "Mrs. Brennan?"

Alice had gotten up and ambled over to see what was happening. As she nudged me aside with a push of her head to my hip, the men took a step back.

"There's been an accident."

I leaned out over Alice and glanced up and down the rain-slicked street. An accident? "Where?" I hadn't heard any sirens. Didn't see any flashing lights.

They exchanged a glance. "Not here. In Falls Church."

"Then why are you—" Realization hit me with the impact of a sledgehammer. "Sean?" With his name came the last bit of air I had in my lungs. Clearing my throat, I tried to swallow an enormous lump of fear. "Is he all right? Where is he?"

"His car was hit. He didn't survive." They exchanged a glance. "We're sorry."

"What are you saying?" I looked from one to the other, trying to decode their words because I couldn't understand them. "Sean's not dead. That can't be what you're saying because he's not— No. *No*, it's just— He just went to get a part." I was so cold all of a sudden.

Alice stepped forward onto the porch, moving the men farther away from the door.

I had to try several times before I could force more words out. "It was a part for the faucet. It's not working. He took the part off so he could match it, to get a replacement. Only sometimes it's not easy because everything in the house is so old. Sometimes there aren't any replacements. Or they have to be special-ordered. It can take a while. So he's not dead. It's just taking a while. He said he'd be back."

"I'm sorry, Mrs. Brennan. Can we come in?"

I felt like I should offer them something. You didn't invite someone into your home and not offer them something. Not if you were raised properly; not if you were raised by my mother. "Can I . . ." Having made it into the living room, I thought for a moment before remembering what it was I wanted to ask them. "Tea? Coffee? Would you like something?"

"No, ma'am."

My teeth were starting to chatter. I clenched my jaw to try to stop them. But then my mother's training kicked in and I opened my mouth again. "Could you, would you like to . . ." I disguised a full-body shudder by gesturing toward the Alice-distressed brown leather couch that sat in front of the window. "Please."

"We just need to ask you a few questions."

I heard what they said. I must have. I remember answering

questions. And I must have asked them some in return because they told me what they knew.

The accident was a hit-and-run.

Sean's car was totaled.

He was dead.

They handed me a card with the phone number of the medical examiner's office. Asked me to go the next day to identify the body. As they were leaving, one of them paused in the doorway. "Will you be okay, ma'am?"

Sean was dead.

"What?" What was he saying? His mouth was moving, but I couldn't hear any words.

He put a hand on my arm.

I looked down at it.

"Is there someone we can call for you?"

I looked back up at him. "No. Yes." What was the question again? "No. No, I'll be fine. I just have to . . ." My hand was groping for something to hold on to. It found something. A leash. I seized it. Held it up. "If you'll excuse me, it's getting late. I have to walk the dog now. Before I go to bed."

I didn't normally walk Alice at night. Sean did. But if he wasn't . . . if he didn't . . . Alice needed someone to take her out. Sam was sleeping; there was no need to wake him. I only went down to the end of the block. I'd forgotten to take my umbrella, but I had remembered my phone. I called Sean again, willing him to answer, willing for it all to be a mistake.

It kept going to voice mail.

Hey. It's Sean. Let me know where to reach you so I can give you a call back.

<beep>

I didn't know what else to do, so I just kept calling, waiting for him to pick up.

When I got back to the house, I decided to try a different number. I called my mother instead.

"Mom? They told me Sean died."

"Georgia Ann?"

"Sean died. Sean's dead, Mom. He died."

She gasped. "What?" It was a guttural, Southern *whut*.

"He went to the store to get a part for the faucet and his car was hit and he died. Mom?" I'd made a list in my head while I was walking Alice. There were things I needed to do. Lots of them. I just couldn't remember what they were right then. "Mom? What do I do? I'm not sure. I don't know what to do now."

"You just hold yourself together."

"Yes, ma'am."

"We were flying in tomorrow anyway. I'll call and make them put us on an earlier flight."

"I just keep thinking I should have fixed the faucet. I could have fixed it when we first moved in and none of this would have happened. I've always been better at fixing things than he is."

"Georgia Ann, you listen to me, do you hear?"

"Yes, ma'am."

"This is not your fault."

Not my fault. She sounded so sure of it that I wanted to believe her.

"Mommy?" The call came from the hall. "Mommy?" It was Sam.

I closed my eyes. I hadn't even thought of Sam. What was I going to tell him? What was I supposed to tell our son?

"Georgia Ann? Are you still there? Georgia Ann! What's happening?"

"Mommy?" Sam appeared at the entrance to the living room, bleary-eyed and pale, sniffling from his cold. "Mommy? Where's Daddy? He was supposed to kiss me when he came home."

3

OCTOBER

I was sitting in the conference room at work surrepti-tiously trying to write my grocery list while my boss, Ted, was talking about our upcoming two-day red-team exercise. We were supposed to be playing devil's advocate on a group of proposals to make sure we weren't so in love with them that we'd overlooked the obvious or failed to anticipate our customers' criticisms. But Sam and I had just gotten back from a weekend trip we'd taken with my parents to the Eastern Shore and the refrigerator was bare.

I'd been doing better handling my parents in small doses since Sean had died. My father passed through DC regularly to visit companies on whose boards he sat or for whom he served as a consultant on classified projects. The trip to the shore, however, had been about a day too long. They just would not let up on trying to get Sam and me to move in with them once my father got confirmed as secretary of defense. They had bombarded me with a barrage of reasons throughout the weekend.

I forced myself to loosen my grip on my pen. Tried to relax my jaw.

Every few moments I sent a glance up at the whiteboard, which was illuminated with PowerPoint slides.

And then I wrote down the next item on my list.

Bananas.

"Georgie, you're going to be red-teaming with Mark, Bill, and Carl on the inertial navigation proposal."

"Right." *Applesauce.*

When I refocused on Ted, he was talking about my quantum encryption project.

"How's the test prep coming?" He was looking at me.

Our company was one of several contractors working on a quantum encryption project for the Department of Defense. The Chinese had taken the lead in quantum communication technology and there was an all-hands-on-deck effort to leapfrog them. If our product worked as we'd been promising, then it would put us one step closer to that objective. The goal was to use entanglement to make transmitted information self-report hacking attempts. If everything went as planned, if it passed its upcoming tests, it would be the ultimate in proactive cybersecurity.

"There's the test scheduled at White Sands in January. We had to cancel the last one because of a subcontractor issue. Everything looks set this time, though." He asked me about the details of the delay, then he changed the slide. He moved on to something else.

Cereal.

Multitasking was bad. I knew it was bad. My mother always said doing two things at once was like trying to catch a greased pig; it wasn't going to end well. When I was little I'd wondered why anyone would want to grease a pig and why anyone would want to catch one. But in my house, you didn't ask questions. You just fell in line and marched along.

I glanced up at the board.

And suddenly I couldn't breathe.

It felt like the bottom was dropping out of my soul. I locked my gaze on the whiteboard, trying to concentrate. If I could just concentrate, if I could just keep myself in the moment, then maybe everything would stabilize.

I tried. I heard Ted talking, but I couldn't decipher what he was saying.

I was used to grief creeping up on me unawares, but it hadn't yet done so at work during a meeting. As I stared at the slide, at the jumble of words, I could feel the tingling of rising tears. I blinked at them.

When that didn't work, I crooked a finger and pressed it beneath my eye, pretending to scratch an itch I didn't feel.

"Georgie?" Ted said my name as if he were repeating it.

"Yes! What?"

"Did you have an opinion?"

Opinion on what? I tried to focus again on the slide. Tried to discern what the topic was, but the words were meaningless. I couldn't even make them relate to each other. "Um . . . there are some things I would need to look into before I can offer an opinion. Can I get back to you on that?"

"On our next meeting? Just taking a vote. Next week or the week after?"

"Oh. Um . . ." My vision started to tunnel. My ears started to buzz. I wasn't going to be able to do it. I pushed away from the conference table, shoved my phone into my pocket, gathered my notebook to my chest. "Sorry." I forced a cough. "Water." I dashed down the hall to the bathroom, where I took refuge.

Any woman working in a male-dominated workplace learns to appreciate the women's bathroom. It's the only place where she can be herself. It was the only place where I could afford to show my grief.

Most of the time I couldn't do it at home. Not the way I wanted to. I couldn't yell and scream and rail against the accident that had taken Sean from me. When I left in the mornings, it was to take Sam to school on my way to work. When I returned in the evenings, it was always with Sam in hand. He stayed at school after classes ended, in an extended-day program, until I could pick him up after work.

I dropped my things on the counter by the sink and sought the privacy of a stall. I shoved the metal door closed. Before I could engage the lock, it bounced back toward me.

I shoved it again. Harder.

It swung back, clipping me in the chest.

I gasped, curling into the pain. Then I reached out and grabbed the door, slamming it shut again. The whole frame shook.

I did it again.

And again.

And then once more for good measure.

But it flew past the stop and bashed into the door of the neighboring stall.

I stood there panting for a few moments. Then, swiping at my tears, I took hold of the door and forced it back into position. I went and pulled my pen from the spiral on my notebook and used the cap to tighten all the screws.

Then I rinsed my face in the sink and patted it dry with paper towels. An advantage of never wearing makeup? I never had to worry about my mascara smudging. It was the one thing my mother had finally given up on. I gave myself a long, hard stare in the mirror, probing for any sign of weakness. Tried a smile.

Wobbly.

Tried again.

It would have to do.

At least I worked with a bunch of men. They would never notice.

The get-down-and-get-dirty process that was grief, the two-steps-forward-three-steps-back, had become the rhythm of my life. Most of the time weekends were better. At least during the day. There was so much to do at home that I rarely had time to think.

That Saturday Sam was with my friend Jenn, so I decided to finally tackle the kitchen sink. It was a day that felt slightly more like summer than fall. I'd opened the windows to let the breeze freshen the air. Then I got out my pliers and applied them to the faucet I had finally found the nerve to fix.

Didn't budge.

I went back down into the basement and dug around for my strap wrench.

I'd found out that work—physical work—was good therapy. I hadn't found the time to see an actual therapist, but I'd read all the books I could find. They offered the same advice. I was supposed to be patient with myself, validate all my emotions, and remain connected to the people around me. And I was.

My neighbors Jim and June had become surrogate parents to me and grandparents to Sam since my own lived so far away. My best friend, Jenn, and I saw each other a couple of times a week.

I couldn't be anything but grateful for the friends we had.

But as I fastened the strap around the pipe, I heard footsteps scuffing up the stairs to the front porch. Since Sean's death, it had been a sound that left me with a sense of profound dread.

4

When I heard the sound of footsteps, my neck began to prickle and my hearing began to fade. In a strange sort of way I was entangled with the memory of the night Sean had died. Though time and space separated me from his death, my body kept reacting as if it had just happened.

I'd learned that it was best to breathe deeply and try to carry on.

The doorbell rang.

Leaving the wrench dangling, I walked through the dining room and living room to the front door. Opened it to find Mr. Hoffman.

"I thought to come by today. I hope you will forgive me. I know today is difficult."

Difficult. That was the perfect word. It had been eight months exactly since Sean had died.

"There's nothing to forgive." I shook the hand he'd gravely offered.

Alice tried to push her way between us. I pushed her back with my knee. Then I opened the door wider to let him enter.

Out in the street, a gray car drove by, leaving the rustle of scattering dogwood leaves in its wake. As I shut the door, a smile lifted the corners of Mr. Hoffman's mouth and animated a face otherwise void of expression. He was wearing his usual dark suit, hat, and solid-colored tie. He was splendidly old-fashioned and quaintly European. He'd escaped from East Germany back in the sixties and found his way to America, where he'd opened a toy shop down in Crystal City.

Next to him, my frayed jeans and my Think Like a Proton and Stay Positive T-shirt looked even scruffier. "I'm trying to fix my faucet."

He shifted the bag he was carrying to his other hand and removed his hat, revealing the bald spot that had been slowly consuming an otherwise enviable mane of hair. He tucked the hat under his arm. "We have a saying in Germany on faucet."

I raised a brow.

"When faucet drips one must call the plumber."

I laughed. "We have that saying here too." I gestured toward the back of the house with a sweep of my chin. He followed me. "Coffee?"

He demurred with a frown and a shake of his head. "Please." He nodded toward the sink. "Continue. I must not stop you."

The aerator finally came loose with a couple of forceful pulls. I unscrewed it and held it up to the light. "A lot of buildup in there." It hadn't been cleaned in a long time. Maybe never. The good thing about mineral buildup was that it acted like cement. It kept everything together. Bad thing: it messed up the seal.

"Little Bear is not here?"

"He's at a friend's. Due back anytime." I was using Sam's play-dates to tackle the enormous to-do list that had accumulated since Sean had died. I kept telling myself I just had to do one thing at a time. But it seemed like every time I crossed one thing off, I added two things to the list in its place.

"Then this, I give you. To give to him." He gestured to the bag he'd placed on the floor at his feet.

I didn't have to look inside to know what it was. "Mr. Hoffman— you really have to stop!"

He shrugged. "He is a boy who misses his father."

"And another toy is going to help?" Actually, another wooden train to add to his collection of playsets probably *would* help. For a while.

Like many things in life, those too were my father's fault.

Dad had presented Sam with his first wooden train set just a few months after he was born. And over the years it had been joined by many others.

When he worked from DC, he'd come to dinner on Saturdays, new toy in hand, and play trains with Sam. Then, after Sam went to sleep, he'd stay and talk with Sean.

I was just the conduit for bourbon.

There was a period of time when Sean's reserve unit deployed and my father was so otherwise occupied that the additions to the playset had ground to a halt. Sam had begged me for something new, but I hadn't been able to find anything of similar quality online. I finally asked my dad where he'd found them. To my relief, his source was a toy shop—Mr. Hoffman's shop—just down the road, in the mall in Crystal City.

That's when I found out he'd escaped from East Germany with only the clothes on his back. His wife hadn't been so lucky. Before he'd been able to get her out, she'd died of pneumonia behind the Iron Curtain. Once he told me that, we'd had him join us for Easter. And Thanksgiving too.

He was a kind, dear man.

I took a mug from the cabinet, dropped the aerator in, and poured vinegar over it. I was hoping it would dissolve enough of the mineral deposits that I could clean it up and put it back on.

The doorbell rang again.

"That's probably Sam. You can give it to him yourself. Be right back."

My friend Jenn and her son, Preston, had returned Sam to me.

I stepped out onto the porch and leaned out over the boys to give her a hug.

When I wore a button-down shirt and jeans it always looked like I was planning on digging around in the yard. When she wore a button-down and jeans, like she was that day, it always gave me the impression of yachts, horses, and expensive estates on the Eastern Shore. She had that thing going on. But that afternoon she looked rumpled. And unhappy.

She kept me close. "Is there any way you could watch Preston for just an hour? I have some things I need to talk about with Mark. So we can come to an agreement on the divorce."

The crimp in her mouth and the line between her eyes let me know she wasn't looking forward to this talk.

"Sure. Yes. Of course."

I stepped aside so the boys could go in. Before they could tear through the house, I caught Sam at the elbow. "Mr. Hoffman's here. Why don't you go back to Sam's room, Preston, and let Sam come say hi first."

As Sam and I walked into the kitchen, Mr. Hoffman held the bag out to him. "Something for Little Bear."

"Cool!" Sam ran over and took the bag from him.

The delight on Mr. Hoffman's face as he watched Sam unwrap the gift? It transformed him. Sam didn't have a very good grasp of the calendar; there was no way he would have known how many months Sean had been gone. But it had been sweet of Mr. Hoffman to bring him a distraction.

Sam pulled a train and an add-on playset from the wrapping. "Wow! Thanks!"

Mr. Hoffman leaned forward. "And tell me: How is hockey lessons?"

"I'm really good!"

When Preston came wandering in, Mr. Hoffman stood. "I must go." He kissed me on the cheek. Nodded at Sam. The two boys ran off down the hall while I walked Mr. Hoffman to the door.

After he left, I went back to work on the faucet. I took the aerator from the vinegar and scrubbed it free of the accumulation of decades' worth of hard-water deposits. Then I applied a toothbrush to the threads of the faucet, trying to do the same thing. But as I screwed the newly cleaned aerator back on, I realized something.

Sean had lied to me.

5

The thought landed in my stomach like a deadweight.

He'd lied to me.

Whatever it was that he'd put in his pocket the night he'd gone to the store and never returned, it didn't have anything to do with the faucet, because those parts hadn't been touched in years. And whatever he'd put in his pocket hadn't come back to me with the effects from the coroner's. At least I didn't think it had.

I stood there at the sink staring out the window into the sun-drenched autumn afternoon wondering what Sean had actually been doing when he died.

As I tried to understand the implications, I started to tune in to Sam and Preston's conversation. They were in the living room.

"Dad says my hockey bag would be a good place to hide."

Sean had told Sam that? When? I put a hand on the counter and turned toward the dining room.

"Like for hide-and-seek?" I didn't blame Preston for sounding confused.

"Just if I ever had to hide."

Preston seemed to accept the explanation. "Want to play hide-and-seek?"

"Okay. Maybe my mom would look for us."

Not a chance. And I went into the living room to tell him so. "Hey, Sam? You said Dad told you your hockey bag would be a good place to hide?"

"Yeah."

"When did he say that?" I tried to sound nonchalant.

"When we played the game."

"The game? What game? Hide-and-seek?"

"The Bad Guys."

"The Bad Guys?" I was starting to sound like a demented parrot. "I don't think I've ever played that game." I looked at Preston, hoping to enlist an ally. "Have you?"

He shook his head.

I knelt beside Sam. "How does it go?"

"So you're in the—you have to pick the room." Sam looked at me, prompting.

"The room? Of the house?"

"Mom." He should have said, *Duh*.

"Okay. Um . . . here. The living room."

"Okay. So you're in the living room and the bad guys come. What are you going to do?"

"What kind of bad guys are these?" And why had I never heard of this game?

"The *bad guys*."

"Uh . . . well . . ."

"You're dead."

"What?"

"You're dead. You took too long. Now it's my turn."

Preston protested. "It's *my* turn!" He raised his hands and jumped. "It hasn't been my turn yet." He jumped again.

"Preston's right, Sam. It's his turn. But just— I need a second here to get used to being dead. That happened kind of quick, don't you think?"

"That's how it happens, Mom. And you don't get second chances. It's Preston's turn now." He turned to his friend. "So where do you want to be?"

I interrupted. "I still don't understand how this works. Could *you* do the living room? So I know how it goes? What do you think, Preston?" I wasn't beyond using peer pressure to plead my case.

Sam sighed the heartfelt, world-weary sigh of a six-year-old. "Okay. I'm in the living room and the bad guys come so I hide in the couch."

"The couch?" Preston and I looked at each other. It didn't seem like that great a hiding place.

"Like this." Sam dove into the couch, shimmying down into the crack between the seat cushions and the loose pillows. He burrowed in and pulled the pillows over himself. By the time he was finished, he'd completely disappeared. "Can you see me?"

"See you? I can hardly hear you."

He tossed the pillows off and pried himself out of the cushions.

"Let me try!" Preston repeated the disappearing act.

I put a hand to Sam's head. "Just out of curiosity, what did Dad say about the couch?"

"He said it was pretty good. Not as good as some of the others, but if you're in the living room when the bad guys come, it's good."

"So you're just supposed to, what? What are the rules? You stay there in the couch until the bad guys leave?"

Preston was crouched on the hearth, trying to pull a big pot over his head. I walked over and took it from him.

"Only if you have to. Because maybe the bad guys will go into another room and then you can run away." It was such a reasonable explanation that I had no doubt Sean had spent some time explaining to Sam how those things worked.

The hairs at the back of my neck stood on end.

"If they leave the living room, I run out the front door to Mr. Jim's house and I ring the doorbell until he or Miss June lets me in."

"Do *they* know about this game? About the bad guys?"

"Then I tell them to call the police."

"Do they know about this?" My voice had taken on a shrill edge that I couldn't quite control.

He shrugged. "You told me Mr. Jim sees everything."

He did. Most things. That's partly why he and Miss June had a spare key to our house; I could trust him. But I didn't think bad guys were on Jim's radar. Not the really bad ones.

"My turn! My turn!" Preston was jumping up and down.

Sam turned to him. "What room do you want?"

"Your room!"

"My room's great! There's lots of places to hide in there."

They raced into the dining room and then swerved down the hall while I stood there trying to count just how many kinds of wrong that game of Sean's was.

6

Sean had been dark and handsome in a mysterious sort of way. He had a five o'clock shadow at noon. And bedroom eyes just about any time of day. He was the sort of man you might overlook until he looked right back at you. That's when you discovered he had a gaze that could see inside your soul. And the sort of slow, sensuous smile that was a serious turn-on.

But when we first met, I hadn't been able to figure him out.

He wasn't constantly eyeing his cell phone the way most people in DC did. And he didn't seem to be looking for better options when he was with me or thinking of what he was going to say next. He didn't monopolize the conversation or play more-in-the-know-than-thou the way people in the area often did. In fact, after several weeks of dating, I realized I really didn't know anything about him. And wasn't a girl supposed to be suspicious of a man who never mentioned his family? Or his job? Or his hobbies? Or anything about himself at all?

With his dark eyes, dark hair, and swarthy skin, he might have been from anywhere.

So one night, as we were walking back from a restaurant to the apartment I shared with Jenn, I went for it. "I have to ask. Are you— I mean, your family. Where are they from?"

His lips lifted in a half smile. "I'm black Irish."

I blinked. "What?"

"Black Irish. Not Italian. Not Hispanic. Not Arabic."

Apparently, though, he spoke Italian. And Spanish.

He took my hand and fit our fingers together as we walked along.

"It's just— I feel like I don't know very much about you."

He sent me a sidelong glance. "What do you want to know?"

Everything.

So he told me. He'd been in the military, special forces; he'd gotten out. He had family—of course he had family, everyone had family—it was just that he'd grown up on the other coast.

Sean had a PhD in history. He worked for the army as a historian. He did have hobbies. *A* hobby. He liked to read: history, any kind.

Friends? He'd never mentioned friends. But that was normal, wasn't it? For someone who had grown up on the other side of the country and never had time to do anything with anyone but me?

"But what do you really know about him?" Jenn asked me the question one Saturday morning about six months after I'd met Sean. She was doing yoga in the living room. Her eyes were filled with concern as she regarded me, upside down, from a pose.

"*Pfft.* Everything."

"I mean, really. How much?"

"Enough."

"Because he's the silent, mysterious type, and sometimes mysteries aren't like, 'Oh, who keeps sending me flowers anonymously?' Sometimes they're more, 'Oh, who keeps torturing all these cute little kittens?'"

"Jenn, he's fine. Trust me."

To my great relief, Jenn shut up about Sean. But eventually I felt like I had to tell my parents about him. My father was still in the military and they were living in the area at the time, so of course my mother insisted that we come for dinner. And that I stay afterward.

Within five minutes of meeting Sean, my mother had managed to convey all the important information: she was from Mobile, born a Sinclair. Some people thought the Sinclairs were French, but they really weren't. Although she'd been brought up country club, she'd somehow ended up officers' club. No one in her family had thought my father would ever amount to anything, but she'd known better. Just look at him now; he was everyone's hero. Regardless, family was important, wasn't it? And a person would do anything for family, wouldn't they? She flashed her beauty-queen smile.

As always, her blonde hair was flawless. Her lightly tanned skin glowed against the red of her jumpsuit and the gold of her bangles and earrings that night.

As she started to ask Sean about his family, my father sent me a wink and diverted her attention. Mentally, I breathed a sigh of relief.

"Look here, Mary Grace! The poor man doesn't care about all that. Here's what you need to know, son: we're having brisket for dinner."

My mother smiled. "And slaw and coconut cake. Which I made."

My father raised his beer glass in her direction. "Which you made. To perfection."

She beamed. "What would you ever do without me?"

"Eat pork rinds and peanuts?"

"Be nice." She sent a glance to Sean. "People have always said we're like sweet and tea."

"Or bats and hell." My father mumbled the words under his breath as he brought the glass to his lips.

My father was gung-ho about life in general. The moment he sat down, he'd invariably get right back up. His favorite exercise, aside from running marathons, was pacing. My mother's job was to manage. She managed everything. If he was guns blazing, full speed ahead, she was the coolheaded analyst who always proceeded carefully, checklist in hand. He was big picture. She was details. All in all, they made the perfect team.

A very attractive, very perfect, quite formidable team.

At least they waited to talk about Sean until after he left. My father looked at the door that had just swung shut, lips pursed, eyes narrowed. "At least his discharge was honorable."

How would he know that Sean's discharge was . . . I felt my mouth drop open. "You checked? Mom!"

She kissed me on the cheek. "Your father loves you, sugar pie. Let him do what he has to do."

My father left the front hall and went into the living room. "He was awarded a silver star. Did you know that?"

I couldn't stop an eye roll. "No. I didn't ask for his evaluations." Not the way my father had apparently done. The stars he wore on his uniform guaranteed him just about anything he asked for.

Dad took up a post in front of the window. "He did the serious sh—"

"JB!" My mother tsked.

"What? It's true."

I joined him.

Sean glanced up before getting into his car. He pulled himself straight and threw a salute. Dad nodded.

For heaven's sake! I left my father standing there and followed my mother into the kitchen.

If I had still harbored the slightest, tiniest, slimmest reservations about Sean, our wedding wouldn't have soothed them. On the Slater side of the aisle: a veritable Who's Who of the Washington and military establishments. On the Brennan side? His sister. A handful of coworkers and the overflow from my side.

My mother approached me just before she was walked down the aisle. She fluffed my veil. Straightened my gown. "I only have one piece of advice."

I'd been hoping that, considering the occasion, I might get by with no pieces of advice that day.

But she grabbed my hand, leaned toward my ear. "In any marriage, there are some things you might not want to know. Understand me? So don't you go asking questions that you don't want to know the answers to."

Before I could think of any reply, she'd pasted her beauty-pageant smile back on and was adjusting the groomsmen's boutonnieres.

I didn't know what to think of my mother's advice, so I decided not to think about it at all. Jenn, my maid of honor, had been flirting with a senator's aide as she waited for her own cue to walk down the aisle. Somehow she'd turned her scoop-neck bridesmaid gown into a shoulder-baring one.

I poked her in the ribs with my elbow. Gestured with my bouquet toward Sean, who was waiting at the front of the church. "See? He's not some sort of ax-wielding serial killer."

"I never said he was ax-wielding."

"You thought it."

"He always struck me as more of a knife-wielding kind of guy."

"Seriously, Jenn."

"Seriously? It's your wedding day. Why are you worried about knives and axes?"

It wasn't until later in the evening, at the country club where my mother had planned the reception, that I had a chance to talk to Sean's sister. She was too reserved to be described as friendly, but she and Sean shared the same brown eyes and the same Brennan smile.

I lifted the massive skirts of my dress and sat down next to her for a moment. I thought I'd been in the market for a simple and plain wedding dress. Somehow my mother had talked me into an extravaganza of ruffles and lace and even more ruffles and lace, and when I looked in the mirror just before I walked down the aisle, I thought it might have been a mistake.

Sean's lifted brow as he offered me his arm at the front of the church during the ceremony just proved the theory.

I'd leaned close. "Pretend this isn't me."

His mouth had quirked. "Really hoping it *is* you under all of that. Kind of why I'm here today."

I stuffed the extra froth of petticoats underneath the table as I leaned close to his sister and thanked her for coming. Kelly was her name.

"I didn't want to miss it. He never said much, but Sean always wanted a family."

It wasn't an odd thought to share. Most people grew up imagining themselves married, having children one day. But she said it in such a strange way. "Didn't you have one?"

"Not really. Not after Mom and Dad died. We got farmed out to relatives. You know how it is. I went to stay with Aunt Colleen and Uncle Bill. Sean got sent to Uncle Mac and Aunt Sue. Then we were together for a while, but Sean was kind of a handful. When we got put into foster care, he sort of fell in with the wrong crowd. Then he enlisted." She shook her head to dismiss the conversation. "But you don't want to talk about all that today."

"I knew your parents had died." Sean told me when we'd been planning the wedding. "But I don't think I've ever heard how."

"He wouldn't have told you. He still feels guilty about it."

7

Guilty about it? Visions of axes and knives floated through my head. "Why? Um, *why* would he feel guilty?"

"It's just that he was so small."

The backs of my ears began to tingle. From across the room, Sean caught my eye and raised his champagne glass in my direction.

"Small? How small?"

"He was six." She said it as if that explained everything.

"I see."

She plucked at her sleeve. "We've all told him there's nothing he could have done. And he saved me, so . . ." Her smile flickered. Died.

Her demeanor didn't exactly shout Crazy Person, but she kept saying the strangest things. "I have to be honest. I've never heard any of this. Do you mind telling me what happened?" So I could have the marriage annulled right away if I needed to?

"Oh." She sent me a searching gaze. "Sure. It was a robbery. I guess they thought no one was home. But we were. The lights were off because my parents had promised Sean a camping trip. But it was raining that weekend, so they'd decided to do their camping in the living room instead. They'd already set up the tent. Sean was coming downstairs when the thieves came in the front door. Sean watched them shoot Mom and Dad, then he went upstairs and took me from my crib and hid me underneath the bathroom sink."

"He saw them do it?"

She nodded. "He went over to the neighbors after, crying, saying the bad guys came."

∞

The only real argument Sean and I ever had happened that first night of our marriage. I brought up the death of his parents.

"I just wish you would have told me yourself."

He was sitting on the bed in the hotel room, pulling off his bow tie. "It wouldn't have changed anything." Those were the words he said, but his eyes were asking me a question. *Would it have?*

"Why should it have?"

He glanced away, but I saw his shoulders relax.

"But it seems like—" I huffed a sigh in exasperation. "That was a big deal. And it changed everything for you. Both you and Kelly. I just feel like if I didn't know that about you, then . . ." I let my voice trail off.

He said nothing.

"Parents, family. They're really important."

"I can see that." He sent a sardonic look toward my wedding dress, which seemed to be expanding like Gorilla Glue, trying to take over the hotel room.

I ignored the barb. "And if you're that closed off about them, then maybe it's something you still have to work through. Maybe you haven't gotten over them."

"Maybe I've never gotten over my parents, but you've never gotten out from under yours."

The sting of his words stole my breath. I blinked back tears as I replied, "My strategy has been to keep my distance." I didn't like what happened, how easily my resolve wavered, when I was drawn into their orbit.

"How's that working for you?" He shrugged out of his jacket and stalked over toward the closet.

But he had to pass me on the way, so I reached out. "It's difficult! They're just so . . . so . . ." They were just so everything that they defied description. "And anyway, how would you know what it's like?" I clapped my other hand over my mouth as soon as I'd said it.

He stepped away from me and held his own hands up as if in surrender. "I wouldn't." He slipped by and hung up his jacket.

The first, some might say foundational, law of physics is that objects in motion tend to stay in motion unless acted upon by an external force. It was vitally important to me that we not start our lives together moving away from each other.

"I'm sorry." I went to him. Put my arms around his waist. Pressed my cheek against his back. "I didn't mean to hurt you. But I don't want you to keep hurting yourself with your memories either." He'd thrown me a zinger, but what he'd said was true. I released him. Stepped back. "So let's try to help each other. Over." I pointed at him. "Out from under." I pointed at me. "Deal?"

We might have shaken on it, but it was our honeymoon. We came up with a different way of sealing our bargain.

Considering his past, it was perfectly logical that Sean would teach Sam to play the Bad Guys. But in another sense? It was completely and horribly wrong.

We weren't living in an industrial, crime-ridden city of the 1980s like he had been when his parents were killed. Our house was smack-dab in the middle of one of the wealthiest counties in the nation. Kids walked to elementary school in our neighborhood. And middle school and high school too. They rode their Big Wheels down the sidewalks and tossed footballs in the streets. There were community movie nights and food truck festivals and bonfires in the park. If Sean had been looking for a safe place to raise Sam, he couldn't have settled in a better area. But clearly, none of that had been enough. Sean had still been worried about something in the months before he died.

I was still trying to figure everything out when Jenn came to pick up Preston.

She looked beyond me into the house. "So where are the kiddos?"

"Playing Bad Guys."

She sent me a quizzical look. "Bad Guys?" She raised her brow. "Do tell."

How to put into words the unease that I felt? It wasn't normal to teach your child the Bad Guys game. But Jenn had enough problems of her own. She didn't need to add mine to them. "It was a Sean thing. He used to play it with Sam." I shook my head. "But never mind. How did it go?"

"It's not. Going." She bit her lip. "I don't know if I'll be able to get residential custody."

That was news to me. "What do you mean?"

"I'll share custody, but you know my schedule. It's crazy. Senator Rydel's a great guy, but working for him will never be nine-to-five. And you know Mark. He's all about being a dad. Since he's got the more flexible schedule, what's the judge going to say?"

As Jenn stood there recounting her meeting, I tried to sympathize in the right places. But my mind kept crunching the new pieces of data I'd discovered, trying to reconcile those glimpses of Sean with the man I'd once known.

Why hadn't he told me about his fears? What other kinds of secrets might he have been keeping?

8

By evening, my unease had morphed into something bigger and darker. I may have banged my pots around as I washed them, and I might have slammed the doors to the cabinets as I put the dishes away. After the kitchen was clean and every spare crumb obliterated by antibacterial kitchen spray, I stood there wanting to *do* something. Solve something. Fix the disequilibrium that had been created.

Using my wrist, I pushed at the hair that had escaped both my ponytail and the confines of my headband.

I went into the dining room and ripped the placemats off the table. And then, as I stalked to the back door to go shake them outside, I nearly tripped over Alice. "Sorry."

All the warmth of the afternoon had been lost to the autumn night. After I shook the mats clean, I took a deep breath of frost-laced air before going back inside. After throwing them back on the table, I returned to the kitchen. Squeezed out my sponge, put it back in its holder. Then I slapped my palm down on the countertop.

Alice was watching me, ears cocked.

"I'd been doing so well, don't you think? Fixing the faucet. Cleaning out Sean's desk." I still hadn't dropped his phone line from my account, but I would. Eventually. I'd called his voice mail almost every night that first month after he'd died. I'd just needed to hear his voice.

My mind had been so fuzzy back then. Without Sean, I'd just been going through the motions.

Then, a few months later, my synapses had begun to fire in fits and starts as I began to take notice of the world around me. As of that afternoon? I was fully engaged, my thoughts razor sharp and singed around the edges with frustration over all the unknowns that were cropping up in my world. "What am I supposed to do, Alice?"

She sighed and settled her chin on her paws.

"I wish I could talk to him about everything. Maybe there was some perfectly reasonable explanation."

People always say you never forget your first. Well, that was Sean: my first, my only.

I hadn't even been thinking about love the night we met at the Clarendon Ballroom.

I'd been thinking about black holes. Because, why not?

The concept of the black hole is a mystery made more enigmatic by a misnomer and more complex by competing theories.

Black hole is an oxymoron. They're created by dying stars. And it's not that black holes signify a giant nothingness, but rather a giant everything-ness. A black hole is the densest mass in the universe. They aren't called black holes because they're unfathomably deep, but because they're unfathomably dense. And they just keep adding to their density.

There's everything *and* the kitchen sink in there. There's so much matter crammed into a black hole that nothing can get out. Not even light. That's what makes them invisible.

That means black holes can only be studied by observing their effect on the matter around them. Millions of black holes exist undiscovered—in our galaxy alone—simply because nothing has passed by close enough for us to detect them.

The funny thing is, people talk about black holes all the time. Even when they don't know they're doing it. Everyone who wishes they could stop time? The only point at which time ever stands still is at the edge of a black hole. Just before mass tips over the "edge" and is drawn into one, time freezes. If people knew that's what their time-stopping moment would be, they wouldn't make that wish.

How many black holes are there?

One hundred *million*. A new one forms every second. There's one at the center of our galaxy.

You'd think scientists would be able to figure out what happens to the things that get pulled inside black holes, but no one actually knows. Energy can't be created or destroyed; we know that for certain. But inside a black hole, it can be honed and compacted down to a single, solitary point. Dump in the entire United States. Throw in Africa and Europe and Asia too. And in the end? They all get compressed down to a single point.

The paradox is mind-blowing.

And yet whatever is taking place inside of them must have some sort of process. Even if it defies description, it can't defy explanation. If someone could just turn their brain inside out long enough to comprehend all the complexities, then physicists might be able to better explain the phenomenon.

Why couldn't that person be me?

Jenn had long ago attached herself to a lawyer type wearing the newest pastel incarnation of preppy chinos. And I had long ago given up on meeting anyone other than a junior Capitol Hill staffer or congressional lobbyist.

So, black holes.

I brought out the topic the way other people pulled out a Sudoku or a crossword puzzle, hoping that time and experience might reveal a different way of looking at things. There was always the chance that a series of unrelated events or mindless daily tasks would provide the trail of crumbs that would lead to comprehension of the scientific mysteries of dark matter, dark energy, or the reversal of time.

And, possibly, a Nobel Prize.

I sighed and glanced out over the wall. The rooftop bar overlooked a bloated median in Clarendon that was meant to be a tree-lined oasis. It was home to an Orange Line metro stop, a fountain that burbled when it happened to feel like it, and an overlooked monument to those who had died in the last century's wars. I was probably the only one who wished I were down there instead of up on the roof.

Everyone else was laughing and drinking. They were making a surprisingly persistent attempt at pretending the song the DJ was playing was danceable.

Poking my straw at the fruit that had settled to the bottom of my ruby-colored sangria, I wondered how long I should wait before I dragged Jenn away. She'd made me promise not to let her go home with anyone but me.

Thirty minutes? An hour?

I gave a piece of pineapple a good poke. As I eyed the steadily growing crowd and all the gyrating bodies, my gaze swept past a man at the bar. Came back to focus on him.

Dark-haired. Dark-eyed.

Hel-lo!

9

I caught a glimpse of his face and he shifted, attention caught by something to the left of me. I still had a few high school tricks up my sleeve, though; I moved left, threading my way around dancing couples, hoping it would place me in his view. And it did.

He saw me.

We saw each other and everything changed.

It was one of those movie moments. He pushed away from the bar and started toward me and suddenly time became elastic. The music faded and people moved in slow motion as I swallowed, wishing I'd actually worn the cute dress Jenn had convinced me to buy.

Then time slammed back into place—the music overloud, people overclose, my cheeks overheated. As he came toward me, I wished he'd stop looking at me. But then, just as quickly, I hoped he wouldn't.

He nodded.

My mouth opened, but I don't think I said anything.

What was it about his eyes? They were dark. Probing. But it was more than that. It was as if I was the one he'd been looking for.

The lock of gel-tipped hair that lifted from his widow's peak? It only emphasized those gorgeous eyes. The tattoo on his bicep that played hide-and-seek with the sleeve of his polo? Intriguing. The fact that his jaw was outlined by a not-too-close shave? Magic. And yes, Robert De Niro, he was talking to *me*.

And he *kept* talking to me! (Honestly, that normally didn't happen. I wasn't very good at flirting.)

When he asked if I wanted to leave, I happily threw all my mother's advice right out the window, as if I didn't have a world-class brain.

Don't ever let a stranger buy you a drink.

He wasn't a stranger; his name was Sean.

Don't ever leave a bar with someone you don't know.

I did know him. His name was Sean.

Always go home with the friends you came with.

I would have, but Jenn had just given me a thumbs-up and disappeared with the guy in pastel chinos. And that left me with Sean.

When all else fails, take a taxi home with the spare twenty you keep in your wallet.

If I hadn't spent that spare twenty, I might have. But again, there was Sean, who seemed more than happy to walk me home. It was odd, really. There'd been no one at all and then, all of a sudden, there was Sean.

I wasn't drunk. I never got drunk. But I was buzzed and I was happy and when he offered to take me home, I accepted. Why? Because somewhere, deep down, I understood that I wouldn't be able to keep feeling like the only girl in the world if he stopped looking at me.

Now I couldn't even think of our first meeting without wondering if there was something I should have seen from that very first night. Was he a liar when I first met him? Was there something he'd been hiding even then?

You never know enough about a person when you first start dating to understand what they're made of. They're a black hole of sorts. You know they're composed of a density of associations and people and experiences, but you can't actually see any of that. You know everything about them reinforces a certain theme of their character. But you can't see that either. Not at first. Not until you get closer. And by that time they have pulled you in past the point of no return and you've lost your objectivity. You've become part of their density, and when that happens you can no longer escape.

So I had questions without any good answers and no foreseeable way of finding any either. But it was clear that there was something, some *things*, about Sean that I hadn't been able to see.

If it had just been the lie about the faucet, I might have gone into our room and rifled through his clothes—which, yes, were still there—looking for signs of lipstick or sniffing for the scent of an alien perfume. Or any perfume, really, because I didn't wear any. Much to my mother's chagrin.

But it wasn't just the lie.

It was the idea that Sean thought Sam might be in danger.

Sean had worn a green beret. It's not like he didn't know what danger was. It might seem strange that I'd never asked him much about his time in service. Probably made me seem impossibly naïve, because that's what pillow talk was for, wasn't it? But I was raised in a military family by a four-star general. Any information I was given had been strictly on a need-to-know basis. And one of my family's cardinal rules was Don't Question What You've Been Told.

Over a million Americans hold top secret security clearances. Among them were probably many of my friends and neighbors. So in the DC area? You didn't pry. People told you what they could. They might say what three-letter agency—Department of Defense, Department of Homeland Security, Department of Agriculture—they worked for, but that's usually where the information stopped.

When Sean had told me that he'd "done stuff," I'd left it at that because people with top secret security clearances honestly don't even tell their wives what they do for a living. Not everything.

So, knowing Sean's background and that he was worried about Sam's safety? That was big news. That meant I should be worried too.

It led me to question my understanding of reality as I folded laundry that night.

In order to make sense of our unanswerable questions in physics, we scientists have begun to think we might have to jettison all of our assumptions and leave behind everything we know. The answers are staring at us—they are right in front of our eyes. Everyone knows they are; we just can't see them because they've camouflaged themselves in our reality. The key to unlocking the mysteries has to be things we've seen a million times and always managed to overlook.

So that was the challenge. How could I unknow the Sean I'd married? How could I re-see the man I'd once known? I needed to look, not for clues, but for something obvious. Something, perhaps, that had been there the whole time.

10

It took longer than normal to get Sam to bed that night. His counselor told me it might take a while for Sam to let himself fall asleep again without a fight.

Subconsciously he was afraid I might die while he was sleeping too.

I called my parents and put them on speakerphone. Sometimes that worked. My father asked Sam about school. Asked me about work. I mentioned Mr. Hoffman had brought Sam another train. Sam sang a song he'd learned at school that included the names of all fifty states, in alphabetical order. Then he sang it again. They reminded him that they'd be coming into town again on Friday and would play with him. But when we said good night, Sam was still wide-awake.

We cuddled for a while on the couch as we stared up at the constellations of glow-in-the-dark stars I'd stuck to the living room ceiling. When he started nodding off, I carried him to bed.

But then *I* couldn't sleep. I kept thinking about Sean.

I'd been looking back at the beginning of our relationship to try to figure out what I'd been missing. It hadn't gotten me very far. I decided, as I lay in bed, that maybe I should start at the end, with the night Sean died. Maybe from there I'd be able to pick up something, some thread, that would unravel everything back to the beginning. It was the same way scientists observed explosions in the universe and then followed them back through billions of light-years to determine where they'd come from.

So I threw on a bathrobe and went into the office and pulled out the documents from the accident. The police report. The medical examiner's report. The death certificate.

As I sat there on the cold wood floor in my pajamas, I read through the medical examiner's report. The descriptions of the actual autopsy meant nothing to me. And I wasn't quite sure what I was looking for.

Sean had died. End of story. But I skimmed the pages anyway. They stated his sex, height, weight. Eyes: brown. Hair color: black. Noted his tattoo, scars, moles. There were descriptions of the evidence of injuries. Next were pathological findings.

He'd been found in the driver's seat. He had blunt-force injuries. One of his lungs had been punctured. I went on to the next page. There had been no video surveillance. No witnesses that they could find. The verdict? He'd died of blunt-force injuries to the head due to a motor vehicle accident.

It was signed and stamped by the medical examiner, Dr. Kyle Correy.

Attached to the report was an inventory of personal effects. The items he'd been wearing or carrying were listed on the left-hand side of the page. The right side noted that they'd been "given to father-in-law." I'd asked my father to identify Sean on my behalf.

The inventory had been taken by the medical examiner as well. I read through the list:

Black coat
Blue plaid shirt
Jeans
Brown leather wallet
Keys
Phone
White socks
Brown boots
Briefs
Watch
Gold wedding ring
Pocketknife

They were all still in the cardboard box my father had signed for. But what would it hurt to go through them again? I pulled the box from the corner of the closet where I'd let it gather dust and went down the list, pulling the items out as I came to them.

With every item came a whiff of that indefinable combination of soap, shampoo, and laundry detergent that had, when combined with the heat of his skin, resulted in a scent that was uniquely Sean.

I had to pause a couple of times, take a few deep breaths, but I got through it.

Everything was there but the pocketknife.

I turned the box upside down.

No knife.

I unfolded all the clothes, averting my eyes from the rust-colored bloodstains. Then I felt in the pockets of the jeans and coat to make sure it hadn't been concealed inside.

Nothing.

I paged back through the report and made a note of the medical examiner's name and phone number.

Had anything else failed to come back to me from the autopsy? I grabbed his wallet and went through it.

Driver's license. Library card. Visa. ATM card. Medical insurance card.

Nothing else.

No receipts. No money.

I picked up the key chain: the car key, house keys for both the front and back doors, key for his bike lock. And one more. A key for what? I fingered it for a moment. Key to his office? It was small and thin. More like a key to a padlock? A filing cabinet?

Probably something at work. And if that were the case, then I needed to return it.

I worked it from the ring and set it aside.

What else was missing?

Struck by inspiration, I went to get my purse from the bedroom, then came back and dumped it on the floor beside the box. I took my wallet and pulled everything out of it.

I had most of the same things in my wallet that he did and some cash in addition to several receipts.

I took my money and the receipts and set them aside. I put my sunglasses on the pile too, along with my mini notebook, pen, assorted hair ties, lip balm, and the coins that lived at the bottom of my purse.

It was an exercise in uselessness.

Nothing was missing from Sean's effects but his Leatherman pocketknife. I sent a quick glance over in the direction of my piles. What about his sunglasses?

He hadn't been wearing them. It had been raining that day.

But then where *were* his sunglasses? I would have noticed them if he'd left them in the house.

I tore a page from my notebook and wrote it down: *sunglasses*. Then I wrote *Leatherman* underneath it.

Oh! Where had I put his attaché? I found it on the floor in the pile of things I'd removed from the closet when I'd brought out the box. I took everything out of it and stacked the contents next to the things I'd found in his wallet.

A couple of pens. A few binder clips. A ruled notepad. It wasn't nearly as packed as it could have been. Or maybe he'd just never carried much in it. I couldn't remember.

Once again, I grabbed hold of my own attaché and compared my contents with his.

Mine had power cords, my security badge from the office, some folders with notes from the office, my work laptop.

Laptop! His was missing.

I added it to my list.

But it was a government-issued computer. Maybe he'd left it at work that weekend. A definite possibility.

Anything else?

My attaché had a security badge. He'd had one too. He'd worn it on a lanyard, putting it on every morning before he left. It usually spent weekends in his attaché. But it wasn't there. And he hadn't left it on the dresser either, the way he sometimes had. I would have noticed long before. I added it to the list.

Mystery item: *key.*

Missing items: *sunglasses, Leatherman, laptop, security badge.* What had happened to them?

11

The next morning I called the medical examiner's office.
It was a Sunday, but I was guessing they were open for business 24/7.
I asked for Dr. Correy.

There was a long pause.

"I don't want to interrupt him. If he's in the middle of . . . of . . ."
An autopsy? A body? I shuddered at the thought. There was a reason
I'd gone into a *theoretical* science. "If he's in the middle of something
I could leave my number and ask him to return the call."

"No. That's not— I mean, you can't."

"I'm happy to call back."

"He's not here."

"Can you tell me when he'll be in?"

"No. It's not that." The voice on the other end dropped. "He was
fired."

"Fired?"

"After he was arrested."

"He was arrested?"

"I mean, yeah. He was taking people's things."

The conversation was making no sense.

"It's not as if they needed them anymore. Not that it was—"

"Dr. Correy was taking things? Whose things?"

"The dead people's. Not like, I mean, you never know what you're
going to find when you do an autopsy."

I had no idea what to say to that.

"Sometimes people hide things. In their . . . you know."

"In their wallets?"

"No! In their cavities."

"Oh." Oh!

"Drugs. People hide drugs. Sometimes Dr. Correy found them. Instead of reporting them, he'd sell them."

Just the thought made me feel icky. "Did the doctor ever use any of those drugs he stole?"

"Don't think so."

"There isn't any chance— It's just, he's the one who performed the autopsy on my husband, and it makes me wonder if—"

"Doc was really good. At autopsies. You should have seen him with that saw. *Zizzz-zizzz.* If it wasn't a 'specially difficult case, he'd be in and out like no one you'd ever seen. Don't worry. If Doc Correy autopsied your husband, he was good to go."

While Sam played with his trains that afternoon, I did an internet search on Dr. Correy, medical examiner. He'd been indicted and pled guilty to charges of racketeering and conspiracy to distribute. He was serving a three-year sentence in a federal prison. That seemed quite generous for a convicted drug dealer. If he'd gotten time off for good behavior, they'd awarded it before he'd even been assigned to a cell.

Strange.

The federal prison was at the extreme southwestern edge of Virginia. It was not reassuring that Sean's medical examiner had been a drug dealer. But I didn't have time to drive down there and ask him about it. And beyond that, what would I say?

My husband didn't happen to tell you what he'd been doing right before he got hit by that car, did he? He was, in fact, dead when you autopsied him, right?

It didn't seem like he'd actually been taking drugs himself. He'd only been selling them.

But strange was strange.

Twenty-four hours earlier, there had been no strange people in my life. Now there were two: the bad guy or *guys*, which Sean had been afraid of, and the medical examiner.

I googled the number for the prison, called, and asked if I could speak to him. Or at least leave a message.

"You want to leave a message? For who, now?"

"For one of the prisoners. His name is—"

"Oh, we don't do that. Nope, nope, nope."

"But I *really* need to talk to him."

"Then you *really* need to get *him* to call *you*." *Click.*

So maybe that hadn't been my best idea ever.

How could I get Dr. Correy to call me if he didn't even know me?

I could write him a letter and ask him to call me, which might entail a several-week turnaround. Or I could contact his attorney. I found the phone number of the attorney's office and added it to the contacts on my phone. Then I added it to my to-do list for Monday.

Reading the medical examiner's report hadn't helped me understand what Sean had been doing when he died. But that didn't mean I had to stop looking for information. As Sam did some coloring, I read through the police report on Sean's accident. When I'd received it, I'd only given it a cursory glance before shoving it into a drawer of his desk. At that point, it was redundant. It had only told me what I'd already known: Sean was dead.

That night I actually read it.

He'd been killed at Seven Corners, which had taken no one who heard about it by surprise. Five major roads converged at that point into one of the worst traffic snarls in northern Virginia. It was a concrete and asphalt nightmare framed by potholed access roads and parking lots that fronted superstores and other blights on modern existence.

The accident had occurred at the intersection of Leesburg Pike and Broad Street. Sean's car had been traveling southeast on Broad Street. He'd been hit on the driver's side by a car traveling up Leesburg Pike and—

Something didn't seem right.

Pulling my phone from my pocket, I googled Seven Corners and zoomed in, trying to make sense of a truly funky intersection. One road split, two went up and over, and a fourth entered from a side, while the fifth just barreled through underneath them all. Okay. So if Sean had been on Broad Street and . . . Why had Sean been on Broad Street?

Broad Street was *past* Home Depot.

I zoomed in even closer. There was no way a car traveling on Leesburg Pike could have hit him. Because at the point where Leesburg Pike intersected Broad Street, it wasn't called Leesburg Pike anymore. It had a different name.

Wasn't that something a police officer would have known?

But a bigger question remained. Where had Sean been coming from?

12

Monday came in the way only Mondays do: with protests, regret, and a vow to do the next weekend better. Clothes, breakfast, vitamin gummy; brush teeth; coat, backpack, shoes. That was the morning routine. But Sam waved off the backpack and sat down on the floor to tug at the Velcro fastenings on his sneakers.

The order didn't matter, as long as he walked out the door with both. That's what I told myself. But I drew the line at superhero capes.

I didn't think his teacher, Ms. Hernandez, would appreciate it. But mostly I was worried that some of the kids might make fun of him. Or try to take it and wear it themselves.

Considering that he was still working at making sense of Sean's death, and that Sean had called him Super Sam, I would have done almost anything, offered any bribe, in order to keep that cape at home.

I pulled it out from the collar of his coat and then turned him around so I could undo the tie beneath his chin.

He batted my hands away.

"Why don't we leave this at home today?"

"Because I can't be Super Sam if I don't wear it. And I have to practice for Halloween!"

"You know what? Superman didn't always wear his cape. But even though no one else knew he was Superman, he knew it. And that was the important thing." The other important thing was that I'd gotten the knot undone and the cape lay in a puddle on the floor behind him.

I leashed Alice, then she and I walked Sam to school past 1920s farmhouses and bungalows with wide front porches; storybook brick Tudors from the 1930s with their arched front doors and steeply pitched roofs; and brick colonials from the 1940s and '50s in sizes small, medium, and center-hall large.

Here and there, raised ranches from the 1960s and a rare split-level from the 1970s made an appearance. And—often whispered about, but largely ignored, like a sprawling seatmate on a regional plane—a few mini mansions bumped up against county height restrictions and strained against the outside edges of their too-small lots.

Alice and I walked back home along her preferred route of boxwood- and liriope-lined walkways. Chris Gregory and his Maltipoo joined us.

Chris walked his dog around the same time I walked Alice, along the same route. There were dozens of Chrises in our neighborhood. People you talked to because you were walking in the same direction. People you shared your life with for ten or fifteen minutes every day.

My out-the-door-at-the-very-last-possible-minute schedule assured that I was usually heading into the school with Sam while Chris had already dropped off his son. Although, once or twice, I'd managed to see his son ignore him as he'd waved good-bye.

I'd found out Chris was a professor at one of the local universities and a fountain of knowledge about all things Boy. He wore a leather-billed baseball cap over his sandy hair and had a penchant for pairing Northwestern T-shirts with his cargo shorts.

He slid a look toward me. "How are things?"

I shrugged. "You?"

"Same. I wanted to offer, with Sean not there, if there's anything you need help with. Kristy was always asking me to do things around the house. You know—change a lightbulb, kill a fly."

His wife, Kristy, had died several years before.

Chris and Kristy. What could be cuter?

But she must not have been handy like I was. Sean and I had an unspoken agreement. The person most bothered by something became the person responsible for the fixing of it. So when the towel rack in the bathroom started tilting toward the floor or the front door started to stick, Sean got out a hammer or a wood file and went to work. But when the fridge started gurgling or the air conditioner stopped working, I got out my multimeter, my power drill, and my set of screwdrivers and unfastened the panels labeled *Do Not Open—Danger of Electrocution* so I could take a look inside and figure out what was going on.

Sean had been the first one to comment on the dripping faucet. It wouldn't have taken me long to fix it, but that faucet had been his.

Chris's hazel eyes crinkled at the corners as he slanted a smile at me. "It would make me feel useful again. And I've got this great set of screwdrivers."

That made me smile.

He glanced at his watch, then inclined his head. "Anyway. Just let me know. Sorry to ditch you, but I've got to go."

As his stride lengthened and his pace quickened, I wondered what it would be like to establish a life with someone so normal. So solid. Someone who was exactly what he seemed.

Alice and I looped toward home. Along the way, a garbage truck stalked us, halting with a grinding shudder and starting up again with a hydraulic hiss. When it drew even with us, we stepped from the sidewalk into a yard, waiting for it to pass.

Alice tensed.

I tightened my hold on the leash and ordered her to sit.

That's when I remembered.

Trash!

I hadn't put out the trash.

I'd meant to. But the previous night I'd been focused on the police report. And that morning there'd been the issue of Sam trying to leave the house with his cape around his neck.

Alice's muscles bunched and then, before I could take any deterrent measures, she'd whipped the leash from my hand and was off down the road, scampering after the truck, legs a-blur.

"Alice!"

She didn't used to run after garbage trucks. She only started after

Sean died. We all had our ways of dealing with grief. Without Sean as her alpha, her preferred method was to pretend that she'd forgotten all of her obedience training.

"Alice, stop!"

Skidding to a halt just before our house, she sat down—with an odd, sharp bark—in the middle of the street, just the way Sean had taught her to do on command.

A pleasant surprise.

As I recovered the leash, she stretched her neck up and let out another short bark. The garbage truck disappeared around the corner, two garbage men hanging on to the back.

I trudged up to the house, scowling at the yellow fall crocuses that had magically appeared the previous week in the front yard along the fence. They were supposed to have been spider lilies. I knew that because Sean and I had planted them with Sam.

I hated fall crocuses. When crocuses pushed up out of the earth in the spring, it was cause for celebration. When fall crocuses did the same, they seemed like latecomers, irritatingly out of season. The party? It's over. Ended months ago. Everyone's gone home!

I was so focused on despising them that I almost ran into my trash cans.

But I hadn't wheeled them out. I was certain I hadn't. I flipped the lids shut and hauled them back up the driveway anyway. God bless Jim. He must have rescued me. Again.

I'd thank him later.

As I came back around the house toward the front yard, a gas company van drove up. Slowed. Parked on the street in front of the house.

Men in white coveralls popped out of the back as if it were a clown car. One of them waved me over.

"Can I help you?"

"Is emergency."

13

"With my *gas*?" I peered past him out to the street. Orange cones had already been placed along the perimeter of my property. "What emergency?"

"System say need repair."

The neighborhood was nearly a hundred years old. Something was always breaking down. One week the fire hydrants would be flushed out. The next week the power company would shut down the lines for a few hours to put in a new transformer. Just as soon as the county repaved a street and filled its potholes, the water company would come along and dig a trench right down the middle to pull up an old pipe or replace the main. If you thought too long or hard about the aging infrastructure, you'd never be able to sleep at night.

I led him through the house to the kitchen. Alice wanted to come too, but I ordered her to stay.

Surprisingly, once more, she obeyed.

We walked down the bare, scarred wooden stairs to the partial, cinder-block basement. Pulling the string for the light, I pointed past Sam's train table to the gas pipes, which snaked along the wall.

He gestured toward the meter. "Is old."

It most certainly was. I'd asked the gas company about the regulator before we'd moved in. They said they'd be happy to replace it. On our dime. Unfortunately, by then we'd already spent all our dimes buying the house, so I'd made myself feel better by reading up on the decades-old, mercury-regulated device. It had the effect of making me feel worse. I finally made my peace with it by inspecting it every week and building a cage of sorts to keep Sam and his friends away from it. Mercury didn't have a discernible smell, but it did leave traces and would give off toxic fumes if it spilled.

I removed the cage and gave it a once-over, then glanced at the floor beneath it. "I don't see any spills or leaks."

"Is, uh . . ." He waved a hand toward the regulator.

I raised a brow.

"Inside."

"The leak? That's impossible." When the units fail, they fail because they've been improperly moved. The spills are *ex*ternal. I'd read all about the incidents near Chicago back in the early aughts.

The man shrugged and nodded at his clipboard. "Is on list."

"For what?"

"For fix."

"How?"

"We fix."

"With a new one?"

He nodded.

Uh-oh. The problems in Illinois had been made worse when poorly trained contractors removed the old mercury regulators. "So you're going to use a vacuum cleaner, right?"

"Yes."

Good grief! "Okay. Know what? I don't see any signs that this is leaking and I need to get to work. Leave me the number of your supervisor and I can call to get this sorted out."

Upstairs, Alice was barking like a fiend. Over across the basement near our bedroom, where an outdoor crawl space abutted the cinder blocks, floorboards squeaked. What was she doing over there?

14

Twenty minutes later, I was showered, changed, and ready for work. But I was also thirty minutes late. As I locked the front door, Jim hailed me from across the street. Sunlight glinted off his glasses. His old, paint-splattered barn jacket was buttoned up against the morning's chill.

I waved back. "Hey—thanks for putting out my trash this morning!"

"What?" He put a hand to his ear.

"The trash. Thanks for putting it out."

He shrugged. "Didn't do it. Not this week."

If he hadn't done it and I hadn't done it, then who had?

I puzzled over it on the drive to work. None of my other near neighbors would have even noticed my trash wasn't out. I finally decided I must have pulled them out without remembering, crediting the lapse to the interminable twists and turns of the grieving process.

Setting my uneasiness aside, I told my phone to call the gas company's customer service line. Five minutes later, as I was turning into the parking garage at work, I was connected to an actual person.

I hit my blinkers and pulled to the side so I wouldn't lose my connection.

Of course, every car behind me felt the need to honk on their way down into the garage.

I pressed a finger to my free ear as I explained about the repairman.

"We don't replace old meters, although we can recommend a contractor."

"I know you don't. He wasn't there to replace it; he said it needed to be repaired."

"We don't repair old meters."

"He said my meter was on his list."

"His list of what?"

"Repairs."

"We don't repair old meters."

Being trapped in an endless loop of conversation with a person was worse than being trapped in an endless loop with an automated answering system. "Can you check to see if my house was scheduled for work today?"

"Can I have the work order number?"

"I don't have a—" I took a deep breath so I wouldn't yell at him. "There is no work order number. Could I give you my address?"

"How about the account number?"

"I don't have my account number at the moment."

"Can you give me the address?"

I gave him the address. And after five minutes of incredibly frustrating conversation, it only took him about five seconds to confirm that my house had been issued no work order and that it was not on anyone's list of anything to be concerned about.

"So you're saying you didn't send them."

"No, ma'am."

Once I got to work, I shut the door to my office and placed a call to the medical examiner's attorney.

"And you need to talk with Dr. Correy why?"

"My husband was one of his . . . um . . ." Patients? Clients? "He performed my husband's autopsy."

"And you want to what? Thank him?"

"No. There was something missing in my husband's inventory, and I wanted to—"

"Let me guess. Your husband had drugs on him? In that case—"

"What? No!"

"—the feds might be very interested in talking to you about your husband's drug—"

There was a knock on the door. Ted poked his head in.

I held up a finger.

He gave me an okay sign and closed it.

"No, he wasn't— That's not what I called about. Dr. Correy's inventory listed a Leatherman pocketknife. My father signed for it when he picked up my husband's effects."

"And?"

"And it wasn't there when I got the box."

"Listen, I can't help you."

"Is there no way you could contact him and ask him to—"

"I did my job when we made the deal with the feds. I'm not his office assistant, okay?"

"Wait. He had a deal with the—"

"Can't you people just leave the guy alone?"

You people? "I was just wondering what might have happened to the Leatherman, that's all."

"Who did you say signed for it again?"

"My father."

"Then why don't you ask him?"

15

My boss, Ted, leaned into my office as I hung up. "We missed you this morning, for the beginning of the meeting. The customer was here."

"I'm sorry. I just—"

He came into my office and plopped into the chair in front of my desk. "Thing is, we were counting on you. Classic entanglement theory as it relates to cybersecurity. Remember?" He shifted, placing his elbow on an armrest, propping his chin up with a loosely held fist. "You're the only one who can answer all those questions in detail."

"I know. I'm so sorry."

"Can't tell the customer"—he cleared his throat—"*prospective* customer, that we could do the job better when you're not doing the talking."

"I know. I—" What was there to say? I'd screwed up. "I'll follow up with them and see if they need anything else. I've been working the clearances for the test in January. Everything's submitted. Admin says we're good to go. I've been told the chairman of the House Intel Committee wants to come." That's how big a deal it was. And it added a whole other layer of anxiety. "Our subcontractor says there shouldn't be any problems. They've checked and rechecked." Ad nauseum. A lot was riding on the test. If everything worked the way it should, then the system would go into production almost immediately. Which meant lots of money, lots of jobs, lots of growth for the company. It would put us in a prime position, riding the leading edge of the technology.

He eased himself from the chair. "Listen, I know it's hard with Sean gone." He sent me a keen-eyed glance. "Do you need to cut back on hours?"

"No! No. I can manage."

"I understand. I really do. They say it takes time." He gave a half shrug and headed toward the door. "You could go to part-time. We'd find a way to make it work. Think about it."

Part-time did sound nice. And I did think about it. For two seconds. That's all it took to remind myself that somebody had to pay our bills. There had been insurance money when Sean died, but I'd used most of it to pay off the car and refinance our mortgage so I could afford the payments on my salary. With the little bit that was left, I'd done some things like fencing in the backyard for Alice and replacing several of our ancient windows. The rest I'd dumped into my 401(k) and a college savings plan for Sam.

My boss disappeared out the door only to reappear a second later. "Before I forget, where do we stand on your contract for next year?"

From long experience, by *we*, I knew he meant *you*. Whether the test was successful or not, the funding for my part in the current phase had almost been used up. I'd had to find a new contract to work on in the coming year, so I submitted a proposal for a quantum encryption project and I won it. But winning a government contract was a double-edged sword. "It's been awarded, but since Congress hasn't approved the budget, they're operating on a continuing resolution." Like they *ever* approved a budget. "The money hasn't been released. Word is, they're going to pass the appropriations bill next week. Then it's a go."

"So we're good?"

I gave him a thumbs-up. Then I called my contract officer and asked if he'd heard anything new about the vote on the appropriations bill.

He scoffed. "It's been twenty years since they've passed an appropriations bill on time, the way they're supposed to. I'd like to see *them* operate on 75 percent of *their* last year's budget."

"How long do you think it's going to be?"

"Till we get the real budget? Who knows."

"Because I can't charge against my new contract until the funding comes through."

"Believe me, you aren't the only one."

I hung up feeling much less hopeful than I had been. I might be forced to take vacation until I was funded. Which normally would be fine, only I didn't have any left. I'd used it up during those first few weeks after Sean's death, and I'd been working through lunch ever since to accumulate extra hours for when Sam got sick or an appliance broke or any myriad other things happened that weren't big enough to qualify as an emergency or a rainy day but seemed to crop up every week since he'd died.

Without the funding, I'd be out of a job, and not many employers were looking for quantum physicists. People tended to look at you strangely when you spoke of things like time travel, parallel dimensions, and wormholes as matters of fact. As my father said, with a wink, when I announced my college major, "Why? Are there too many people out there with useful skills? You have to major in unuseful ones instead?"

Why?

Because I wanted to get to the bottom of things. I wanted to know the reasons.

Most people would conclude that my research didn't really matter. Regardless of what I discovered, the world would keep turning the same way it always had. But those of us who were traditional quantum physicists poked at the foundations of our science for the sake of principle, invalidating assumptions one by one just to see what would happen.

When we removed one assumption too many, when our theories suddenly started to fall apart, then we'd know where we stood. We'd know what was foundational and what wasn't.

Before I left work, I wrote Dr. Correy a letter, printed it, and put it in outgoing mail.

As I drove home, I thought to send out an email to the neighborhood loop and ask if anyone else had run into the gas people. I didn't have any other way of figuring out who they were.

Next problem? My meeting with Sam's teacher that evening.

Despite Sam not wanting to fall asleep, his occasional lapse into present tense when he spoke about Sean, and his reversion to wetting the bed, I'd thought he was doing a pretty good job processing his father's death. That's what his counselor had told me.

And that's what I'd told Ms. Hernandez when she asked for the meeting.

But she asked me to come in anyway.

She was working at her desk when I walked into the classroom. Standing, she teased a folder from a pile in front of her, then gestured toward one of the miniature round tables that dotted the classroom.

She was a vivacious woman with vivid features and an ever-present smile. The children took to her like sunflowers to the sun. The fact that she wasn't smiling as she took a seat next to me was not a good sign.

"I just wanted to talk to you about Sam." Her dangly earrings trembled as she tilted her head toward me. She pressed her hands to the folder. "In the afternoons I call the children aside one by one and ask them for their happy thoughts." She opened the folder. "I write them down and have them color a picture about them." She passed me some papers. "What I'm trying to do is help them order their thoughts and strengthen their motor skills in advance of writing."

I began to read.

Daddy says I'm Super Sam. I have a red cape.

I picked another.

When Daddy plays trains with me.

She gave me a few moments before she spoke again. "I would have kept these until the next parent conference, but I thought it might be better to show them to you now."

The happy thoughts were each different, though they all had to do with Sean, but the picture was always the same. Sam had drawn the same thing over and over again.

"It's been six months since his father died?"

"Eight."

"That a child would speak of a dead parent in the present tense sometimes is normal. Especially for a child so young. But combined with his illustrations, I'm a little bit concerned."

I was too.

"Usually children at this age draw pictures of their families or pets. Their house or apartment building."

Sam's pictures had none of those things.

"I was hoping you might be able to help me figure out what he's drawing. He keeps telling me it's 'the firm.'" She frowned. "It might look like he's scribbling, but I've watched him. He's clearly not. It's, uh . . . it could be slightly alarming, the color he keeps choosing."

Black. He drew them all with a black crayon.

"Not necessarily, of course, but considering that his father recently died—" She looked at me, brows drawn together. "It's concerning."

My heart ached for my son.

"I've watched him do these. He's not angry. He's not clenching the crayon." She ran a finger over one of the images. "You can see that he's not pressing down very hard. I just would like to understand. And to help if I can. Do you know what he's trying to draw? Do you know what he means by 'the firm'? Which firm he might be talking about?"

He'd drawn a long black spiral, or series of circles, that stretched from one end of the page to the opposite corner.

"I've just never seen a student draw something like this before. On purpose. Then associate it with a happy thought."

I could only shake my head. "I don't know what it is. I wish I did, but I don't." I told her I'd ask Sam's counselor to talk to him about it. Then I left.

I made it down the hall to the bathroom before I started to cry.

After grabbing a hunk of paper hand towels, I locked myself into a stall and tried hard not to make any noise. I couldn't quite keep from sniffling, but I did manage to squelch most of the sobs as I dabbed at my tears with the towels.

One thing I knew. We were going to get through it.

We had to.

16

By the time I put Sam to bed that night, I was ready to kick something. I'd found all sorts of odd things associated with Sean's death, but none of them seemed to be connected to the questions I was trying to answer. I had to talk it through with someone, but there wasn't anyone I could trust.

I didn't want to give my parents one more reason to worry about me. They had enough to do with my father's upcoming confirmation hearing in November. It was only three weeks away. My neighbors, Jim and June, had been lifesavers, but they already did too much for us. I didn't want them to think I was having a breakdown. Jenn? She had too much going on with her job as chief of staff to a senator, let alone her divorce. And at that moment she was completely anti-male.

One thing, one *more* thing, still bothered me.

You people.

The medical examiner's lawyer had lumped me in with *you people.* People who, for whatever reason, were calling the lawyer about his client. And either there were so many of them or whoever *they* were had called the lawyer so many times that he was beginning to feel harassed.

Why?

There were too many *whys* and not enough *becauses.*

I had the feeling that the *whys* might matter, but I didn't know—wait for it—why. The ratio of things I knew about Sean to the things I didn't seemed to be rapidly decreasing. It was unnerving. I'd had the same feeling when I started to study dark matter.

That's when I'd found out that physics can account for only 4 percent of the universe. Nobody knows what makes up the other 96 percent. Ordinary matter, the kind we can define and measure and experiment with, actually *isn't* the most common kind. Of course there are theories—physicists have lots of theories—but that mysterious, undecipherable, unexplainable 96 percent, that dark energy and dark matter, is something upon which we're entirely dependent.

I didn't like knowing that I hadn't even known what I didn't know about Sean. I'd depended, to an extraordinary extent, on someone who was becoming increasingly opaque.

I needed more information. I called Sean's old office at Ft. McNair and left a voice mail message for Brad asking for a callback. He was the person Sean had worked with most closely at the army's Center of Military History. Then I called my father.

"Peach. Hey. We're looking forward to coming out your way in a few days. Just have to finalize some appointments up on the Hill before we get there."

"Sam can't wait to show you his new train." We talked for a few minutes about his confirmation hearings, then I got down to business. "I have a question about when you went to the morgue. Do you remember there being a Leatherman in the box of things you brought back?"

"Don't think so. Don't know that I'd really have noticed, though. But hey, Clyde and Harry and the others are having some Halloween thing for their grandkids on post at Fort Myer. Do you think Sam might like to go?"

"Clyde and Harry?"

"Westerman and Ladowski. You know. The joint chiefs."

Right. Yes. The joint chiefs of staff. That collective governing body formed by the heads of the branches of the military, otherwise known as Clyde and Harry and the Others. "I don't think so, Dad. But thanks for asking."

"Sure. No problem. Gotta go. I'm live on cable in five."

Before I could say anything else, he was gone. At least he hadn't put my mother on the phone. I wasn't up to hearing about all the things I could be doing better.

It's not like I had expected Sean's autopsy to be the key to some secret code. But still, I'd been hoping for something more. For some hint as to what Sean had been doing.

Alice woke me up in the middle of the night, barking her short, sharp bark. It was the one that told me she knew she'd get in trouble for it, but for whatever reason, she'd decided it was worth it.

"Alice!" I hissed her name.

She lumbered to her feet, left her cushion-bed, and scratched at the hardwood floor.

"Stop!"

I'd been hoping she'd turned a corner on the obedience thing, but she just looked at me, whined a bark, and scratched again.

Sighing, I got up and went to the bedroom door. "You need to go out? Is that what this is?" I was halfway down the hall before I realized she wasn't following me. Turning back, I found her right where I'd left her.

I flicked on the light.

She was staring at the floor, head cocked, ears at attention.

"Alice!"

She flinched as if I'd startled her, gave me a long look, and gave off another sharp bark.

"Shh!"

Still staring at me, she lowered the front of her body toward the floor and dug into it with both paws. Her long, quavery whine ended with a yip.

I took her by the collar and tried to lead her back to her bed. She wouldn't budge.

So I walked around her, bent toward her behind, and gave it a mighty push.

She scrambled away from me, came back in a U-turn, and curled up right on top of the place she'd been scratching. After a few more whines and barks, she settled into sleep.

She was acting the way I felt. Out of sorts. Disoriented.

Our world had seemed so safe and ordered. But like a dying star, going through the motions, sending out its last rays of light, I felt like my reality was collapsing. I was being drawn into the darkness of something I couldn't fathom.

17

The only way I knew to solve a problem was by asking questions. Sean had been afraid of something. Someone. Bad guys. In my search for the truth, I didn't want to ask the wrong people my questions. I did, however, need some answers.

So the next day, during lunch, I called someone I knew was safe. I went outside and walked across the street to the Crystal City Water Park, where I sat down in a chair by one of the fountains and called Sean's sister, Kelly.

"Georgie! I've been thinking so much about you lately. How is Sam?"

I gave her the executive summary version.

"And how are you?"

That was where things were getting tricky. "I was wondering, do you have a minute?"

"I have about twenty minutes. That's how much longer the baby's going to sleep." Sean had missed the birth of his nephew by three months.

"Could you tell me a little more about Sean? About your childhood?"

She went back over the part I knew—about their parents' deaths, about being passed around to relatives.

"But what happened after that? You told me once that he fell in with the wrong crowd." Were those the people Sean was afraid of?

"Well . . . the wrong crowd. Yes. I'd say so."

I waited for her to expand on that idea, but she didn't. "Could you tell me a little more?"

"I don't think it's anything he'd want Sam to know. It would be a shame to remember him that way."

"I won't tell Sam. I promise."

"It was something he really tried to put behind him. It seemed like he was trying to close that door when he joined the army. I don't think he'd like me talking about it."

Which was probably why *he'd* never talked to me about it. "It's just— I was hoping maybe understanding Sean better would help me process everything." A cool wind stirred the trees and tugged some of my hair from my ponytail. I pulled the zip on my jacket all the way up to the top of the collar.

"What can I say?" There was a long pause while I hoped she'd say *something*. "He was in a gang, Georgie."

"A gang? You mean a *gang* gang?"

"It's not like he wanted to be. He tried not to be. He really did. But where we grew up wasn't very nice."

"But he didn't do things, did he?" Surely he hadn't done things. Gang things. Girls, guns, drugs. Not my Sean.

"Honestly, I don't know what he did. He never told me and I never asked."

My mother's words came back to me. *In any marriage, there are some things you might not want to know.* "But he got out."

"Yes. By that time I knew what gangs were. And I was really scared for him. I kept begging him to get out, but you couldn't leave the gang. And if he'd tried, I don't know what they would have done to him. I was only in sixth grade. And I was with a foster family; I was stuck there. Looking back on it, I think he was worried that if he tried to go, they'd come after me. They probably would have. And there was this one boy. He was not a good person. He was in Sean's gang . . ." Her words tapered off, and I was worried that might be all she was going to say. "He wanted me to be his girlfriend. But Sean found out about it. He told me he was going to take care of it. That I wasn't going to have to worry about that guy, about any of it, anymore. I was so excited. I assumed Sean was going to take me away somewhere with him."

The regional train must have pulled into the station behind the park because a horde of people suddenly appeared. They walked en masse to the sidewalk and dispersed in all directions.

If Kelly had been in sixth grade, then Sean would have been a senior. "That was just before he enlisted, right?"

"Yeah. But I didn't understand that at the time. To me, it felt like he'd just disappeared."

"So he did leave the gang." He'd found a way to do it. "But what about that boy? He didn't bother you after Sean had gone?"

"No. He never bothered me again."

"That must have been a relief."

"Well, yeah. Sure. I mean, they died, so . . ."

"What do you mean *they* died? Who died?"

"That boy. And his best friend."

"When did they die?"

"It was just before . . . just after?" A pause hung in the air. "I think it was just before. I don't know. So much happened right then. Like I said, Sean enlisted. I didn't see him again for years. But one of my aunts took me in right after, so I ended up moving. But I think, at least I'm pretty sure, it happened just before he left."

"*Both* of them died?"

"Yeah."

"How?"

"They were shot. It was some sort of gang thing."

My heart stopped beating for one long moment as the implication of that statement made impact. Then it started again in double time.

In the background, a baby cried.

"They never sleep as long as they're supposed to, do they? Don't tell me. I don't want to know."

She made me promise to call again soon and hung up.

What were the chances that Sean had absolutely nothing to do with those gang members' deaths? The ones who'd been interested in his sister?

I considered what I knew about Sean. The medal he'd received during his service had been awarded for gallantry in action. The vehicle he'd been traveling in had been hit in an ambush. It overturned. He'd dragged his fellow soldiers to safety, killed the dozen enemy combatants who'd ambushed them, and used their own vehicle to transport him and the wounded soldiers out of danger.

All by himself.

That was heroic.

And I would know. I'd grown up around heroic people, people who risked their lives for the safety and liberties of others. Could I really say, if Sean had been responsible for those long-ago gang deaths, that it was any less heroic? If he'd done it, he'd done it to save his sister; he'd done it to get out of a gang. And after having been in foster care for so long, to have an aunt suddenly agree to take Kelly? I didn't think it was too generous to attribute that to Sean as well.

I was not going to think less of him for doing what he'd done back in high school, nor think more of those two gang members who'd been trying to coerce a *sixth grader* into a relationship.

When his sister had been in danger, he'd done what he had to do.

The resourcefulness and determination that had led to Sean's medal had also led to a bachelor's and a master's and a PhD. But back there, in that gang? That's where his resourcefulness and determination had developed.

I had to work with the facts I could find. Those facts told me Sean had been afraid of someone. Those facts told me he'd lied to me. But they also told me something about his character. In conjunction with Kelly's story, they told me he would do literally anything to protect someone he loved. I was beginning to see the outlines of a pattern.

18

Later that afternoon Brad returned my call.

"Georgie. Hey. How you doing?"

I appreciated it when people asked, but by that point, I figured they didn't really want to know. "We're doing all right. But hey—I was sorting through some things the other day and I found a key I think might belong to the office. And I realized I never returned Sean's badge." Not that I could have, had I wanted to, because I didn't have it. But how would Brad know that? "Do you want me to bring them in?"

"I'm pretty sure he would have turned those in when he left."

"When he left? You mean at the end of the day?"

"At the end of his job."

End of his job? "Because I know he brought his badge home every night."

"He probably had one from his other job too. But I'm sure we're fine."

"What other job is that?" There was a long enough pause that I wondered if we'd been disconnected. "Brad?"

"Yeah. I'm here. It's just— How do I say this? I thought you knew. Sean stopped working here last year. About six months before he died."

"When you say he stopped working there, I don't understand."

"He left."

"But he was still working. He was working somewhere. He went to work every day."

"He did say he had something else lined up."

I hated to put him on the spot, but it was the first I'd heard of it. "Do you remember when that would have been? Exactly?"

"Sure. Yeah. It was toward the end of August. I remember taking him out for lunch during Restaurant Week. You know, in DC? Cut-price menus at all the fancy restaurants?"

"He wasn't *fired*, was he?"

"Fired? No. Don't think so. It didn't seem like it. He was just moving on. Sort of vague about the job he was going to, but that's not unusual around here. Whatever it was, I got the impression that he was just switching agencies."

After the call I sat there behind my desk, holding on to my head with both hands. It seemed best. I was trying to grab hold of my thoughts. Maybe I was wrong. Maybe the core of Sean's character *wasn't* the desire to protect. Maybe it was a pathological drive to obfuscate. To lie.

I'd always kind of seen myself as A Seeker of Ultimate Truth. I'd taken pride in it. But the new information about Sean? I almost wished I'd never uncovered it. Any of it. I sat there trying to look at everything objectively, and the problem was, I couldn't figure out one way for it all to make sense.

Someone knocked on my door. Opened it. "Georgie?"

"Ted. Hi!" I took my hands from my head. Tried to make it look like I'd been smoothing back my hair.

"Meeting at eleven? You coming?"

"Yes. Sure. Yeah. Just give me a minute."

The door shut and I heaved a sigh, closing my eyes and rolling my chair way back so I could rest my head on my desk.

What was I supposed to tell Sam about his father?

I could hardly play the role of adoring, trusting wife when my perfect life had been blown to pieces.

Actually, probably I could.

Most definitely.

I sat up, opened a drawer, and rummaged around for a pen.

Pretending would be easier than telling him the truth. Because what truth would I tell him? "Hey, Sam, turns out your father was a big liar"?

Saying that could be problematic. Because it might create a ticking bomb of self-loathing that would explode upon impact in adolescence. So maybe not.

I sent a file to the printer.

But what if I didn't tell him the truth? What if someday way, *way* down the road I met an actual nice guy, someone like Chris, and fell in love again? Maybe not *again* again, because obviously I hadn't really fallen in love with Sean if the Sean I knew wasn't a true representation of the real Sean. I'd fallen in love with an illusion. So if I happened to fall in love with a real, honest, truthful person? What would Sam think?

That I'd thrown over the memory of his sainted father.

What defense would I have? Other than that I was a fickle woman, faithless to the memory of her beloved first husband?

I closed my eyes once more and forced myself to breathe. I didn't know the truth. Yet. I opened my eyes as I thought about the implications. So the best thing to do was nothing.

Nothing. I wasn't going to do anything. "There's nothing to do."

I'd said it out loud. My head didn't burst. The world didn't explode. For the moment, everything was all right.

I grabbed a notebook and my water bottle and headed out down the hall. As I walked, I tried to ignore the voice in my head, but I couldn't quite silence it.

Who were you really, Sean Brennan?

19

Jenn came over that night with my half of our farm share.
Her au pair picked up the box on Wednesdays.

I hustled us all inside, out of the cold. "Tell me there's some Halloween candy in there. I could have sworn I bought some last time I went to the store. And the time before that too. But I can't figure out where I put it."

"No candy. But there's broccoli and carrots and turnips." She dropped the large, waxed cardboard box onto my kitchen countertop.

I peered inside. "Turnips? Great." I wasn't a fan.

"Hey—I'm taking Preston down to that toy store in Crystal City on Saturday for story time. Want to come?"

"To Mr. Hoffman's? Maybe."

"Margarita?" Jenn opened my fridge, not bothering to wait for my reply. She brought out the mix, poured it into a pair of glasses, then mixed it with a generous pour of tequila. Jenn and margaritas and I went way back. "So spill it." She pointed at herself. "Best friend. Maid of honor. Person you can tell anything to, otherwise known as me. That would be *moi* in French. Come on. What's going on?"

I should have known I couldn't hide anything from her. It had always been that way. We'd met in high school and had been part of a group that included the daughter of the Pakistani deputy chief of mission at the Pakistani embassy; the daughter of the president of the American subsidiary of a big multinational conglomerate; the daughter of . . . I'd forgotten what her mom had done, but she'd been mentioned in the *Post* a lot; and me. Typically Arlington. I'd lost contact with the others soon after high school, but Jenn and I kept rotating in the same orbit. "Bad day. Bad week. That's all."

"Seriously, G. What's the deal?"

Did I really want to tell her? If I told Jenn, then it would all seem real. It would be like opening a door to a haunted house. I didn't know what might come out. Besides, she had enough to deal with on the Hill. She had a hand in everything Senator Rydel did and was trying constantly, as any chief of staff would, to weight the scales of political power in his favor. She was a master in the Byzantine art of keeping track of who owed favors to whom. And my father's upcoming confirmation hearing was probably making everything worse. Since Rydel was the head of the Armed Forces Committee and would be chairing the hearing, that was now on her plate too. She didn't have time to deal with my extracurricular stress.

I shook my head.

"We're still good, right?"

"It's just that I've been wondering . . ."

She straightened as if bracing for something. "Spill it. Just say it and get it over with. It's more efficient." She rolled her eyes. "That's what my father says, anyway."

Jenn had issues with her father. He was a big, serious, intimidating Supreme Court justice who'd only gotten more serious and more intimidating after her mother had died during our sophomore year. It wasn't easy pleasing someone who demanded perfection. It was even harder to find ways to get his attention. Back in high school Jenn had seesawed between trying hard to coax him into her life and shutting him out because she didn't think she deserved his time or attention. Since she'd left home after college they'd reached a sort of truce, although sniping had a tendency to break out now and then.

But if I couldn't talk to Jenn, then I couldn't talk to anyone. And I had to talk to someone. I decided to take a chance. "Do you think Sean ever cheated on me?" The thought had been lurking in the back of my mind.

Her brow furrowed and it took a moment before she responded. "Why would you ask that? You and Sean, you were like, I don't know, all those perfect 1950s TV couples. You weren't just Georgie. And. Sean. You were GeorgieandSean."

"I don't know. Just some things I've discovered lately."

"About *Saint Sean*? I can say this as the honest truth: I don't think he ever looked at anyone but you."

"But he was hiding something from me, Jenn."

"How do you know?"

I shook my head.

"Did he say something? Before the accident? Is that what this is about?"

"No." I shook my head. Tried to shrug it off. "It's probably just me being paranoid."

"Did somebody else say something? You want me to beat them up for you?"

I laughed and determined to put the topic away.

Jenn and I finished our margaritas, then she rounded up Preston.

As I walked with them out the door and onto the porch, Sam lured Preston down onto the lawn where they ran around like loons. As we were standing there, I caught sight of all those fall crocuses waving their spring-colored petals at me, showing me a detail I hadn't noticed before.

I must have pulled a face because Jenn raised a brow. "Something wrong?"

"I just—" I sighed. *"Those flowers."* I gestured out toward the fence. "I hate fall crocuses. I thought they were going to be spider lilies."

"So dig them up."

"We naturalized them. They were supposed to be naturalized." But they weren't. They mocked me from their ruler-straight rows.

She gave me quizzical look. "Yeah, flowers are natural."

"Naturalized. Planted as if they'd grown naturally."

"Which kind of contradicts the idea that they were planted at all. What do they call that? Oxymoron, right? Compassionate conservatives. Practical progressives. Principled politicians."

"The point is, we gave Sam the bulbs and had him throw them up in the air. Wherever they landed, Sean planted them."

"And?"

"And those are planted in rows. And they aren't lilies."

"So maybe he bought the wrong kind. Mark was famous for doing stuff like that. Send him to the store for toilet paper and he'd come back with a bag of potato chips."

"No. I saw them. Have you ever seen a spider lily bulb? They aren't the same. You can tell the difference. And it looks like he dug them up and replanted them."

"You know how Sean was. Always anal about— No, wait. That's *you*."

"Ha-ha. But that's what I mean."

"Okay. So he dug them up and replanted them. But why does that have to *mean* something?"

"Jennifer—we planted all those bulbs! Dozens of them. Why would he replant them? And when? And he knew I hated that kind of crocus. Why would he do that?"

Jenn's look of concern was being overshadowed by confusion. "He was probably joking. It's no big deal."

I might have believed her if Sam hadn't been there. But he'd had so much fun helping that day. And the Sean I knew never would have tried to erase that memory.

20

There was about an hour of daylight left. I texted June and asked if they would mind watching Sam for a while. She met us at the door, wearing a pair of Halloween-decorated sneakers. She enfolded him with a hug. "It's my favorite Sam!" As I left they were discussing whether to make cookies or brownies.

I found the shovel in the shed. It was hidden behind the rake and the plastic sled. I tugged on some garden gloves and went to work. "Jerk!" I muttered the word as I forced a shovel into the ground and jumped on it to drive it down farther. Blinking back tears, I overturned the dirt onto the grass. Sean had called me from the store to verify what kind of bulbs I wanted. I'd told him spider lilies; the red ones, not the pink ones.

And still he'd somehow managed to end up with yellow crocuses. So that meant he'd bought both? Because I knew we'd planted spider lilies.

Good grief, how many had he planted? If it had been just a dozen, I might have left them. As it was, the whole artificial-looking display insulted both my sense of aesthetics and my sense of fair play. I peeled my quarter-zip fleece off and draped it over the fence. My Don't Trust Atoms, They Make Up Everything T-shirt had seen better days, but then, so had the crocuses.

I jumped on the shovel again, but the ground wouldn't yield. Moving it a bit to the right, I tried again. That time it worked. Levering the soil out, I turned it over on top of the pile I'd created.

When I dug back into the ground, though, I hit that same hard patch of earth. Was it a stone? A brick? It wouldn't have been surprising. Whoever had built the house ninety years before had used the front yard as a trash heap for construction debris. Whenever we did yard work we couldn't dig anywhere without finding bricks and boards and nails.

Using the shovel more like a trowel, I excavated around the spot and was finally able to lift off the layer of earth from its top. It wasn't a stone or a brick. It was a box. A metal box.

Kneeling, I brushed the dirt off and exposed a corner.

"Hey!"

Jumping at the greeting, I turned to find Chris and his Maltipoo on the other side of the fence.

I stood. "Chris. Hi."

"Need some help?" He'd already released the latch on the gate.

"No." I tried to push the mound of dirt back into the hole with my foot. "All done."

He eyed the crocuses that I'd thrown into a heap. "I'm not really a flower guy, but aren't you supposed to let them, I don't know, stay in the ground while they bloom?"

"I meant to dig them up earlier in the season, but I never got around to it. They're the one flower I just can't stand."

"So you're ripping them out midseason."

I shrugged, then dumped a shovelful of dirt back into the hole on top of the box. "My yard, my rules."

"Remind me never to cross you."

I picked my way out of the bed—away from the box—toward the driveway and the shed behind the house, hoping he'd follow.

He did. "Where's Alice? She okay?"

"She's inside. She's fine." Mostly. When she wasn't trying to dig a hole through the house. Which reminded me. "Have you ever had mice?"

"As in pets?"

"As in pests. Something's driving Alice crazy in our crawl space."

"My neighbor had raccoons last winter. It's amazing, the tiny holes they can fit through. Rats too."

If I ever found a rat in my house, I would move out. Immediately.

"I could take a quick peek. See if there's anything down there."

"You know, I might just take you up on that." If anyone had to confront a creature, better him than me. "But I've got to get Sam to the rink tonight for a lesson."

"Sure. No problem. I'll see you tomorrow." He gestured with his thumb toward the end of the block. "Gotta get going too. Soccer practice."

As soon as he had turned the corner, I went back to the flower bed and dug the box free.

Kneeling, I brushed the dirt from it. It looked like a metal cashier's box. The finish was still shiny, untouched by corrosion. I might have convinced myself that it had been left there by kids playing buried treasure if it hadn't been placed right beneath all those replanted fall crocuses.

I nearly opened it right there but thought better of it. After glancing up and down the street, I shook the rest of the dirt from it and took it with me into the house.

In the kitchen I set it in the sink and put on my cleaning gloves. I didn't want to be at the mercy of any bugs that might come crawling out. But there was no need to worry. It was locked. If only I had a key.

But I did.

I had a key. I had the mystery key from Sean's key chain.

I peeled off the gloves, ran to the office, and dug the key out of the cardboard box. Then I slipped it into the lock with a trembling hand. The top swung open easily, silently. The inside was pristine. It contained just a single book enclosed in a gallon-size Ziploc. I undid the fastener and slipped it out.

It was some sort of diary or journal.

I opened it.

Sean's handwriting.

21

I set it on the counter. Ran my hand across the pages as if touching them would somehow put me in direct communication with him. I flipped through it. Only a quarter of the pages had been used.

The alarm on my phone beeped.

Time to get Sam ready for his hockey lesson.

I put the phone into my giant catchall of a purse and went across the street to get Sam. June gave him back to me along with a dozen still-warm brownies. I sent him to his room to get dressed for skating. Sooner than I expected, he bumped back down the hall, dragging his bag behind him.

"Are you sure you need all of that? It's going to take you half an hour just to take everything out and put it on."

"It's only my helmet. And my stick. And my pads and—"

I took the bag from him. "It's fine." He was small for his age, but even so, it seemed like the bag shouldn't be taller than the kid who owned it. I would have swung it forward to tap him on the butt, but I was afraid I might give myself a hernia.

Once we got to the rink, we stood in line to get skates. I wrestled them onto his feet and must have tied and retied them ten times to cries of "But they're too loose" and "Now they're too tight."

"Is your name Goldilocks?"

He giggled.

"You ready?"

He nodded. At least I thought he did underneath that massive helmet.

I held his hand as he tottered on his skates through the glass double doors to the rink. There, he joined the crowd of wobbly-legged kids waiting for the session to start.

"Want me to stay until they let you on?"

He nodded.

I held Sam's hand as he shuffled along toward the door. Then I watched, holding my breath, as he put a tentative foot to the ice. He grabbed the rail and wouldn't let go, but as he inched away from the door, he glanced back and sent me a triumphant wave, which very nearly caused him to lose his balance. I stayed to make sure he made it to his lesson in one piece.

Once he did, I went up to the glass-fronted mezzanine and found a seat overlooking the rink. And there, I pulled the book out of my purse and opened it.

The book I was holding wasn't a journal. In fact, I wouldn't have said Sean had even made entries. The pages were filled with numbers and names.

Some had been crossed out.

Others had a question mark drawn beside them.

They were all written in the same format.

E/Abbott/David/DS
E/Ornofo/Lee/DS
E/Beckman/Beck/DS
E/Wallace/Reginald/DS
E/Conway/Paul/DS
2/Denunzio/Bobby/BW
2/Jenkins/Peter/BW

It was like a logbook. A roster.

Or a record of some sort of investigation?

I felt my eyes widen. I shut the book and buried it at the bottom of my purse. Glancing around, I looked to see if anyone had been watching. A woman's glance intersected with mine. She smiled and then her gaze shifted to the rink.

I picked up my purse and transferred it to my lap, threading my arms through the strap.

But as I sat there watching Sam pick his way back and forth across the rink, something niggled at me.

I brought the book back out and flipped through the pages again until I found it.

E/Conway/Paul/DS

Conway.
It seemed to me I'd heard that name before.

After I put Sam to bed, I picked up the book again. I took a picture of all the entries with my phone so I could look at them without having to access the actual pages. Sean had gone to a lot of trouble to hide it, so I figured I should do the same. I'd find a safe place to put it.

I turned back to the Conway page.

Abbott
Ornofo
Beckman
Wallace
Conway

On a whim, I turned on my computer and typed in the names as I flipped through the pages.

A search returned nothing but the random hits a person would expect with common names like Abbott and Conway.

Costello. Twitty.

I searched several of the combinations of names and numbers from Sean's notes.

Nothing there either.

I woke myself that evening with a snore. After going through Sean's book, I'd been too wound up to go to sleep. I'd turned on the TV instead and fallen asleep watching cable news. I woke to the sound of my father's voice. It took me a moment to realize it was coming from the TV.

"Listen—we've tried being enemies with Russia. We tried it during the Cold War. Was the world any safer? Why don't you ask the children of the eighties, who grew up having nightmares about nuclear wars."

The news anchor was frowning. "So you're saying we should *trust* Russia? Because that's what I'm hearing."

"Trust them?" My father held up his hands as if that was going a bit too far. "I think trust has to be earned. What I'm saying is, why can't there at least be a dialogue? Talking never hurt anyone. And talking about small things can sometimes lead to bigger things. That's all I'm saying." He leaned forward, tone earnest. "I'm not talking about making promises. Not talking about signing treaties or defense agreements. I'm just talking about . . ." He stopped and chuckled. "I'm just talking about talking."

I turned off the TV and went to get myself a glass of water from my perfectly working faucet. Out in the night, past my backyard, a light went on in the house behind mine. A man appeared in the window.

He lifted a hand.

I nodded and clicked off the light.

It was strangely comforting to know that there was someone else besides me awake so late. Especially since I'd found out that Sean had done something. Some *things*. Things that were undecipherable.

And definitely not like him.

Or maybe they were completely in character. Things that I had been so certain of the previous week were now open to question.

As I climbed into bed, I tried to corral my thoughts, but they were restless. I hadn't yet fallen fully into sleep when I heard something. Some noise that reverberated through my head loudly enough to wake me.

I lay there listening, trying to turn the sound into something familiar.

But it hadn't been the refrigerator or the radiator or any other thing that I was used to hearing. I knew that because it had come from beneath me.

From the crawl space below my room.

I sat up and turned on the light, hoping, I suppose, that illumination would help with clarification. I drew my knees up to my chest. The sheet up to my chin. It was an ages-old reaction to the fear of monsters underneath the bed.

Alice had heard it too. She listened along with me, head lifted, ears cocked.

What was it?

I was listening so hard that I could almost hear myself listen.

It hadn't been a creak, a squeak, or a rustle.

Alice whined.

Wanting to listen, hoping to hear it again, I hissed at her to stop.

She pushed herself to her feet, left her bed, and started pawing at the floor just like she'd done two nights before.

"Alice!" I whispered her name. When that didn't make her stop, I snapped my fingers at her. "Alice." She turned around and lumbered back to her bed.

I'd heard *some*thing. An animal, maybe? A mouse running between the floorboards?

There it was again!

Some sort of shifting. Not a shifting *of* the floorboards. A shifting *beneath* them.

Alice froze as I swept my blanket aside and eased toward the side of my bed, closer to where the sound had been.

It wasn't a mouse. I'd heard mice before. They scratched and scurried. This thing, whatever it was, hadn't been that. It was a heavier sound, with more force behind it. It had been something bigger.

Alice let out one of her quavery barks.

I heard a metallic *clink*.

I picked up my phone from the bedside table and dialed 911. Then I pulled Alice away from her post and took her into the living room with me. Whoever was out there would have to make it past Alice and me before he could even think about going down the hall for Sam.

While Alice sprawled on the couch and went to sleep, I pulled back an edge of the curtain and stood there, heart pounding as I stared into the darkness, waiting for the police to arrive.

22

"But you had to have heard them, Jenn. You're only three blocks away." I switched my cell phone from speaker as I heard Sam flush the toilet. He'd be coming down the hall for breakfast; no need for him to hear about what had happened the night before. I lowered my voice. "They sent two squad cars."

"I didn't hear a thing."

In the background I heard the sound of . . .

"What are you doing?"

"Teeth."

"Sorry. Didn't mean to catch you in the bathroom."

"'S okay."

"There were lights and sirens. Thank goodness Sam didn't wake up."

"Did they catch whoever it was?"

"No." I'd been afraid they wouldn't. Because who would hang around when he could hear the cops coming?

Jenn murmured something I couldn't hear.

"What?"

"Sorry." Her voice was more distinct. "So what'd they say?"

"They said there may have been someone, but they couldn't find any signs." Which was probably cop code for "just another crazy lady."

"None?"

"No footprints. No signs of forced entry into the crawl space. But then, it wasn't locked. There was no lock." Stupid, stupid. Putting a lock on it had become priority number one. "And that side of the yard is mulched."

"You want to spend a few days at my place, G?" Her voice seemed to echo. I heard heels clicking across a floor. "I could put you two up on the couch."

"We're fine. There's nothing to be afraid of." Funny just how little reassurance those words provided.

"I'd be afraid. Just saying."

"I'll put a lock on the crawl space. Should have done it before. It was probably just a drifter looking for someplace to spend the night." The more rational I sounded, the more afraid I felt. But I was thirty-six years old. I wasn't supposed to be afraid of the dark anymore.

"It wouldn't be a problem. It really wouldn't."

And I really wanted to say yes. But I knew I shouldn't. "We'll be fine."

"Just so we're clear, when the police find you and Sam murdered and they come to question your best friend, I'll tell them I offered, but you declined."

Chris asked how our night had been as I was walking home from school that morning. I just smiled. "Fine." I didn't want to think about it any more than I already was. But when I got home, Jim was waiting for me at the front gate.

"You okay?" He peered at me from behind his glasses, worry sketching lines between his eyes. "Heard the sirens last night."

"I'm fine. I had a prowler."

His brows peaked. "You should have called. I would have sent June right over with her rolling pin."

I laughed.

"Seriously. You should have."

"We pay enough in taxes, I figured I should make the police handle it."

"Did they catch him?"

"No."

"He get inside?"

"In the crawl space. That's where I heard him."

"Want me to take a look?"

"I don't have time right now. I've got a meeting at work. Can't be late." Not to another one.

"Doesn't take two people. I'll check it out for you while you get your things."

"You wouldn't mind?"

"'Course not!"

"You don't have to."

"Hey, kid, I want to, okay?"

By the time I'd made a lunch for myself, exchanged my yoga pants for a pair of jeans, and grabbed my attaché, Jim was nailing the door shut. "I'll swing by Cherrydale Hardware and pick up a lock later in the morning. But this should do the trick for now. Once I get that lock on, I'll leave the key on your dining room table, okay? I'll let myself in with your spare."

"You don't have to do all this, Jim."

"Maybe not, but I want to."

"Thank you. I can't even tell you—" I couldn't finish my sentence. I felt too much like crying.

He patted me on the shoulder. "Hang in there, kid. It'll be okay."

It didn't feel okay. It didn't feel okay all day long. And it still didn't feel okay when I picked up Sam from school. But I tried not to let it show.

"Mom!" He ran over, backpack bouncing, when he saw me. "Mom! Ms. Hernandez wants to know what you do. She's looking for parents to talk about their jobs. I told her you were a fizziest. She didn't know what that was, so I told her you're a scientist. And now she needs to know what kind."

"A physicist."

"That's what I *told* her. I told her you work with holes. She said she needs to talk to you."

"It's *worm*holes. Although they're not really what I work on."

"But that's what I told her."

Because that's what I'd told him. What kid wants to know that their parent just sits around all day and thinks really hard? So I'd told him about parallel universes and wormholes and black holes. "I'm a special kind of scientist. I try to explain things that are hard to understand. Kind of like magic."

"So maybe I can tell Ms. Hernandez that you do magic tricks!"

"It's not really magic tricks."

"You could say it was. And I'd let you wear my cape."

I stopped walking, pulled my son close, and kissed him on top of the head. Hard. It was easier to keep from crying that way. "Thanks."

Jim came over that evening to make sure I'd found the key on the table. After he'd gone, I left Sam playing in his room with Legos, grabbed a flashlight, and went to see what Jim had installed for the crawl space.

A large Keep Out sign was nailed to the door, and it had been secured with a very big, very formidable-looking padlock.

I unlocked it and opened the door. Then I clicked on the flashlight and squatted, peering inside, just to make sure everything looked okay.

Nothing to note except a glint. Back in the corner.

Were they eyes?

I beat the flashlight against the wall, hoping whatever it was would scurry away, but it didn't move. I shifted the flashlight up and down, back and forth.

Still glinted. Still didn't move.

I so didn't want to crawl around down there. I was fine with electricity and motors and machines and lasers, but I was not fine with spiders. Or mice or rats or other things.

"I'm coming in!" I said it with a confidence I didn't feel.

23

"I'm coming in there right this second." I paused, listening for any noise that would require an actual, certified pest removal expert.

Nothing.

Crouching, I stepped over the threshold and swept the space with the flashlight. I hadn't been down there in a long time. Outside had been Sean's domain.

At least it wasn't musty. It smelled of damp earth and old wood.

Duckwalking, I headed toward the corner where I'd seen the glint. My light bounced around as I tried not to let any part of my body or clothing touch the ceiling or the dirt floor.

Huh.

There weren't any cobwebs.

And it wasn't all dirt at my feet. Here and there, bits of sawdust powdered the ground.

Termites?

I hoped not. Not on top of everything else.

I swept the arc of light up to the ceiling. Was that . . . ? I took one duck-step closer and put a hand to the ground to get a better look at a shadowed area between two long wooden support beams.

I didn't see any evidence of termites, but there was a cable running along the length of the crawl space, right up against one of those beams. Following it with my light, I traced it back to where it took a right-angled turn and headed down the outer wall toward the door.

Taking a look outside, I saw where it went up the side of the house and then joined a set of other cables that ran from the house to the electricity and telephone poles along the street.

Back in the crawl space, I traced it in the other direction toward the other side of the house. Exploring further, I could see where that long central cable was joined by another that came from the basement.

A circuit?

But we'd had the house rewired after we'd bought it. And there was no reason why any of those new wires would have been routed through the crawl space.

I shined the light up toward that cable again.

Definitely a puzzle.

My flashlight hand sagged and something caught the light, reflecting it.

The glint.

Setting the flashlight on the ground, I rolled forward from my feet onto my knees. One hand on the ground, I reached out toward the object with the other, fingers closing on it. I brought my prize into the flashlight's beam.

Then I brought a trembling hand to my mouth.

Sean's Leatherman.

I closed my eyes as I remembered.

"Ow." I shifted positions on the couch, placing space between my hip and whatever it was that had gouged me. "What *is* that?"

Sean was already reaching for me, pulling me back into his embrace. After a month of dating, it had become my favorite place to be. "What is what?"

I slid a hand up under his shirt and around his waist.

He cringed. "Cold hand!"

"Warm heart." I smiled, pulling my hair away from my face as I pushed away from him. "What is this thing that keeps poking me?"

I edged up his shirt and grabbed at whatever it was near his belt.

He glanced down. "My Leatherman." He sat halfway up, wrapped an arm around my waist, and pulled me back beside him, nuzzling my neck.

"Your Leatherman?"

He sat up, adjusted himself, then pulled it off his belt, offering it to me.

"It's a pocketknife."

He scoffed. "Does it look like a pocketknife?"

It was shaped like a pocketknife, albeit quite a bit larger. And it had all those metal pull-outs on both sides, with slits in them like a pocketknife. I started pulling them out. A saw. A knife. A wire cutter. Pliers. Some sort of little brush. All the kinds of things that would come in handy in a research lab. I'd figured out what to ask for at Christmas!

"Why do you wear this?" He didn't work in a lab. He was a historian. He worked in an office. And spent a lot of time going through files in archives.

"Why do I—" He snatched it from me as if worried I might break it. "It's an old habit. From my army days. Any soldier worth his rank wears one of these. I mean—" He broke off as if he couldn't find the words. "Okay. Before we go any further, we don't *wear* them. We *carry* them."

I tried my best not to laugh.

He turned to face me. "They do a hundred things." Now he was sounding like a used-car salesman. "Your father must have one of these."

It was my turn to scoff. "My father has people to carry one of those for him."

He smiled. "Fair enough."

I kept on pulling out tools. A wire stripper. An awl. A screwdriver. Several of them. "A wire crimper?"

"For crimping wire." He took it from me, folding everything back up.

I learned something new about myself. Men with pocketknives. It was kind of dorky. And adorable.

Sean had never gone anywhere without his Leatherman.

Ever.

It could be considered a weapon, granted. So he couldn't take it anywhere there was a metal detector or a security checkpoint. But anyplace he *could* take it, he did.

On the weekends it was one of the first things he put on in the morning and one of the last things he took off at night.

He'd shoved it into his pocket as he left the house the night he was killed, hadn't he? I was sure he had, but maybe I was wrong.

I had to be wrong because I was holding it in my hand.

But then, the Leatherman had been listed on the inventory from the morgue, even though it hadn't made it back to me in the box of Sean's effects.

How did any of that make sense?

I put a fingernail to one of the slits and pulled out a tool.

Screwdriver.

Maybe the medical examiner had been mistaken. Maybe the Leatherman had never been among Sean's effects.

I discounted that theory almost before I'd finished thinking it. That didn't make any sense either. Some things, almost anybody brought into the morgue might have: keys, a wallet, shoes. But a Leatherman?

You wouldn't make a mistake about something like that.

So somehow the Leatherman had disappeared between the medical examiner's office and the cardboard box. Then reappeared.

In my crawl space?

Like I'd told Sam, my job was trying to explain things that are hard to understand.

But the disappearance and reappearance of the Leatherman just wasn't possible. Not in our universe. Not without the presence of something like a wormhole.

24

I tucked the Leatherman into my pocket, took one last look around, and backed out of the space. I pushed the door shut with a scrape and closed the padlock.

Then I went inside and performed an inspection of my basement.

I'd found a cable of unknown origin. That much was clear. Its function, however, was a complete mystery. As was the date of installation. It looked new . . . ish. But how new was new? Had Sean had something put in that I hadn't been aware of?

I called both the phone company and our cable TV/internet provider. Nothing had been recently installed.

In frustration, I grabbed a pair of wire cutters and stood staring at it with indecision.

There was no reason for the cable company to install a wire that ran from the basement into the crawl space. The only point in that would be to provide either service or access. I discounted service. Obviously there were no computers or TVs in the crawl space and there never had been.

Access? Possible. But why go all the way out there and then to the street, when the cable box was easily accessible on the outside of the house?

I heard the thump of small feet across the floor above my head. "Mom?" The call floated down the stairs.

"Down here."

"Mommy?"

"I'm down—" I raised my voice. "I'm in the basement!" I reached up and snipped the piece of the cable that ran through the wall and into the crawl space. No green lights flickered on the router. No red lights appeared. It hadn't made any difference. "Coming!"

Later that night, after sleep had finally claimed Sam, I tested all my cable connections. In spite of my having cut that cable, my internet, TV, and Wi-Fi were all up and running.

Someone who was not the gas company, the telephone company, or the cable company had a very odd interest in my basement. A very marked interest in keeping tabs on what?

On information being accessed by my computer?

Was that why the not-gas-company people had wanted access to the basement?

A cold sweat of fear broke out on my forehead.

Who were they? Why would anyone be interested in me? And why now? Whatever Sean had been involved in, whomever he'd been involved with, they had to know he was dead.

My computer, and quite possibly my Wi-Fi, had been compromised. I'd severed the connection, but that didn't mean whoever *they* were wouldn't try again. If I assumed they would, then I would keep myself from doing anything stupid.

I rebooted my router, then reset my password and renamed the network. I adjusted the Wi-Fi settings on my phone.

Phone!

My phone was even more susceptible. Every time it was turned on it could function as a tracking device. And every time I made a phone call, it pinged a cell tower. Of course, monitoring my cell phone required a court order. Or a personal decision on my part to download an app that would share my phone's location with family and friends or help me find my phone if I lost it. I went to my phone settings and app manager and made sure I hadn't granted those permissions.

I could power off my phone when I didn't absolutely need it, but that would risk me missing emergency texts from the school or a call about Sam or even a phone call *from* Sam. My phone number was the only one he'd memorized. Considering how often he mixed up his words, I didn't trust that he could memorize a new phone number without mixing it up with the old one. I needed to know he could reach me in an emergency situation.

One thing was certain: I also needed to figure out what Sean had been involved in. Because, apparently, it now involved me. And soon, whoever *they* were would figure out I'd blocked their access.

I took advantage of the window of opportunity to do one more search on Paul Conway. I was hoping it would jog my memory. There were hundreds of Paul Conways, but I got a hit on a local internet news site. The link led to an article on a hit-and-run fatality that had happened the previous night.

Paul Conway was the victim.

25

I had a lunch meeting the next day in Ballston and decided to swing by home on the way back to work. I could hear Alice whimpering even before I opened the door. Once I stepped inside, it took me a minute to understand what I was seeing.

And another minute to take it all in.

Alice had been muzzled with a Velcro tie around her snout; her legs had been zip-tied together. And the living room?

There was no place left for Sam to hide from the bad guys.

The sofa cushions had been sliced, the pillows punctured. The curtains had been torn from their rod.

Sean's campaign desk had been overturned. My hovering Bluetooth speaker had been grounded; a dent marred its smooth surface. And my replica da Vinci clock was shattered.

A hole had been punched through the plaster wall by the fireplace.

The TV had been knocked over.

Nothing, absolutely *nothing* was as I had left it that morning.

A white-hot rage swept over me.

Alice was eyeing me with a look of profound shame. I knelt beside her and freed her from the muzzle. For her legs I needed scissors. Or a knife. But as I moved toward the dining room, intent on finding one, she barked and let out a long, rolling growl.

I froze.

So intent had I been on freeing her that I hadn't stopped to consider that whoever had ransacked the house might still be there. I retreated to the door and then, leaving Alice, I fled to Jim and June's.

"What?" Jim put a hand to my forearm. "Just slow down. One thing at a time."

"I need a knife." I also needed to find some way to keep my teeth from chattering.

June had come from the kitchen to join us. "What kind do you need? Paring knife? Bread knife? I've got this great—"

"They tied up Alice and I have to get her free."

Jim and June exchanged a glance. "Tied up Alice?" Jim peered down at me, concern etched between his eyes. "Back up and start again from the beginning."

By the time I'd finished, June was calling the police. Jim had retrieved a gun from somewhere and was shoving it into his waistband. He saw me watching him. "Don't worry. I know how to use it."

Over June's protests, I went back to the house with Jim. While I freed Alice, he inspected the rooms. We were standing together on the front porch when the police pulled up.

Though the living room had been vandalized and Sean's study was a complete wreck, I couldn't say for certain that anything had been taken.

"Did you check your jewelry, ma'am?" The officer paused in her writing while she waited for my answer.

"I don't have any." Aside from my wedding ring. My mother had given me lots of jewelry over the years. Necklaces. Bracelets. Earrings. As soon as she sent them, I'd donated them to local charity silent auctions.

"Any cash in the house? Credit cards?"

"No."

"Electronics? Any of those missing?"

"Missing? No. Broken? Yes."

"Anything else of value?"

Memories? Souvenirs of my life with Sean? A sense of security that would take a long time to restore? "No."

She told me she would file a report. After she left, I got in touch with my insurance company. Then I called a locksmith to come change out all my locks and add deadbolts, agreeing to pay extra for immediate service.

June and Jim helped me clean up the mess. I didn't want Sam to see anything out of place when he got home. I found an old college poster down in the basement to tack over the hole in the wall. While June ran the vacuum cleaner up and down the hall, Jim duct-taped the sofa cushions back together. When he was done, I fit them back into the couch, wrong sides up. I crossed my fingers that Sam wouldn't notice.

I sent June and Jim home with a promise that I would call them if I noticed anything suspicious.

I knew I should call my parents. I knew I should tell them what had happened to the house. They would have wanted to know. But if I did, they'd swoop in and make us stay with them. All my reasons for not moving in with them would be moot.

But would that really have been such a bad thing? Why couldn't we stay with them a few days? Why shouldn't I let them help us?

Because after a few days we'd still have to come back home.

I'd still have to get used to living in a house that had been broken into and pondering questions that didn't have any answers. I'd still have to be brave and strong. I'd still have to figure out how to keep on keeping on.

It was something my parents couldn't do for me.

The chill, crystalline morning yielded to a blustery evening. The wind pushed at my car as I drove from work to school that evening to pick up Sam. Ms. Hernandez was waiting with him. She pulled me aside to fill me in on something that had happened earlier in the day.

I waited until after dinner to address it with Sam.

"Is there dessert?" He was looking up at me with hopeful eyes.

"I need to talk to you for a minute."

"Then can we have dessert?"

"Yes. Then we can have dessert."

He sat there in his booster seat, cape tied around his neck, waiting for me to continue.

"Ms. Hernandez told me about something that happened in class today. Sam, did you push someone at school?"

He sucked at his bottom lip. "Guess so."

"Why?"

He shrugged.

"Can you tell me what happened?"

"She was mean."

That shouldn't have made it any worse, but it did. "What happened?"

"She said mean things to me."

"What things?"

He shrugged again. "Things."

"Sam!"

He looked up at me, startled.

"I need you to tell me the truth."

"She said Daddy was dead."

"The thing is, Daddy *is* dead." It was one of the hardest things I'd ever had to say. "You went to Daddy's funeral. Don't you remember?" He'd sat right beside me. We'd held hands the entire time.

He said nothing.

Maybe he didn't remember. Maybe he'd been more emotionally impacted by his father's death than I'd thought.

"He's in a hole now."

Relief washed over me. Of course he remembered. "That's right."

"He went into the firm hole."

"*Firm* hole?" Sean had been cremated and I'd explained they were going to put him in a little hole in a big wall and put a plaque on top of it. The wall was made of stone. I supposed it *was* an unusually firm sort of hole.

"You know." He looked at me as if he was waiting for me to say something. "You go in one side and come out the other. Like a tunnel."

"A *worm*hole?" *Dear God.* "You think he went into a wormhole?"

He was playing with the strings of his cape. "Yeah."

"The thing is, Sam . . . The thing is . . ." I couldn't tell him wormholes weren't real, could I? I'd always tried hard to tell him the truth. No one had ever found one, but theoretically, they could exist. There was a possibility.

His eyes sought mine. "Welp, what if . . . what if when Daddy went into the firm hole—"

"Wormhole."

"What if, when he went in, he was still alive?"

How to tread carefully? "If he was still alive when he went in, then it would be possible that he could come back out."

His face brightened. "That's what I told her. He just went into the hole, that's all. That's what I said. But she wouldn't believe me. She said her grandpa went into a hole and he was still there and he wasn't ever coming out and—"

"Sam, Daddy would have had to have been alive if we expect him to come back out. And we know that he wasn't."

His gaze sank toward the table.

"You know that he wasn't. Remember?"

He nodded.

"So your father *didn't go into a wormhole.* Do you understand?"

"But if he went in there before he died and he was still alive, then—"

"Sam, your father didn't."

"But how do you know?"

"Because he died, sweetie."

"But how do you *know*?"

"Because his car was hit and he died. Remember?"

"But if—"

"So if Dad was dead, then he couldn't be anywhere else. He couldn't be in a wormhole. Do you understand?"

"But—"

"He's not coming back. He can't."

"But if he went into the hole—"

"Sam!"

He looked up, eyes wide in that small, dear face. "But—"

"He didn't go into a wormhole. He's dead! Your father is dead. He's dead and he's *not coming back*!"

He slid from his booster seat and tore off down the hall, cape flapping behind him.

"Sam!"

26

I would have given Sam anything. I would have moved heaven and earth if I thought I could. I would have lied, cheated, or stolen if I had to. I wanted Sean back just as much as he did. Mostly so I could yell at him for what he'd done to his son.

And to me.

Bedtime was a subdued affair that evening. As Sam brushed his teeth in the bathroom, I did a quick check of his closet. Knelt and looked underneath his bed. I don't know what I would have done if I'd found anything odd there, but it made me feel better.

Sam came into the room and pulled his pajamas out of his drawer. When I tried to help, he gathered them up and turned away. When he got in bed, he turned away from me and refused to say his prayers. I said them for him.

"Sam, I'm sorry I yelled at you. I shouldn't have done that."

There was no response.

"Sometimes adults don't know the right thing to say. Sometimes they get scared. And sometimes when you're scared, it's easier to yell than it is to say something the nice way."

He turned to look at me over his shoulder. "You get scared?"

Yes! I'd spent the rest of the previous night awake, listening for noises. I was sleeping with Sean's Leatherman under my pillow. And someone had just ransacked our house. But still, maybe I shouldn't have admitted to it. Maybe my being scared would make Sam more scared. No matter, it was done. I'd said it. Best thing to do was to own it. "I do get scared. Everyone gets scared sometimes."

He rolled toward me and put an arm out to hug me around the waist. "It's okay, Mommy. That's why we have Alice."

I kissed him. "You're right. That's why we have Alice."

"And if you get scared in the middle of the night, you can always come and sleep in my bed with me."

Tears slid from my eyes at the words of my kind, brave boy. "And what would you tell me if I did?"

He let go and settled onto his back. The hall light shone in his eyes as he looked at me. "I'd say, 'Mommy, it's okay. Don't worry. Everything's going to be all right.'"

The wind whipped into a temper that evening as it sometimes did. I heard it the way I heard planes going into and out of Reagan National Airport: from a great distance, as a hum in the background. Then, quite suddenly, it was beating against the house.

I jumped.

My heart had just dropped back into its normal pace when the floorboards creaked somewhere in the front of the house, in the living room.

Alice didn't even flick an ear.

I reminded myself that we lived in an old house. It was just settling.

But the wind stirred up a great restlessness inside of me. Suddenly I felt much too isolated. I wanted to talk to someone besides myself.

I wanted to talk to Sean.

I wanted to tell him about the break-in. I wanted to tell him what I'd said to Sam. I wanted to tell him off. To demand he tell me what the heck he'd been doing the night he died.

But I couldn't. He was dead.

That's what I'd told Sam, wasn't it?

I vowed that in the morning I would finally take his number off our phone plan. It was time. But that night, listening to the wind howl through the trees and beat against the windows, I just needed to not be alone. I needed to hear his voice one last time. I picked up my phone to dial his old number and realized I had a voice message of my own. I thumbed over to my voice mail log to see who it was.

Sean Brennan.

At 6:43 p.m.

How was that even possible?

I brought up the call information; it listed his old number. I went back to the voice mail log and pressed on his name. Held the phone to my ear.

Hey. Georgie. There was a long pause. *Do you still trust me? I need you to know that—* His words became garbled, as if he'd turned away from the phone, and then the message ended.

27

Sean?

Had I just heard . . . Was that *Sean?*

How could it be?

Sean was dead.

As I was trying to figure out what had just happened, the voice mail ended with a beep.

I stared at the phone in my hand, trying to think of a reasonable explanation for what I'd just heard. But the more I stared, the more my hand shook.

I set the phone down on my bedside table and pushed it away.

Swiped at the sweat that had formed above my lip.

My ears felt thick. They were buzzing.

Maybe my doubts about Sean's trustworthiness were manifesting themselves in audible voices. Maybe I'd been wanting to speak with him so badly that I'd brought him back to life.

I tried to pick up the phone but dropped it.

With a shaking hand, I retrieved if from the floor and brought up the message again.

Hey. Georgie. Do you still trust me? I need you to know that—
<beep>

Sean.

It truly sounded like Sean. And the call had been made from his phone number.

It was as if something in my brain had crossed circuits and I was receiving messages from the twilight zone.

But that wasn't possible. I tried to refocus myself on what *was* possible.

Maybe Sean's phone had been stolen during the break-in. I hadn't even checked to see if everything was still in the box. I went to the office and pulled it out of the closet to check.

It was still there.

But maybe someone had traded out his chip for theirs.

I took the phone into the bedroom and used one of the tools on Sean's Leatherman to take it out. I used my phone to verify that it was his.

That meant the call had to have come from Sean's phone.

Where had I been at 6:43? Eating dinner with Sam.

Fear knotted my stomach.

Had someone been in the house, in the office, while we'd been in the dining room?

I tried to power up the phone, but the battery was dead.

There was no way the call could have come from Sean's phone. It wasn't possible.

And there was no way Sean could have made that call. He was dead.

I sat on the bed, phone cradled in my hands.

What should I do?

First thing I couldn't do: tell my parents. They were coming into town to get ready for the confirmation hearing, and I'd invited them for dinner. But crazy was not something the Slater family did. Period. End of story.

I couldn't tell Jim and June. They worried about me enough as it was.

I could tell Jenn, but she'd looked at me so strangely when I asked her if she thought Sean had ever cheated on me. I didn't want to have to explain all the other odd things that had been going on. So that left no one.

No one but me.

✎

I couldn't sleep that night. I have to admit I didn't try very hard. I was afraid to. I was worried I would wake up certifiably insane. But I had more than enough distractions to keep me from those thoughts. The next day, Friday, was Bring a Parent to School Day. And after that, my parents were coming to dinner. I called in sick to work so I could have the day off. They assumed I had a physical ailment. I didn't tell them I was afraid it might be mental.

Ms. Hernandez beamed her thousand-kilowatt smile in my direction when she saw me. "I've put you right after Dr. Thomas."

I wished she had put me before Dr. Thomas. Dr. Thomas was a veterinarian and she brought real live animals. After she put the guinea pig and the baby chick back in their cages, Ms. Hernandez asked Sam to introduce me.

He took my hand and pulled me up from my place on the carpet beside him. "Welp, this is my mom. She's a doctor too, but she can't help anyone."

That was me. Academically brilliant but practically useless. It didn't, however, keep me from performing the magic tricks Sam had requested. I made a glass fill itself with water, I turned liquid into gas using a bicycle pump, and I made a boiled egg slide through the narrow mouth of a glass jar. I wished I could figure out the magic that had created Sean's message as easily. The only thing I could figure: someone was playing a cruel trick.

After me came Mr. Carter. He was a journalist with the *Post* and he came armed with handouts: bookmarks, colorful cartoon books, and puzzle pages that explained the importance of the First Amendment.

Later, as I was standing in the lunch line with Sam in the cafeteria, Ms. Hernandez motioned me over. "When the students go outside to play, would you mind coming by the classroom?"

I ate my lunch in record time and waved at Sam as he ran from the cafeteria out onto the playground. In the classroom Ms. Hernandez was sitting at one of those tiny tables, waiting for me. She pushed a folder across the table. "He's still drawing these."

I opened the folder.

It was another long black spiral that stretched from one end of the page to the opposite corner. But this time there was a difference. This time I knew what it was.

Realization sank into my stomach. I couldn't keep the tears from coming. I dabbed at them with the cuff of my sweater. "They're wormholes. He's been drawing wormholes."

28

I waited until Sam came back from recess before I left. I didn't want him to freak out if I wasn't there. As I walked home—coat collar turned up, hands shoved deep into my pockets—my cell phone rang.

I turned into the wind as I answered so my hair would stop blowing into my face. "Hello?"

"Mrs. Brennan? This is Kyle Correy."

Kyle Correy? Kyle *Correy*! The medical examiner from Sean's autopsy. I'd written him a letter. "Yes. Dr. Correy. Hi."

"You asked me to call you? About your husband?"

"Hi. Yes. My husband. You did his autopsy. And you also took his inventory. I had thought there was something missing, but I found it." Or maybe *it* had found *me*. "I'm sorry. Sorry to have bothered you."

"No. I remember." He paused. "Could you do me a favor? I'm sure you've got it all figured out by now . . ." His voice trailed off. When he resumed talking, it was in a whisper. "But the feds didn't want that to get around. It was different from the others."

I stopped walking. "Sorry?"

"Everyone knows I swung a deal. But not many people, not even my attorney, know about *that*. So please, let's keep it that way."

"Dr. Correy, I don't understand what you—"

"I have to go. Sorry."

"Wait! Dr. Correy?"

Silence.

I stood there on the sidewalk trying to figure out what had just happened.

I'd been operating under the assumption that Sean's death was a hit-and-run.

Had I been wrong?

Dr. Correy had seemed to suggest that there was some sort of relationship between the feds and Sean. Some sort of relationship they didn't want anyone to know about.

Maybe Sean's death hadn't been an accident.

As I sat there, it felt as if the world was collapsing in on me.

I tried to push it back. In order to think, I had to focus.

What else had Dr. Correy said? *The feds didn't want that to get around. It was different from the others.* What did that mean? That Sean's death didn't have to do with drugs? Or that whatever deal Correy had made, when it came to Sean, it had been done in a different kind of way?

And why didn't the feds want it to get around? What were they trying to hide? Who were they trying to hide it from?

I didn't have enough information to determine what Dr. Correy had meant when he said that.

And what about the other part? *I'm sure you've got it all figured out by now.*

What was there to figure out? And why was he so sure I would have been able to do so?

I spent the afternoon tidying the house for my parents' visit. As I cleaned, I worked on solving the mysteries of Dr. Correy's words and the notes in Sean's book as well as trying to make sense of the mysterious voice message.

I needed a theory that would explain everything.

The voice mail message almost made me want to change my mind about the existence of parallel universes.

Had someone somehow recorded him speaking before he died? And then used it to create a message? But then, how had they been able to use his phone number? I was still paying for that phone line. The number was still assigned to my account.

I shook my head in an effort to focus on the problem at hand.

Dr. Correy.

Sean's notes.

And the prospect of something disturbing, something nefarious, that Sean had gotten mixed up in. Maybe whoever was trying to wire my computer and ransack my house was looking for something, some information, that Sean had left behind.

Information like the notations in the book.

I took Alice for a long walk as I tried to sort it all out.

Midafternoon I was interrupted by a call from my mother. She was calling from their layover in Atlanta to make sure I had something "smart" to wear for my father's confirmation hearing. I assumed she wasn't talking about my Resistance Is Not Futile—It's Voltage Divided by Current T-shirt.

I kept going back to the names and numbers from Sean's book. If I knew what the two-letter designations after each name were, it might have helped. It would have given me some hints as to what Sean had been doing. As it was, I felt like I was trying to define dark energy.

Physicists knew dark energy existed—for numerous reasons, it had to—but beyond that? We knew nothing about it at all. In the same way, Sean's notations had to mean something, but it was easier at that point to say what they weren't—a grocery list, a car, a ball— than what they were. I didn't know how to start thinking about them; there was nothing to put my hands around.

29

I let Sam stay at school until the end of extended day. I'd already paid for it and, considering the things that had been happening, he was safer at school than he was at home.

My parents arrived soon after I picked up Sam. I saw them pull into the driveway and alerted Sam. He already had his new train ready and waiting to show my father.

My mother came bearing gifts. "Just a little something." She dipped toward me so I could look inside the leather tote she was carrying. The little something turned out to be some cheese straws, a gallon of sweet tea, and container of pimiento cheese.

She winked. "I know you never have any."

I didn't. Hadn't. Not for a number of years. I kissed the cheek she offered as I took them from her.

"So I thought I might as well bring my own." She smoothed her hair as she glanced around the room, raising a brow when she noticed the galaxy of stars on the ceiling.

I didn't want to hear her thoughts on those. "I'll run these into the kitchen."

Sam was already well into telling his grandfather about his new train.

Out in the kitchen, I set the tote on the floor and put the cheese and sweet tea in the fridge. When I lifted out the package of cheese straws, I saw— "Mom? Mom!"

"Georgia Ann?" Her reply came floating from the living room.

"Mom? Come here!" Right now!

She appeared a moment later. "Sugar pie?"

I gestured toward the tote at my feet.

She came over to peer down inside it.

"Did you know that was in there?"

"The gun? Well . . . you can take the soldier out of the army, but you can't take the army out of the soldier."

"Mom!"

"Your father has a permit to carry."

"And I have Sam. What were you planning to do with it?"

She lifted a slender shoulder. "Take it with us when we leave."

"But why did you bring it here?"

"With the world the way it is? You just never know."

"Do you always take—" Parents! "You know what? I'm going to put it here." I stretched up toward the refrigerator and placed her bag on top of it. "And when you go, you'll take it, and you won't bring it back."

She smiled. "All right."

"I mean it."

She went back to Sam while I took a few moments to get myself together. Deep breaths; some ice cold water patted on my face. Once I had myself under control, I rejoined them. My father had already shed his sports coat and was playing with Sam's new train.

But my mother wasn't having it. She'd taken out her phone. "Come on, everyone. I need a picture for Instagram. And the blog. And Facebook."

She gathered us together. Then she stood back from us, hand on hip. "Tsk. Georgia Ann, does your child not have any socks to wear? Samuel, go find something to put on your feet!" She shooed him off to his room. "And comb your hair while you're there!"

Once Sam came back, dressed to her standards, she took a selfie. And then another. And then—

"Mom! Seriously." She was annoyingly techie. But she ran a military-spouse support website and spent a good part of every morning clicking through the apps on her phone, visiting the sites and pages of all her acolytes in the military community and leaving comments.

My father was fiddling with the wheels of Sam's new train. "When did Sam get this?"

"Saturday. Mr. Hoffman brought it for him."

My father's brow rose. "To the house? Because it seems like the wheels are already a little loose." My dad cupped a hand to Sam's shoulder. "But it's no problem, buddy. Nothing a screwdriver can't fix." He glanced over Sam's head at me.

"Downstairs. In the toolbox beneath the workbench. But—" I stepped toward them, offering to take it.

My father pushed to his feet with a groan. "Don't worry about it. We can do it, can't we, Sam?"

Sam had taken the train from my father and was clutching it to his chest.

My mother intervened. "Georgia Ann, you never answered my question from before."

I dutifully turned toward her as my father and Sam went to fix the train. "Which question was that?" There were lots of questions she'd asked that I'd never answered.

"The confirmation hearing. What are you planning to wear?"

That question. I caught myself mid–eye roll.

"Because you just know, sitting right behind him, that we'll be on television the whole time. I've already made an appointment for us at a spa downtown. I'm going to have them give you just a little trim. I was thinking a couple inches off the bottom and some more layers. With hair like yours, layers are the only thing that help. And I really need you not to frown while we're sitting there." She pointed at me. "Like that. It makes you look like you're scowling. And everyone will see you and they'll wonder why. Just—" She paused, remolded her features into a look I could only label angelic. "You can do that, can't you? I know you can."

"I, um . . . Alice! She needs to go for a walk."

At the sound of her name, Alice lifted her head from her paws.

I nodded toward the door. "Let's go for a walk."

Her ears flicked forward. She stared at me as if questioning my sanity. She'd already been for a walk earlier. A really long one.

I had to grab the leash and walk over to her in order to clip it to her collar. And then I had to plead with her to get up.

"You sure she wants to go?" My mother asked the question with a frown as she stared at me over the top of her reading glasses.

"She's going. I'll be back in fifteen minutes. Maybe twenty. Then we can all go out to dinner. My treat. How's that sound?"

Before she could say anything else, I slipped out the door.

The wind had picked up. And with the sun's decline, it had turned frosty. In my haste to get away, I hadn't thought to grab a hat or gloves. In retrospect, it might have been better to stay and deal with my mother. We turned left, away from the school, at the end of the block. It took us past Mrs. T's house.

I hadn't thought about Mrs. T in forever. She'd lived in a bungalow that was the same era as ours. She was big on walking, and her route took her past our house in both the morning and the evening. Soon after we first moved in, she'd decided that Sean was her personal project. She baked him cakes and knitted him sweaters and recorded television shows for him about the Dalai Lama on her VCR. She flirted with him outrageously. It wasn't difficult to understand why. When Sean smiled, it was like Christmas and the Fourth of July combined.

After she let it slip that her ninetieth birthday was fast approaching, Sean had started checking in on her in person every Friday, to see how she was doing, to make sure she was okay. We discovered she made a mean martini. *And* played a competitive game of Nertz. And just like that, Friday-evening cocktail hour at Mrs. T's had begun.

She'd passed away several years before Sean died. Her son had rented the house out for a while, then decided he could make more money by selling it. Her old house with its tattered garlands of Tibetan prayer flags and its collection of stone Japanese lanterns had been torn down during the summer and a new mini mansion was being built in its place.

As we reached her lot, the last of the contractors' mud-splattered pickups was pulling away.

Mrs. T wouldn't have liked the McMansion. I stood there for a moment, trying to take it all in. It was too big. It was too much. Alice must have sensed my inattention, because she bolted toward the front yard, pulling her leash from my grasp.

"Alice!"

She ran up the front steps and disappeared into the house.

"Alice!" I picked my way through the debris that was strewn around the front and climbed up onto the porch.

I pushed the door open wider and put a foot to the threshold. Took a listen.

Heard nothing.

Slipping inside, I closed the door behind me, then stood in what would eventually be the front hall. "Alice!"

A whimper came from a room off to my right.

"Alice?" I walked into it.

A yelp came from the room beyond.

"Alice, what have you—"

At the back of the house was a great room with soaring ceilings and a full wall of windows that provided a view into the backyard.

Alice was there, lunging at a construction worker who was trying to calm her.

I jogged toward him, trying to explain myself. "Alice! I just— Sorry. Alice—stop! I know we're not supposed to be here, but my dog got away and— Alice, sit!"

Alice sat, but her tail kept thumping.

The construction worker took off his hat and tucked it under an arm.

I reached for the handle of the leash. "I'm sorry she jumped—"

He put a hand to his sunglasses and pulled them off.

"—all over—" All the air left my lungs. I gasped. Felt my knees buckle. "Oh my—"

30

He was beside me in a minute, grasping my arm, keeping me upright.

"Sean?"

"Georgie, I—"

It was *him*. It *was* him. Underneath the beard and the too-long hair, it was truly and unmistakably him. But still, as he put a hand on my forearm, I moved away. "Don't touch me! Don't!" I recoiled, retreating in the direction of the wall. "Don't touch me! I can't—" I turned away from him, folded my arms around my waist, and closed my eyes. I wasn't okay. I wasn't going to be all right. I leaned my forehead against the wall for a moment. It was solid. Cool. I turned to face him and slid down the wall, sobbing.

He reached out.

I held up a forearm to fend him off. "Don't!" My chin began to tremble. "You're not alive." I whispered the words.

"I am alive."

My mouth was drawn down like a bow, my voice dissolving into hysteria. My whole body was trembling. I was deathly cold. "Don't you—" I could hardly speak. Sobs, deep and guttural, were pulsing upward from deep down inside. "Don't you just come here—" I grimaced as I wrapped my arms around myself, trying to hold everything together. "Don't just come here and—" A sob broke through. "And tell me that you're alive and show up as if—as if—I should be *glad*? Glad that I had to bury you? Glad that I had to listen to my son try to explain to me why he thinks you're alive when you're dead?"

"I'm not—"

"But you're not! You're *not dead*."

He squatted and tried to put his arm around me.

"Don't try to apologize. Don't—" My resolve crumbled. "You were dead."

"Georgie?"

"Don't."

"Georgie." His voice was closer.

"Just—"

His arm came around my shoulders.

"You can't—"

He went to one knee and pulled me to his chest.

I clung to him, weeping. I wept for him and for me. I wept for our son.

When he tried to pull away, I clutched at him. "Don't go!"

"You listened to my message."

"It was you. I tried everything I could to make it not you, but it was you."

"I've been trailing you for two weeks, but there's always been someone around. We need to talk."

I sat up, putting distance between us, and swiped at my tears with my forearm. Then, drawing a shuddering breath, I nodded.

He sat down next to me, back against the wall.

Alice came over and curled up beside him, placing her head on his thigh with a sigh.

He gave her one of those rubs behind her ears that she loved so much. "Remember that Gulf War project?"

I nodded.

"I was helping write the army's history of Desert Sabre. Pulling together documents. Collecting oral histories."

Where had Sean been all this time? What had he been doing?

"Georgie?"

I blinked. Nodded. "Desert Sabre. My father was there."

"And I was writing about his battalion, down to the company level, looking back through everything I could get ahold of—oral histories, field reports, orders of the day."

If I hadn't interred Sean, who had I interred? Who had I— I heard myself gasp. I'd had someone else cremated!

"Georgie, are you okay?" Brow furrowed, he touched my arm. "Are you—"

"Fine. I'm fine. Haven't been sleeping. There was someone in the crawl space on—"

"That was me."

"That was—that was *you*?"

"I was trying to—"

"Wait. Stop." Everything was starting to make sense now. It was as if I'd been looking at everything backward and upside down. "Alice chases the garbage truck. She started doing that after you died."

"Because it's me."

"*You're* the one who hauled out the garbage cans this week."

He nodded.

That was *him*? "Those were all *you*? All those times she chased the truck? You'd been there? *Right there?* The *whole time*?"

"I needed to make sure you were okay. So I pay one of the guys off every Monday morning so I can make sure that no one is—"

"So you've been, what? Working construction here? In my own backyard, all this—"

"No, I've just been wearing this the past few days so I could blend in. Lots of construction in the neighborhood."

"—time and moonlighting as a garbage man once a week? Did you never stop to think, *Gee, Georgie looks a little sad. I know! Maybe I should let her know I'm alive!*"

"I couldn't because—"

Maybe that's what Dr. Correy had meant. Maybe he assumed that I already knew Sean hadn't died. Why would he have assumed that? Because I was *Sean's wife*. "I cremated someone and put your name on him. I don't even know who he is."

"Just— I need you to listen." He shifted to face me and gripped my hand. "I can't keep you here much longer. I noticed there were—"

"The Leatherman. It was on the inventory from the medical examiner's office, but it never made it to the house. At least, I didn't think it had, but then I found it under the house. It's because you—"

"—because I took it with me when I left the medical examiner's office. When I didn't die."

"Then how did— The autopsy?"

"I only have a few minutes and I need to explain." He squeezed my hand. "Are you with me?"

The questions could wait until later. "Yes. Okay. Yes. I heard you: Desert Sabre."

"Right. I was working on your father's part in the war. It seemed like a no-brainer, assigning that to me. I had an inside connection."

I nodded.

"So I started contacting soldiers in his old unit, scheduling oral interviews, asking questions about the night they made that breach in the Iraqi lines."

My father's company had stumbled on the Iraqi Republican Guard during a scouting mission the first night of that war. The Iraqis outnumbered them, but the company fought them off and blew up their base, destroying their weapons. That's how he breached their lines and that's what put him on the road to the four stars he eventually earned. It was the one story from that war almost everyone knew. "Okay." It all sounded like standard historian work to me.

"That's when things started getting weird."

"Things? What things?"

"Just . . . little things. All of a sudden I had to turn in a daily report on who I'd talked to, what questions I'd asked. My files were being accessed without my knowledge. Some of my source material disappeared."

"Did you tick someone off? Was someone jealous of your assignment?" That seemed remarkably petty. Even for the army. "Maybe someone just wanted to keep tabs on how the project was going."

"Maybe. But no one else's materials vanished. And no one else had to file a daily report."

"What kind of questions were you asking?"

"Nothing unusual. State your name. What was your rank and duty? What are your memories of that first night of the war?"

"You were *given* this assignment, though, right? Someone asked you to do it. It's not like you were freelancing."

"I was given the assignment."

"I don't understand."

"I don't either. I don't understand any of it. But when things start disappearing and people start following you—"

"People *followed* you? You were just doing what everyone else was doing."

Sean nodded. "But the company I was researching was your father's. And I think something happened out there in the desert. Something that shouldn't have."

31

Outside, footsteps scuffed up the front stairs to the porch.
Paused. A voice called out, "Georgie?"

Alice pushed to her feet. Barked.

Was that . . .

Sean rose to a squat and lunged toward the shadow along the far wall.

From my location I caught a glimpse of Chris's face through the front door.

Sean sprang toward me, grabbed my hand, and pulled me to a sliding glass door at the back of the house that should have led to a porch but at that moment led to—nothing but empty space. The ground was a half-story down. Inside my shoes my toes tried to grab on to the door's track. My free hand clawed at the cutout, trying to leverage me back from the hole.

But Sean's hand clamped around mine. "Jump!" The word was low but vehement, and his momentum was already carrying me with him over the threshold. As he hit the ground, he let go of my hand and reached upward. Pulling me to his chest, he broke my fall and then rolled us away from the house. And even then, he kept moving, heading toward a pile of discarded lumber and scraps of trim that had been stacked at the back of the lot.

Alice galloped along at our heels.

Once we ducked behind it we were out of view of the house.

"It was only Chris."

"Who?"

"Chris."

"Who's Chris? I don't know any Chrises."

"Chris. The dog-walk guy."

Sean's brow folded.

"We walk our dogs together."

"Georgie?" Chris's voice came from the direction of the house. "You okay?"

"He must have seen me chase Alice up the stairs."

Sean grabbed my hand for just a moment. "Go home. Be careful. Meet me tomorrow; walk at dusk. Wear dark clothes. I'll find you."

Hidden from the house, he disappeared around the far side of the pile before I could say anything. I scrambled after him, but by the time I could take a peek, he'd gone.

As I rounded the pile, I saw Chris standing in the opening for the sliding glass door, staring down at the ground.

"Hey!" I waved an arm.

He looked up. Saw me. "You okay? I saw you come in here. Didn't see you come out."

"Alice chased a squirrel into the house. They really should lock these things up when they're working on them."

He made the jump to the ground. Then he walked through the side yard and down the street with me, back home.

"Georgia Ann? Is that you?" My mother's words were accompanied by the click of her heels, and she soon appeared from the dining room. "I was just doing a little tidying up and I went into Sam's room. Did you know he didn't make his bed?"

"He doesn't know how, Mom."

"You were three when I taught you that!" She blinked at me, put a hand to her hip, and gave me a once-over. "What happened? You're a hot mess!"

Coming over, she put a hand to my chin and turned my head to pick something out of my hair. Tsking, she held out a tuft of dried grass.

"I, uh—" I put a hand to my head, feeling for more. "I fell."

She licked her thumb and used it to smudge at something on my face. "You all right?"

No. "Yes. Yes. Yeah. I'm fine." I shied away from her touch, trying for a smile. I'm not sure it worked. "I'm fine." Doubting I could pull off nonchalance, I tried a different tactic. "So! Where are we going for dinner?"

She stood there looking at me, eyes narrowed. "I don't like your color. And your eyes are puffy. You look like you've seen a ghost." She flapped a hand toward the couch behind me. "Go on and sit down. I'll bring you some tea."

"So I said to him, I said, 'Sergeant, I don't care what you *can't* do, I'm only interested in what you can.'" My father was regaling Sam with stories from his past. I was pretty sure a military career wasn't going to be in Sam's future, but Sam never passed up a chance to hear a story. Not even those he'd heard before. My father chuckled as he shook his head. He glanced around the table to make sure we were listening.

My mother and I had heard it a million times, and I was mulling over what Sean had told me, but Sam was rapt with attention. He picked up a piece of Korean-style fried chicken and started pulling meaty strands of it from the bone. That's what we'd decided on for dinner: takeout.

"And do you know what Sergeant Conway said? He said, 'Then I don't think I'm going to be of much interest to you, sir. Because I can't get the phone to work.' Can you believe it? There we were, trying to fight a war, and I couldn't have gotten an order if I'd wanted one because the phone wouldn't work!" My father wiggled his eyebrows at Sam.

Sam obliged by giggling.

"Wait. Dad?"

"Hmm?"

"Sergeant Conway. Do you remember what his first name was?"

"Started with . . . an *M*? No. Started with a *P*. Pete? Pat?"

My mother surprised us by answering, "Paul."

He blinked. "How do you remember things like that?"

"Because the first hundred times you told the story, you used his first name too."

"Huh." He gave Sam a wink. "So there we were, sitting in the middle of the desert, stuck tighter than a hair in a biscuit . . ."

My father continued, but I didn't hear him. The only thing I could think about was Paul Conway. That's why the name had sounded familiar. I'd been hearing about him for years.

"Peach?" My father had fastened his eyes on me.

"Hmm?" I'd been trying my best not to talk. I was afraid that if I opened my mouth the words *SEAN IS ALIVE* would leap out before I could stop them. Right then I was afraid I'd babble something about Paul Conway too.

I forced my lips into a smile instead.

"Got any intel on dessert?"

"Dessert. Right." I collected the plates and took them with me into the kitchen where I put them in the sink. I retrieved the carton of ice cream from the freezer and took it out to them.

My mother frowned. "Bowls?"

I blinked. "Yes. Sure." I went back into the kitchen, but by the time I got there I'd forgotten what I needed. Sean's revelation kept running through my head in a loop. *I think something happened out there in the desert. Something that shouldn't have.*

The thing was, the actions of my father's company were widely known. My father talked about that night all the time, just like he had with Sam. He wouldn't do that if something odd had happened.

Unless he didn't know about it.

Bowls.

And spoons. *That's* why I was there.

I got them and returned to the dining room. Then I scooped the ice cream and handed out the bowls.

"Do you keep up with anyone from your company, Dad?"

"Which one?"

"The one from the desert. The one you were telling Sam about. Anyone like Paul Conway?"

"From E Company?" He thought for a moment. "Can't even remember the last time I talked to anyone from there. Probably that History Channel retrospective. The twenty-five-year anniversary show, maybe? But that was mostly people from the headquarters level; it wasn't any of my troops."

"Would you ever want to see any of them again?"

"What? People like Conway? Sure." He winked at me. "I'd even buy him a beer. Ask him how life's been treating him."

I tried to ignore the chill that crept up my spine. "They were good guys, then?"

"The best. Never served with any better."

32

Being the sole recipient of his grandparents' attention that evening tired Sam out. He went to bed without any problems.

As I came back into the living room, my father stood and unfolded a blue T-shirt with a flourish and held it up across his chest. "I brought you another one, Peach."

"She doesn't want another T-shirt, JB." My mother was shaking her head.

I read the words. "Quantum Entanglement Is Neither Here Nor There." I smiled. "Good one."

He balled it up and tossed it to me. "You can never have too many T-shirts."

"I kind of think I might. But thanks." My wardrobe of pithy physics-themed shirts was entirely due to him.

He was the first to admit that he knew nothing about physics, but whenever someone asked about me, he'd say, "Georgie? She's a genius. Don't know where she got it from, but it's true."

He sat back down in Sean's old chair.

My mother got up. "I'm just going to powder my nose before we leave for the hotel." She passed by my father on her way.

He reached out for her. "Best thing I ever did was marry you."

She bent down, took him by the chin, and kissed him. "Don't you ever forget it."

"Like I could." He kissed her back and then sent me a wink. "You're always reminding me."

She straightened. Laid a hand on his shoulder and sent me a glance. "Can you believe this man didn't know a butterfly from a boutonniere when I first met him?"

He took her hand. "It was in first grade."

"Well. It's been my life's work, but I think all those rough edges are just about buffed off." She ruffled his hair and turned to walk away.

He pinched her on the butt. "All but the ones you like."

It used to be that I was both profoundly embarrassed by and incredibly proud of my parents. Who else had a mom and dad who looked like Ken and Barbie? And who else could say their father was a general and their mother was a no-kidding beauty queen? However, it had been embarrassing in the extreme when they kissed in front of my friends, or when my mother wore her fur coat to shop for groceries.

In college, *incredibly proud* had evaporated, leaving only *profoundly embarrassed*. It wasn't cool at the time to cheer America's swagger on the international stage. And when your professors were grappling with new theories of light and matter, beauty pageants just seemed so trivial.

By the time I met Sean, I was swinging away from embarrassment and back toward proud. To have two parents who took care of themselves just as carefully as they took care of those around them? Who were still deeply in love with each other? The more I'd seen of the world, the more I'd realized just how rare they were.

But I was a grown-up with a son of my own. And I knew that people weren't good or bad. People were people. They were good *and* bad. All of us had weaknesses and strengths.

My parents' strengths were many.

Ever since I was old enough to notice, my parents had been tirelessly, *relentlessly* patriotic. Military-themed symposia, panels, seminars? My father had been part of them. Visiting professor, cultural ambassador, talking head? He'd done all that too.

And my mother had been at his side the whole time—comforting military spouses, cajoling Congress for more support for veterans, and fundraising for myriad nonprofits.

If there was good to do in the military community, they had done it.

Their weaknesses?

Appearances seemed so important to them. But considering who they were, wouldn't appearances have to be important? In order to advocate for others, to present yourself as an expert in something, you had to be a person who could be trusted, didn't you?

Even *I* didn't wear yoga pants and my Physics—I Can Explain It to You but I Can't Understand It for You T-shirt to customer meetings.

Sometimes their squabbles became heated. And my father could be a little controlling.

But all couples experienced friction, didn't they?

Even Sean and I had had our moments.

Moment.

And part of the job description of a general was to control.

Knowing Sean, there had to be something behind his suspicions. If he said something happened in my father's company, then something probably had. The question was, why didn't my father know about it?

Sean was alive!

The moment my parents pulled out of the driveway, I said the words aloud. I whispered them to myself. "Sean is alive!" Okay, I might have more than whispered them. Alice's ears pricked as her head swiveled toward the door.

I was every emoji on my phone, all at the same time.

Ecstatic that he was alive; mad that he had let me believe he was dead for so long. I still didn't understand why he'd done that. But as soon as he could clear up what had happened during the Desert Sabre project, we could get on with our lives.

I heard a whisper in the back of my mind, but I was too busy exulting over Sean's appearance—planning how we would let Sam know and figuring out what to say to people like Jim and June—to listen.

Sean was alive!

It wasn't until I had slipped into bed and turned off the light that the volume on my exultation was turned down enough that I could finally hear.

Sean was no choirboy. Trouble followed him for most of his youth. If he thought something had been going on, then experience said he was probably right. And what had his instinct always been? What was at the core of his character? The desire to protect the ones he loved. Sean would have left us only if he thought he had to.

33

The next night Sean found me walking past an ivy-covered wasteland in a dip along the road that no streetlight could reach and no window seemed to overlook. I'd invited Jenn and Preston for dinner earlier in the week. Considering that Jenn was going through a tough time with her divorce, I hadn't wanted to cancel. But when they arrived, I asked her if she could keep an eye on the boys while I took Alice for a walk.

Finger to his lips, Sean led me through the vines to the far side of a decrepit old shed that was falling apart at the back of the property. Alice yipped and did a joyful two-legged dance as Sean tried to quiet her.

I put a hand on his arm. It was solid. Real. He was real. And I didn't want to be hiding in the shadows. I wanted to walk down the street with him and take him home to Sam. It made me angry that I couldn't.

"I still don't understand any of this, Sean. We had a funeral. You were cremated." *Someone* was cremated. "After you left that voice mail message, I thought I might be making you up, that I was having a breakdown."

"No, Georgie."

"How did you leave that message?"

"It was a caller ID spoof. I didn't want to do it that way, but I needed to talk to you. I was going to ask you to meet me, but then I got interrupted."

"What is this? What's going on?"

"I don't know. I didn't have time to find out."

"Then what *do* you know? You're saying someone was worried about you finding something out. You're also saying you *didn't* find anything out. You've got to give me something. Something to think there was a reason you've been dead for eight months. I cried real tears for you. My heart broke for you. Sam can't sleep because of you. I want to know there's a reason why." My tone was sharp. My fists were balled. I took a step back, consciously uncurled my fingers as I waited for him to reply.

He turned away from me, ran a hand through his hair again. Turned back. "Here's one thing I can tell you: the Iraqi Republican Guard didn't have any defenses in the area where your father was."

"But they had to have been there. He made a breach through their lines."

"I know. And he destroyed an arsenal of top-of-the-line weapons. It's all documented."

"Maybe those Iraqis were originally somewhere else. Maybe their new location just hadn't been logged."

"That's what I thought too. I might still be thinking that, sitting at the table in our house drinking coffee every morning and walking my son to school, if someone hadn't intervened."

"Do you know Sam thinks you're still alive? He thinks you're in a wormhole somewhere and that at some point you're going to—" My emotions had overcome my capacity for words. My throat closed. I took a deep breath. "Have you seen Sam since you died? Have you talked to him?"

"No. Why would I—"

"Why didn't you talk to me? Why haven't we done this before now?"

"Shh."

I lowered my voice. "Why didn't I know any of this? I'm your wife! I thought we were in this marriage together."

"We are. I just couldn't—"

"You do not get to walk out the door and leave. Not without telling me."

"Why would I have left you if I could have stayed?"

"I don't know. But you destroyed our family, Sean. Whatever this is, you let it in and then you left."

"I'm sorry, I just—"

"No. I'm sorry. I'm sorry I've wasted eight months trying to get over you, telling myself I should move on, trying to fix myself by reading— I've been reading *nonfiction*!"

"I know I should have—"

"I am beyond mad at you."

"Georgie."

"What have you been doing for the past eight months?"

"I've been disappearing. Covering my tracks. Trying to stay alive. And I've been trying to figure this all out. I have been reading every book about the war, watching every interview, tracking down every article I could find. And I've been trying to stay out of sight at the same time. And keep an eye on you. And make enough money for food and somewhere to stay. None of it's been easy."

He was telling the truth. I could read it in the slant of his shoulders and the haunted look in his eyes.

"Someone ransacked the house. Tore it all apart."

"Someone ransacked the—"

I held up a hand to preclude his questions, because I had questions of my own. "Do you have any idea what they might have been looking for?"

"They were probably looking for information. My notes?"

"What were you doing in the crawl space the other night?"

"You were gone the weekend before—"

"My parents took us to the beach."

"—and the first night you were gone I noticed activity. There was someone in the basement. Someone in the crawl space. I wanted to see what they'd been doing."

"They tried to wire your computer."

"I know. I know what they've been doing. What I still don't know is why."

34

Dark energy was at work again. Sean didn't know who he had provoked or why, but we knew he'd happened onto something that mattered because of the reaction that had occurred. Something invisible was at work and it was powerful.

"Tell me about work. Your files were accessed. Things disappeared from the archives. Someone was following you."

"They had me write up my research. And once they had all my materials, they transferred me to a different job. Out of the army. It was straight DoD. They sent me to the Pentagon."

The new job.

"That was last August? When they transferred you?"

He nodded.

So at least that cleared up one question. But it left so many more. "What did they want you to do in the new job?"

"Update the list of all the military-related museums in the country and put together a spreadsheet of their addresses, contact information, and boards of directors."

Busywork? Ouch. "And why didn't you tell me about it?"

He sent me a sardonic look. "Why do you think?"

"You worked it for half a year. That was important. I would have wanted to know. I embarrassed myself just last week calling Brad about something."

"About what?" His gaze sharpened.

"Keys. Your security badge."

"Why?"

"I realized you'd lied about the sink the day you died. You weren't trying to fix it that afternoon. That thing you took with you. It wasn't a part from the faucet. What was it?"

"It was a thumb drive."

"Well, it never came back from the medical examiner's. And that led me to wonder what else was missing, or not, from what you'd left behind. So I went through everything. I found a key I couldn't identify, but I didn't find a security badge. And I knew you'd had one."

"What did you say to him?"

"To Brad? I don't know." I searched back through my memories, sifting through the emotions I'd been experiencing. "I just told him I was sorting through some things and found a key I thought might belong to the office. And that I realized I'd never returned your badge."

"But you just said you *didn't* find my badge."

"I lied, okay? Crucify me."

"Just—" He stretched out a hand, tucked some hair behind my ear. "You asked if you should return it?"

I nodded.

"So he must think you have it."

"Right."

"Okay, I should be fine then."

A chill crept up my spine. "*What* is going on, Sean?"

"You found my notes, right? In the front yard. In the book?"

"Yes, and—"

"I knew someone was following me and it felt like I needed to hide it somewhere. I knew if crocuses came up in the fall, you'd want me to dig them up. I could access it then if I had to. And if anything happened to me before, I wanted you to know why."

"That's just it. I have no idea what any of it—"

"It's in a safe place? It needs to be in a safe place."

"It is. I put it—"

He gripped my hands. "Don't tell me!" He took a deep breath. "Sorry." He drew me close, enfolding me in his arms. He planted a kiss on my forehead. "Sorry. But as long as it's safe, it's better if I don't

STATE OF LIES | 143

know where it is. It would be even better if *you* didn't know where it
is. Safer. Maybe we should just burn it."

Suddenly not even his embrace felt safe.

He let me go.

I stood beside him, back against the shed, slipping my hands
into my sleeves to keep them warm.

Alice sighed and sat down in front of us.

"So I changed jobs, but I couldn't let it go. That's when I started
that list of names. I was looking for anyone connected with your
father. Anyone who could help me figure it out. Back in October, I
got in touch with the FBI."

"And?"

He lifted a shoulder. "And they wanted my help in passing them
all the information I'd found."

"But you said the army took it all."

"They took my files, but I knew what I'd read. At first, the FBI
wanted me to find out who was wanting me to cease and desist, at
what level that decision had been made."

"So you were working the new job, and also working for the FBI?"

"*With*. I was working *with* the FBI."

With. Knowledge dawned with startling clarity. "You were an
FBI source?"

He frowned.

"Sorry. *Asset*. You were an asset."

"They were *my* asset. *I* was trying to get *their* help. That's what
I was doing that night."

That night. "The night you died."

"You'd just told me that afternoon that your father was going
to be nominated as the new secretary of defense. I thought the FBI
should know since whatever had happened out there had involved his
company. So I went out and met my contact. The FBI took care of
the car accident. They even swung a deal at the coroner's for a fake
death certificate and autopsy report."

That's what Dr. Correy meant.

"They needed the DoD, the army, to think I was dead; someone over there was getting nervous."

"Wait, wait, wait. The Department of Defense tried to kill you?"

"No. The FBI just wanted to make it look as if I had been killed."

"They did a good job of it. My father identified your body."

"What?"

"He identified your body. I couldn't do it. I couldn't go. Sam wouldn't let me out of his sight. So I asked my father to do it for me."

Sean's eyes narrowed. "But there was no body. The agency told the medical examiner to write out a death certificate and fill out the transfer paperwork for the crematorium. It was supposed to seem like my body had already been sent. When you came to identify me, he was supposed to give you my effects and a phone number in case you wanted to lodge a complaint. It would have been a number at the FBI. But your father said he'd *identified* my body?"

We stared at each other for a long moment.

I was trying to sort it all out. "Maybe he just got caught in the plan. The FBI thought I'd show up, but he went in my place. Maybe he thought I'd be even more upset if I knew there'd been some mistake with your body."

"What did he tell you when he came back?"

"From the medical examiner's? He said they had to know what to do with you. That there was no point in having a viewing, considering the effects of the accident, so he asked them to cremate you." There was something distinctly odd about discussing someone's cremation when they were standing right in front of you.

He sighed and ran a hand up the back of his head. "Anyway, the plan was that I'd be able to move around more freely if I wasn't being watched. But—"

"By the Department of Defense? They were the ones watching you?"

"Yes."

What kind of world did we live in?

"But then something must have happened because the FBI reprioritized; things with me were put on a back burner. I wasn't interested in that, so I disappeared."

Disappeared? "What does that even mean?"

"It means that I made sure even the FBI didn't think I was alive anymore."

"Why? How?"

He sent me a sidelong glance. "I had ways."

Ways. The hairs at the back of my neck stood on end.

"But now they're looking for me again. Both the DoD and the FBI."

There was something about what he was saying that didn't make sense. "If the DoD didn't want to hear what you discovered and the FBI didn't care to follow through on what you found out . . ." I forced myself to think it through, one piece at a time. Realization came with an overwhelming sense of dread. I had to force out my words. "You *can't* be alive, can you? Because you think that someone thinks you know something. And whoever it is—maybe even the FBI—doesn't want that something known and would kill you for it all over again."

He didn't answer.

"Only, you don't know. You don't know what they think you do. But if they find out you're alive, then—"

"Then they could threaten *you*, you and Sam, in order to make me reveal myself. So I took you both out of the equation. I made sure there was no reason to threaten you."

I took you both out of the equation. He'd done the same with Kelly. He'd disappeared from her life when he thought his presence endangered her. Without hesitation, without warning. "That's why you had to die."

"A second time. And that time, I had to stay dead."

I had it. I understood it. All the pieces of the puzzle had fallen into place. But I still couldn't make any sense of the picture. "So then why are you back? Why now?"

"Because I think they suspect I'm alive. It's what I was afraid of. Maybe I should have stayed away—I tried to stay away—but I just can't stand by and watch anymore. And you needed to know what's going on. They're using you as leverage. This could escalate."

35

Standing there by the shed, we talked it through. "You've been at this for eight months. More than eight months. The only thing you know is the Republican Guard shouldn't have been where it was?"

"I also know somebody thinks I know more than I do. I can infer that person, those people, want the information—whatever it is—to stay hidden."

"Agreed."

"Beyond that? Whoever it is must be in a position of power. If they were able to demand reports on my progress and access my computer, take documents from the archives, they had to be doing it from a level above my pay grade."

"You're thinking officer or civilian?"

"I'm not sure."

"And it has to do with my father's old company?"

"It almost has to, doesn't it? That's what I was working on."

"I asked my father about Paul Conway last night. He was one of the names in your book."

"He was a sergeant."

"Right. But he died. Hit-and-run at the beginning of last week. My father didn't show any signs of knowing that, though."

"This might not have anything to do with your father. Not directly. I've been trying to find out more about the commanders further up the chain. Maybe someone had information about that Republican Guard position. Maybe your father should have been given that information. Maybe that's what this is all about."

"Does that make sense, though? Everything turned out all right in the end for everyone. Maybe we should just ask him. Maybe it would help us figure it out."

"By you asking him questions all of a sudden? If they tried to shut me up, what would they do to him? And what would you tell him when he asks why you think there's a problem? That your dead husband was just wondering? We need to keep me out of this and you as far away from it as possible."

He was right.

"With your father's nomination, people are probably poking around his career anyway, trying to see what they can find."

"Everybody likes my father."

"But not everyone likes the president. Think how many people would like to embarrass him."

"You think it's the *president* who had you reassigned?"

He shook his head. "There's no way to know."

"What could have gone hidden for this many years when a whole company of men was involved?"

"We don't know it was the whole company. It could have been just one man. And he could have been someone at the battalion or brigade level."

"We need to figure out what this is. And then we need to make it known."

"That's all I've ever wanted to do. But I've been working on this for months and I can tell you everything about the war but that."

"Let me help."

"I can't. I refuse to put you in more danger than you already are. I never should have left that message on your voice mail. I shouldn't be here now."

"But you did. And you are. And now I know. We're in this together. Tell me how to help. How did it all start? If we back up, then maybe—"

"It started with the project. But you don't have access to the archives."

He was right. "But you said you did interviews. Let me talk to the people you talked to."

"They weren't helpful. If they had been, then I would have figured it out long before now."

"It's worth a try. You never know. What if I ask a question you didn't? Or they think of something they forgot to tell you?"

He shoved his hands into his pockets. "I'll give you a name. It's the first person I interviewed. I don't have a phone number, but you can find it. Lee Ornofo. He lives near Philadelphia. Ask him about that first night of the Gulf War." He leveled a look at me. "Be careful. Whoever is behind this, we have to assume they're watching and listening."

Lee Ornofo.

It was one of the names in Sean's book.

Sundays were Samdays as far as Jim and June were concerned. After Sean died, they'd made a point to do something with Sam every Sunday. It let me have time to get things done.

That Sunday I went to Central Library, signed up for computer time, and started googling. Considering that extraneous cable I'd discovered, I didn't trust my home computer network.

I couldn't find an email for Lee Ornofo, but after tracing the name to a radiosport organization in Philadelphia, I was able to find contact information from their website. I went out to the car so I could have some privacy. People walked in and out of the library, stacks of books in hand. Two teenagers hit a ball around the tennis courts beside me. I phoned Mr. Ornofo, explaining that I was doing a report on Desert Sabre. "Are you the Mr. Ornofo who served in Captain Slater's company?"

"I am."

"May I ask you a few questions about your time in Iraq?"

"Sure. Yeah. I served. I did." He sighed. "That was back when they give you a parade when you came home from a war. Marching band. Convertibles. The whole shebang." He coughed. "Different times now."

"I'm just trying to understand the war better, how exactly it went. That sort of thing. Would you mind helping me?"

"You with that project? The one that other fellow was with?"

"I'm working with the military history office. Just following up. You spoke with someone last year?"

"That's right. Happy to help. What do you need to know?"

"Let's just start with the basics, Mr. Ornofo. Name, rank, position. All of that." I opened up the notebook I'd brought.

"You can call me Lee."

No, I couldn't. I hadn't been raised that way.

He gave me the information, then I asked him what particular job he'd done.

"I was the company RTO. The radio telephone operator."

"What did that mean, practically speaking?"

"Meant I was the captain's shadow." He cleared his throat. "Anywhere he went, I was there too. Stuck like glue."

I asked him to describe February 24, from the time he woke up until the time he went to bed that night.

He laughed. "Well, I didn't go to bed, that's the first thing. So I didn't wake up either. Desert Storm was a month and a half. Started in January. Desert Sabre was the actual ground campaign. The war itself. It was fought in five days. Probably didn't sleep five hours for the duration."

"As RTO, you were used to receiving communications from headquarters?"

"Sure. Message traffic. Orders. We communicated with the other companies too. And kept in contact with all our platoons. There were five of them in our company. And I kept in contact with the commo too." He replied to my unspoken question. "That's the communications sergeant. Wouldn't have wanted to be him."

"Why not?"

"Sand. And all that wind. Later on in the afternoon and evening—that's when everything started to go south."

"How so?"

"We didn't have our ground-to-ground comms. At least not dependably."

"What did that mean for you?"

"Didn't really matter what it meant for me. It's what it meant for the captain. We had a job to do, but we couldn't do it if we couldn't coordinate with our platoons. And the battalion couldn't do its job if they couldn't coordinate with us. See?"

"Makes sense."

"You tend to think the battalion commander gives an order and the companies like ours go out and get it done. But it's not like that. 'Specially not out there."

"So what happened?"

"The commo would know better than me. He got all the communications. Everything from the battalion on down. My job was just communicating for the captain. I sent out what he wanted to say, and when someone wanted to say something to him, I took the message or put the phone to his ear. The commo made sure all the message traffic, all the calls got through."

"And who was the commo?" I waited, pen poised above my tablet of paper.

"Conway. Paul Conway."

36

Paul Conway. **My knuckles turned white as I wrote his** name. "So the company stumbled onto a Republican Guard unit that night. How did that happen? Do you remember? You must have been there because you were with the captain the whole night, right?"

"Mostly I was with him the whole hundred hours. Yeah. So things started off as planned, everyone all lined up. Nice and straight. Tidy, you know? Then someone runs into an enemy position. Slows 'em down till they can wrap it up. Pretty soon, some units who don't encounter any resistance are out ahead; other units get hung up, they fall behind. Relatively speaking, you see?"

"Sure."

"Then the comms start going in and out. We weren't receiving messages. Or only receiving partial messages. Drove the commo crazy."

"What did you do?"

"You just press on, do what you're supposed to do until someone tells you otherwise because that's what everyone's expecting you to do."

"So you pressed on."

"Yeah. Captain was a little uneasy. Early on, the companies could see each other. Later on, you could see the dust-ups. Know what I'm saying? Explosions. Smoke, when there was contact with the enemy. After that, couldn't see anything at all. And it was dark that night. Sand in the air. Cloud cover. Radio was on the fritz. Seemed like an order came through telling everyone to pull back, but it cut out. We couldn't confirm receipt. Captain and I just looked at each other. Shrugged."

"Wait. You got an order but you didn't do anything about it? Why?"

"Because the general, he was all set before the whole thing started on how important it was to do the job. Just keep doing the job. He didn't want anyone getting all hung up. Had to keep up the pace, keep going, because of the strategy. There were multiple countries' forces involved. If we weren't all where we were supposed to be at the time we were supposed to be there, then the plan wouldn't work. So we hear half an order and it just doesn't make sense. Why would the general tell everyone to pull back when he'd been dead set on going ahead full throttle before it all started?"

"So what did you do?"

"We talked it over."

"You and the captain?"

"Yeah."

"He asked for your opinion?"

"Yeah."

"Did he do that a lot?" The father I'd grown up with had always had a plan. Had always known what to do. He never asked anyone's opinion, never asked anyone's permission. He just stepped out and expected that everyone else would follow along.

"Ask me what I thought? Sure. And sometimes he'd just talk, work his way around to a decision. That's part of the job. To be the guy the captain can talk to. The RTO is like a black hole. Lots of stuff goes in through the ears, but none of it's ever supposed to come out."

"So what did he decide?"

"He decided to just keep going. That's the only full order we'd received. And that's when we discovered that minefield and met up with the Iraqis."

Minefield? I made a note to ask Sean. "What happened then?"

"Well . . . turns out, they had us surrounded. But the captain, he went out to talk to them."

"And you went with him?"

"No. In that case I didn't. He left me behind."

"So you don't know what was said?"

"Not exactly. But I know the end result. The captain found us a breach. It's what the general had wanted. Once we got our breach, everyone else could go through."

Maybe that's all there was to this. Maybe my father was just embarrassed that they hadn't obeyed an order. My relief, however, was short-lived. That didn't seem like enough to need to kill someone like Sean over. "But it didn't cause anyone any heartburn that he hadn't obeyed the order to fall back?"

"Thing about the captain is, once he decided something, he was all in. I stayed with him for a while as RTO after. Through the desert. Into that mess in Bosnia. After that, they booted me out. Whatever it was I brought back from the desert, I wasn't any use to the army anymore."

I didn't get it. "What did you bring back?"

"Nobody knows. Felt like I was an old man at thirty years old. Gulf War Syndrome. That's what they called it. At least it wasn't just all in my head. Shame to leave the captain, though. Felt like I was letting him down. He was a major by then. Best officer I ever had the pleasure to serve under. He might not have known exactly where everyone else was out there in the desert, but I can tell you, no matter where we were after that, he always seemed to know where the enemy was. It's like he had some sixth sense or something." He coughed again. "Captain Slater? He was good people. That's about all I know."

My father had gotten himself way out ahead of the line and then he'd chosen not to obey an order. He'd come across the enemy and gone to talk to them by himself. But what did that signify? I still hadn't heard anything that was worth killing Sean over.

But I had heard about Paul Conway, and that bothered me.

A lot.

Because Paul Conway was dead.

Paul Conway probably knew more about what had happened that night than Lee Ornofo did. And now he would never be able to tell anyone.

37

"Georgie!" The receptionist caught me as I was passing through the lobby on Monday morning. She waved a slip of paper at me.

I smiled my thanks and took it from her as I continued on down the hall. I'd only taken a few steps before I turned right around and went back to see her. I held it up. "I'm not quite sure what this says."

"That was your ten o'clock who called."

"My ten o'clock what?"

"Meeting. Your ten o'clock meeting. Said he didn't have time to come by the office, but he could meet you down at Starbucks."

"Starbucks?"

Her brow folded. "Isn't that what I put down?" The phone rang. She held up a finger as she answered.

I waited as she transferred the call through.

"Did he leave a name?"

She shrugged. "Just said he was your ten o'clock."

"Did he say *which* Starbucks?"

"I just assumed you'd know. I'm sorry. I should have asked."

"He didn't leave a number?"

"I just assumed . . ." By that point she was getting flustered.

"Don't worry. It's not important. Thanks for—" I held up the message.

Starbucks.

There were three in the general area.

I'd just have to assume that the Starbucks in question was the closest one. The one beneath my building, in the Crystal City Shops. It was the same mall that housed Mr. Hoffman's store.

The identity of my ten o'clock appointment?

It was a male; that's what she'd said. I wanted to think it was Sean. But what if it wasn't? Who else might it be? It could be those nameless, faceless DoD or FBI people Sean thought were after him.

If I didn't go, then I wouldn't be putting myself in any danger.

But I might miss an opportunity to talk to Sean.

I went early. That way, I was there first.

I got a venti brew. If anyone tried anything funny, a huge cup of hot, scalding coffee in the face could be my first line of defense.

Second line of defense? I took a seat along the mall-facing counter back in the corner where it met the interior wall of the store. That way I could see everyone who came in, and if anyone tried to drag me out of the store, I'd have a chance to make a scene.

I watched from my perch for half an hour. Ten o'clock appeared to be break time, so there were lots of professionals, company lanyards looped around their necks. There were military people. Artsy types. There was a guy draped in an oversize hoodie and a woman with really long red fingernails. Retail associates from other stores in the mall stopped in, name tags pinned to their shirts and sweaters.

The guy in the hoodie leaned against the stool next to mine while he waited for the barista to make his drink.

I shifted away from him.

He was talking to someone over a Bluetooth headset that was stuck in his ear. "So what did you think of my guy?"

I kept my eyes on the entrance to the store as I waited for Sean.

"You had the chance to talk to him?"

I shifted once more, securing my purse between my elbow and the wall.

The man shifted too, adjusting his Bluetooth, putting his heel to the rung of the stool. "I don't have much time, Georgie. Did you get to talk to him or not?"

At the sound of my name, I jerked. Tightened my hold on my coffee. Then I looked past the baggy jeans, past the hoodie and the beard, and . . . "Sean?"

38

He put a finger to his Bluetooth and glanced over toward the counter. "Don't look at me."

Uh. Okay. "Yes." I opened my purse and pulled out my phone. Pretended to pull up a number and dial. Then I put it to my ear. "Hi. Yes. I talked to him."

This was not the Sean I'd known. The Sean I'd known was articulate. And rational. And most definitely not paranoid. "Yeah. It was very interesting. Did you know there was a minefield that night?"

"Not one of the things that everyone talks about, but yeah."

"And my father didn't draw back when he was supposed to."

"Comms went out. I know."

"Apparently my father talked through a lot of his decisions with his RTO. That's something I can loop back to if we need it."

"Anything else?"

"He stayed with my father. Went with him to Bosnia. Did you know that?"

"No."

I asked him a question I should have asked long before. One that was vital to our collective safety. "How did they figure out you're still alive?"

"I don't know."

"Was it my phone calls? I called you every night that first month."

The barista called out someone's name. Sean slipped from the stool and sauntered over, hand in a pocket, to get his drink. When he came back, he sat fully on the stool, positioned to see out the window. "No. It couldn't be. When I call in to access the voice messages, it's from a different number every time. That voice mail box is like a dead drop now." He put a finger to the Bluetooth again as he held his cup in one hand.

I pulled out a pad of Post-its and a pen as I spoke. "But they think you'll show up at the house." I wrote on the top Post-it. Slid it out in front of me so he'd be able to read it.

I'm scared.

I was scared about what it all meant for Sam and me, but I was also scared in a broader sense. I was scared of what was out there lurking.

"Yeah. I get it. I really do. You've just got to trust that I'm doing what I can."

"I don't know what to do."

"I need you to be careful."

Right. I turned my back to him while a tear slipped down my cheek.

"I'll figure out what to do, but in the meantime, just be careful . . ."

"They're not trying to kill us?"

He didn't answer for a long moment.

My knuckles grew white as my fingers clenched around the phone. "Are they?"

Something brushed against my arm.

I glanced over and saw that he'd stood.

He hitched up his jeans and put his finger to his Bluetooth again as he grabbed his coffee. "I think they're using you to bait me." His eyes scanned the passersby who strolled the mall.

"It seems to be working."

There had to be a solution. A way that Sean could come back to life again. The FBI might suspect that he lived, but they couldn't truly know for certain. And if the DoD figured it out? My son had already lost his dad once. I didn't know if I could handle him dying again. For real. I had to know he understood that. "I'm in."

He squinted. "What?"

I pulled the pad of Post-its back. "I'm in. Whatever it takes." I put them back in my purse as I spoke. "I'll do whatever it takes, but you have to promise not to die again."

He fiddled with the cardboard sleeve around his cup. "I can't—"

"I can't go through that again. I won't."

"Can't promise you anything."

I held the phone out in front of me and pretended I was making another call. Put it to my ear. "I don't care if you can't promise. I need you to do it. Just say it."

"Georgie—" He flipped the lid off his coffee. Put it back on.

"*Say it.*"

"I promise."

"Good. Okay. Now we just need to figure out what it is that everyone thinks you discovered."

He grimaced. "Get a phone. A throwaway. Leave the number on my old voice mail."

39

I needed to figure out what Sean had discovered and why people were so intent on keeping it hidden. And if I wanted Sean to be able to come back from the dead, if I wanted Sam to live in safety, then I would have to figure out how to make all of it known. No one kills to protect information that's freely available.

First things first. Back at the office, I muted a conference call in which I was peripherally involved so I could contact a security company. A supervisor with an eye toward customer service, plus the guarantee of a much higher-quality system than I could afford, made the impossible possible. Waving a credit card was like waving a magic wand. They scheduled the consultation *and* installation for the next day. I crossed my fingers that Jim would be able to supervise.

I would feel safer if I knew who was watching me. Not in a global sense but in a particular one. I wanted a name I could recognize, a face I could identify. That way I would know who to look for.

In the absence of definite knowledge about the bad guys, I needed to play defense. Anyone could create a hypothesis. That's where conspiracy theories usually started. And ended. In order to turn Sean's suspicions into a plausible theory, I needed facts.

At lunch I went out and bought two prepaid phones. I called Sean's old number and left contact information for one of them on his voice mail. The other I decided to use for talking to people like Lee Ornofo.

I stopped by Mr. Hoffman's on the way back to the office. He greeted me, asking about Sam.

"My father was playing with him the other night and he mentioned there's some sort of train that has things you can take on and off?"

He frowned. "I don't know this one."

"Things like boxes? Crates?"

"Ah!" He walked behind the counter and pulled out a well-thumbed catalog. I probably could have found it faster online, but I loved that in his shop at least, things were done the traditional way. He flipped through it and turned it around toward me, pointing. "This one."

It looked pretty cool. It was a cargo set with an engine and a couple of cars. "Do you have it? I want to give it to Sam for Christmas." Mr. Hoffman's store wasn't large; his stock was limited. If he didn't have it, if he had to make a special order, sometimes it took a while to arrive.

He went to the shelves to take a look. Then he went into the back. He came out empty-handed. "I can order it." He made a phone call as I browsed and arranged to have it delivered to the shop later in the week.

My burner phone vibrated as I was walking back to work. I pulled it out. A text from Sean. It was blank, but at least I had his phone number.

When I came out of the school from dropping off Sam the next morning, Chris was petting Alice. She nudged his hand aside when she saw me. He turned and then straightened. "Hey."

"Hey." I freed the leash from the holder.

We fell into step with each other as we headed out toward the street.

He glanced over at me from beneath the leather brim of his hat. "How's Sam doing with everything? Keith wasn't much older when Kristy died."

"His teacher's keeping an eye on him. And he's been working with a counselor."

I asked him about what kind of help he'd gotten for Keith. By the time we made it back to the house, the security van was waiting on the street.

Chris nodded toward it. "You have a system?"

"I'm going to. Just as soon as I can have one installed."

"Been getting quotes?"

"I'm just going to do it. Consult and installation on the same day."

"Don't sign up for anything yet. Let me give you the name of the company who did mine."

"I already basically gave them my credit card and told them to charge whatever they wanted."

"Tell me you didn't."

"With Sean gone, I just want to feel safe."

"You could feel safe for cheaper. I can guarantee it. Want me to see if I can haggle for you? Work the price down?"

"You're sweet, but in this case, the cost of being able to sleep at night? It's priceless."

He shrugged, waved good-bye, and continued toward home.

I watched him walk away. He'd seemed concerned about my not being taken advantage of. Which was nice. And kind. And maybe it spoke more to my state of paranoia than anything else that I couldn't just accept his interest at face value.

He'd shown up at Mrs. T's. He'd been interested in my new security system. In terms of how much it was going to cost me. I caught myself frowning. Sean had ruined me for nice people who just wanted to look out for their friends.

The installation began. Jim had agreed to come over and stay at the house so I could get to work.

I took my lunch break in my office, closing the door. That's when I pulled Sean's book out of its hiding place behind my bookshelf. It was easier to read the actual pages than to zoom in on my phone to see the entries.

The letters and numbers finally made sense. E was E Company. 2 was 2nd Battalion. DS was Desert Sabre. BW. I assumed that was the Bosnian War. The names, I guessed, were all people my father had commanded.

There was nothing to indicate that Paul Conway's death had anything to do with Sean's inquiry into Desert Sabre, but why not take precautions as I made contact with the people on the list? If there was a truth to be revealed, those people could tell me what it was. I googled the names, filling in ranks and positions when they were available. Noting phone numbers when I could.

Before I picked up Sam, I stopped by home and met Jim. He came equipped with operating manuals and instructions about programming the system, setting a security code, and contacting the monitoring center.

"So if you're home, you turn the system off. That way you won't activate it. And when you head to bed or when you go out, you turn it on."

Mostly I was worried about when I was at work. That seemed to be when strange things happened.

"If one of the sensors gets tripped, then they'll call you from this number." He pointed to it in the manual.

I entered it into my phone's contact list.

"Remember: you had them set the alarm to silent."

I had. I'd debated whether I should. But because the security company called the police when the sensors were tripped, I figured they'd have a better chance of catching an intruder if the alarm wasn't clanging a warning.

"So all you have to do to disable the alarm is punch in the code." He showed me the four-digit number. "The year I was born."

His security code lasted the length of time it took me to change it later that evening. I knew I'd never remember his birth year. I changed it to the year Sam was born instead.

I had new locks and deadbolts on my doors and sensors for every room, window, and door of the house. By the time I brought Sam home from school, I felt like I might actually be able to sleep.

My new phone buzzed as I was getting ready for bed.

There should be a better way to earn money than panhandling

40

What?

It was from Sean. It had to be. Same number as before. But I had no idea what he was trying to say.

A better way to earn money than panhandling?

I tried free association. Panhandling. Money. No money. Poor. Homeless. Street. Corner.

Street corner!

I thought—I *hoped*—I knew what Sean wanted me to do. There was an intersection about five minutes away, in Pentagon City, just after the exit ramp from the interstate. A man stood there every morning panhandling. Cars would back up in the left-turn lane, giving him the perfect opportunity to walk up and down the median and ask for money.

I'd made the comment more than once that some company could have a captive advertising audience if they'd just pay the man to hold up their sign instead of his. And that way maybe he'd be able to earn some decent money. *A better way to earn money than panhandling.* I'd just have to cross my fingers that I'd guessed right.

A storm blew in during the night. I'd expected to run into Chris at the school the next morning, the way I usually did, but I didn't see him. Not surprising considering that the entire fifth-grade class was bunched together on the curb huddling under umbrellas, duffels and pillows in hand, as they waited to be whisked off to the county's Outdoor Lab for an overnight. He was probably still inside, filling out last-minute forms or hauling luggage.

I walked home by myself and got ready for work.

Sure enough, as I waited in the left-turn lane at Pentagon City, I saw the man at the edge of the intersection. He was wearing the usual battered camouflage jacket and Nationals baseball cap. Rain dripped from the brim. As he stood there holding a handwritten sign, he hunched his shoulders against the wind. Today, however, the man looked a lot like Sean. I tried to time it just right so that I'd have the full rotation of lights to speak to him. But still, I had to stall for a couple of seconds before the light went red.

Several horns blasted in protest behind me.

Sean walked over, holding his sign.

I rolled down my window.

He leaned toward me.

My phone rang.

I ignored it.

"Can you maybe just leave a voice mail for me? Instead of sending crazy texts?"

"Burner phones aren't hack-proof. They can be traced."

True. I eyed the traffic light. Still red. "I had a security system put in. I need to identify who it is that's doing all these things. Then we can figure out whether it's the FBI or the DoD. We can be working on this from both sides."

The phone stopped ringing.

"I just want you and Sam to be safe."

The intersection cleared. My light would be turning green soon.

My phone pinged. Text message.

"You should talk to Abbott next. I couldn't figure out what to think about what he told me."

I glanced at my phone. Home Security. Intruder Alert. "I have to go."

"What's wrong?"

"Someone just broke into the house."

He gripped the door. "Let me come."

"You can't. You're dead."

As the light turned green, I whipped around the median, making a U-turn, and barreled back onto the interstate.

41

I could have left it up to the police, but I was so close to home. I wanted to see who it was. If I saw him—them, whomever—before the police scared them off, then I would know who I was up against.

After parking the car several houses down, I jogged up the driveway and around the house to the back door. I opened it as quietly as I could and then stepped inside and listened.

Alice wasn't barking like she would have if a stranger had forced their way in. She wasn't even whining the way she had when she'd been muzzled.

Maybe the system had glitched?

I tiptoed into the dining room.

That's when I heard a voice. It was out in the living room.

My phone rang. I grabbed at it, turned the ringer off, and sent it to voice mail.

The voice stopped talking for a long minute. Then it started again. This time I could hear it clearly.

"Georgie?" Is was a she, not a he. "Hi. This is June. Jim and I are over at your place and—"

I walked into the living room to see June and Jim standing by the front door.

The look on June's face as she noticed me was one of utter confusion. "I was just—" She took the phone from her ear. Looked at it. Looked at me. Held it up. "I was just calling you."

Turned out they'd gotten a big Halloween yard inflatable for Sam. They'd decided to leave it inside so it wouldn't get wet. They'd used the house key but plugged in the old security code. I gave them the new one. We got it all sorted out.

But not before the police got there.

It was getting to be a regular thing with me.

That afternoon I got word that everyone was cleared for the big test in January. I put in a request with the travel office for plane tickets and hotels. Congress was still moving forward on passing a funding bill, so I was good there. But I had phone calls to make and emails to send and a list of new government requests for proposals to scan. Several to start working on. And I had a presentation for one of the American Physical Society's conferences to outline.

When I came home with Sam that night, Jenn and Preston were sitting on the porch swing, shivering as they waited for us. A box filled with my half of our farm share sat in front of the door. At least I wouldn't have to go into the house by myself. I'd expected that installing the security system would make me feel more secure, but it hadn't.

Jenn hefted the box to her hip as I opened the door. After punching in the security code, I let everyone in.

Sam discovered the Halloween inflatable right away. He and Preston wanted to take it outside. I persuaded them we couldn't blow it up in the rain and herded them toward the kitchen instead.

"Sorry about the delay." Jenn followed me. "Got home too late last night to bring it over. But guess what's in our box this week— You'll never guess."

"Kale, broccoli, turnips, onions, and cauliflower?"

"O-kay, so maybe you will guess. But there is *one* surprise."

"No idea."

"Apples!"

"Really?" I took it from her and carried it into the kitchen. Apples were a gift from heaven. I didn't have to think about how to disguise them or make them yummy. They already were.

"I know, right? I'm thinking we should drink to them."

Rain splattered against the window over the sink. Where would Sean go on a night like this? Where would he sleep? What would he eat? Was he safe? "You'd drink to anything." I pulled a bag of veggie chips from the cabinet and shook them into a bowl for the boys.

Jenn raised a brow. "Let's just say I'm not picky. Usually people think that's a virtue, G."

I shot her a look over my shoulder. She'd been drinking far too much lately, in my opinion. "They say women are drinking just as much as men now, but because we have a higher fat-to-water ratio than—"

"Please, don't mention fat." She put up a hand. "Let's think positive thoughts: agave. There is agave in tequila. Agave is green. Greens are green, ergo, when I drink a margarita it's basically like eating spinach."

Divorce was tough. I got it. But she seemed manic. Borderline destructive. "I count at least three fallacies in your argument."

"That's just because you're a scientist. Normal people would agree with me. I say we deserve doubles."

"You can deserve a double. Make me a single." I pulled the tequila from the cabinet and set it on the counter next to her.

"Only if you promise to drink it twice as slow."

I held up three fingers in a Scout's promise.

She poured herself what looked like a triple shot to me.

We sipped the drinks while Sam and Preston chattered about the Halloween party that would take place the following Friday. Sipped some more as they told us the latest rounds of their hilariously unfunny knock-knock jokes.

Sean used to knock-knock Sam right back with even crazier, screwier jokes. Whatever wavelength Sam lived on, Sean had been a frequent visitor.

Jenn leaned toward me. "Do you mind?"

"Huh?"

Jenn snaked the bottle of tequila from the cabinet and poured herself another shot while the boys acted out a scene from some super-hero movie. When they ran out of the kitchen, Jenn trailed them, taking a seat at the table in the dining room.

Pushing thoughts of Sean away, I pulled out a chair across from her and sat down. "What's going on?"

She blinked in apparent innocence. "With what?"

"The divorce."

She made a face.

"I just worry about you."

She downed about half the tequila in one long swallow.

"Seriously worry."

She shook her head. "Don't." Jenn worked hard and partied hard. She always had.

"Have you talked to your dad lately?"

She took another drink. "Chief Justice Andrew Cunningham Baxter IV?"

I raised my brow.

Her gaze dropped toward the table. "No." It came out in a whisper.

When Jenn's mother died, her father had conquered his grief by pouring his heart into his career and his religion. Which left Jenn no one to help her through her own grief. No wonder she was messed up. In high school, we'd had parent envy. I gladly would have given her my type A parents for the bliss of benign neglect. She'd tried everything she shouldn't have at least once by then. But she'd finally figured out that being the best was a better way to get her father's attention. Therefore, Harvard. Therefore, Georgetown Law. Therefore, her position on the Hill in the office of the most powerful politician in Washington. Senator Rydel chaired the Armed Services Committee that would be conducting my father's hearing. He was rumored to be exploring a run for president. If that happened, if he got elected, Jenn would be able to ask for any position in his administration she wanted.

"I really do worry." About her. About Sam. And about Sean.

"It's not worth it. I mean, think of how many times you've already worried about me. And here I am." She saluted me. "I'll be fine."

"You'll be drunk."

"Too late." She snickered.

At least I didn't have to worry about her driving. She and Preston only lived a couple blocks away. I leaned across the table and reached for her drink, but she held it out of reach.

"I just want you to be happy."

"I *am* happy. In my odd, perverse, screwed-up sort of way."

"Is it Mark? Has he changed his mind? Is he asking for full custody?"

"No. He's just about perfect. Except he married me. We still have to hold that against him." She took another drink.

Jenn wasn't the sentimental type. Especially not about her exes. "You realize you just said something nice about him."

She nodded glumly.

"Sean always thought he was a good guy."

"Sean." She sighed, closed her eyes, and leaned against the back of the chair. "Here's to Sean." She raised her glass. "The perfect gentleman who, even when presented with the possibility of a sure thing, chose fidelity." She tossed back the rest of her tequila.

42

"*What* did you just say?"

"What did I what?" She sat up, wiped her mouth with the back of her hand, and set the glass down, hard, on the table.

"That thing you said. About Sean."

Something flashed across her face as her gaze shot away from me. "What did I say?"

"Something about when he was presented with 'a sure thing'?"

"I said that out loud?"

I nodded.

"Funny story . . ."

"I don't think I want to hear it."

"No. Wait." She didn't seem drunk anymore. "I think you should hear it. I think you should hear how one day last January I came over when you were gone and asked Sean if he wanted to—"

I stood up. "You should leave. Now."

She put a hand to her eyes. "I'm such a mess. I can't even tell you—"

"No, really. You should leave." I stepped into the hall. "Sam?"

He answered a moment later, yelling, "What?"

"Preston has to leave." My call sounded more like a screech.

"Can we have five more minutes?"

"He has to leave *now*."

"But, Mo-om!"

I went down the hall to Sam's room and started scooping up Legos and tossing them into bins.

Jenn had followed. "If I could just—"

Glancing up, I saw her lean into the room. Alice nudged her aside and came in and stood beside me.

"You have to understand. Please, Georgie."

Understand? What could there possibly be to understand? Once she'd blown up her own marriage, she'd decided to blow up mine? I ignored her, focusing instead on Sam. "Don't worry about picking up. I'll do it."

"'Kay."

I looked over at Preston. "Your mom has to go."

His bottom lip edged out into a pout. "But we weren't done playing."

Jenn stepped forward to grab Preston's hand, pulling him toward the door. "Sorry."

I wasn't sure who she was saying it to, but I hoped it was Preston. Because sorry wasn't going to be enough for me.

After we'd finished dinner—after *Sam* had finished his dinner—I took him to the public skate session so he could practice what he'd learned in his lesson the night before. I laced up his skates and helped him over to the wall of the rink where he could wait with the rest of the kids.

"I'll meet you down here when it's over."

"What if I get tired before that?"

"Of skating? You love skating!" And I knew I'd need the whole hour to process Jenn's revelation.

"Can you skate with me?"

"Tonight?"

I could barely see his eyes through his helmet. But I probably wasn't imagining they looked hopeful.

"I can't, sweetie. I didn't bring any thick socks." And my heart was breaking.

His shoulders dropped.

"I'll skate with you sometime next week."

"You will?"

"I promise."

One of the skate guards unlocked the door and swung it open.

I stayed until Sam made it to the end of the rink. The chill in the rink reinforced the chill in my heart. After verifying that there were two fluorescent yellow–hoodied skate guards on duty, I went upstairs to the mezzanine, which overlooked the rink. It was warmer there than it was rinkside, and I could keep an eye on Sam. I could have watched him the whole time if I'd wanted to. And I did want to. But my gaze kept veering off into nothingness as I contemplated Jenn's betrayal.

Forty-five minutes into the public skate session, I'd done absolutely no work on hunting down Mr. Abbott, even though my purse, papers, and phone were strewn across the seat next to mine. On my other side, a woman had sat down, book in hand. She was a typical skater mom, dressed in one of those puffy down jackets and a pair of fuzzy boots. She spent more time watching one of the figure skaters who was using public ice to practice than she did reading.

When I looked down into the rink the next time, Sam was stumbling more than he was skating, but he was making a valiant effort of it.

Far away, on the other side of the ice, two other kids were skating around in hockey gear. They were much more solid on their skates, elbowing in and out of the crowds, crisscrossing back and forth. Maybe someday Sam would skate like they did.

I glanced at the clock on the scoreboard that hung suspended over the middle of the rink. Five minutes of public skate left.

Looking down at the rink, I found Sam at the far end. He was holding on to the rail with one hand. The two would-be hockey players were at the other end, racing along, zigzagging around the other skaters. As I sat there watching, the taller one looked up in my direction. Following his gaze, I noticed a man standing by the mezzanine window.

The man gave them a thumbs-up.

The kid nodded, pulling at the arm of the other. They continued on, careening down the long side of the rink.

I looked over at the man again.

He was nodding as he watched them.

Seriously? Shouldn't he be reining in his kids rather than encouraging them?

Sam shoved off the wall and moved toward the crowd that was circling the ice.

"Watch out!" I knew he couldn't hear me, but it was the only thing I could do to help him.

I breathed a sigh of relief as he narrowly avoided colliding with a girl who had just completed a jump.

He threw his arms out, trying to balance.

"Just—" I held my breath.

An adult who was skating past paused a moment to steady him.

I promised myself I'd skate with him at public skate for the rest of the year. It would be less exhausting to be out there with him than to watch him.

A blur of red streaked into my vision.

Those kids.

They were bent forward, skating fast, and seemed to be heading right toward— Did they not see Sam?

I sat up straighter. "Don't— Stop—" Dumping my computer on the seat next to me, I stood. I put a palm to the glass and pounded at the window.

It didn't help. They couldn't hear me.

It seemed like it happened in slow motion. One came at Sam from behind and pushed him. As Sam flailed, the other came at him from the front, slamming into him. Then my son crumpled into a heap on the ice.

43

I headed for the stairs at a run.

When I got to the ice, those two boys were at the end of the rink, opposite Sam, and my son was still sprawled face-first on the ice.

"Hey!" I tried to wave down a skating guard, but he didn't see me. Nobody saw me.

"Hey!" I tried again. Gave up. Stepping out onto the ice, I started off down the rink toward Sam.

The skate guard came flying at me and slid to a stop with a scrape of his blades and a shower of ice. "I'm sorry, ma'am, you can't—"

"My son!" I pointed out to the end of the rink where a crowd was now, *finally*, gathering.

He skated off and soon returned with Sam.

I took Sam from him and carried him to the nearest bench. Propping him up against the wall, I knelt in front of him and pried his helmet off. "Are you all right?" I felt his head for bumps. Pressed trembling fingers to his face to feel along his jaw. "Did you know those boys? Did they hurt you?"

The buzzer sounded the end of the session and skaters exited the rink. I leaned forward, an arm on either side of him, trying to create a buffer as the bench filled. "Does anything hurt?"

He shook his head and winced.

"Where does it hurt? Can you see okay?" I rolled forward on my knees to get a better look at him. There was no bruising. No blood. "How many fingers am I holding up?"

"Two."

"How old are you?"

"Six."

"What day is it?"

"Thursday?"

Wednesday. But that wasn't a fair question. He mixed up the days of the week on a regular basis just the same as he mixed up yesterday and tomorrow. "Can you move your arms?"

He lifted them up.

"Can you move your head? Slowly."

He moved it up and down and then from side to side.

"Can you—" I paused, distracted by a pair of red hockey jerseys. It was those two boys. "Hey!"

I stood. Keeping one hand clamped around Sam's forearm, I used the other to reach for them.

They glanced at me, glanced at each other, then made a break for those double glass doors.

Luckily, they ran right into that man who'd been watching them from the mezzanine.

"You! Sir!"

He glanced over at me, then quickly looked away.

"Sir! Yes, *you*!"

The other children on the bench were staring up at me, mouths agape. Parents, kneeling beside them, busied themselves with untying skates.

I couldn't leave Sam by himself, and the man was standing his ground. But I was in a mood, and I could do Crazy Lady better than just about anyone. I raised my voice. "You told those kids to attack my son!"

He held up his hands as if in defense.

"I *saw* you! My son could have been hurt!"

The skate guard lurched over and offered an ice pack to me.

I rounded on him. "And *you*!"

He quailed, dropping the pack.

"You're a *skate guard*! How could you not see those kids were being reckless? Did you not notice how many times they—"

He held up his hands. "I— They were practicing hockey moves— they were just deke-ing."

"By weaving around all over the place?"

"That's what—"

That man was steering the boys toward the doors.

"That's what deke-ing is." His teenage voice climbed the scale a full octave.

Bolting from Sam, I caught up with the man and grabbed him by the sleeve. "I want your name."

He stopped. "Boys will be boys. They were just practicing."

I tightened my grip on his sleeve. *Your name.*

"Mommy?" Sam had left the bench to follow me. He was holding a finger up to his nose. Blood was dripping out beneath it. "I think my nose is bleeding."

Letting go of the man, I knelt beside my son, drawing him close within the circle of my arm. "Let me see."

I'd left my purse upstairs, so all the hand sanitizer and Band-Aids and Kleenex I carried in it were useless. I shepherded him to the bathroom and used up most of a roll of toilet paper trying to stop the bleeding. By the time it had tapered off, the benches that had been filled to capacity were empty. The ice that had hosted the public skate crowd was now occupied by figure skaters executing graceful spins and effortless jumps. The Top 40 music had been replaced by a symphonic rendition of the latest Disney movie theme song. I felt as if I had emerged from a wormhole into a parallel universe.

I held out a hand to Sam. He grabbed on. "My things. They're upstairs." At least I hoped they still were.

The skater mom who'd been sitting beside me looked over with concern. "I saw it all. I'm sorry. Is your son okay?"

"He's fine." I wasn't. My hands were shaking. My knees felt like they'd come undone. "Thanks for keeping an eye on my things."

She smiled, then turned her gaze back to the figure skaters who were gliding across the rink.

I got Sam checked out at the emergency room. No sign of a concussion, just a mild sprain to his wrist where he'd tried to break his fall on the ice. It was soon clear my phone, however, hadn't survived its time at the rink.

At random intervals, the alert light would blink when I had no incoming email, and the camera flash even went off once. I resigned myself to asking the tech group at work to take a look at it.

In all my time at the rink over the past year, I'd come to recognize most of the parents. But I'd never seen that lady before. She acted as if she'd watched my things, but who had watched her?

At home I texted Sean. What I really wanted to do was call him, but he was right. Even disposable phones could be identified and hacked. And people who attacked children were just the type to do it.

> S got hit at rink. No accident. S fine.

I meant to get ready for bed after I tucked Sam in, but I couldn't. My hands were shaking too hard to brush my teeth.

The attack on Sam hadn't been random and it hadn't been a childish prank. It had been deliberate.

I went into the kitchen to get a glass of water. Alice followed me, pausing in the doorway as if unsure what to do.

"I don't—I don't—" I put down the glass and gripped the lip of the sink. I couldn't seem to take in a breath. So I stepped back, bending over to let my head fall between my arms. "I don't know, Alice." I took in a deep, gasping breath and then lifted my head. "What do I do?"

Ransacking my house was one thing. But attacking Sam?

I glanced out the window over the sink, into the dark, out into the night where people were watching. Sean, perhaps. And the FBI.

Or the Department of Defense. Or grown men who told their children to beat up little boys.

I grabbed my glass. Or tried to. It toppled over into the sink and shattered.

"Alice—" I couldn't keep the sobs from coming any longer. I slid to the floor and pulled my knees to my chest.

Alice shuffled over.

I grabbed hold of her neck and buried my face in her fur.

The tears didn't last long because I knew they wouldn't help. And I knew it didn't make any difference how afraid, how terrified I was. The only way out was through.

44

I was surprised to see Chris at school the next morning with his Maltipoo. Wasn't Keith supposed to be at the Outdoor Lab overnight trip? As I bent to pull Alice's leash from the holder, he joined me.

"Is Keith all right?"

"What? Sure. Yeah. He's fine. Had soccer practice last night."

We started walking. "He must be really dedicated. That's quite a drive, isn't it?" The lab was at least an hour west of Arlington.

He shrugged. "It's not that bad."

"He must have been disappointed to leave."

"Homework waits for no man. Or boy."

"I thought—" It seemed, somehow, that he was talking about something different. Keith was in fifth grade, wasn't he? Had I remembered wrong? That would be embarrassing. Only one way to find out: ask. "Is he worried about middle school next year?"

"Middle school!" He blew out a breath. "He's not worried. I am, though!"

So he was in fifth grade, just like I'd thought. And if so, he should have been on that trip. Even Sam had heard about it. "Sam's already looking forward to the Outdoor Lab."

"Outdoor Lab? Is that in sixth grade?"

My step faltered as my blood ran cold. "Pardon me?"

"The Outdoor Lab. Sounds fun."

He didn't know. Chris didn't know about the Outdoor Lab.

"I, uh—shoot! There's something I forgot to give Sam. I'd better—" I gestured back toward the school.

"Sure. Okay. See you." He nodded and walked off down the street.

I jogged with Alice back toward the school until he was out of sight and then I stopped. I stayed where I was until my legs stopped shaking and the fear that had broken out in a cold sweat behind my ears had evaporated. Until I could think clearly. And even then, one thought echoed in my mind.

Chris doesn't have a son.

I forced myself through the motions of getting changed, making my lunch, getting into the car.

Two things I needed to know. Who was Chris? And who had ordered him to watch me? We'd been walking our dogs together since when? The week after Sean died? Fear stole my breath. He'd been watching me for that long and I'd never once suspected.

Halfway to work, one of those red dashboard warning lights came on. It was an exclamation point enclosed by a circle. And parentheses. At the next stoplight, I pulled the car's manual out of the glove box.

Immediate attention was required.

Of course immediate attention was required. And I'd have to pay for it with all the money I didn't have. I pulled off into the nearest parking lot and called my mechanic. He was happy to take my car but vague about when he'd be able to fit the work in or get it back to me.

The next call I made was to Jim. He drove out and followed me to the mechanic's shop in his car, then dropped me off at work. He lifted a hand as I got out. "When do I pick you up?"

"I can take a taxi home."

"Not when you've got me as a neighbor."

I smiled my thanks. He'd been so good to us. They both had. "Five?"

"I'll be here."

By the time I got to work, I was already in a deficit. I hadn't slept well. Again. I had to turn my cell phone over to the tech group so they could figure out what was wrong with it. And my thoughts kept jumping randomly to Jenn, to Chris, and to the problem of what had happened over in Iraq.

I pulled out Sean's book and surreptitiously worked at deciphering his notations. It quickly became apparent that the names he'd struck through had died. Those notated with a question mark? I had no idea. So I texted him.

Looking at records. Question about ?s

His answer came a few minutes later.

Couldn't find any info

During a conference call, I created a new email account and then sent emails to some of the people in Sean's book. Toggling back and forth between the call and the emails didn't do my concentration any favors.

I heard back from David Abbott. He gave me a phone number for the USO lounge at Dulles International Airport where he volunteered. I pulled out the notes I'd taken from Lee Ornofo, then I gave Mr. Abbott a call as I ate lunch at my desk.

"You want to know about Desert Sabre? What can I tell you?"

"I believe you spoke to my colleague about the war. He was working on a history of the conflict, but he died not long after you spoke to him."

"Sorry to hear that."

"I was just wondering, could you tell me what you talked about?"

"The war. Mostly."

"You were with Captain Slater's company? Can you tell me about the twenty-fourth of February?"

"Day one? You want to know what it was like? Not what you expect. You think desert, you think hot. Sun. All that. Well, it wasn't. It was rainy. Rained more there that month than it did back home.

Least we didn't get stuck like some of the other units. So, yeah. Rain, early in the day. Then the rain stops and the wind kicks up. We had us one of those desert sandstorms. Went from miserable conditions to just pure misery."

"And what was your position?"

"I was a platoon sergeant."

"And what were the orders for the day? Do you remember?"

"Sure wasn't to take a mud bath. That was extra."

"So you woke up at, when?"

"We were awake. We were all awake. Don't think none of us slept. We knew the war was starting."

"So what happened?"

"What happened? What didn't! Start of a war isn't like the start of a race. One-two-three-bang! And you're off and running. More like one of those big marathons. Someone must be right up against the starting line ready to go, but most everyone else is piled up behind them just waiting. Sometimes takes a good twenty, thirty minutes for the guy in the back to get to the start line where he can do some running. That's how it is. So the war starts when the general says it starts, but we didn't get to move out until the guys in front of us started moving out because the guys in front of them had started moving. See what I mean?"

"Sure. Makes sense."

"And even then, to start fighting, you got to get yourself to the war. We were all waiting in Saudi, right? But to fight the Iraqis and liberate Kuwait, we had to get ourselves to Kuwait. So we're cold. We're getting rained on. Antsy. Finally start moving. Got to get through their first defenses. Just trenches in the desert, through the sand, manned by those Iraqis. Good thing: we got lots of sand to work with. Bad thing: we just plowed them over."

"Sorry? What did you say?"

"Plowed 'em. They wouldn't surrender so we just went right along their trench lines and plowed all the sand they'd dug out right back on top of them. Their fault, I suppose. If they'd have thrown all that sand they dug out over on the other side of their trenches, then we couldn't have done it. Us grunts didn't want to say it, but it didn't sit right. See what I mean?"

They *plowed* them?

"You sign on to be a soldier, you expect you might get killed by a bullet, but you don't consider that you might be buried alive. In sand. That's one thing I wish I'd never seen."

I resisted the urge to shudder.

"But after that? Things opened up real nice. Guys in front of us took care of the minefields, laid lanes out over them, and we were set to go. Wasn't that hard. The Iraqis we ran into, they weren't the Republican Guard. Most all of them saw us coming, they surrendered. Just like that. So we were going pretty good. Rain stopped. But then the wind started. Came on something fierce toward evening. Messed with the communications. Our company commo, he was having fits, trying to keep us connected to headquarters. Terrain started changing too. More dips and valleys. Some rocks thrown in. The battalion got spread out. Wasn't long before we were out there on our own."

"And what happened then?"

"Well, we stopped. You have to understand that all those sand dunes look the same. Not like here: Potomac to the east. Blue Ridge Mountains to the west. You can always kind of figure out the lay of things. And if there's any doubt, just look for the Washington Monument, right? Well, out in that desert, there was only sand. Here, you see sand like that, you look for an ocean. There? Nothing. It's odd. It's disorienting."

"It must have been."

"If you didn't see the sun rise, you'd have no idea where east was. And if you didn't know where east was, you didn't know anything. Those Iraqis, though, they seemed to have a sixth sense. Had some prisoners by then. We were trying to pass them back but couldn't find anyone to pass them to. Anyway, I'd noticed when we were sitting back there in Saudi two, three weeks before, didn't matter what time of day it was, when prayer time came, those Muslims, they'd get on their knees and pray toward Mecca. Really something to see. So we're sitting there, who knows why, night coming and I guess it's time for prayers, 'cause all of a sudden, those guys, they're down there in the sand. They were praying. Toward Mecca."

"Right." That made sense. Because Mecca for Muslims is, well, it's Mecca.

"Mecca was south and west. It's always south and west if you're in Iraq."

"Sure." I was a little spotty on my Middle Eastern geography, but that sounded reasonable to me.

"So if they're praying toward Mecca, and orders were that we attack from the west, we're supposed to be heading east, right?"

I nodded.

"So they're praying toward southwest and the company's sitting there, middle of the desert, and we're kind of pointed at an angle from them, maybe hundred fifty degrees, hundred sixty degrees."

"So?"

"So Mecca is *west*. We were supposed to be going *east*. Should have been going opposite, right?"

"You're saying that the company was going the wrong direction?"

"That's what I'm saying. Not by much, maybe, but still."

"Did you do anything about it?"

"Not a lot *to* do. I was a sergeant. Company commander was a captain. He wins. Still didn't sit right, though. So I went up and had a word with top. That's the company first sergeant. He said the captain was dead set we were going the right way. Top said to just go along. If it came to it, he said the captain's the one who'd hang for it, not us."

"Who was top? Do you know how to get ahold of him?"

"Top? That was Sergeant Wallace. First name? Sarge." He laughed.

I wrote it down. "So it was known among the NCOs that the captain was off course?"

"Oh yeah. But Captain Slater, he was one of those—if he was heading to hell in a handbasket, most folks'd say, 'How do I hop on?' It was the desert, you know? We had people lining us up with a compass, standing out there in the sand, directing us with their arms. Little bit off course here, little bit off there, and then we got so far ahead of everyone."

"Can I ask, did you know someone named Paul Conway?"

"The commo? Sure. He was a good troop."

"Do you know what he might have been doing that night?"

"Conway? He was just trying to keep everything working. Sucked to be him that night." He laughed. "But you should talk to him. He's the one who'd know what messages managed to get in and out."

45

Mr. Abbott had corroborated Mr. Ornofo.

The company had lost contact with everyone else.

Even so, that wasn't a major crime or even a minor one. It was more than a little embarrassing, leading two hundred men out into the middle of the desert and not being in quite the right place, but it wasn't court-martial terrible, not kill-to-keep-it-quiet terrible. The only thing it established was that my father wasn't where he was supposed to be. That was the theme: no one was where they were supposed to be. I can see why Sean hadn't known what to think. It seemed like it ought to mean something, but what? There had to be more to the story.

One of the tech gurus brought my phone back midmorning. She handed it to me. "You had some nasty stuff on there. Didn't find any record of anything having been downloaded, though."

"But you got it all off?"

"Yeah. 'Cause I'm kind of awesome that way." She flashed me a smile as she left.

At least all my communications with Sean were through my new phone. But I deleted my personal email account from the mail program on my old phone just to be safe.

Who had planted the malware? The FBI? The Department of Defense?

"Georgie."

"Huh!" I was startled out of my reverie by Ted.

"There's a—" His words were drowned out by the sound of a vacuum cleaner down the hall. We worked so often with classified information that cleaning staff had to be escorted. It was easier to have them come during the workday and make everyone take escort responsibility for their own office.

"Sorry, Ted. What?"

He stepped inside my office. "There's a problem with your contract."

"The appropriations bill. I know."

"Besides that. Someone's challenged the award. They say you had inappropriate contact with the contract officer."

What? "I didn't talk to anyone in the government after the request for proposal came out. Not until after they published the award of the contract."

"I know. Of course you didn't. But you're going to have to sort it out. Make some phone calls." He dropped the folder on my desk. "Just answer the challenge, will you?"

"I resent having to charge billable hours to someone else's unfounded accusations when—"

"Then you're really going to resent having to get it done before noon tomorrow."

"Seriously?"

He didn't answer. He was already out the door.

I made a few calls trying to determine who had challenged the award. I narrowed the possibilities down to two.

By that time it was noon. I dug into my purse for my sandwich. Looked at my phone. The old one. Then the new—

I'd missed a text from Sean. He'd sent it several hours before. It must have been during all the vacuuming. I hadn't heard it buzz.

Meet me downstairs

I grabbed my purse and left my office at a run.

I was heading for the Starbucks, like before, when someone stepped out from a store right into me. His coffee spilled all over my sweater and down onto my purse.

He stepped back. "I'm so sorry. I didn't mean to—"

I glanced down at the stain. "It's fine. It's all right." I looked at him. It was Sean. "Sorry I'm late. I didn't see your—"

He grabbed my arm. "Let me wipe this up for you." He pulled me over to a bench. Handed me a napkin. Then he took one himself and dabbed at my purse. "You need to tell me what happened with Sam."

"There's not much to tell. Two of those little hockey punks sandwiched him. He fell."

"He's okay?"

"He's fine." I used a napkin to squeeze the coffee out of my sweater. "It took a while to stop his nosebleed. That night I realized my phone was acting strange. It was spyware."

"From the rink? How did they do it?"

"When I ran down to get Sam, I left everything upstairs. It couldn't have been for more than ten minutes. Or maybe fifteen."

His gaze had settled over my left shoulder as he'd listened to me speak. "So they knocked Sam down on purpose."

"Georgie!" The call came from behind me.

I stiffened.

Beside me, Sean did too.

46

"Georgie, hey—" It was one of my coworkers. One who'd actually met Sean. We'd all gone to a baseball game together back in the day. "How's that presentation for the conference coming? I was hoping we could talk about it this afternoon. I had some ideas." His gaze settled on Sean.

Sean smiled. "Hey."

I gestured to my sweater, trying to distract him. "I ran into him as I was heading for Starbucks. Wasn't quite the way I'd imagined getting coffee, but—" I dabbed at it again with the napkin. "Anyway, yes. I'll swing by your office later."

"Great. Okay. Later."

I breathed a sigh of relief as he walked away. "Do you think he recognized you?"

Sean shook his head. "People only see what they expect to." His eyes scanned the crowd. "Flirt with me." He turned the full force of his attention back to me and I remembered exactly what it had felt like when I'd first met him.

"What?"

"Flirt with me. We'll draw less attention as we talk if it looks like there's a reason we're doing it."

He didn't know what he was asking. Even back when I was single and flirting, I wasn't very good at it. And somehow, just then, I couldn't quite catch my breath. He didn't look like a panhandler anymore. He was wearing a tailored sports jacket, trim trousers, and an open-neck shirt. His hair was slicked back. Had he trimmed his beard? He looked European.

He put a hand on my arm. Looked down into my eyes. Then his

gaze dropped to my lips. Went back to my eyes. "I like being with you."

My cheeks bloomed. "Sean."

"I do. It's been way too long." He flashed a smile again. "Did you learn anything from Abbott?"

He didn't seem like Sean. He was so suave. It was as if he were playing a role. But he was so good at it. It was like he'd done it all before. A lot.

"Georgie?"

I blinked. "Yes. My father let the company get off course."

"Right. I know."

"Is that why they ran into the Iraqis?"

"Less frowning. More flirting."

I smiled.

He smiled.

"Maybe the company was in the wrong place; maybe the Republican Guard was right where they were supposed to be."

He winked. "I checked that out at the Pentagon. Neither group was supposed to be where they were."

"They buried people alive, Sean. In the sand. Is that what this is about?"

"Everyone knows that. Nobody talks about it."

For good reason.

He smiled once more and extended his hand.

As I put mine into it, I felt him press something into my palm.

He winked. "See you around maybe?"

"Yes. Sure. Yeah."

He turned around, threw his empty coffee cup into a trash can, and walked away.

I plunged my hand into my purse, letting go of whatever it was he'd given me. Then I brushed at the coffee stain one last time. It was useless. I tossed the napkin away and continued on to Starbucks. At least that would provide a reason for my trip.

If anyone was watching.

As I stood in line waiting to place my order, I fished Sean's gift out of my purse. It was a hotel key enclosed in a cardboard pouch.

I'd never spent much time thinking about Sean's past. Not as it related to his relationships with women. He'd seen so many terrible things. Done, perhaps, some terrible things. He'd been in a gang. And he was *really good* at flirting. Just how much experience with women did he have? Granted, he'd turned Jenn down, but how many others had thrown themselves at him?

If I could have beat myself over the head with something, I would have. I didn't have time for that kind of nonsense. And I wasn't fifteen years old. But after talking to Kelly, after hearing Jenn's betrayal, after seeing Sean's performance, I was starting to question what we'd had. How could I trust *us* again?

The hotel was connected to both the mall and the office complex. It was a fancy hotel, the kind we put our consultants in when they came to meet with us. I strode through the lobby as if I did it every day of my life. As if I belonged there.

I lectured myself as I rode the elevator up to Sean's room. I told my stomach that it was *not* allowed to turn over. I told my knees that they were *not* allowed to melt. I practiced what I was going to say when I saw him because I needed to ask him about Jenn. I wanted to hear what he had to say. I used my key to unlock the door, pushed it open, and then all those good intentions fell right out of my head.

Sean was there.

And he wasn't wearing his shirt anymore. Or his jacket. Or his shoes.

I held up a hand. "Don't come any closer."

He ignored me.

I pressed my back against the door and closed my eyes so I wouldn't lose focus. I wanted to be able to say what I needed to. "There's something I really need to talk to you about. I need to talk to you about Jenn."

His hand cupped my elbow.

My eyes flew open.

His gaze held mine. "What about her?"

"Sean. Seriously. You know. January?"

He sighed. Ran his hand up the back of his head. "It was that Saturday when you were doing that Kids and Science day downtown. Jenn brought Preston over. She'd been flirty before, but I'd kind of written it off as her trying to get attention."

"Jenn's flirty with everyone."

"I know the difference between fun flirty and sexy flirty. I'd been brushing her off. You know, deliberately misunderstanding the cues. But that day there wasn't any way to misunderstand. So I told her I wasn't available. End of story."

"And you didn't tell me, why?"

He took hold of my hand. "Because I figured I could handle Jenn, and whatever it was that you got out of your friendship with her was something you needed on some level. I just made sure I was never alone with her again."

He was trying to meet my gaze, but I didn't let him. I needed to sort it out on my own. Either I trusted him or I didn't. But I wouldn't be persuaded into it. "I just . . ." I put a hand to his chest.

He covered it with his own.

"I want to trust you, Sean."

"You *can* trust me."

"I'm not—" A sob was trying to work itself out and I didn't want it to. I swallowed. "I'm not good at any of this."

He let go of my hand and cupped my face. "Any of what?"

I closed my eyes. "I never even thought—it just always felt like—" My voice had gone ragged. "*I* wanted to be the one."

His hand slid to my shoulder. "You are the one."

"I just— I think I would have wanted to know."

"Then I'm sorry I didn't tell you." He scooped me up and carried me to the bed.

47

After, as I lay there next to him, I would have sworn I was floating if my head hadn't been cradled in the crook of his elbow.

Sean pressed a kiss to my forehead.

"I don't want to leave."

He pulled me closer. "I don't want you to."

I slid my arm across his chest. "Should I worry about how you paid for this? You did pay for this, right?"

"The important thing is that there's no trail that will lead to me. Or you. Right now the only thing I want is for you and Sam to be safe."

"I wish we could talk to Paul Conway. I think he's the key; he knew everything. He's the one who sent and received all the messages. I don't think it's an accident that he died."

He entwined his fingers with mine. "I don't think so either."

I curled into his torso. "They don't get to choose what happens to us."

"I couldn't save my parents, but I'm doing everything I can to save you."

He was doing what he'd done when he saved Kelly. He was withdrawing in order to pull away the danger. I could feel it. "I want you back."

"I need you to understand. I might not get to come back." He said the words slowly. Distinctly.

The illusion of safety, of togetherness, vanished. I propped myself up on an elbow. "Why not?"

He glanced up at me and then rolled onto his side to face me. "How can I? I don't even have an identity anymore."

"We figure this out and we tell the truth." I reached out and traced one of his eyebrows. "We tell the truth and it's not worth it for them to try to kill you anymore."

He rolled onto his back. "Sometimes I wish I'd just kept my mouth shut. Decided that it was just an oversight—that someone forgot to mark that Iraqi position. I could have convinced myself it didn't matter the Iraqis weren't supposed to be there."

"Once we figure this out, maybe if we told someone *else*. Someone different. Someone not at the Pentagon or the FBI. Isn't this the kind of story someone would publish?"

"Maybe. Probably." He looked over at me. "Let's say they did. It'd be a twenty-four-hour sensation. Then what would happen? I'd get arrested and prosecuted for leaking classified information."

"They couldn't—"

"The only one who'd know all those things, who could have pulled it all together from all the different sources—the message traffic, the people, the maps—is me. And how would I know them? Because I had access to classified materials. And worse, the other historians would be brought in to testify against me. There's no way for me to publish my story without revealing classified information."

"But wouldn't it be a whistleblower suit? Intimidation by the government? Conspiracy?"

"Maybe. But what kind of money would I need to defend myself in a case like that? And how many years would it take? And even if I were exonerated, what kind of job could I hope to apply for? I'd never be eligible for a secret clearance again. No one in the federal government would want to touch me. Academia? I'd always be the crazy conspiracy guy. So why would I come back?"

"You have to."

"Most people, had they put two and two together the way I did, would have looked at the other side of the equation. They would have realized it wasn't worth it."

"The truth is always worth it."

"Is it? Always? Really?" He searched my eyes.

"It has to be. The confirmation hearing is less than two weeks away. We need to know what happened. There has to be a way."

"All roads still lead to me. And classified information."

"But what if they didn't?"

He raised a brow. "How could they not?"

"What if they lead to me instead? That way you wouldn't be implicated."

"It won't work." Sean didn't even pause for a moment to reflect before discarding my proposal. He threw back the sheets and got out of bed.

I followed him to the bathroom. "It *will* work."

"It won't. You'd have to have access to message traffic and the files and interviews in the archives." He turned on the shower.

"Not necessarily. You could tell me."

"But what I know is based on that information."

"*And* all the research you've been doing in the past eight months."

"You'd have to know what people to interview."

"I do. I have the names in your book."

"But you'd have to know what the orders for the day were—"

"I can get that information."

"How?"

"It's like a geometry proof. You got there one way. All I have to do is figure out an alternative method."

"In academia we call that researching with a bias."

"That's quaint. In geometry it's called proving a postulate."

He closed his eyes and leaned back into the water.

I raised my voice so he could hear me. "Do you want to come back from the dead or not?"

He straightened, opened his eyes, and looked at me. "This isn't safe." His eyes softened. "If they'll kill me for what I know, what do you think they'll do to you? This isn't academic, Georgie. This is good guys and bad guys."

"And that's absolutely what gives me hope."

"Hope?"

"That's right. Because you're not dead yet, are you?"

"I might as well be."

"You aren't. And after I'm done, you'll be even more alive." I stepped into the shower with him, reached up, and took his face between my hands, treasuring the opportunity, knowing from experience that I might not ever be able to do it again. "I love you. And I want Sam to have his father back. That's why I have to do this. Just trust me. Okay?"

Underneath the desolation in his eyes was something I hadn't seen in them since he'd turned up alive: hope.

48

By the time I finished washing and drying my hair, Sean was gone. But that was okay. My body was still warm, my heart still singing from his having been there. I walked out of the hotel and back down to the mall. As long as I was passing by, I decided I might as well pick up Sam's Christmas present.

Mr. Hoffman came out from his storeroom as I walked into his shop.

When he saw me, he stopped. Then he smiled. "You are happy."

If only he knew. I blushed. Then tried to cover it up. "How could I not be happy? Walking into your store is like walking into a fairy tale."

He returned to his storeroom to get Sam's train. It was already boxed, bagged, and ready to go. "Little Bear is well?"

"I think things are going to work out for him."

I went by Ted's office on the way back to my own.

"Hey—Georgie. Thanks. I need to talk to you." He took in a hiss of air through his teeth. "I hate to do this to you, but I just heard Congress is going to pass another continuing resolution today."

A continuing resolution? "You mean an appropriations bill." A resolution meant nothing. It wouldn't release the funding for my contract. I couldn't do anything, I couldn't get paid unless they passed the actual bill.

"Nope. It's going to be a CR."

"Another one? For how long?"

"Four months."

"Four—"

"I know. Sucks, right?"

That meant I wouldn't be able to charge any money against the new contract until February. At the earliest. "Can you put me on someone else's contract until then?"

"That's the thing. We saw this coming and already did the old shell game, you know? Switching people to other contracts until they can get funded on their own."

"And?"

"And thing is, we don't have any moves left. Your contract was a sure thing and it seemed like they were going to pass the bill, so—"

"It *is* a sure thing. It's already been awarded."

"Point is, we didn't come up with a plan B for you. I need you to go on PTO—"

He needed me to go on vacation? For *four months*? "But I don't—"

"—and since you don't have any left, I need you to go."

"Go. Go where?"

"Go home."

"Go *home*?" What was he trying to say? "Are you *firing* me?"

"Well, I'm . . ." He opened his mouth to speak, but no words came out. He tried again. "We're letting you go. Because of the contract. Or lack thereof. If it comes through . . ." He shrugged.

"When. *When* it comes through. It's coming through." But not until the appropriations bill passed.

He shrugged. "When it comes through, we'll have a welcome-back party."

"So you're—" I really was quite sure I hadn't heard him correctly. "You're letting me go. I'm fired."

"Not for any *bad* reason. It's not personal." He sent me a thumbs-up. "I'll give you a great recommendation if you feel like you have to find something else."

"But the fiscal year just started. Can't we run into the red a little bit and make it up—"

"Wish we could, but we've been told to clamp down on that sort of thing."

One of the security guys stopped outside Ted's door.

Ted gestured toward him. "He'll escort you out. He can help you carry the heavy stuff." Ted winked. "Okay?"

I simply stared at him. Not okay. Not okay at all.

There wasn't much to pack. Just a few pictures. My framed diplomas. Some well-thumbed college books I used for reference. The pen I liked the most.

It all fit into two cardboard boxes.

After downloading my personal files and Outlook contacts, I tossed the thumb drive into one of them. "Guess that's it."

The security officer held out his hand. "Badge?"

Right. I slipped it off and gave it to him. We were halfway down the hall when I remembered Sean's book. "Just— I forgot something. Be right back!" I sprinted down the hall before I remembered I didn't have the badge to access my office anymore. I had to wait for the guard to catch up with me.

But my badge had already been deactivated and he had to get special permission to let me back in. Then he had to watch me.

Did I ever feel like an idiot on my hands and knees reaching back along the wall behind my filing cabinet.

Nothing.

I moved even closer, jamming my shoulder up against the metal.

Still nothing.

"What you got behind there? Stack of *Playgirl* centerfolds?"

"Just, um, my son. He visited. His ball. It rolled back there."

He leaned against the cabinet and levered it away from the wall for me.

There it was!

"Huh. No ball, but at least I found this book I'd been missing." I pulled it out and slid it down the side of the box.

I called the car mechanic from the lobby of my building, asking when the car might be finished. He said the parts they needed were on back order and since they'd torn the engine apart, they couldn't guarantee when they'd have it all back together.

I asked if they'd found anything unusual.

"Like?"

"A bug."

"A bug? What? You mean on the windshield or something?"

"A bug. An electronic bug. You know. For tracking someone?"

"Oh. Oh! Like in James Bond? That kind of thing?"

"Right."

"Nope. I mean, I haven't looked. But aren't they supposed to have red blinking lights? I would have noticed something like that. Unless, wait. No. Red blinking lights are the car bombs, right? Not the trackers?"

I told him not to worry about it.

The security guard asked me to stand outside since I was no longer employed by the company and I wasn't a visitor. I shivered in the wind while I waited for a taxi.

It's not like Congress hadn't punted on the budget before. And it wasn't unusual to have contract funding delayed due to a continuing resolution, but for Ted not to even *try* to find interim funding for me? That was strange.

And wasn't the timing just a little suspicious? The DoD or FBI had already tried to bug my computer and my phone. They'd already broken into the house. They'd beat up Sam to distract me. Why wouldn't they take my job away too? Most of the company's business came from government-funded contracts. How would Ted be able to say no if they asked him to fire me?

I texted Jim that I wouldn't need a ride home.

206 | SIRI MITCHELL

Ms. Hernandez texted me, asking if I could meet with her again.

I texted her back, setting up a meeting. I hoped Sam wasn't still drawing wormholes. I'd meant to sit down with him and try to talk things through again—without raising my voice—but then the house had been ransacked and Sean had come back from the dead and Sam had gotten beaten up by hockey hooligans. Maybe I really was a bad mom.

My mother called on the way home, as I sat in the back seat of the taxi clutching what remained of my professional life. Being fired from a job was definitely not Slater-condoned. Maybe my mother had been right about everything. Maybe I should have been following her advice. Maybe I should have studied business like she'd told me to. I sent her call to voice mail because she had an uncanny way of ferreting out the truth.

I walked into the house, dropped the boxes on the floor, and barely remembered to punch in the security code in time. Then I pulled Sean's diary out and took it into the kitchen with me. Taking Sam's box of Fruity-O's from the cabinet, I removed the bag of cereal and dropped the diary inside the box and put it back in the cupboard.

After retracing my steps to the living room, I peeled off my coat and let myself sink into the couch. "I'm not that bad a mom, Alice, am I? I've never forgotten to feed you, have I?"

I hadn't. Ever. At least not that I remembered.

"And you always get at least two walks a day."

In fact, Alice got more planned, more regular exercise than I did.

"I don't add sugar. To anything. I only serve real juice. And I have a CSA subscription. I've tried."

Really. I had.

"Isn't the thought what really counts, Alice?"

Silence.

"Alice?" Normally Alice gave some sort of response when I came home. And when I talked to myself.

"Alice?" I pushed myself to sitting. Where was she? I'd assumed she was close because she usually shadowed me around the house.

But she wasn't on her dog bed in the living room.

She wasn't in the kitchen where she sometimes liked to cool her belly on the old linoleum floor.

"Alice?"

As I walked down the hall to my room, I heard panting. Then I saw the mess. "Oh, Alice!"

49

Jim drove us to the vet and helped me carry Alice into the exam room.

"Are you sure she hasn't had any chocolate?" The vet gave me a searching look as I tried to keep Alice from pacing the length of the clinic's exam room.

"I don't know where she would have gotten it." I kept all of ours in a cupboard.

"She's been vomiting? Had diarrhea?"

I nodded.

"Tell me about her daily care. Have you changed anything? Food? Shampoo? Medications?"

"Nothing." I was kneeling on the floor beside her, trying to stroke her head, but she kept shifting positions—sitting on her haunches, then pushing to her feet—as if she just couldn't get comfortable.

"Has she been anyplace new? A dog park? Someone else's house?"

"No. And we've been walking the same route for years." I tried to embrace her, tried to ease some of her discomfort, the way I did with Sam, but it didn't seem to help.

"She hasn't spent longer than usual in one place on her walks? She couldn't have discovered any old food containers on the street or anything?"

I had no answers.

"Something's poisoning her system."

Fear clutched me. Something or *someone*?

"Do you keep fertilizers or pesticides within reach?"

"No."

Alice whimpered again, shifting her weight from foot to foot.

I stroked her head. Her ears.

She lay down and then immediately got back up.

The vet lifted Alice's tail with one hand and wielded a thermometer with the other. But before she could insert it, Alice began to seize.

It took a while for the doctor to stabilize her, and there were some harrowing moments, but by the time I left the veterinarian's office, I was told she would recover.

I got back in enough time that I was able to walk down to pick up Sam right when school ended that afternoon. There was no reason for him to stay for their extended day program since I was home. I had to figure out how to cancel him out of the program anyway. Even if I managed to bring Sean back to life soon, with security systems and car repairs and vet bills and the loss of my job, we were going to have to save every penny we could.

Sam and Alice had always had some sort of telepathic connection. First thing he asked when he got home after school? "Where's Alice?"

I'd meant to ease into telling him. Could nothing go right? I shoved my keys into my front pocket and took off my coat, trying to buy myself some time. "She has to stay at the doctor's overnight."

Sam looked at me, concern coloring his eyes. "Why?"

"The doctor thinks she found chocolate somewhere and ate it." No need to tell him of my own suspicions. "She can't eat chocolate; it's not good for dogs." It wouldn't hurt for Sam to know that. "If they have too much they can get super sick."

His mouth dropped open. His eyes went wide. "Is Alice going to die?"

"The doctor says she'll be fine. But she got really sick and she'll need to stay there a few days."

Tears were welling up in Sam's eyes. "I'm sorry."

I knelt and gave him a big hug. "I'm sorry too."

"It's my fault." He wrestled himself out of my hug and took me by the hand and led me to his room. I had discovered Alice in the hallway, so I hadn't seen Sam's room until just then. The mattress of his bed had been pushed askew and the floor was littered with candy wrappers. "Sam?"

He was sobbing. "It's all my fault. Alice is going to die and it's all my fault."

"Shh." I tried to hug him again, but he wasn't having it. He beat my arms back and sat on the floor, pulling at his hair.

"Sam. It's okay. Alice is going to be okay."

Gulping back his sobs, he looked at me. "Are you sure?"

"I'm sure." Pretty sure. I sat down next to him.

He scooted onto my lap.

I put my arms around him and rocked him back and forth.

He turned and snuggled into me.

"How come you had so much candy for Halloween in here? I thought I told you we were keeping it all in the kitchen."

"I took it for Daddy. In case he was hungry after the firm hole."

I cheered him up with his Super Sam cape, tying it under his chin. Then I made him half a peanut butter sandwich as a snack.

When tears threatened, I thought up another diversion. "Hey! Guess what—I have a surprise for you. Want to see it?" I slipped my old phone into my back pocket, in case the vet called, and the new one into my front pocket in case Sean texted. Then I grabbed the bag containing the new train from one of the boxes on the living room floor.

"What is it?"

"You'll see." I'd been meaning to keep it for Christmas, but he seemed to need it just then. And so did I.

We went downstairs into the basement where he could play with it.

The delight in his eyes when he pulled it out of the box was worth it. "Grandpa was telling me about these!" He offered the train and its crates to me. "You can use them with the crane."

I handed them back. "Show me."

Sam took them from me and pushed them along his intricate network of intersecting tracks. He made the crane take off the crates, ran it around again, and then made the crane put them all back on. Pretty soon he forgot about me, so I sat cross-legged on the floor and checked my email. Already word had gotten around that I'd been let go. I drafted an email to send to all of my business contacts.

Sunlight had retreated from the basement windows; it was getting dark. I got up and turned another light on.

Somewhere above us, a floorboard creaked.

"Can you do this for me, Mommy?" He held up two of the trains. He was trying to secure the connection between them.

I cocked an ear toward the ceiling. Old house. Just settling. "What?"

He dumped the trains into my lap. "Can you make them fit together?"

"Sure." I picked them up.

But there it was again.

I put a hand to his arm. "Just a second, buddy."

I held a finger to my lips as I glanced up at the exposed ceiling. He followed my gaze with his own.

Another creak.

I set the trains on the table. Put an arm to his shoulder and eased him away from it. I bent so I was looking directly at him and spoke quietly. "This is very important. When you and Dad played that game, the one about hiding?"

He nodded. "The Bad Guys."

"Did you ever play it down here?"

He nodded again.

"I think we ought to play it, you and I. Can you show me how?"

"Not really, I mean—"

"This is a real game, Sam. Do you understand?" There was another creak upstairs. That time it sounded like it was coming from the dining room. "There's someone up there. And Alice isn't here to protect us."

50

"But Daddy says—"

"Can you tell me some other time? Right now I need you to hide."

"Welp, there isn't any laundry piled up." He glanced around behind him. "And you moved Daddy's big backpack and his bike, so—"

"Sam!" I hissed his name. "What did Dad tell you to do?"

He took my hand and pulled me toward the back of the basement where the water heater and boiler sat. But Sean had always been compulsive about keeping the area around them clear. I yanked him back. "There's no place to hide over there."

"Mom!" He tugged back so hard that my shoulder felt it.

I put a finger to my lips. The creaks were moving toward the kitchen now. Whoever it was might soon notice the stairs.

He let my hand fall and ran over to the water heater. Then he pointed toward a metal flap set high in the cinder-block wall.

There was a ledge beneath it, but even if I hoisted Sam up there, he'd be in plain sight. "I don't think that ledge is big enough for—"

"You're supposed to open it."

"What?" I spoke the word a bit louder than I meant to, but he was jumping at it, trying to reach it with his hand.

"Open it, Mom. Just push it open."

"But even if it opens, I don't think—" I gave it a push and it swung straight up into the outside air.

"Dad says it's a coal chute."

The door to the basement creaked open and a footstep fell on the stair. I boosted Sam up and he scrambled through. Then he lifted the door from the outside. "Come on, Mom!"

"Listen to me. I want you to run over to Mr. Jim and have him call the police. Tell him there's someone in the house."

"Mom! Come on!"

Now the footsteps were coming down the stairs. In just a few moments I would be seen. "I can't make it. Just go!"

"Stand on the pipe. Climb up."

I put my foot to the pipe. Two steps more and I was holding on to Sam's hand. "I don't think I can fit through here." I might have, pre-Sam, but my hips were wider than they used to be.

"Dad fit. Just go like a snake."

I wriggled a bit, testing the sides of the chute and the sides of my thighs. The chute wasn't very forgiving. My thighs, on the other hand, compacted quite a bit.

The chute was masked by a tall, chubby euonymus bush that hid us from the driveway behind its green and yellow leaves. The deep shadows of dusk also helped.

I eased the flap closed behind me and crouched next to Sam. "I never noticed that before."

"Dad says nobody remembers them." He put his head to the ground and looked out between the branches of the bush. "I can't see anyone."

Neither could I.

Holding on to Sam's hand, I led the way around the bush. Then, keeping to the darker parts of the yard, we moved out toward the street. As I pulled him along, I sent a glance back to the house. And as I was doing it, I ran right into—

"Oof!"

Chris. It was Chris.

I put a hand to his arm to steady myself. "Sorry!"

He'd recovered his balance and now he smiled. "Georgie. Hey." He glanced toward the house.

Was he the intruder?

No. I discarded the thought. He wouldn't have had time to meet us out in front. But maybe he was an accomplice. I followed his gaze, trying to figure out the best way to get rid of him. "We were just leaving." I gestured toward Jim and June's. "We really need to—"

He released my arm. "I was just wondering if—"

A door slammed. Then a strange light illuminated the backyard for an instant as a shadow went racing away toward the house behind ours.

The sudden contrast with the darkness hurt my eyes. Squinting, I put my hand up to block it even as I backed away from Chris. It wasn't safe to be on the street. I had to get Sam out; had to get him away. "Sorry. Can we talk tomorrow? Sam and I were—"

There was a percussive boom.

Chris put up a hand to shield his face. "What the—"

I felt it in my chest, like the slap of a wave, before I heard it. The sound started low, then mushroomed. It swelled, threatening to obliterate my ears, and then it retreated, leaving me staggering.

Ears ringing, I reached out for Sam.

He'd been knocked to the ground, but he was pushing up from his knees. Arm extended, brow crumpled, he reached for me.

I pulled him up, turned us away from the house, and folded my body around his as I felt to make sure he was okay.

"Mommy?" I felt Sam's mouth move against my cheek. He clamped his arms around my neck.

"It's okay. It's going to be okay." I spoke the words into his ear as I scooped him up and started running.

But it wasn't.

Heat licked at my backside. The pavement, the houses next to ours, stood out in graphic relief. Windows had been blown out of the cars that were parked on the street.

It was not okay.

Our house had just exploded.

51

"Why didn't I call about it? About the intruder?" My voice had climbed an octave in disbelief.

The police officer sat across from me at June's table, pen poised above his notebook. "That's right."

"Because I didn't have time. Literally." I clutched at the blanket June had wrapped around my shoulders. "We escaped from the basement and then the house exploded."

"You didn't notice any fumes beforehand?"

"I noticed the sound of someone walking around in my house. That's what I noticed."

"Setting that aside for the moment—"

"Setting that *aside*? Setting aside the fact that someone was prowling around my house? While we were *in it*?"

June put a hand to my shoulder as she leaned in and put a mug of coffee on the table in front of me.

I cupped it, pulling it close.

"There's no one who might be able to corroborate—"

"Chris Gregory was there. Outside the house with us. He saw it explode."

"Chris?"

"He's the one who called 911."

"And he's . . ." The police officer glanced out into the living room where Jim and Sam were working a puzzle. "Is that him?" He gestured toward Jim.

"No. Chris is—" Where had Chris gone? He'd been there, at the explosion. He'd made a phone call. "I don't know where he is."

"Do you have contact information for him?"

"I— No. He's just a neighbor. We walk our dogs together."

"Address?"

"He lives . . ." Where *did* he live? He always dropped me off on the way home and then continued on. I didn't know anything about him really. Except that he didn't have a son in fifth grade. "Um, he lives farther down this street." Or maybe the next one up? Or maybe he didn't live in the neighborhood at all. Maybe Chris wasn't even his real name.

Jim had pulled the curtains in the living room shut so Sam and I didn't have to see the firefighters or watch flames devour our house, but against the darkness outside, the curtains still glowed. And they still pulsed red from the lights of the fire trucks.

The police officer flipped his notebook shut. "It will probably take a while for everything to stop burning."

Everything. Every single thing I owned.

"We'll be in touch."

I knew why my house had exploded. I knew who had done it. The FBI or the DoD. Agencies that shouldn't have been trying to intimidate me in order to reach Sean.

By the time my parents drove up, I was crying big, ugly tears of rage.

My mother pulled me into her arms.

I let her.

My father stood outside in Jim's yard, watching the house burn, one hand clutching his side, the other pressed to his mouth.

We stepped out to join him.

My mother tightened her hold on me. "At least you weren't at home."

Pulling away, I very nearly yelled. "We *were* home. We were in the basement when I heard someone in the house. Had we been two minutes later in getting out"—of our own house!—"we wouldn't be standing here now."

She blinked. "Pardon me?"

"We were *there*. At home. In the basement."

Somewhere inside the inferno, something popped. Flames flared. A window exploded.

The orange and yellow of the fire reflected off my mother's face. She clutched at me, drawing me close, and whispered my father's name.

He eyed her. Dropped his hand from his mouth and extended it to her. But she didn't see it. She just stood there holding me, transfixed by the flames.

My father glanced beyond her to me. "I, uh, maybe . . ." His shoulders slumped as if all the air had suddenly left his lungs. "I don't know. Why don't we get your things? Sam shouldn't be seeing this."

He wasn't. He was still inside with Jim. "I don't have any things."

My father's brows collapsed in uncharacteristic confusion. "What things?"

"Any things. I don't have *any* things. I have nothing." Nothing but the clothes we were wearing and two cell phones. Everything else was gone.

"Nothing." The word hung in the space between us for a moment. "Well." He cleared his throat. "I just think that it would do you a world of good to get out of here. Leave all of this behind you. Your mother and I have found a house. A big one. There's room for you. There's no reason you couldn't move in with us."

"We can't." My tears had dried up as the weight of reality had settled onto my shoulders. For myriad reasons we weren't going to do that. I chose the easiest one for protest. "Sam's school is here."

"But the new house is in a good school district and—"

"His friends are here."

"He can make new—"

"I'll have to deal with the fire. The insurance company. There might be things that can be salvaged. If there are, I want to know about them."

"But your father's right. Maybe this is a good time to start over."
My mother had reengaged.

"Start over?"

"Completely. Leave the past behind."

I choked down a laugh. It left me feeling strangled. "Leave the past behind?" My own father, her husband, was the reason I couldn't. Because somewhere out in the desert in Iraq, something had happened. "Sean wouldn't want me to." But if I wasn't careful, if I didn't say just the right thing when I told him about the fire, he was liable to throw all caution to the wind, come back to life, and have to die all over again. For real. I gestured toward the fire. "That was my life. Everything we'd built together." I wanted it all back.

"It's been eight months, Georgia Ann. Let us help you. We'll be here now. Let us take care of you."

"But Sean was trying—" I'll never know what I might have told them, what I might have admitted to, if my father hadn't interrupted me.

"Sean doesn't matter!"

I blinked.

"JB." My mother's voice was low. She was sending him a warning.

"Do you really think it was fate that led Sean to you? *I* sent him to that bar to find you. So whatever loyalty you think you still owe him is misplaced."

"You—you what?" The bottom dropped out of my world. My memories, the very foundation of my life with Sean combusted, turned to cinders, and disappeared through the huge, gaping hole my father had just blown in my heart. "But he'd gotten out." Sean had gotten out of the service by then.

My father dismissed my words with a frown. "Strong character. I could tell that about him. I'd thought I could trust him. I was hoping I could count on him. And truth is, I knew you were floundering—"

"I wasn't floundering!"

"—so I asked him if he'd do me a favor."

Asked him? He'd *asked* Sean? Then it might as well have been an order. No one ever refused a general anything. I'd thought I was blossoming. That I'd finally become the butterfly bursting from her chrysalis. That I was pretty. Maybe I was, maybe I wasn't. But it didn't matter. None of it had mattered. Sean had been sent on a mission. Like any good soldier, he'd done what had been asked of him. I was the mission; he'd done his duty. Which made me wonder. Was he part of all of this too?

52

I left my mother and father standing there, walked up the steps into Jim and June's house, and locked the door behind me.

After plying us with multiple mugs of hot chocolate and a dozen freshly baked chocolate chip cookies, they settled us into their guest room. It would have been nice if Sam had been a cuddler. I would have liked something to hold on to. But he was a spinner, rolling in his sleep. At least he always spun in the same direction. I kept myself out of his way as I stared into the dark, trying to wrap my mind around all there was to do. At one point I almost got out of bed to make a list, but then I realized my attaché had burned along with everything else.

I'd have to ask June in the morning if I could borrow a piece of paper. And a pen.

And shampoo. And a hairbrush. And a towel.

And a cereal bowl. And a spoon.

And maybe a clean pair of socks.

And some dental floss.

I'd have to ask the DMV for a replacement driver's license. I'd have to contact my bank for a new credit card and ask the post office to forward my mail to a new address. And then . . . and then . . . I couldn't quite remember . . . and finally, I fell asleep.

I didn't text Sean about the house until morning; I didn't know what to think about him anymore. I didn't figure there was any way for him to help, and I didn't want him to do anything rash. Which is probably what someone had been hoping for.

I put some effort into figuring out how to tell him, but I finally gave up.

House exploded last night.
S ok
At J Js

It was Friday and that was both good and bad. I could send Sam off to school and he wouldn't have to see the smoking ruins of our house, but all his fears about leaving me had come back. Jim and June tried to make him feel better about everything by telling him it could be Samday every day now, but he wasn't buying it. They offered to take him to a movie and out for lunch over in Ballston the next day. That cheered him up.

I borrowed June's car that morning, went to Kohl's, and picked up some basic essentials. Pajamas, a change of clothes for us both. A purse for me. A backpack for Sam. I used a phone app to pay.

When I got back, I wandered over to the house. It looked as if someone had doused our entire lot with a bucket of charcoal-colored paint. My nose wrinkled at the acrid scent of burnt wood and burnt wiring.

"Georgie!"

I turned around to find Chris walking down the sidewalk toward me. "Hey. How are you doing?"

I slipped my hand into my pocket and grabbed my phone. I didn't think he knew that I was on to him, but I was wary just the same.

"I keep wishing I'd been able to do more for you than just call 911." He shrugged. "I'm sorry."

"It wasn't your fault." I tried to sound convincing.

"You guys okay?"

"The police were asking about you."

Did his eyes sharpen beneath his baseball cap? "Me? Why?"

"I told them you were there with us. They wanted contact information, but I realized I don't have any."

He pulled at the brim of his cap. "Right."

I pulled my phone out of my pocket, pretended to open an app while I opened my camera instead. I held the phone up, gesturing with it, and took a picture of him. "If you give me your phone number, I can pass it on to them."

"Sure."

I opened up my contacts and thumbed it into my phone as he gave it to me. "Thanks. Well. I should go. Lots of things I have to do. About the fire."

"Sure. If I can do anything, let me know, okay?" He lifted a hand by way of good-bye and left.

I let out the breath I'd been holding.

A lawn maintenance crew had gone to work blowing leaves in the yard next door to mine. They came every Friday. As the leaves began to swirl, I stood there staring at the ruins of my house.

The picket fence dipped toward the street as if trying to escape the wreckage. The gate had been blown off its hinges.

There was just so little left.

And what the fire hadn't destroyed—the massive support beams, the fireplace and chimney, the concrete laundry basin in the basement—wasn't anything I would have wanted to save.

Ten years of life together and there was nothing. I didn't have the strength to stand anymore, so I squatted. As I swept a hand over a pile of ashes, something brown and lumpy caught my eye. I pulled it out of the debris. A melted Lego brick. Next to it was a picture frame. It was a photo of Sean and me on our wedding day. The frame was blackened. A corner of the photo was singed.

One of the lawn workers approached the edge of the property line. His leaf blower sent a stream of powdery, acrid ashes in my direction.

I stood, spitting ashes from my mouth. "Hey!"

He didn't appear to notice.

Clutching the picture to my chest, I stomped over, skirting a pile of still-smoldering embers. "Hey!"

He turned.

"Can't you see what you're doing?"

He idled the leaf blower.

I looked past the work boots. Past the company jacket. Past the sunglasses. It was Sean. Of course it was Sean.

He held the leaf blower away and leaned close. "Argue with me."

Argue with him? He wanted an argument? Well, I had one for him! I raised my voice. "I always really liked our story. The way we met at the Ballroom. The way we found each other." I tossed the picture behind me onto a still-smoldering pile of charred wood. "My father told me last night that he put you up to it!"

"What?" He powered the leaf blower up a notch and swung it back toward the house, sending up another stream of ashes.

I kept pressing him. "Did he? Did my father ask you to find me that night?"

"What night? What are you talking about?"

I grabbed hold of his coat. "Did my father set you up with me?"

He twisted away.

"How am I supposed to trust you? What am I supposed to believe?"

"Georgie—"

"Is my father telling the truth?"

He pointed the leaf blower out toward the street. "No! You have to believe me, Georgie."

"How?"

"I am not the bad guy here." He gestured to the ashes. "Our house blew up. My son got beat up. I got run out of my job. You're not asking the right question. You need to ask yourself why your father would lie to you about something like that."

"I want to believe you." I closed my eyes. "I want to. Just tell me how."

Everyone trusted someone until they realized they couldn't. Everyone thought they knew what love was until they discovered they didn't. Everyone thought they knew the truth until they found out it was a lie. But how do you let go of one to take hold of the other?

"I have always tried to act in your best interests, Georgie. I might not have always succeeded, but I have always tried. Because I love you. And that's what love does."

Love. Sean claimed that he loved me. He'd never stood me up beside him to portray the perfect American family. He'd never used me to bolster enthusiasm or display patriotism or recruit supporters. He'd never made me part of an argument that made him look better than he was. If Sean had used me at all, it was to make *me* better, not him. When it came down to it, the decision to believe him was simple. It didn't have anything to do with anything he said. It had everything to do with all the things he'd done, including lying to protect his family. "I believe you." Maybe he wasn't Saint Sean, but he was something better. He was my Sean. "This is where it stops."

"This is where it stops."

I pulled my phone from my pocket, showed him the picture of Chris.

"He's FBI," Sean said. "Be careful."

53

As I walked back across the street to Jim and June's, I called the number Chris gave me. Just to see what would happen.

No one answered.

No voice mail picked up.

My mother called while I was helping June clean up from a batch of Rice Krispies Treats she'd made for Sam. "Georgia Ann. Sugar pie."

June waved me toward the living room. I handed her the sponge with an apologetic smile and went to sit on the couch.

"I just wanted to tell you how bad your father feels about last night. I want you to know that I'm on your side."

My side.

Maybe she was.

"He wants you to know how sorry he is. He shouldn't have told you that."

"Is he there?"

"Your father?"

"If he's there, I want to talk to him."

There was silence for a moment and then my father came on the line. "Georgia Ann?"

It was a measure of just how much trouble he was in that he didn't call me Peach. "Why did you do it, Dad? Why did you set me up with Sean?"

"Why?"

"Why."

"Because he was a good man. I could tell. I can always tell a good troop. He was everything I'd always wanted for you. If we'd ever had a son, I would have wanted him to be someone like Sean. It was time for you to find someone." My father was warming to the topic. "I told myself, if I'm picking family, I might as well pick the best."

It was clear to me that he was making it up as he went along. I was trying to figure out why. Regardless, one thing he'd said was true. "He was. Sean was the best."

He sighed. It was the sound of relief. "Can I take you out for lunch maybe?"

"I don't think—"

"Here. I'll pass the phone back to your mother. She'll set it all up."

My mother came back on the line. "Georgia Ann?"

"Dad wanted to do lunch, but today is not a good day."

"Tomorrow then. We'll both come by. We can go to McLean and show you the new house. Even if you decide not to move in with us, we want Sam to know there'll be a room just for him. Whenever he wants to visit."

"Tomorrow we can't. Have you already bought it? You don't want to jinx anything."

"You know your father. Senator Rydel might be a bear, but everyone likes him. We're not expecting any trouble with the confirmation."

I asked June if she would mind if I borrowed their computer for a while. She set me up at their dining room table. I got out my phone and brought up the pictures I'd taken of Sean's diary. Then I logged in to my new email account and checked some emails I'd sent to several of the names in Sean's book. I called a couple of them as well. After several hours of talking to people who'd fought in Desert Sabre, I felt like I was spinning my wheels. Every person I'd talked to who had served with my father had known that their unit had been far out ahead of everybody else. Some of them had even known about the order to draw back. None of it was breaking news.

There had to be more to the story.

Maybe I was looking in the wrong places.

I wished I could just look at everything from a different angle.

Or maybe figure out how not to do what I was doing. If I'd had my notepad, then I would have taken it out and made more notes. But I didn't have it. I had to borrow some paper from June.

I wrote down the names *Conway, Ornofo, Abbott.*

What did they have in common?

They were all there during the first Gulf War.

What else?

They were all part of my father's company. And those were, quite logically, the people who could tell me what had happened. If anything had happened at the company level at all.

Frustrated, I drew a circle around their names. I needed to think outside that circle. Although they'd been there, they didn't have the information I needed.

Who else had been there? My father. Obviously. Who else? Almost two hundred other men. Whom I didn't have time to interview individually.

I put my fingertips to my temple. Closed my eyes. Forced myself to focus. I needed to speak to people who were not those three men. I needed to speak to people who were not the communications sergeant, a platoon sergeant, or the radio telephone operator sergeant.

My eyes sprang open.

There it was. I needed to speak to people who were not sergeants, people who hadn't been noncommissioned officers. Maybe I needed to speak to someone who wasn't my father's subordinate. Outside the circle that I'd drawn, I wrote down *peer* and *commanding officer.*

If choices had been presented that night and decisions had been made, just like Mr. Abbott had said, it wasn't the NCOs who had made them. It was the officers.

What else did those names inside the circle have in common? At least two of the three had really liked my father. Whatever had happened out there, they were likely to have given him the benefit of the doubt.

So what if I came at it from a completely different angle? If I was going to find out the truth, then maybe I should talk to people who hadn't liked him. At least it would provide me with a different perspective.

I just had to find out who my father's enemies were.

54

I called my father's staunchest supporter.

"Mom. Hey."

"Georgia Ann! Did you change your mind about lunch tomorrow?"

"No. But I was out running errands and, funny thing, I thought I saw that guy. The one who never liked Dad." It was a complete shot in the dark. For all I knew there might have been no one on earth who disliked my father, or there might have been hundreds. But it was worth a try to see what my mother came up with. "What was his name again?"

"Steven Edgars? Lord have mercy! If that man—" The pause was full of vitriol and venom. "If that man'd had his way, your daddy would be in Leavenworth to the end of his days, turning big rocks into little rocks. I've never a seen a soldier more just plain mean than Steven Edgars."

"Right. That's the name. He served under Dad?"

Steven Edgars. I wrote it down.

"Nothing but trouble."

"Just out of curiosity, what was it with him and Dad?"

"Oh, just—things not worth repeating."

"None of it's true, is it?"

"Georgia Ann!"

"I mean, how could any of it be true?"

"That man was poison. Pure spiteful poison."

"Didn't mean to bring back bad memories. Do you know what happened to him? After he got out?"

"Edgars? Who knows? Although I heard he started one of those watchdog websites. Always going on about corruption in the military. Figures."

A few internet searches and I found him: Steven Edgars, CEO, Integrity in Government. It was an Alexandria-based company. I pulled up their website and read some of their press releases. They were mostly fact-based accusations that tended to veer off into rambling tirades against the federal government and the powers that be.

I imagined there were people like Mr. Edgars in every field. People who seemed reasonable at first glance but on closer inspection turned out to be just a little bit odd. If the goons at the Department of Defense and the FBI had considered him credible, he might have met the same fate as Paul Conway. Or Sean.

I signed up for another free email account, using a fake name, and sent an email asking him if we could meet.

> Dear Mr. Edgars,
>
> I'm working on an account of Desert Sabre and am in search of new source materials beyond those that have already been so widely referenced. It's been pointed out to me that you served in Captain JB Slater's company. Is it possible that we could meet?
>
> Regards,
> Gina Porter

Jenn came over that night, after dinner. Jim invited her in. She enfolded me in a hug and sat down right next to me on the couch, taking my hands into hers.

"I'm really worried. Jim said there was someone in the house? Before it blew up?"

I nodded.

Her face was pale, her eyes wild. "First the guy in your crawl space. Then your house blows up. You have to come stay with us."

I freed myself from her. "Jenn, I can't—"

"Say whatever you want. I'm a terrible person. I know I am. But you need someplace to stay. Come home with me."

I stood. "Are you insane?"

She blinked. "No. Why? No. The boys would love it. I really think it would be safer."

"Jenn. You tried to sleep with my husband."

"I know I did. I just want to make it up to you." She was pleading. "Can't we get past it?"

Make it up to me? Get past it? I could only stare at her.

She held up her hands as if fending off an argument. "I mean, I know I could never make it up to you. But we've been friends—we *were* friends—for a very long time. Please. I have to find some way to make this good."

"There's nothing that would make this good. You'll never make this good. We're not good."

"But I really need to—"

"I don't know how many ways I can say this. I don't know why you're not understanding this. We will never be good."

"Don't say no yet. Okay? Please don't. Maybe once the insurance people have come out and everything is settled?"

I said nothing.

"I want to help."

In some weird way, she probably did.

"Just tell me you'll think about it. I'm hardly ever at home. It would be like I'm not even there."

That, at least, was probably true.

"So we're good?"

Good? No. Not even close.

After Jenn left I put Sam to bed. At least he didn't put up a fight; there weren't any stars on June's living room ceiling to look at. I tucked the blanket under his chin. "You okay, Sam? It must feel strange, sleeping here. You probably miss your things."

"Daddy told me things are just things."

I smiled. Sean had always said that when Sam had lost or broken one of his toys. I kissed him on the forehead. When I was sure he was asleep, I wandered back down the hall.

Jim waved me over. "Hey, sweetie! Your dad's on the news."

When wasn't he?

"Come watch with me."

I sat in an armchair next to his.

It was mid-interview and the host was beaming at my father. "I can't think of any reason anyone would contest your nomination."

"You just haven't talked to my wife yet. She'd give you at least ten."

They both laughed, though the commentator quickly followed up. "Seriously, though." She leaned closer, as if hoping for a confidential word. "You're one of the only retired generals I can think of who hasn't thrown in with any of the political parties."

My father sat back, raised a hand. "Not my place."

"You must have a preference. Some opinion? An allegiance?"

"Sure I do. To the American flag. Truth is, the American people don't care who I vote for. They just care that they can count on me. Give me a commanding officer, give me a marching order, and I'll get the job done."

"Don't you think that's a little simplistic in our modern age?"

"You think that's simple? Here's what I learned in the army: it really is do or die. You either achieve the objective or you don't. You win or you lose. There aren't any awards for trying real hard. Know why? Because usually those guys end up dead. If you're going to play the game, then you gotta win it. Simple as that."

"Simple as that," the host echoed. "Well. Nothing simple about being secretary of defense, and I know everyone on the Hill is pulling for you. Best of luck at the hearing."

My father nodded, acknowledging the compliment. "I'm just here to serve."

55

The next morning an email from Steven Edgars was wait-ing for me.

Dear Ms. Porter,

I'm happy to tell you everything I know about that fraud. Please advise on best way to contact you.

Cheers,
Steve

Through an exchange of emails we arranged to meet in Crystal City on Monday. He suggested lunch at a local burger joint. I demurred, afraid I might be recognized by one of my father's many friends who now populated the desks of the region's defense contractors or who had become some of DC's most powerful lobbyists. I suggested a hotel restaurant instead. Nobody ever ate at hotel restaurants. At least not for lunch. I was hoping he would be able to offer further insight into what had happened in Iraq.

I answered emails from colleagues at work for a while. Forwarded some files to people who would have to deal with them in my absence.

I glanced at my watch. Nine o'clock.

Time had gotten away from me. I borrowed June's car again; mine was still at the shop. I was due to pick up Alice from the vet's. When I got there, she seemed like her normal self.

As we wound through the parking lot on the way home, I could see the traffic light change to green at the far end. I sped up. When it turned to yellow I sped up even more. The light turned red as I passed the middle of the intersection.

At the edge of the parking lot, behind me, a gray car skidded to a halt.

Sam was in heaven when I got home. He'd been playing with Legos that Jim had found somewhere in the attic. I didn't think it had quite registered with him that all of his trains had burned up in the fire. He told me June had promised they could make cookies later.

"Cookies? But we just made Rice Krispies Treats yesterday. Did you already eat them?"

"No. It's just Miss June said she needed help."

"Why?" She'd seemed fine when I'd left. "Did something happen to her?"

"She just doesn't have a whole lot of kids to lick the scraper clean anymore. That's what she says. They've all grown up and moved away. And she says she's going to make me a cake on Monday while I'm at school! Any kind I want. And I sang her the concert song. She liked it!" The school's fall concert was on Wednesday night and his class had been practicing their song for weeks.

I expected him to be cranky after dinner when I asked him to put away the Legos, but he was so happy to have Alice back that he didn't protest. He got into his pajamas without any pushback and went straight to sleep.

Alice rolled from her side to her belly when I came back into the living room. Jim and June didn't have a fenced backyard, so I had to take her for a walk. It made me uneasy to be out in the dark. I tried to stay underneath the streetlights and I took my phone with me.

The neighborhood was respectable, friendly during the day. At night it was downright menacing with its looming trees and deserted streets.

My breath fanned in front of me as we started down the front walk.

Alice tugged on the leash and started off across the street toward the place where our house used to be. I yanked her back and stayed on Jim and June's side.

I walked her down to the end of the block. We'd just turned to start back when Chris found us.

"Georgie. Hi."

I kept walking, knowing every step took us closer to safety at Jim and June's. "Hey." It was too bad Alice knew him, otherwise she might have been a deterrent. I needed a strategy. And fast!

Moving away from the cars that were parked in front of the houses, I pulled Alice toward the middle of the street.

Chris kept pace with us. "I haven't really had the chance to catch up with you. Not since the fire."

"It's fine. We're fine." Just two more houses and I'd be safe.

"I've been worried about you."

Not as much, probably, as I had worried about him.

He put a hand on my arm.

I recoiled.

He put his hands up. "Sorry. I'm sorry."

I kept walking. "It's fine. I'm fine. Things are just a little tense right now."

"Sure. I understand."

I put a hand to Jim and June's gate, pressed down on the latch.

He caught me by the wrist.

I pulled it to my chest, but he didn't let go.

He stepped forward, toward me. "I just need to know, Georgie. Do you need help?" His eyes searched mine.

Help? Yes! I most certainly did.

The porch light turned on and Jim stuck his head out the door. "You all right out there?"

Chris let go of my wrist.

I slipped through the gate and latched it behind me. Held a hand up to Jim. "We're fine." I took a few steps up the walkway before I turned to answer Chris.

But he had already disappeared.

Midmorning Sam and I were playing with Legos in the corner of the living room. It was Sunday—Samday.

There was a knock on the door. Jim answered.

I paused to listen.

It was a reporter wanting to know if he knew what had happened to JB Slater's daughter. She asked if Jim knew where she was staying or if he knew how to contact her.

Jim had fun playing Clueless Neighbor.

"Slater? There aren't any Slaters on this street. Did you try the next block over?"

"It would be Brennan. She married."

"Brennan. With a *B*?" He called out over his shoulder to June. "Honey? There's a reporter here asking about the house that burned down across the street. Were there any Brennans there?"

I glanced at Sam. He was intent on building a spaceship. I didn't think he'd heard anything.

June gave me a wink as she walked past us on her way to the front door. She joined Jim. "What's that?"

"Brennan. Were there ever any Brennans living across the street?"

"Wasn't that the previous family?"

The reporter cut in. "The house is listed in the property records as belonging to Sean and Georgia Brennan. Georgia is JB Slater's daughter. Do you know what happened to her? Or where she's staying? Her father's been nominated to be the next secretary of defense."

Jim nudged June with an elbow. "I was just telling this reporter that there have never been any Slaters there. At least not for the past thirty years."

June agreed with him. "I don't even know if I know any Slaters. Do you?"

Jim and June talked for a while about all the people they knew who *weren't* Slaters and the reporter finally gave up.

But word must have gotten out because they kept coming. June and I peeked out the window at one point in the afternoon and counted four different people canvassing the street, going from door to door. She sighed as she let the curtain fall back into place. "I don't think they're going to go away."

I agreed with her. "I might have to say something. Maybe if I give them what they're looking for, they'll leave."

We came up with a plan. She sent Jim out to gather them all up. That way, when I stepped out onto the front porch, they were all waiting on the walkway, cameras at the ready.

I explained who I was, confirmed that JB Slater was my father and that, yes, it had been my house that burned down.

A reporter tilted a microphone in my direction. "Do you know why?"

"You would have to ask the people who are doing the investigation."

"Are they treating it as an accident?"

"You'll have to ask them."

"Have you been in contact with your father?"

"My parents are aware of the situation."

"Is this connected in any way with his confirmation hearings?"

"I wouldn't think so. Generally, when senators have differences with nominees, they talk about them; they don't set out to destroy each other's homes. Sometimes a house fire is just a house fire. That's all I have right now. Thank you."

56

It felt oddly like a betrayal, the meeting I'd arranged with my father's enemy.

Steven Edgars looked just like the picture from his company's website. He had a square, ruddy face softened at the edges by a beard. His hair stood up at the top as if it hadn't quite realized it was no longer cut in a military high-and-tight.

"Mr. Edgars?" I held out a hand as he stood.

"Ms. Porter!" He gave me a searching look and took my hand in his. Giving it a couple of pumps, he squeezed it tightly. He gestured to a seat beside his. "Call me Steve."

I chose the seat across from him instead.

"Looking for new source materials, huh?"

A waiter brought us menus. We put the conversation on pause to inspect them and to order. Once the waiter had disappeared, I got down to business.

"I'd like to hear your version of what happened during Desert Sabre on the night of February 24th."

He scoffed. "My *version*? Listen, the truth doesn't come in co-ordinated colors. It either is or it isn't. Collecting 'versions' won't get you any closer to figuring it out; it'll just confuse you. So what I'm going to tell you is what actually happened. And it's the truth. You can have it, but you'll have to take it all. Understand?"

I nodded.

"Good." He leaned back into his chair with a scowl and fell silent as he crossed his arms over his chest.

"Can you start by telling me the rank you held at the time? What unit you were assigned to and what your duty was?"

"I was a brand-new captain, the company XO. That's executive officer."

"So with regard to General Slater—"

"Captain."

"Sorry?"

"He was a captain at the time."

"You were the same rank?"

"JB was my commanding officer, but yes, we were the same rank. I'd just become a captain and he was promoted early out of that war to major. But we were comrades in arms. Or so I thought at the time." He fell silent as the waiter returned with glasses of water.

I waited until he left before I spoke. "Can you take me back to that morning? Starting with when you got up?"

"When I got up?" He snorted. "I'd never gone to sleep. Have you ever been in the desert?"

"I've been to Palm Springs." My mother had held one of her fundraisers there for the survivors of military members who had been killed on duty. But I hadn't even finished speaking before he was dismissing my words with a derisive snort.

"A *real* desert. Where there's nothing but sand. Sand upon sand. Miles of sand. It's not like driving through Arizona or New Mexico, where there's sagebrush, cactus, and scrub brush to tie things down. That desert, the one over there, it's real. It's alive."

Okay then.

"It slowly eats away at you. Starts with sand across the road. Sand in the Hummers. In between the seats. In the engine. Sand in your pockets. In your boots. Inside your socks. Gets into your ears and your mouth."

I was getting the idea that he really did not like sand. At all.

"Annoying. But that's not all. Everything's different there. The sun. The night. Sounds. Stars. It's like you're trapped inside an hourglass, just waiting to be upended. You start wondering, just how far down does it go? I mean, how far down would you have to dig before you got to something else? Is that all there is? Just sand?" He paused. Stared, vacant-eyed, at something just beyond my shoulder.

Then he shifted, pinning me again with his ice-blue gaze. "So I was awake."

"Did you know where you were?"

"What do you mean? I was sitting there in the desert. Sure wasn't back home in Kansas."

"I mean where. *Where* were you? Exactly? Did you know?"

"We were where the division told us the satellites told them we were."

"Are you sure?"

"Well, yeah." His eyes tracked the hostess who was seating a couple at the other end of the room. Then he turned his attention back to me. "I mean, we all had compasses too, right? And the company had maps. But the real triumph of that war was that GPS worked. Granted, there weren't that many satellites back then, so it was limited, intermittent coverage, but still. Can't imagine a world without it anymore."

"So the war started. Did you know where the Iraqis were at that point?"

"Didn't matter. If we found them, we were supposed to neutralize them and move on. We weren't supposed to get bogged down or committed to any conflicts. The Iraqis we made contact with weren't the Republican Guard; those guys were the elite, the best of the best. Most of the guys we met that first day surrendered before we even fired a weapon. The real mission was supposed to happen the next day. We were supposed to make a breach through their lines so that everyone else could pass through it, *then* we were supposed to find and destroy the Republican Guard."

"So what happened?"

"What happened? What happened is we got so far out in front of our line that we actually made it through *their* line. By accident. How it works is, you start out in formation and then stuff happens. You're supposed to stay in communication with everyone so you know where the friendlies are."

"But?"

"But sand happened. And wind. And weather. It was a regular mess. Before you know it, we were out there in the middle of the desert. I'm looking around realizing we haven't seen anyone in a while. It's like we're on our own planet. Know what I'm saying? And it's not conducive to life."

"You were supposed to be scouting, weren't you? It wasn't unexpected that you'd be out in front of everyone."

"Sure, but problem is, we hadn't encountered anyone. Scouts go ahead of the main contingent until they encounter the enemy, and then they report back where he is. No enemy, no reporting back, no stopping. We could have gone completely through their lines into Kuwait and back into Iraq for all I knew. And then we start noticing the terrain looks a little sketchy. One of our trucks thinks they spot a mine. And that's when JB ordered us to stop."

"Do you know what the orders from headquarters were at that point?"

"No. But I heard later we were supposed to fall back. The general wanted to regroup and start up again with the sun."

"What happened next?"

"I'm wondering what's going on, so I go up to JB. He takes me aside. Turns out, he thinks we're smack in the middle of a minefield. But it's not on any map. JB orders everyone to stay put. We argued about whether to call in our position. JB, you can tell he's worried about how it's going to look. He has no idea where we are in relation to anyone else. Do we have support behind us or have we gone so far ahead of everyone into Iraq that we're on our own? But that's not the worst part. We're sitting out there in the desert just waiting to blow up, and all of a sudden, the guys with the infrared scopes start spotting people. Lots of them. All around."

"How many?"

"More than us."

"What did the captain do?"

"He leaves me in charge of the company and goes out there on his own to meet them."

"What about his RTO? Isn't he supposed to stick with the captain?"

He took a drink of water. "Supposed to. But JB ordered him to stay with me and the rest of the command group. If someone's going to shoot the captain, we needed to be able to tell headquarters about it. So JB's out there on his own."

"Does anyone else know about this?"

"Besides me, the RTO, and top? No. Thing about minefields is, you don't want anyone panicking. So JB goes out there, hands up. Talks to them. Then he turns around and tells us to put our rifles down. I'm thinking he's surrendered us, right? But then he goes out there again, talks to them some more. Brings one of them back with him. Guy opens a map, starts pointing to this and that. Turns out he shows JB a lane through that minefield, back to their position."

"Back to the *Iraqi* position? The Iraqis, who outnumbered you, led you back to their own position?"

"That's what it seemed like. JB takes the map and orders us to head out. So I argue with him. Why are we trusting the enemy? In the middle of the night? As we sit there in a minefield? Only due to the grace of God we hadn't blown ourselves up by that point."

"What did the captain say?"

"Said to trust him. Said it'd work out just fine."

"So you let the Iraqis lead you through it?"

"We did. JB said he'd convinced them the rest of the corps was right behind us and they might as well just cooperate."

"That's what he said? But it sounds like you didn't believe him."

"I did at first. The others thought JB had balls of steel, but I figured those Iraqis were like all the other units we'd come across. They couldn't surrender fast enough. They just wanted the war to be over. But then I get a look at them. They're weren't regular Iraqi army."

"How could you tell?"

"They cared too much. They had actual uniforms. Other thing? Their place wasn't bombed to crap. We'd been bombing the Iraqis every day since the middle of January, and that place hadn't been touched. Camouflaged pretty good. And it was state of the art."

"So you went there and did what?"

"Guy opens the gate and invites us in like it's some hotel or something. Takes the captain on a tour."

"Did you go along?"

"No. But I saw enough to know their equipment, the weapons, they were top-of-the-line. Straight from Mother Russia. And recent."

"The Iraqis fought with Soviet weapons. That was widely known." At least that's what I'd gathered from my father over the years.

"Not those weapons. We fought all kinds of Iraqis for the next four days, and I never saw the kinds of things I saw there."

"Did the captain make any remarks about them?"

"Yep. He lined us all up and used them as target practice."

I felt my brows peak. "The Iraqis?" My father had ordered a slaughter?

"No. The installation. The weapons. Destroy everything. That was his order. We blew it all up."

"That was the overall mission, right? To destroy the Republican Guard."

"Right. That was the mission: to destroy them and their weapons so the pathway to Baghdad would be clear. JB kept us away from them, and could be everyone else thought they were Republican Guard, but I got close enough to hear some of them talking. They weren't speaking Arabic. They were speaking Russian."

57

I heard myself gasp.

Edgars sent me a wry smile. "He never talks about that when people ask him about the war, does he?"

Russians? Had my father made some sort of deal with the Russians? *That* might be a fact worth killing someone over. "The Russians were known to have sent military advisers to the Iraqis. They helped build up the army."

"Yes. But those people there that night weren't advisers. They were *soldiers*. A whole unit of them. They weren't there, out in the desert, to advise people. They were there to fight against us."

"Against us? On the Iraqi side? If that's true, then how come none of this ever came out?"

"Because our boys were focused on the firepower, not the personnel. And as we were blowing things up, those Russians disappeared."

"Where did they go?"

He shrugged. "Don't know. Poof! Vanished."

"Did you ask the captain about it?"

"He said to let it go. The next day we'd be heading out for the big battle and there was no time for prisoners."

"But you weren't satisfied with that explanation?"

"I saw what I saw. I heard what I heard."

"What do you think happened?"

He took another drink of water. "I think he made a deal. I think JB traded a lane through that minefield and their installation for the Russians' freedom. Think about it. It would be embarrassing, come dawn, if we'd been found miles in front of our line, in direct contradiction to the general's orders. And it would have created an international incident if those Russian soldiers had been discovered in that position. It would have given away their whole game and their lie about just trying to be honest brokers."

"Honest brokers of what?"

"You're probably too young to remember, but this was the Gorbachev era. It's still the USSR back then. They're warming to the West, right? But inside the Kremlin, there's people who liked things the way they were, and the way they were is that the Soviets were Iraq's allies. Big-time. They had a treaty with them. For a while there no one knew what the Soviets were going to do. *They* didn't know what they were going to do. What they *said* they were doing was trying to negotiate a peace treaty between Baghdad and the allies. But here's what I think. I think someone in the Kremlin wanted the good ol' days back. They liked it better when the Evil Empire was a force to be reckoned with. Someone wanted to fight. But the war accelerated too quickly. We got too far out in front. They weren't expecting it; we weren't expecting it. I think that's what happened." He sat back. "Hadn't heard that before, had you?"

"No."

"Didn't think so."

The waiter came with our food. We paused our conversation as he set the plates in front of us. There was something about Steven Edgars that I didn't like. I just wanted to get the interview over with and leave.

"Can anyone verify what you've told me?"

"JB could. But he won't. Never said anything about it in any of those TV interviews, did he? And now he's General Slater on the way to becoming the new secretary of defense. Think he'll tell anybody about it now?"

"There wasn't anyone else who figured it out the way you did?"

"Let me tell you what it's like out there in the middle of a war. You know there's only two outcomes: you survive or you don't. Any given moment, you're dead. So those times when you aren't dead, when you *don't* step on the mine, when the grenade *doesn't* explode, when you *aren't* hit by a bullet, you don't stop and think, *Why the heck haven't I died yet?* You tend to celebrate your incredible good fortune. Who was going to raise his hand that night and say, 'Pardon me, Captain, sir, but this doesn't make much sense. We were supposed to end up dead'?"

"So even if someone did put two and two together, the way you did, no one ever said anything."

"*I* said something. I took Slater aside and gave him a talking-to. Because what were we supposed to do after that? And how were we going to account for countermanding a direct order?"

"What did he say?"

"He said he'd take care of it. And he did. Once the commo got the communications going, JB had the RTO radio in that he'd made a breach. He had that map the Russians had given him; he gave it to the commo so he could tell headquarters right where we were. It identified the entire minefield. And there you go: he became one of the heroes of Desert Sabre."

"So to summarize, the truth is—"

"The truth is that Captain JB Slater illegally collaborated with the enemy. That's what happened. And you know what he always said in all those interviews he gave afterward? He said, and I quote, 'Truth is, I'd rather be lucky than good.'" Mr. Edgars snorted. "Rather be lucky than good. But here's the thing. He was unusually lucky during his career. There were those times in Bosnia and those others in Iraq—again—and then in Afghanistan. How many times did his units find the enemy where they weren't supposed to be? Or just narrowly miss being hit by air strikes? I'd say he had more luck than one guy deserved."

I tried to ignore the twist in my gut. Tried to view what he was saying about my father objectively. "Are you accusing him of something?" I wanted to be crystal clear about what he was saying.

"I'm saying that not only did he collaborate with the Russians that night in the desert, I think he also collaborated with them his entire career."

I tried not to show any outward emotion, but beneath the table, on my lap, my napkin was twisted into knots. "Do you have anything specific? Any proof?"

"Nothing but suspicions." He scowled.

"I would like to believe you, but I really need proof." He was talking about my father.

He blinked. "I just laid it all out for you, like I've been laying it out for everyone for years. And you know what I've gotten for my troubles? Nothing. Nothing but raised eyebrows and dismissals. JB Slater didn't get any smarter in the years after Desert Sabre. You'd think if you were going to cheat your way to four stars, at least you'd try to look competent about it. You know, when I first met him, I used to think that good-old-boy, country-hick talk of his was a prop. That he was using it to put people off guard. But the more I was around him, the more I discovered that he wasn't even smart enough to use it as a tool. It's the only thing he was ever truthful about as far as I know: he really was just a country boy from the backwoods of Arkansas who was lucky enough to marry Miss America."

"Miss Alabama."

"What's that?"

"His wife. She was Miss Alabama."

"You know what I did instead? What career path I took? I busted my butt for twenty years doing what they told me I should do."

At the beginning he'd come off as intelligent, though understandably bitter. At that point? Dangerously obsessed and slightly unhinged.

"Only 3 percent of second lieutenants are ever promoted to general. Did you know that? And do you know how many of those 231 generals have four stars? Seven. That is point-zero-zero-one percent of the active army. Know how many other soldiers deserved those stars JB Slater eventually got?"

I shook my head so I didn't have to say anything.

"All of them! *Every. Single. One.*" He picked up his knife and slashed into the steak he'd ordered. "Guess you can report to your father that I'm just a crazy relic from his past. No one will believe a word I say. Not enough proof to keep him from that fancy desk in the Pentagon."

"Sorry?"

"Your father. That's what you're here about, right? To do opposition research for his confirmation hearings?"

"I have no idea what you're—"

He leaned toward me over the table. "You can tell him there's no one who's listened to me for the past twenty-five years. Don't know why anyone would listen to me now."

I felt along the floor for my purse, grabbed the strap, and pushed to my feet. "I'm sorry, I—"

"Sad, what happened to your husband."

I shoved the chair toward the table and took a quick step back, in the direction of the lobby. "Thank you for your time."

"I feel sorry for your son. Sam, isn't it? You should probably tell Miss America to stop posting pictures on Facebook."

"I really don't—"

"At least you live in a nice part of Arlington. Good neighborhood. Nice homes. Good neighbors?"

I turned around and fled.

58

"Georgia. Georgia Brennan!"

Was he following me? Dodging the lunchtime crowds of government contractors and the al fresco diners eating at tables on the sidewalk, I took a quick look over my shoulder.

Yes, he was.

"Georgia Brennan. Wait!"

I plunged into a cluster of passersby, half stepping to match their pace and then sidestepping to move through them, away from the curb.

Then I heard a thud. The squeal of tires.

The diners on the sidewalk around me let out a collective gasp. They stood in unison as if they were controlled by a puppeteer. Steven Edgars lay sprawled on the street. As I watched, a gray car sped away toward the Washington Monument, which rose like a sentinel above Long Bridge Park. If he wasn't dead, he would be in the hospital for a very long time.

As several bystanders ventured out of the roped-off eating areas toward the street, I kept on going. Kept moving forward, kept putting distance between myself and Edgars. Because there had to have been someone watching us, someone who notified the people in the car that we had left the hotel. Someone who might still be out there, watching.

Edgars had told me my father collaborated with the Russians, but he'd offered no verifiable proof. If Edgars could no longer tell anyone what he'd heard—and since everyone at the Department of Defense had written him off as a bitter, angry person—I needed more than just his word.

But the things he'd said about my father had to be true. They made sense. And it was the only thing I'd heard that would make Sean worth killing. It would be devastating for the Pentagon if that information were revealed. They'd promoted a collaborator to their highest ranks. And on a personal level, if Edgars's information was revealed publicly, my father would be ruined. Past, present, and future.

What I still needed, however, was actual proof.

If I took Edgars at his word, maybe if I went forward through my father's career, dug into his follow-on assignments, I'd find some hard evidence that would link everything back to the Gulf War.

I'd almost made it to June's car when I keeled over, retching. A cold sweat had broken out on my forehead. I don't know how I even opened the door, but suddenly I was sitting in the driver's seat, hands clenched around the wheel. I closed my eyes.

In my mind I saw Steven Edgars lying in the street.

In my soul I remembered every time my father stood next to a flag talking about duty, honor, and country. Every time I ever heard him say, "God bless America." I thought of all the soldiers he had served with, all the people he had led into combat. And deep inside, I felt something shift.

I started the car. Left the garage.

I didn't have time for a breakdown. My father's confirmation hearing was in six days, and I was the only one who could stop it.

I went to the library, sat down at a public computer, then brought up the pages of Sean's notes on my phone. There was one name left from Desert Sabre that I wanted to find. Reginald Wallace. Top. He'd been mentioned in both interviews. I had to do some research to find his contact information, but I found an address in Maryland. The address led me to a phone number.

I stepped outside to call him.

Mr. Wallace answered. He wasn't available to speak just then, but he agreed to talk with me midmorning the following day, if I would drive out to see him. He didn't like telephones. Couldn't hear very well.

I chose a name from one of my father's other units. The one from Bosnia. But when I called and told him what I wanted to talk about, he hung up. The next name I chose from the unit did the same.

What had happened in Bosnia?

Though I only vaguely remembered the Gulf War, I remembered next to nothing about Bosnia. I typed *US Army* and *Bosnian War* into a search engine.

It came back with a lot of summary articles. Looked like the United States didn't really put boots on the ground in the region until the actual war was over.

I found another name identified with my father's unit, spent time on the internet, and came up with some contact information. I called the number I'd found and asked for Bobby Denunzio.

"Speaking."

I told him what I wanted to talk about.

"The Bosnian War?" His disgust was apparent, even over his New York City accent. "What a mess. Who ever heard of fighting a war with three sides?"

"*Three* sides?"

"Yeah. Give me a minute. Have to think about this." There was a long pause. I heard the sound of a TV in the background. "See, it used to be Yugoslavia, right? Remember that? Part of the Union of Soviet Socialist Republics. Well, those Soviets crammed lots of countries into one in order to make it. You had Bosnia and Herzegovina. That's actually one even though it sounds like two. You got Croatia. You got the two *M*s: Macedonia, Montenegro. You got Serbia and what's the other *S* one? Slovenia, right? Bunch of alphabet soup. So when the Soviet Union started busting up and everybody wanted out, well, those Serbs decided they wanted out too. But all on their own."

"This is before the war?"

"Right. So pretty soon it's a regular slugfest over there. Serbs on Croats on Bosnians. Only they used guns and bombs."

"And Major Slater was your commanding officer."

"Yeah. Now I told you there were three sides, right? So you got Serbs. And you got Croatians. Only—and this is the tricky part— you got your Croatian *Serbs* who, if Croatia decides they want their own Catholic country, well, those Serbs don't want to be a part of it. They want to be part of Serbia because Serbs are Orthodox. Now Bosnians are Muslim; they were the third side. Unless they were Bosnian *Serbs*, in which case they're Orthodox. So you got your Orthodox Serbs and Catholic Croats and Muslim Bosnians most of the time, but not always. And I don't mean to speak out of turn, but I'm a good Catholic boy and normally I'm on the side of the angels, you know? Except this time, the Orthodox Christians and even sometimes the Catholics, they were the bad guys. They were massacring the Muslims. So you got good guys who are bad guys and bad guys who are good guys. Couldn't keep 'em straight."

Maybe that's why I didn't really remember much about that war.

"And the politicians? They screwed it all up. At the end there, know what they did? The politicians went to the bad guys—those were the Serbian Serbs, the Orthodox types—and they basically said, 'Just tell us what you want. If we give it to you, will you just pack it up and go away?' That's basically how that war ended. Bad guys got everything they wanted and the good guys declared victory. Us grunts? We were going, *What was that all about?* All those cities destroyed? All those people killed? They were slaughtered. Serbs mowed 'em down and bulldozed them into mass graves. So if you were just going to give them what they wanted in the first place, then what was all of it for? Know what I'm saying?" He took a deep breath. "Sorry."

"So what were you doing there?"

"Me? I was finishing up my enlistment. We were fighting on the allies' side even though it seemed like we were helping the Serbs.

Stupid politicians. They were trying not to choose sides. But basically it was everyone against Serbia. Mostly."

"I was under the impression that there weren't any Americans on the ground until after the war ended. But you were there during the actual war?"

"Sure. Yeah. Serving under Major Slater."

"What did you do?"

"Mostly we were in Bosnia helping them communicate with the UN forces and the allies. We weren't supposed to be helping them *fight*, right? But we helped them out with comms. And we helped them spot military targets. When NATO dropped their bombs on the Serbs, it wasn't the U-S-of-A officially fighting. It was more like NATO just got lucky when they were dropping their bombs and magically hit important targets. That's what we did. We told 'em what to hit."

"Did you ever come into contact with any Russians?"

"Thing is, Russia said they were on our side, but you could tell their heart wasn't in it. 'Cause those Serbs, they were Orthodox. Russians were Orthodox. Know what I'm saying?"

"Did the major ever communicate with any Russians? Do you know?"

"You had to. You couldn't talk to a Serb unless it was the good kind of Serb. But Russians weren't Serbs even if they liked Serbs. So if you wanted to communicate with a Serb, you went through a Russian who knew how to get in touch with a Serb. That's the way it was. It was a crazy war."

"So the major had a Russian contact."

"Yeah."

"So this wasn't any secret."

"No."

Was this another dead end? If everybody knew, then my father had nothing to hide. Maybe Edgars had been wrong. "Were there ever any complications?"

"Well, it was like this. The Serbs were monsters. But we weren't necessarily there to fight them. We were there to support the Bosnians who were fighting them. For the Russians, it was kind of the same. So sometimes you had to do the dance."

"What dance?"

"You had to say, 'Hey, Ivan. We got to get from here to there. Do me a solid and don't let those Serbs drop a bomb on the road while I'm on it. That would be on such and such a date at such and such a time.' *That* dance."

"You coordinated movements."

"I wouldn't say coordinate. We *facilitated* things."

"And there were complications?"

"Well . . . I don't know." He paused. "I don't know."

"Can you tell me what happened?"

"I don't really know that anything did."

"What might have happened?"

"There was this, um, this group. This group of wounded. We were evacuating them. We assumed that it was all good. Turned out it wasn't. Serbs bombed the convoy. But see, that's the kind of thing that would have been coordinated. We would have told Ivan. He would have told the Serbs."

"How many people got bombed?"

"Lots. One of those Bosnians, one of the wounded, turned out he was one of their commanders. He bit it. And they got some of our guys as well. The good guys. The ones who were helping with the evacuation. It's not like that kind of thing didn't happen all the time. But usually it was just the Serbs bombing the other alphabet soup guys. That's what made that war so crappy. It happened *all the time*. Mostly all we were allowed to do was stand there and watch. But that time? That time it put a real dent in the Bosnian forces when their guy got killed and some of the good guys got killed too. Someone must have screwed up. I felt sorry for the major."

"Was that the only time it happened?"

"Happened a couple times."

"Were any other Bosnian commanders killed those other times?"

"Yeah. I mean, that was the tragedy, right? Not to mention allies. I mean, the Bosnians were fighting. You can kind of think, 'Well, that's the breaks.' But when the good guys got killed? It just wasn't right."

"Were you with the major's unit the whole time it was there?"

"No. When my enlistment was done, I got out. I didn't sign up to just sit around and watch people kill each other. That's not what I was in it for."

I thanked him for his time, and before he hung up, I told him to be careful.

"Careful? Me? Lady, I'm talking to you from Brooklyn. And not the good part. Born and bred. If anyone should be careful, it's the other guy."

I thanked him again and hung up.

I couldn't help wondering if maybe those bombings *hadn't* been a mistake. What if my father had passed information to the Russians? Not so they could keep the roads clear, but so the Serbs could bomb them and take the Bosnian commanders out?

59

My parents showed up just before dinner. They came bearing boxes.

"Just a few things," my mother said as she knelt on the floor and offered one to Sam.

It was almost bigger than he was, so I took it from her and set it beside him. She'd put all those years of charity work with disaster and military relief organizations to good use. It was filled with clothes. Shoes. A coat. A scarf and gloves. And down at the bottom were several smaller boxes.

Trains.

"Wow! Thanks!" Sam pulled them out and held them up toward Jim like prizes. "Want to play, Mr. Jim?"

"Sure thing, kiddo. But I want to show your granddad something first."

Sam didn't wait. While Jim walked down the hall toward his office, Sam dumped them out of their boxes. I knelt beside him, collecting the packaging.

Jim came back, a piece of paper in hand. "Just drafted up a little something." He tipped the sheet so my father could see it.

"Don't show the president!" My father flashed a grin.

"What is it?" My mother leaned over to have a look. "Well now."

I got to my feet and walked over so I could see too.

Slater for President.

Jim had drawn up a campaign logo for my father. Somehow he was able to hit all the right notes: patriotism, leadership, strength.

Horror swept over me. I hadn't realized until then just how lofty my father's ambition was. And just how close he was to achieving it. He had to be stopped.

My father extended his hand toward Jim.

Jim took it. Shook it. "Just a little nonsense." He winked. "I might be retired, but I can still have some fun."

My father chuckled. "Hey, mind if I keep it?"

"As long as you put it somewhere you can always see it." Jim tapped his forehead. "Keep it in mind."

"Sure, sure." My father clapped him on the back.

My mother put a hand on my arm. "There's a box for you too." She indicated one that my father had set near the front door. "I didn't know what you need, so I put in some toothbrushes, toothpaste. Some clothes."

What was she going to do when she found out about my father?

"There are a couple pairs of shoes. As well as a purse with some Visa gift cards to get you by for a bit." She gave me a look. "And some unmentionables. You know, we have a suite at the Hay-Adams. There's more than enough room for you and Sam."

"No."

"That way you wouldn't have to continue imposing on these kind people."

June must have heard our conversation. She walked over and put an arm around me. "It's no trouble at all."

June invited them to stay for dinner. They left when I put Sam to bed. Just before I went to bed myself, I decided my best move was to call Sean. There was too much information to be conveyed in a text.

But the phone didn't go to voice mail. He picked up. In the moment before he spoke, I could hear talking. There was the sound of dishes, utensils. And beneath it all, there was music. "Yeah? Hey. I can't talk right now. Can't slip away. I'll get back to you." He hung up.

I stood there staring at my phone. We only had six days left to figure it all out and he didn't have time to talk? Couldn't slip away? I was trying to save his life and mine. And our son's! I wanted to throw my phone at the wall. But I didn't. Mostly because I was my mother's daughter; it wouldn't have been polite. So I powered it off and pulled my new pajamas from the box my mother had brought. Pondered my next move as I put them on.

But that music from the call refused to fade away.

That music.

I'd heard it before.

As I eased the blanket away from Sam and put a knee to the mattress to crawl into bed, I finally remembered where.

I put the blanket back, pulled my pajamas off, and put my clothes back on. I left my old phone on the dresser; Sam was safe with Jim and June, and there was no need to make it easy for anyone to track me through a known device. But I slipped my new phone into a pocket.

If Sean wasn't going to come to me, then maybe I could go to him. I glanced at my watch.

Ten o'clock.

Jim was still up, watching the news, when I tiptoed into the living room. He glanced up. "Sweetie? You okay?"

"I just need to go for a drive."

He searched my eyes before he answered. "Not a problem. Keys are on the table in the hall. We'll have some cocoa when you get back."

The restaurant I drove to was just one of dozens located in the shabby strip malls lining Columbia Pike. Redevelopment was relentlessly chewing up Latin American groceries and halal delis, and spitting out gleaming condos and sleek office buildings. But along that stretch of the Pike, restaurants were still numerous. On offer in that block were five continents' worth of food. Rai music competed with punchy mariachi. On summer evenings, when the doors to the restaurants were propped open, it was as good as going to the Smithsonian Folklife Festival down on the mall in DC.

When we first moved to the neighborhood, Sean and I must have passed the restaurant a thousand times before a taxi driver called it to our attention. *Best kebabs in town.* It soon became our go-to takeout, though I hadn't been since Sean had died.

My eyes swept the restaurant.

No Sean.

I was trying to be surreptitious, but the other three customers were looking quite pointedly at me.

I stepped up to the register and ordered what had, at one time, been my usual. After ordering, I took a seat in one of the darker corners, facing the kitchen. I listened, trying to imagine how the sounds would filter through a cell phone. The kitchen door opened and the strains of rai music drifted out into the dining room. It made me think of the desert. Of minarets and cool oases. The door swung shut, muffling the music.

He was there. He had to be.

I glanced at my watch. Ten thirty. I looked at the other two tables. Their occupants were eating with *plastic* utensils. From *paper* plates. My hopes spluttered and died. On the phone I'd heard the clatter of dishes. The slide of metal utensils against plates.

The music was right, but the setting was wrong.

60

I left the restaurant, clutching a bag of unwanted food, trying to push back my fears. I needed Sean's help to figure out what to do. After navigating the uneven sidewalk, I stepped over a broken curb and left the spotlight of the streetlights for the bleakness of the alley where I'd had to park.

The back door to the restaurant opened with a metallic scrape, flooding the alley with light. Music poured out of the door, along with the clatter of dishes. A man appeared, backlit on the doorstep, as a voice called to him in words that were indecipherable. He paused. Pivoted toward the interior as he answered. Then he bent, picked up a cardboard box, and carried it out to the dumpster. After balancing it for a moment on his thigh, he lifted the lid and hefted the box over the edge. As he turned, the streetlight drenched him in its glow.

"Sean." I whispered his name.

He was wearing a worn pair of jeans and a T-shirt. Fastened around his neck was a stain-blotched apron. With his bushy beard and longer-than-I-was-used-to-seeing hair, he fit right in with the restaurant.

He sent a sharp-eyed glance toward the edges of darkness and retreated to the building. As he took a pack of cigarettes and a lighter from his back pocket, I stood there fascinated. Sean didn't smoke.

Shaking a cigarette out, he put it to his mouth and cupped a hand around it while he lit it.

Had he smoked in his former life? Back when he'd been in the gang?

Holding the cigarette between two fingers, he raked his hair from his forehead. Massaging the back of his neck, he closed his eyes and leaned his head back against the wall.

I stepped forward from the shadows. "Smoking can kill you."

His mouth curled before he even opened his eyes. "I'm already dead." He tossed away his cigarette and came toward me. "They're closing in on me." Without breaking his stride, he took me by the arm, pulling me with him back into the shadows.

I'd come to talk to him, but right then I just wanted . . . him.

He glanced back over his shoulder. "You shouldn't be here. I think I'm being watched. That's why I can't meet you. It's too dangerous."

I put a hand on his arm and the other on his chest, reminding myself that he was real. This was what I was fighting for. I slid one hand to his shoulder. Used the other to tug at the too-long ends of his hair. "I know."

He closed his eyes. Bowed his head.

I moved my hand to his beard-covered jaw. This was where he was. This was what he was doing. I'd come to talk to him, but instead I stood on tiptoe and kissed him.

His lips were unyielding.

He smelled of cumin and grease and cigarettes. His beard was scratchy. My hands moved beyond the tangle to his temples, my thumbs splaying down toward his cheeks. Bringing his head toward mine, I kissed him again.

He exhaled, heavily. Then he removed my hands, pressed a fleeting kiss to my palms, and dropped them.

In the shadows, I couldn't read his eyes. I didn't want to let him go. I moved to embrace him.

He blocked me, slipping from my grasp. "I can't—" He stepped away, out of my reach. "I can't be here for you, Georgie. Not like this."

"I just— I need you." I approached slowly, took up his hand. Skimmed my other hand up his bare forearm.

His muscles tensed. "Don't."

"Sean." I kissed what I could reach. I kissed his shoulder, through the T-shirt. I stepped closer. Kissed his neck. Kissed just beneath his ear, a spot his beard hadn't reached. I kissed—

His hand fisted into my shirt, at my waist.

I put a hand up to his jaw. Encountered his beard where it used to be smooth. Pulling, just a tiny bit, I turned his head toward mine so I could press a kiss, just a single kiss, onto his lips.

His embrace came swift, fierce, so tight I couldn't breathe. He pulled me in to himself and then his mouth descended on mine. Hungry, desperate.

I wanted.

I wanted him. I wanted everything. Everything I didn't have. I wanted him turning to me in the night. I wanted him waking up next to me in the morning. I wanted him catching up our son and throwing him over a shoulder.

I wanted him.

I wanted us.

A shout came from the kitchen.

He raised his head. Answered in that unknown tongue. Then, breathing heavily, he let his forehead dip down to touch mine.

I kissed him again. Once. Twice. "What language?"

"Arabic." He kissed me back. Once. "I can't do this."

"Sean."

"I can't." Even if he hadn't been whispering, his words would have been hoarse. He gripped my forearms, tightening his hands when I tried to loosen their hold. Gently, he held me off. Held me apart. "I can't. Not again. Not until this is over."

"But—"

The man from inside the kitchen opened the door and called out.

"I have to go."

I grabbed his head, pressed his forehead to mine. "My father met Russians out in the desert that first night. It wasn't the Republican Guard. It was a Russian outpost. Not advisers; soldiers. They were there to fight. They traded a way through the minefield and their position for their freedom. But there's no way to actually prove it unless my father admits it. In Bosnia, he met up with Russians again. He gave them information about the positions of Bosnian commanders to pass to the Serbs. The Serbs bombed them, along with some of the allies."

He stepped away from me, though he kept his gaze on mine. "That's what this is. That's who they are, who wants to keep this quiet. They're not FBI or DoD. They're Russians."

Once again, everything shifted. "I thought—I assumed—" I'd interpreted everything wrong. It wasn't the DoD trying to protect their own, hoping to cover for a mistake. It was the Russians. "My father is a traitor and a murderer." They were words I'd never imagined I would ever say.

"Yes."

"You were wrong, you know."

"About what?"

"About your parents. You said you couldn't save them. But you were young, Sean. You were just a child. It wasn't your job to save them."

He tried to move away, but I stopped him. "But Sam and me? This is going to work. It is. You're saving us. This is going to work and you're going to come back. You are not going to lose us."

He was watching me.

"Because I won't let you." I took a breath. Blinked back the tears that pressed against my eyes. "So tell me, what do I do? I need actual proof. How do I find it?"

"I don't even—" He broke off helplessly.

"I don't know how much longer I'll be able to talk to people. They keep getting—"

The man from the kitchen came out onto the stoop and yelled.

Sean yelled back. "I've got to go. This job is how I get the money to pay people off. I need to keep it. But we'll talk. Soon."

"But—"

He strode away toward the kitchen.

"—they keep getting killed." I said the words to no one at all.

61

June let me borrow her car again the next day; mine would
be in the shop for the rest of the week. It turned out that Reginald
Wallace lived about an hour and a half away, out past one of the small
farming communities that populated Maryland between the border
with Delaware and the eastern shore of the Chesapeake Bay.
The land was cut by small streams and pocked by ponds. The trees
were gilded, the grasses golden. It was one of those bright, burnished
autumn days when the sun still gave off warmth.

But it was dry. The windshield soon collected a fine coating of
dust. I pulled the lever for windshield washer fluid, turning the dust
to mud. A few more pulls washed it all away.

As I followed my GPS through the twists and turns of the
countryside, a gray car bobbed in and out of my rearview mirror.

There were a lot of gray cars on the road in the region, but there
always seemed to be one in close proximity to me in particular. I was
too paranoid to chalk up my suspicions to coincidence. If someone
was following me, why oblige them by leading them straight to my
contact? I approached the next T in the road without signaling and
didn't slow down as I turned away from my intended destination.

The gray car turned the same direction I had.

I was starting to worry. It was one thing to be followed discreetly,
another thing entirely to be followed brazenly. With one hand on the
steering wheel, I widened the view on my GPS program to take a look
at my options.

There were more streams in that part of Maryland than roads.

The longer I drove in the direction I was going, the closer I got
to the Potomac River. The closer to the river, the fewer the roads.
There looked to be only one possibility to escape being dead-ended.

I glanced into the rearview mirror.

The gray car was still there.

I looked back at the GPS. I was coming up on what had to be farm plots because they were bounded by roads that formed a grid of tight, even squares. I could turn down one and then, by making a series of turns in the same direction around the grid, I could resurface on the same road I was currently on. Then I could head back down it, in the right direction, toward Reginald Wallace's.

And if I took those turns fast enough, maybe I could lose the car behind me.

Of course, the driver of the gray car might intuit what I was doing, and if he was clever, he could use the same method. Only he could come at me from the opposite direction. And in that landscape of narrow roads and deep ditches, I didn't want to play chicken with anyone.

I gripped the steering wheel tighter. It was time to make a decision.

In three . . . two . . . one— I turned hard to the right. Glanced back to see the gray car do the same. I stepped on the gas and flew down the road, then gritted my teeth and got ready for my next turn. In three . . . two . . . one.

My back wheels fishtailed, fanning a cloud of dust.

No time to think. I just tried to counteract the fishtailing.

Was the gray car still there? I couldn't see for the dust. When it began to dissipate I saw that the answer was yes.

I'd broken out in a sweat. Making that first turn at the T had been a mistake. What I needed to do was get back to a main road. If anything happened to me, it was more likely to be noticed there. I was more likely to be found.

One more turn and then I could head back in the right direction. And once I hit that road, I was planning to hit my accelerator too.

Behind me, the gray car honked. Once. Twice.

What did he think I was going to do? Pull over?

I glanced back to see him turn off onto a rutted lane. Farther down a pickup truck waited. A man was standing in the bed. He straightened. Gave a wave to the driver of the gray car. Then he held up something dark. Something long and narrow.

Reflexively, I cringed.

It was something that looked . . . just like a fishing pole.

It wasn't until I made that last turn that my heart started beating again.

Gradually, my fingers held steady. As I got back on the route to Reginald Wallace's, my muscles began to relax. As I turned off onto the narrow ribbon of a lane that led from the highway to his house, I was nearly run off the road by a car that shot past me in the opposite direction.

I hoped it wasn't Mr. Wallace; due to my detour, I was late. But after that, I crept around every bend of the road. I passed several other houses before I finally reached his.

The lane ended in a driveway that curved up to an old-fashioned white farmhouse and a tidy metal-roofed barn. I parked in front of the house, behind a sun-faded pickup. Then I walked up the front steps to the wide, covered front porch, rang the bell, and waited.

There was no answer. No sound of footsteps coming toward the door.

I rang again.

Nothing.

Stepping off the front porch, I walked over to the barn.

"Mr. Wallace?"

The sun filtered in through the open door, making the dust motes sparkle as they drifted through the air.

"Mr. Wallace?"

Over in the corner, a light shone from a workbench of sorts. Tools lined the walls.

He'd said he was hard of hearing, so I went in and walked toward the workbench, my feet scuffing against the concrete floor of the barn.

"Mr. Wallace?"

My view was blocked by a riding lawn mower. As I moved around it, I saw a body lying on the floor.

62

I froze. Then I dropped to the floor in a squat. Old men have heart attacks more frequently than they get murdered, but knowing what I did about my father and the Russians, I couldn't take any chances. What if he had been killed? And what if the killer was still there? I didn't want to be the next victim.

Keeping my profile low, I crept over to Mr. Wallace and shook his arm.

No response.

I stretched over him so I could see his face. Then I wished I hadn't.

Vacant eyes stared up at mine. A hole had been blown right through his forehead. I rocked back onto my heels and took a deep breath, forcing air into my nostrils and down into my lungs to try to keep from retching.

I had a sudden, nearly overwhelming urge to stand up right there and reveal myself. To shout, "I'm out. I'm done."

But the people who had killed Mr. Wallace wanted to kill Sean. And they wanted to kill me and Sam too. In fact, they almost had. So it wouldn't be over until we managed to get through.

I worked my way around to the entrance of the barn and then I stayed there, in a crouch, watching. Waiting. Listening for any sign that someone was still there.

How had the Russians known who I was going to talk to? They were there the day I'd talked to Steven Edgars. They were just ahead of me in coming to Mr. Wallace's. Actually, if I hadn't been late due to my detour, I might have walked right into them.

Somebody was watching me. And closely enough that they knew my habits. They knew when I went to work; they knew when I came home.

There *was* somebody. There had to be. They were watching me as closely as Jim kept watch on his neighbors. He knew everything that happened on our street. He was the first to notice visitors. The first to help me with the garbage cans or yard work. The first person I'd been turning to when I needed help.

No one knew more than Jim did.

And whose car was I borrowing? June's.

Which might make a person start to wonder.

Eventually I made my way back to the car.

There was nothing I could do for Mr. Wallace. And if I called for an ambulance or reported the killing to the police, then who would be their chief suspect?

Me.

As it was, I'd probably left far too many traces of myself in that barn.

I drove all the way up to Waldorf before I pulled off at a gas station and took my phone from my purse with shaking hands. I'd been making a tally. They'd killed Paul Conway. I assumed they killed Steve Edgars. They'd just killed Reginald Wallace. Who else was on their list? Who else had I talked to?

I called Mr. Ornofo.

It rolled to voice mail.

I hung up.

Just because he didn't answer didn't mean he was dead. But I wanted to be certain. I googled his name. It brought up the same pages on radiosport that I had accessed several days before.

I moved the cursor back to the search box. Typed in *Lee Ornofo death*. But I couldn't quite bring myself to tap the Search button.

It wasn't as if I would be summoning Death. Tapping Search had no bearing on whether he was alive. But still I felt like an executioner.

He was Schrödinger's cat. Both alive and dead as far as I knew. And I wouldn't know for sure until I could find more information.

I tapped Search, but it returned nothing new.

I deleted *death* and typed *killed*.

Nothing.

My hope renewed, I tried once more, searching *Lee Ornofo dead*.

It returned a link to an article published the day before in the Philadelphia *Inquirer*.

"Lee Ornofo, aged 65, found dead in his home."

Conway. Edgars. Wallace. Ornofo.

Four names. Four deaths.

I needed to find proof of my father's crimes and find it fast.

As I drove, reason did battle with my paranoia. By the time I reached Arlington, I realized my watchers couldn't be Jim and June. They'd grown up in the area; they'd been living in their house for fifty years. And we'd moved in long before Sean started working on the Desert Sabre project.

Once I got back, I took out my old phone and pulled up my pictures of Sean's notes. I selected another name from my father's time in Bosnia. Perry Jenkins. On June's phone I searched for his name and his unit number. Got a hit on an oral history project that had been collected by Baylor University. Hoping they were focusing on veterans in their own state, I searched for all the Perry Jenkinses who lived in Texas. After calling several phone numbers, I found the right one.

I asked Mr. Jenkins for basic information, the same as I'd asked the others. Then I asked him what his particular job was.

"I kept the guns."

"What guns were those?"

"The ones the patrols would take. We were assigned with a unit of Russian paratroopers, patrolling along the zone of separation. That was the border between the Muslims and the Serbs. We were supposed to keep the Serbs on the Serb side and the Muslims from coming over."

"And how did the guns figure into it?"

"The Muslims would sneak over and, come to find out, they were hiding guns on the Serb side. They were stocking arsenals. Just 'cause we said the war was over didn't mean it was over for them."

"And what happened?"

"Depended on the night. Sometimes it was quiet. Sometimes they rushed the border. But once we figured out where an arsenal was, we'd raid it and take their weapons. My job was to keep track of the guns."

"The Muslim guns."

"Right."

"Was that difficult?"

"Shouldn't have been. There were a lot of guns, though. One night the patrol brought back about a thousand."

A *thousand*? "You said *shouldn't* have been difficult. Does that mean it was?"

"I don't know. Something funny was going on. We'd have x number of guns come in one night when the patrol came back, then a couple days later we'd only have y number of guns. Guns don't have legs, but there had to be some way they kept walking out."

"What did you do about it?"

"I told the major."

"Major Slater."

"That's right."

"What did you tell him?"

"I said those guns keep getting out. I think it's the Russians. I think they're passing them back to the Serbs."

"Why did you think that?"

"I had my suspicions. They were friendly with the Serbs. So that's what I thought and that's what I told the major."

"What did he say?"

"He said he'd take care of it."

"Did he?"

"I don't know. I got reassigned the next week."

"Considering what you told the major, didn't that strike you as odd? That you were reassigned?"

"Not really. I mean, the timing? Okay, maybe some people would say it seemed a little fishy. But the major told me he'd take care of it and he was always good for his word. He wasn't like some officers. And I'd just re-upped and requested assignment to a different post. Guess you could argue the point if you wanted to, but I didn't."

I called more names. Many of my calls went unanswered. And according to the search I did on my phone, several of the people on Sean's list had recently died. But those I got in touch with offered similar stories of my father's time in Qatar, Afghanistan, and through his rise at the Pentagon.

Putting the stories together filled out a pattern. If I'd harbored any hopes that he was just some pawn in a larger scheme, they'd been dashed. It was easy to see how his actions had been overlooked, though. His assignments had been discrete. Once they were over, he'd moved posts, changed positions, left behind the people he'd worked for and with. No one had been able to observe the pattern.

The impression he'd left over the course of his career? My father was a good officer who took care of his people. When circumstances seemed suspicious, every single person I interviewed gave him the benefit of the doubt.

But how much of a pass did one person deserve? And if he kept putting himself, and his men, in incriminating situations, at some point wouldn't any normal person start to wonder? If the pattern kept proving the pattern, then couldn't we just admit there was a pattern?

It almost made me feel for Steven Edgars.

The best defense for my father's actions appeared to be that he was a good guy and everyone knew it.

My witnesses were dwindling; people on Sean's list were being poached. The Russians were trying to make sure the information about my father would not get out. But what could I do about it? The deaths were in different states, different localities, different jurisdictions. Nobody was going to be looking for a connection; I was the only one who knew there was one. And if I alerted someone to it? There were several problems with that.

Who would I tell? Sean and I were pretty sure the FBI wasn't after us, but until I could prove what was going on, we could take no risks.

But more importantly, how long would it take them to follow up?

And what would keep them from throwing *me* in jail? I'd spoken to Mr. Ornofo. I'd spoken to Mr. Abbott. And I'd been the one to find Mr. Wallace dead. That made me a prime suspect.

Should I warn the rest of the people on the list?

Morality warred with expediency. I only had five days left. Either I could spend my time building the case against my father, or I could spend it warning the people on the list that their lives were in danger.

How many people were left?

There had been almost two hundred men in his Desert Sabre company alone. And the further my father went in his career, the more people he had commanded. I could never hope to contact them all in less than a week. But I *could* hope to stop his confirmation hearing.

At least I knew the significance of what Sean had discovered and why people had been so interested in keeping it hidden. I had the truth. I might not exactly have proof, but maybe it would be enough to convince someone to start an official investigation. Even the *suspicion* of scandal had been enough, in years past, to roil Washington.

I borrowed June's computer again and put my notes together. Then I printed out a copy. There was one obvious way to set everything in motion, but it required that I swallow my pride. If it could bring Sean back from the dead and stop my father from being confirmed, it would be worth it. So I did it.

I called Jenn.

"Georgie?"

"I need to ask you for a favor."

She agreed to meet an hour later near the metro stop by the capitol.

I stepped out of the metro train and onto a platform at the Capitol South station. Skirting tourists and government workers, I walked through the impersonal, brutalist concrete tunnel and took the escalator up to the street. As I emerged into the sunlight I squinted, turning as I ascended in order to get my bearings. A line of flat-roofed brick rowhouses stood behind me. The white stone Cannon House Office Building sat in front of me. Tourists milled around the entrance to the station, consulting their guidebooks and maps to no avail; there was no Capitol Building, Library of Congress, or Supreme Court in sight. Anyone who spent time in Washington soon came to realize, unless you knew exactly where you were going, it was almost impossible to get there.

Jenn was walking down the hill, toward me. She waved.

I waved back.

"So, favor?" Jenn asked as she approached.

I pulled my notes out of my coat's inside pocket and handed them to her. "Can you read this? Then pass it on to Senator Rydel?" He would be chairing my father's confirmation hearings and he considered himself the president's archenemy. If anyone could put to use what I'd found out about my father, it was him.

"Should I read it now?"

"No! No. Just read it later. Back in your office. Then pass it on.

It's about my father's confirmation hearing. I'm hoping the senator can do something with it."

"*Before* the hearing? The hearing's on Monday."

"I know. But it's important. Please."

63

Less than two hours later, she called me. We agreed to meet again that night at Northside Social.

Northside Social was as close to a subversive, college-style coffee shop as Arlington had. It wasn't the county's fault. People in Arlington didn't subvert. They did things the Arlington Way. They published letters to the editor. They set up working groups and advisory boards. And they generously funded things like veteran support services, affordable housing nonprofits, and free health clinics.

The coffee shop itself was perched on an odd, triangular-shaped lot that projected into a busy intersection. I bought my coffee and joined Jenn outside. The warmth of the day still lingered. She was sitting at one of the square black metal tables. It was located along the sidewalk, well away from the other customers.

I took a seat in the chair opposite her. "So did you talk to Rydel? What did he say?"

She leaned toward me. "First, let me ask you, how did you find out about all of this?"

"I have my sources."

"Are they DoD? FBI?"

"Does it matter?"

She looked at me for a long moment and then sighed. "Fair enough."

"You did show it to him, right?"

"I read it. And I did show it to him." She dug around in her tote, fished out my papers. "He read it. He agrees the information is explosive. Game-changing. But he can't do anything with it." She offered them back to me.

I took them, trying to make sense of her words. He wasn't going to do anything? "Why not? He's the chairman of the Armed Services Committee. He's the one who'll run the hearing."

"I know, but—"

"Is it because he doesn't believe in exposing espionage to the American people?"

"It's more complicated than that, Georgie." Her face registered frustration.

He wasn't going to do anything at all? "Know what? I'm tired of complications. What about integrity? What about justice?"

"I know you're upset about Sean, okay? What I did was wrong. But what can I say? I'm sorry. I really am. But you can't exact revenge by expecting Senator Rydel to hold up a hearing based on allegations that—"

"Who *are* you?"

"Excuse me?"

"*Who are you?* My friend, Jennifer Baxter, used to be interested in justice. She used to be a rebel. She used to talk about honor and integrity and working for the good of all Americans."

"That Jennifer grew up and went to Capitol Hill. You know what they say: You go to Washington to do good. You stay to do better."

"You're seriously going to sit there and tell me this isn't important."

She shifted. Glanced down at the papers in my hand. Rubbed her lips together. "I know it's important. I know what it says about your dad. But in context—"

"Context is just an excuse. You know it is. So tell me: What's going on?"

She said nothing.

"Jenn?"

She looked out into the intersection, then turned around and scanned the street behind us that served as a parking lot. Then she leaned forward. "There are things going on. Things you don't know about."

"Yes!" I hit the papers with the back of my hand. "Things like this!"

"No, I—" When she started speaking again, I could barely hear her. "You know how my dad is. Mr. Goody Two-Shoes."

I nodded.

"He made a mistake. It was after my mother died."

"What kind of mistake?"

"It involved what turned out to be a female Russian agent and a long weekend in the Hamptons."

My gut clenched. That would mean that this was about more than just my father. Bigger than just a secretary of defense nomination. "Jenn—"

She took my hand in hers. "And ever since, *ever since*, it's been okay. It really has. The Russians have *never* asked him to come down on a certain side of any case." Her gaze bored into mine. Searching. Begging. "It's not like that. It's just . . ."

"It's just that every now and then, he's asked to do someone a favor."

Her shoulders relaxed. "Exactly."

"Are you a part of it too?"

She stiffened. "I just need you to know, it wasn't me hitting on Sean that afternoon, Georgie. It wasn't my idea, okay? *I* never would have done that."

"But you did. You did do it." I pulled my hand away. "Just another one of those favors?"

"You have to believe me. It's never my idea."

"What else have they asked you to do?"

"It would have been really nice if you had taken me up on the offer to stay with me. After your house exploded."

"That wasn't— You weren't—" What was she saying? "The Russians wanted me with you? Why?"

She said nothing.

"Because if I was with you, then they could—" It felt like my brain had frozen. I was trying to work through the possibilities, but my mind wouldn't cooperate. "If we had stayed with you, then—" What was it the Russians were after? "Sean. We would have walked right into their arms and Sean wouldn't have had any choice then but to appear." And then the game would have been over. The Russians would have won. How close I'd come to taking Jenn up on her offer after I'd heard Sean in the crawl space!

She didn't seem surprised that I was talking about him as if he were alive.

"That's the reason you came on to Sean. Who else have you had to—"

"It's not like that." She sat back and her face warped into an ugly, unrecognizable mask. "If I didn't do what they asked, then my father would be in jeopardy. Can't you understand?"

I understood completely.

"And he's never hurt anyone. He's never done anything against the law. Not really."

"Who else?"

A tear slid down her cheek. She glanced away toward the street again and headlights glistened on her cheek. "It's never what I've wanted."

"Jenn. Listen to me. This is not okay. The Russians aren't Americans. This is standard high school government class stuff. They don't get a say in our government. They don't get to do things like this. You have to make a choice. Either you're for us—you're for liberty and justice and democracy—or you're not."

"It's not like that."

"Who? Who else?"

Her gaze drifted back to me. "They asked . . . They wanted . . . Senator Rydel."

The chairman of the Armed Services Committee who had presidential ambitions. The chief justice of the Supreme Court. The soon-to-be-appointed secretary of defense, who also hoped to be president one day. My breath caught. It was civics class all over again. What were the three branches of government? Executive, legislative, and judicial.

The chief justice had been the tie-breaking vote on cases of campaign finance and internet oversight. The senator, chairing one of the most powerful Senate committees, had made decisions on weapons systems, nuclear energy, and national security. And my father? He would have access to top secret government programs and intelligence. He would be charged with the readiness of the military, developing strategies and priorities, and prosecuting war. Or not.

My father and Senator Rydel were already being talked about as presidential contenders. One for the Democrats, the other for the Republicans. To the Russians it wouldn't matter who won. They had both been compromised.

It was a once-in-a-generation achievement. The three branches of government, which were supposed to function as a check and a balance to each other, rendered impotent because they were working together on behalf of our enemy.

She reached out and clutched my hand. "I didn't know about *your* father. I didn't know—"

"But think about what you did know. You knew they had your father and you knew they had your senator."

"I know. I know. What should we do?"

"Did Rydel read this?"

"Yes."

"So he knows about *my* father." My universe was rearranging itself; I was seeing things through new eyes, from a new perspective. There were different rules in operation now. If Rydel held my father's treason over him, then he could effectively make my father do whatever he wanted. And what the senator wanted was what Russia wanted. It was double jeopardy. The Russians could pressure my father from one side. The senator could blackmail him from the other. "Does the senator know about *your* father?"

"Yes." The answer came quickly.

"Your father knows about the senator."

"No. I would never tell my father that I had to—"

I held up a hand. Of course she wouldn't. That meant her father was in the same situation as mine; he could be pressured from two sides. But only the Russians knew about Rydel. "So the senator lets the president's nominee be confirmed as the new secretary of defense, and the Russians get access to the highest level of American military secrets."

"And my senator can't say anything about it"—she eyed my papers—"because he's in the same position."

Right. She'd drawn a very clear picture. "Then can you give this to someone else?"

"How would Rydel *not* know where the information came from? And how would my father not be exposed?"

"At this point, does it really matter?"

"I'm sorry." She swiped at a tear with the bottom of her sleeve. "For all of it. I'm so tired." She closed her eyes for a moment. When she opened them I read weariness in their depths. "I'm in this as much as you are. As much as your father and mine. If this blows up, then I'm in prison, federal prison, for life. If they don't execute me first. And . . . Preston?" She swallowed a sob. "I'd lose everything."

She was asking the wrong person for sympathy. "You've got to do something. You have to. Don't tell me you won't."

"But my father—"

"Your father is one person in a democracy of millions. Are you really telling me you're going to protect him at the expense of everyone else? That you're going to put one person above the principles we all say we subscribe to? How can you put his needs and his rights above all the rest of ours? That's not what we do here."

"But your father's in the same position. Don't you want to protect him?"

"This is what makes us different: I think the rules apply to everyone."

"But he didn't mean—"

"This is kindergarten stuff. It doesn't matter what he *meant*. What matters is what he *did*."

"I used to believe that too, then I got stuck trying to make him look like what he was supposed to be. I told myself it was okay because he's making a difference. He has real influence and—"

"He's been compromised by the Russian government!"

She shook her head. "There's no way for me to get out of this now." She grabbed my arm. "Give it to someone else. Do whatever you need to. Just please, do me a favor. Don't link it to Rydel. Or me."

I shoved the papers into my purse. Then I pushed my chair away from the table and stood to leave.

64

She stood too.

I was beyond caring what Jenn did, but as I rounded the table and started down the sidewalk, she followed me. A jogger was coming up behind us; I picked up my pace, heading for a wider spot in the walkway so I could let him go around.

Jenn called to me, "Just— Wait up!"

As I turned back, she paused and pulled out a chair from an empty table, indicating I should sit. "Please. Let's not leave it this way."

The man coming up behind us veered out toward the curb and began to jog around me.

I took a step toward Jenn to give him more space.

Instead of passing, he pivoted toward us, pushing me away from the table with one arm.

I stumbled and fell.

With his other hand he drew a gun from his hoodie pocket. It had a silencer attached and—

Jenn's eyes widened.

Out in the intersection, a car honked.

I was scrambling to my feet.

Jenn stretched her arm out toward the man. "Hey—" But her protest was stilled, her confusion calmed by a small, bright-red star that bloomed between her eyes.

My strength left my legs and they folded, leaving me stranded on the pavement.

As Jenn slumped forward, the man caught her by the arms and shifted her weight. He pushed her backward, propping her up in the chair.

My heart had stopped when I saw his gun, but it slammed back into motion. "What are— You can't just—"

A sweep of headlights illuminated the scene. It glinted off the star-shaped spot on Jenn's forehead and animated the reflective stripes on her running shoes.

He turned to me and for one long moment looked me straight in the eyes before slowly pulling his hood up over his head and jogging on.

Jenn just sat there, eyes wide open as a thin trail of blood snaked down her nose, onto her cheek.

The people sitting over by the front door kept talking. Cars passed. Out in the parking lot, a door slammed.

I pushed to my feet. My mouth kept opening and closing, but it couldn't seem to collect any air. Then my last ounce of breath came out in a keening cry and I doubled over as if I'd been hit in the gut.

Someone grabbed my arm. "You okay?"

Turning my head, I saw Chris standing there, hunched beside me. I didn't know how to answer.

He braced an arm around my back and pulled me straight.

I tried to recoil, but I couldn't.

"Walk!" The word was a command.

Cars passed, headlights sweeping through the asymmetrical intersection and glancing off the aluminum sides of the Silver Diner. Up ahead to the left O'Sullivan's, an Irish tavern, glowed in the night.

I shook my head. "I can't—I can't—"

Chris's arm came around my shoulder like a vise. He leaned down to talk in my ear. "Just walk!"

"I can't—I can't just leave her there."

Clamping me against his side, he lifted me and strode forward, past the coffee shop, toward the darkness of the parking lot where the glare of headlights didn't reach. The tips of my toes dragged along the ground. "You don't want to be there when they find her."

"They?" I wriggled out of his grasp. "What about *you*?" I beat at him with my fists.

He dodged my blows. "I didn't do anything."

Tears coursed down my face as I continued yelling. "You've been watching me for months now! You've been here the whole time! Why did you let them kill her?"

Catching my wrists, he spun, turning me toward him. Then held me to his side. "Hey! Calm down." He spoke the words into my ear.

I bucked, trying to break his hold. "You're the FBI. You're supposed to get the bad guys."

"I'm trying. That was my fault. I should have identified him as a threat."

I slumped to the ground.

He let me. Then, glancing down at me, he reached inside his coat and pulled out a gun.

I shut my eyes and curled up into a ball, bringing my knees up to my chest.

After a long moment, he hooked his hand around my elbow. "Get up. We're okay. It wasn't them. I think they're gone."

65

As he walked me to my car, he kept his hand hidden away
inside his jacket. I panicked for a moment when I didn't see my car.
Then I realized I'd driven June's to the coffee shop. Chris took the
fob from my hand, beeped the car open, and shoved me in. Then he
jogged around and got into the seat next to mine. "Talk."

I had to be very careful in choosing my words. "I found out my
husband was one of your assets."

He said nothing.

What more could I say? I couldn't tell him that Sean hadn't died.
He might suspect, but did he know for certain? And I couldn't let
him know what I knew about my father. I had to tell *someone*, but
I still wasn't sure if the FBI and the DoD were part of the problem.
It hadn't been the Russians who'd taken Sean's files or gotten him
reassigned. "He was killed in a hit-and-run accident."

"Yes?"

"It just seems suspicious."

"By which you mean a deep-state conspiracy?"

I shrugged.

"We're not—" He paused. Took a deep breath. "The FBI does
not assassinate US citizens. We might jail them, but we don't murder
them. Why on—" Another deep breath. "Let's live in reality for just
a minute. I'd like to help you, Georgie. I think your life may be in
danger." He gave me a long look. "But I need you to trust me."

"I can't."

"I'm being honest with you."

No, he wasn't. There was no Keith. I suspected there had never
been a Kristy either. "It's difficult for me to trust people."

"I understand. But you seem to have the black widow's touch.

You talk to people; they die. What I need you to do is start asking yourself why. If it's not me—and believe me, it's not us—then *who is it*? Seems like you're the only one with answers right now." He got out of the car and left me to drive home alone.

I had to pull over at the first intersection, so I could throw up.

And again at Glebe.

Jenn was dead. We'd been friends since high school. Granted, she hadn't turned out to be as good a friend as I had thought, but no one deserved to be murdered. And what about Preston? What was going to happen to her son?

What about my son? I tried not to let myself think about Sam. I was doing my best to keep him safe.

My eyes darted, scanning the street behind me, as I tried to determine if anyone was following me.

Should I return to Jim and June's? I didn't want to take danger back with me.

Should I try to hide? Try to lose them?

From Glebe, I turned onto Wilson Boulevard. As I approached the coffee shop again, ambulances were coming down the road in the opposite direction, lights flashing. Once they passed, I turned, repeating the loop.

By my next pass, police cars had joined the ambulances.

The Russians were after Sean. But they hadn't been the ones who cost him his job. Someone in the DoD had helped my father do that. With Sean's help, the FBI had been trying to identify him. Or her.

But what about Jenn? Who would kill her? The Russians? But why? Her death had to mean something. It had to fit with the other pieces of my puzzle.

Sean had wanted to investigate what he'd found out; Jenn had wanted to keep what she'd known silent. She'd been doing exactly what the Russians wanted. So why had she ended up dead?

Something else didn't fit: I'd seen the man who killed her. He knew I'd seen him. He *let* me see him and still, I was alive. Our house had blown up and still, I was alive. That was twice I should have died but didn't.

Why?

If the intruder in my house had been intent on killing Sam and me, he would have blown up the house when he was certain we were in it. But I'd been thinking about that. Alice had been at the vet's that afternoon and the car had been in the shop. Sam and I were in the basement. It probably seemed as if we weren't home.

The only logical conclusion was that they *hadn't* been trying to kill us.

Sean was right. They were trying to send him a message.

That made sense; that served a purpose.

But I kept circling back to Jenn. How would killing her serve a similar purpose?

If killing her was supposed to send a message to someone, who would it be?

I was missing a piece of the puzzle. Sean and Jenn had to fit, but they didn't.

It was like the gap between quantum physics and general relativity. The first described the smallest particles in the universe while the second explained its vastness. The problem was, neither could describe the other. When you tried to join them together, the theories fell apart. We all kept hoping that someone, somewhere could figure out a way to bridge the two and reconcile both branches of physics. There had to be a solution. We just didn't know yet what it was.

The Russians were after Sean; the Russians killed Jenn.

There had to be a connection. I just had to find it.

I texted Sean at the next red light.

Jenn killed

Have new info

Everything worse than thought

When I was sure no one was following me, I made my way back to Jim and June's.

In the netherworld between wakefulness and sleep that night, I had a profoundly clarifying thought. I might not have understood the reason for Jenn's death, but one thing I did know. The gunman had let me see his face because, for some reason that was not yet clear to me, it didn't matter that I saw him.

Because I saw him, I could identify him.

I'd gotten what I'd been wanting. I had a face. I knew who to watch for. The contours of his features were seared into my memory. I could easily help a police artist draw a sketch that would help determine his identity.

If he could be caught and questioned, he could be the proof that the stories I'd collected about my father, the reports of his treachery, were true. In fact, that killer was the only real proof we had. And yet that hadn't mattered. For some reason they didn't think leaving me alive posed any risk. If I could figure out why, then I could make sense of Jenn's murder. Until then I had to do my best to keep Sam and me safe.

66

I drove Sam to school the next morning instead of walk-ing. Things were getting too dangerous. As I drove, I tried to prepare him for what he might hear at school.

"Preston might not be in class for a while. In fact, he may be switching schools." Jenn's ex lived in the north part of the county in a neighborhood with a different elementary school.

"Will he be at the concert tonight?"

"I don't think so."

"Why?"

"His . . . um . . . Miss Jenn died last night." I shot him a glance through the rearview mirror.

He was chewing on the string of his hoodie. "Like Daddy?"

"Right. Like Daddy."

"Did she get hit?"

"She did. Not by a car, though."

"By a ball?"

A ball? "No." Well, kind of. A small metal one.

"Because that's why we can't throw balls in PE. We might hit someone."

"She did get hit by something, sweetie." I realized my hands were gripping the steering wheel, my knuckles turning white. I flexed them, trying not to remember the way that bullet hole had bloomed on her forehead.

"Is she going into the hole?"

"She's going into the ground. She's going to be buried. And Preston is going to be really sad."

"Yeah." He went back to chewing on the string.

We pulled into the school parking lot and I drove all the way down to the end to find a spot.

I got out. Did a check of the area immediately around us. No one on the playground. No one suspicious in any of the vehicles immediately surrounding ours. The apartments that abutted the school property? It was hard to tell. There were too many windows. As I helped Sam out of the car, I shielded him with my body.

He grabbed my hand as we walked down the sidewalk. "Maybe Preston could borrow Alice for a while."

"Alice? Why?"

"She doesn't mind when you cry. And when you lie down next to her, she gives you a hug."

The last time I'd been in the classroom was for Bring a Parent to School Day. Back then the featured motifs had been apples and pencils and rulers. Now it was pumpkins and scarecrows and ghosts.

Bring a Parent to School Day!

I tugged Sam back as he went to put his things in his cubby. "Hey, do you remember Bring a Parent to School Day?"

"Yeah."

"Do you remember whose dad spoke after me? The one who brought you guys the comics and bookmarks?"

"Yeah."

"Whose dad was it?"

"Emma's dad."

"Is Emma here yet?"

He glanced around. "No. Yes!" He pointed to the door. "There she is."

There were several mothers walking into the classroom with their daughters at that point. I had Sam go over with me to make sure I talked to the right mother.

I introduced myself. "Are you coming to the concert tonight? I was wondering if I could meet up with your husband to discuss an article for his paper. I think I have a story he'd like."

We arranged to meet later that evening.

I kissed Sam on the cheek as I left. Told myself that he was probably safer inside the school than he was with me.

Sam whispered in my ear as I hugged him good-bye. "Grandpa and Grandma are coming!"

"Where? To what?"

"The concert."

"Tonight?"

He nodded.

"What?!" They couldn't come to the concert. Not when I was planning to pass information on my father to a journalist! "Why? How do they know about the concert?"

"I called them."

"How?"

"Grandma gave me their phone number. I know it by heart!" He proceeded to recite it.

"You called them? By yourself?"

He nodded. "Miss June helped me. They want to hear me sing."

I doubted it. No one in their right mind wanted to sit in a school gym for two hours and listen to a bunch of kids sing. "That's super nice of them."

On the way back up the hill, Sean texted me.

I'm thinking of getting back in touch with old friends

I took it to mean he wanted to go to the FBI. But I hadn't worked everything out yet. I texted back.

What if they aren't very friendly?
Not a good idea

I called my mother as soon as I got back to June and Jim's. "You guys don't have to come tonight. It was nice of you to offer, but—"

"We can't wait!"

"Really, Mom, that would definitely be above and beyond." And I didn't want my father anywhere near my son.

"Sam wants us to. I wouldn't dream of disappointing him."

"But what about the hearing? I'm sure Dad has a million things to—"

"You know your father. Everything that had to be done already is. So we'll be there tonight with bells on. We'll pick you up."

"How about we just meet you there?"

67

We ate dinner with June and Jim. After that, we met my parents at the school. We dropped Sam off with his teacher and then I led them to the gym where chairs had been set up in front of the stage. It smelled like fresh paint and basketballs. Footsteps squeaked as parents walked across the wood floors. Conversations echoed off the concrete walls and high ceilings.

I settled them in chairs as close to the front as I could find. Then I excused myself and went in search of Emma's mom. I found her sitting on one of the aisles toward the middle, holding a tablet up in the direction of the stage. She smiled as she saw me. Nodded at the tablet. "Just getting it ready to record."

The man I recognized as the journalist from Bring a Parent to School Day was sitting next to her, holding a bouquet of flowers.

She elbowed him. "This is Georgia. She's Sam's mom."

He extended a hand. "I remember. From career day." He had an open, genial face with intelligent eyes. "Hello, Sam's Mom."

I shook his hand. "Is there somewhere we can talk?"

He glanced at his watch. "If we make it fast. If I don't hear Emma sing, well, what's the point of going through the trouble of finding a parking spot?" We ducked out of the gym into the hallway. "My wife said you had a story for me?"

"I'm hoping I do." I pulled my notes from my purse. "If you wouldn't mind, can you read this? And then we can talk?"

He pulled a pair of reading glasses from the inside pocket of his coat. It didn't take him long. When he was finished, he refolded the papers and sent me a look over the top of his glasses. "If this is true . . ."

I let his question hang in the air for a moment before I answered.

"It is. All of it. And I would like to give it to you. I know there's no smoking gun or solid proof—"

"No, and—"

"—but I've lived in this town long enough to know that lots of people know things. And journalists hear things. Things like that"—I eyed the papers he was holding—"are never really secret. Someone knows. And sometimes all it requires to put a big story together is taking what you've heard and adding what someone like me knows and pretty soon, people are willing to talk and—"

He held up a hand. "Listen. I'm sure you're hoping for a big readership for this—before the hearing, right?"

I nodded.

"I have to tell you that's impossible. Not with the timeframe involved. The fact-checking alone could take—"

"But it's true. All of it is true."

"How do you know?"

"Because—" Because I'd lived it. And because my dead husband had told me so. And so had other people who had died because of it. "I checked as much of it as I could. And my father is General Slater."

"Your father!" He handed me back the papers as if he couldn't get rid of them fast enough. "I don't do family feuds. You might want to try one of the television newsmagazine formats instead. It would get great ratings."

"This isn't a feud. And I don't care about ratings. This is a matter of national security. It's a failure at multiple levels of the federal government. If this story doesn't get told, then—"

"Thing is, I can't just take your word for it. And your father is . . . Right now? After all the government, all the DoD scandals we've had? He's indestructible. And even if he wasn't, I get the sense that people have had enough. They're tired of watching a circus. They want someone to believe in. They've picked him. He's it."

"But—"

"And setting aside all of that, I would have to interview these people you've referenced. I would have to trace your story all the way back to the first Gulf War. Because with allegations like these, I'd be called up to the Hill. There would be congressional inquiries, and special committees would be formed. This would shake the administration. This one and the last four." He pointed to the papers in my hand. "That would be the next five years of my life. And if I don't do it right, then I put my paper, and myself, in legal jeopardy. So while I would love to take this story, and while I really hope you do find someone to publish it, I can't do it justice in time for the hearing. And my editor wouldn't let me."

"It's a story of national importance."

"It has Pulitzer all over it. If you'd given me a couple months' lead time?" He shrugged. "Stories of national importance are—" He broke off to bark a bitter laugh. "They're important enough that they have to be done the right way. I hope you understand."

68

My parents said they'd drive us home, but I wasn't about to let my father drive us anywhere. I begged off, telling them a walk would do us good. I figured there would be enough people walking back through the neighborhood that we would be safe.

My mother hugged me close before she let us go. My father bent down and gave Sam a high five. Sam asked for one "up high." He jumped several times to reach it, then kept on jumping even after he'd made it.

I let him keep at it so he could get out some of his pent-up energy.

My father leaned close to me. "Hey, I ordered a new train thing for Sam."

"Dad, you didn't—"

"For Halloween. Think you might have time to pick it up tomorrow at work?"

I hadn't told them I'd been fired, so I didn't have any excuse not to. "No problem." One thing he'd done right through the years: cultivate a relationship with his grandson. I wasn't looking forward to having to explain to Sam one day what his grandfather had done.

"Thanks, Peach."

Sam pestered me all the way home about when we could start trick-or-treating this weekend and what I would wear as a costume. He saved his biggest salvo for when we got back to Jim and June's.

"Mr. Jim! I was really good tonight. And Daddy said I can go to Gilman Street this year for trick-or-treating."

"Wow. Gilman Street! Put it here, kid." He held out his closed fist for Jim to bump. "If you get any Milk Duds, save them for me, huh?"

"Sure thing, Mr. Jim."

Gilman Street? Really? "I don't know, Sam. I think maybe—"

"That's what Dad said. I'm six."

"I know, but—"

"Dad said. He promised. He said when I was six."

"Hey. You know that church down the street? I think they're having a party that night. We could go there instead. I bet they'll have lots of candy."

Tears instantly welled up in his eyes. "But Daddy said—he *said*!"

We were coming perilously close to a mutiny. "I just don't know if it's safe." Strolling around outside in the dark? With Russians on the loose?

But then, I could make a reasonable argument that Halloween on Gilman Street might be safer than walking around outside any other night of the year. And what would be the alternative? Passing out treats with Jim and June? That raised all sorts of nightmares about costumed Bad Guys forcing their way into the house and doing terrible things to all of us.

"We come home when I say so, okay?"

He nodded.

"I mean it."

"I promise, Mommy."

"And you're holding my hand the entire time."

I texted Sean after Sam fell asleep.

We need to talk
See you soon?

He answered about half an hour later.

I'll be on ice tomorrow
Sounds like offense needs defense
See you there

Offense. Defense.

It sounded like a sports reference. Thing is, I wasn't a sports fan. I'd always kept Sean company, though, on the couch at night when he'd watch his games. He only followed two sports: football and hockey. But hockey was his favorite. He used to take Sam to the rink sometimes when the Capitals, the town's NHL franchise, were practicing. They used one of the rinks at the Iceplex, where Sam skated.

Ice rink.

I'd figured it out.

I logged on to June's computer and googled the rink's website to access their events schedule. The Caps were practicing at the rink the next morning at ten thirty.

Bingo.

The next morning I went to the Iceplex, driving up seven stories to the roof of the parking garage. In a display of innovative community development of the kind prized by Arlington, it had been built right there on top. I walked in through the glass entrance, then slipped through the lobby and into the bleachers where I worked my way up and over a few rows. There were Caps fans and then there were *Caps fans*. Only the truly devoted would be at a rink midmorning on a Thursday to watch the team practice.

The players were doing some sort of shooting drill.

When they missed the net, pucks thwacked against the sideboards. I flinched every time it happened.

Once, when one of the pucks hit the glass in front of the bleachers, I even threw up an arm. I couldn't help myself.

It was *cold*. As the players performed drills, I sat there on the metal bench watching. My feet went numb by degrees. So did my butt. I wished I'd brought a hat.

A man sat down next to me.

It wasn't Sean.

I slid down the bench a bit and watched for a while longer. When I started shivering, I decided to move inside to the heated mezzanine and watch from there. I took a seat on one of the benches that looked down on the rink.

One of the custodians was cleaning the windows. I moved my feet aside so he could pass. When he didn't I looked up, past the uniform, to see Sean.

"You have to stop showing up like this. It scares me."

"How else am I going to meet up with you?"

He had a point.

"No one ever looks at people who do the jobs they don't want to do. As long as I wear the right color, have the right props, I blend in and no one really sees me." He squirted some cleaner on the window and wiped it off with a cloth. "Tell me about Jenn."

"I was with her when she was killed."

He paused. Turned toward me. "What?"

"I'd put together my notes and given them to her so she could give them to Senator Rydel. I was hoping he could stop the confirmation hearing."

"And?"

"It's like I said. Worse than we realized." As he went back to work on the window, I told him what Jenn had told me, about both her father and her senator being compromised by the Russians.

"Then your father's part of a trifecta."

"But I don't think he knows about Jenn's father. Or her senator."

"This is big."

"We were leaving when they killed Jenn." I had to force myself to concentrate on the words I was saying. That way I couldn't dwell on the image in my mind. "She was shot."

"But they didn't get you."

"They didn't want to. They could have. The killer gave me a good, long look at his face. But then he left. They've been targeting those names on your list. They've been killing the people I talked to."

He sent me a glance beneath his brow and gave up on the window, setting the cleaner down on the ledge.

"They killed Paul Conway before I even had the chance to talk to him."

"They're trying to protect your father. And Jenn? That was a warning to me." He stuffed the cleaning cloth into his pocket. "I want you to take Sam and leave. Get out of town."

"I can't. We're so close. We've figured it out. It's just that I can't get anyone to take the story. If I could just find actual proof."

"The hearing is on Monday."

It's not as if I needed a reminder. "I know. If we just had proof, then I think it would be an easier sell. But I haven't found anyone who actually saw my father and a Russian together in an incriminating way. There was never anyone who caught them passing information or doing anything illegal. And yet people are getting killed to hide the connection. It's all there."

He was facing the window. Anyone watching us would have thought that his attention had been caught by the hockey practice. "Those Russians your father came across in Iraq couldn't have been the only ones. They had to have someone with the government in Baghdad, even if they weren't representing the official Russian position. They wouldn't have sent soldiers to fight without the Iraqis' knowledge. So maybe we need to come at it from a different angle, a different side. If we get proof that the Russians were there in the desert, then maybe someone rethinks what they thought they saw. Or maybe your father comes clean. Let me see what I can dig up."

"In three days?"

"It's not like the confirmation hearing is a firm deadline. Once the hearing's over, they'll still have to vote to confirm him. That won't be scheduled until afterward."

"Even then, it might not be long enough."

"It's all the time we have."

69

I drove down to the Crystal City Mall to pick up Sam's train after I left the rink.

We had to figure it out. If we didn't, the Russians would have the United States by the throat, and my husband would be one step closer to actual death.

While Sean dug through the past, I concentrated on the present.

My father still had to be communicating with the Russians. How could he not be in the run-up to the hearings? He was just days away from being installed at one of the highest ranks of federal government.

But how were they doing it?

The conversations of Russian nationals were routinely tapped. After the government controversies of previous years, everyone knew that. And we weren't in some cheesy spy movie where the characters wore black trench coats and talked over the phone in code.

They couldn't be using technology to pass information, could they? An anonymous Facebook account? Odd messages on Twitter? I thought about it as I waited at a light.

I had to assume they weren't. Russian digital movements could always be subject to hacking or tracking. But they still had to be coordinating. It couldn't be a face-to-face exchange. If anyone had any suspicions, they'd put a tail on a Russian, wouldn't they? And they'd notice whenever my father met with him. What they could use was a dead drop, leaving information for each other in a place to which both had access.

But then how would they signal each other to check it?

There had to be some bridge between my father and the Russians that I wasn't seeing.

I tried to flip the options, rotate the angles.

Something connected them to each other. Something had to connect them.

Something or some*one*.

My mother?

I discarded the thought as soon as it formed. My mother was too close to my father. Too obvious. If there was a person, it would have to be someone who knew them both. Someone who could receive a message and pass it on without suspicion.

One of my father's old aides-de-camp? One of his deputies?

No. They'd changed every couple of years and that would have been too risky. Each person drawn into the network would have meant more chances for the story to leak. For sure the FBI, the CIA, the DoD would have noticed if my father talked to a foreigner on a regular basis. And my father would have had to report that person on his security-clearance applications.

If it was a person, it had to be someone else. Someone different. Someone outside that world. Someone they could both contact, separately, without suspicion. It would have to be someone doing a job like Sean was doing. Someone unremarkable.

Dry cleaner. Plumber. Restaurant or hotel staff.

That seemed too cumbersome. And too geographically dependent.

I drove down the ramp into the parking garage, took a ticket, circled as I looked for a spot close to the elevator. Eventually I gave up and just pulled into a spot back where I'd first come down. As I sat there, thinking through the options, I raked back my hair, grabbing a fistful. Why couldn't I see it? The link had to exist. It had to.

Mr. Hoffman was busy with another customer, so I looked around while I waited. It was kind of funny that my dad had never pushed any army toys on Sam. He'd never bought him green men or guns of any kind. Which I appreciated. I had honestly never known how much my father loved trains. Not until Sam had come along. Maybe it was because I was a girl.

The customer left.

Mr. Hoffman greeted me. "You are here for the train. It's in the back. I'll get it."

I hadn't told him about the house. I didn't want him to worry more about us than he already did. I figured I had a few more weeks, until Thanksgiving, to figure out how to tell him.

He soon returned with it. "Your father has very good taste in trains." He put it into a bag for me to carry.

"I think Sam would agree. I'll let him know."

I'd meant to put the bag aside so that my father could give it to Sam, but I forgot.

Before I could stop him, Sam tore into it when he came home from school. It didn't take long before he was on his knees on the floor, fitting it into the track he'd built in the corner of Jim and June's living room.

I sat down beside him and asked him about his day. As he played, he told me about lunch and recess, which seemed to be his two favorite subjects. He was trying to put together a new crane, but he didn't seem very happy. He took one of the parts and hit the carpet with it once. Twice. Then he offered it to me.

"It's broken."

"What do you mean, it's broken?"

He shook it.

Something rattled.

"Grandpa always fixes them for me."

Always? "Do they usually break?" Those trains and playsets didn't come cheap. And European toys were supposed to be better made than most.

He'd set down the part and was absorbed in pushing a train around the track.

"Sam? Do they break a lot?"

"Yeah."

"Really?"

"What?"

Never mind. "Here." I held out my hand. "Let me see if I can find Mr. Jim's tools."

Jim offered to do it for me, but they'd done so much for us. Too much for us. He finally showed me where his toolbox was and left me to it.

I shook the part. Whatever had come loose was inside. How to get to it was a bit of a mystery. It looked to be solid wood. I tapped at it with the handle of a screwdriver until I identified a hollow area. But it still took some looking to find a way to access it. There was an opening at the bottom about half an inch wide. It had been covered with a wooden plug. I pried it up with the screwdriver and then I tipped it upside down and shook it.

A thumb drive fell out into my palm.

70

Grandpa always fixes them for me. Sam's words echoed in my head.

Sam's toys were always "broken"; my father always "fixed" them.

That bridge between my father and the Russians?

Was it *me*?

The truth hit me with the force of a fist.

Was it—could it be—me?

I tried to view the problem analytically. Tried to insert myself—scientifically, objectively—into the equation. But even as I tried, I knew I couldn't really do it. It was a physics problem as much as it was a problem of perspective. The very act of measuring or even just observing something changed its very reality. Inserting myself into an equation would change it.

But what if I had always *been* a part of the equation?

I reined in my thoughts, stopping them from galloping away in panic and fury. I had already assumed the bridge between my father and his handler was a person. I had known the communication had to have been going on for years. One of them would have to contact someone, leave that person with some piece of information, and then that person—the intermediary—would pass it on to the other.

When had I started buying toys from Mr. Hoffman's? It was four years ago. Sam had been two. My father hadn't been around very often—he was working a job out of California—and Sean had been deployed with his reserve unit. I'd asked my father where he'd gotten the toys and he'd told me.

My father and Mr. Hoffman. That was the network.

I was the link to Mr. Hoffman. At least in one direction. I still didn't know how my father got information back to him. But that's why it hadn't mattered that I had seen Jenn's killer. I was one of them just as much as my father was. Just as much as the killer was.

The realization shattered my world—past, present, and future.

That bridge was me. More than me. It was my son too.

I put a hand to the floor and lowered myself to my knees.

Me.

I'd never known my father liked trains because the truth was, he didn't. Not especially. He'd just needed a way to get information from his contact. He'd used me, used his grandson too, as pawns in his scheme. What could be more innocent than buying a toy for a little boy? And those trains? They were perfect. The iterations of playset add-ons were infinite. And they were all made of solid wood that could easily be drilled to make a hiding place just the right size for a thumb drive.

My father and Mr. Hoffman.

And me.

There really were parallel universes. I'd been living in one. It was a place where enemies were friends and lies were the truth.

How many times had my father told me he'd ordered a new train set for Sam and wondered if I could pick it up for him so it would be there when he came to visit? I remembered all the times I'd brought thumb drives back to my house at his request.

My father had sucked me into his black hole right along with him.

No one really knows what happens inside a black hole. Its gravitational force pulls in everything without discrimination. Escape is impossible. Surrender is inexorable.

In that moment everything I was, everything I'd had, all of it disappeared into the vortex of my father's betrayal.

It had swallowed me whole.

∞

On automatic pilot, I helped June with dinner. Like a robot, I moved through space and time, but I found myself curiously detached from reality.

My father was a traitor.

I was his accomplice.

That meant I was a traitor.

No wonder Jenn's assassin hadn't cared about me seeing him. He had nothing to fear from me. If I told anyone about him, tried to identify him, the trail of investigation would eventually lead to me. In the eyes of the law, I was just as guilty as he was.

It was a disorienting feeling, to know that you were absolutely Other. That you were completely different than you'd always thought you were. I felt like I was trapped in a body that was not my own.

After Sam was asleep I went for a drive. I ended up at Sean's restaurant. Once there, I parked, got out, and waited in the alley, hoping my husband would eventually appear.

Twenty, thirty, forty minutes later, once the cold had driven my hands deep into my pockets, he finally did.

The door scraped open. His form appeared on the stoop.

"Sean." I could hardly say his name without my voice breaking.

He squinted into the night. "Georgie?"

I moved into the light.

He nodded toward the shadows from which I'd emerged and I retreated back into the dark, where he joined me.

Looking down into my eyes, he put a hand to my cheek and smoothed back a lock of hair that had escaped my ponytail. "What happened?"

I reached out and grabbed hold of him, pulling him close, pressing my cheek to his jaw. "I need to know that you know me." I released him, raking my hands through his hair, and met his lips with mine.

He tried to step back. "Georgie, look, I don't think—"

But I didn't want to think anymore. I let my hands drop to his shoulders. From his shoulders, down his arms, to his belt loops.

His hands seized mine.

"Please." I turned my hands, meeting his palm to palm. I threaded my fingers through his. "Sean." I needed him to love me. No matter who I was, no matter what I'd done.

He took one last, long look at me and then gave in.

In a crush of lips and bodies, my arms around his neck, his weight pinning me to the wall, I found my redemption. But even as we rediscovered a long-dormant rhythm, as I arched against the wall, I wept. I wept without dignity, without restraint. And as we buried ourselves in each other, I let the old Georgie go. I would never be that person again.

71

The next morning I walked Sam to school. He wasn't in any mortal danger. And neither was I. He skipped along beside me in his Super Sam cape, oblivious to the world having turned inside out. He couldn't wait for his class Halloween party.

Chris was there with his Maltipoo just the same as always; he must have still been assigned to me. I hadn't told him I knew he didn't have a son.

But I'd been hoping to see him. I unfastened Alice's leash, took a deep breath, and then made my move. "I want to turn myself in."

He blinked. "What?" He took me by the elbow and moved us away from the other parents. "Turn yourself in for what?"

"Espionage."

He dropped my elbow. Stepped back, one hand up, fingers splayed. "I am not taking you in."

"I want to turn myself in for esp—"

"*Shut. Up.* As your friend, I'm telling you to shut up."

"But—"

"*Right now.*"

"But—"

"I'm going to pretend I didn't hear you, okay?"

"But I—"

"We haven't been watching you. I mean, we have, but not— You're not the one we're after. So just—" He put his hand up again. A warning. Then he glanced down the street, put his arm through mine, and dragged Alice and me off down the road. "Let's just turn this into a nice, normal walk, okay?"

"I am in this up to my ears. Over my ears." I tried to swallow the fear that had lodged itself in my throat. "Over my head. And I can prove it. I want to turn myself in so you can wire me."

I spent the day in DC with Chris as I was questioned by the FBI. I gave them the thumb drive, then I sketched out the broad outline of my father's career and associations with the Russians. I explained Mr. Hoffman's role in it. I told of finding Sean's notes after he'd died and following up with the names he'd left.

I gave them the names of the men the Russians had killed.

I did *not* tell them I knew Sean wasn't dead. If things somehow went wrong for me, I wanted to keep him out there, free of surveillance, and able to care for Sam. I also didn't tell them about Jenn's dad or Senator Rydel. One thing at a time. The most immediate goal was stopping my father's confirmation hearing.

In exchange for cooperating with the FBI's investigation and providing names and details, they agreed to give me immunity from prosecution. That didn't mean, however, that I wouldn't have to testify about what I'd discovered. I agreed to it all. I agreed to everything.

I asked the agent who was questioning me, "Can you tell me—how long have you known about my father?"

"First learned of it from your husband. But the Department of Defense took it."

I wasn't supposed to know. "Then why haven't they stopped this before now?"

"It's complicated."

He didn't know the half of it.

"Your husband didn't trust them, so he came to us with the story."

"And you what? Sat on it?"

Chris was in the chair beside me. He put a hand on my arm. "We've been trying to corroborate it. You have to have grounds to arrest someone. You have to make sure a crime's actually been committed."

"Were you going to let my father be confirmed?"

He said nothing.

"You were?"

They said nothing.

"So why have you been watching *me*?"

They exchanged a glance. Chris answered me. "Because things weren't adding up." Which I interpreted to mean that, once again, Sean had been right. They suspected he wasn't really dead. "And we didn't have enough to put it together until now, okay? At this point all of this is still conjecture. But with you agreeing to be wired . . ." He left the possibilities open.

The other agent was sitting across from me. "You ready?"

I nodded.

"Here's the plan."

72

My parents came over that evening. Sam immediately took my father's hand and dragged him over toward the trains. My mother started talking about Halloween. "We just stopped by to confirm the plan for tomorrow night."

"Plan? For tomorrow?" What plan?

"Georgia Ann—it's Halloween! You can't tell me you've forgotten. So what time should we come over? For trick-or-treating?"

My father was surreptitiously picking up pieces of the new playset and shaking them.

"Georgia Ann?"

"Oh. Right! Um." I focused my attention back on her. "You guys don't need to come. We're not really going far."

"But I want to take pictures. And we thought we could take Sam to Fort Myer."

"Fort Myer?" I wasn't letting my father take Sam anywhere.

"Peach?" My father was trying to get my attention. He already had it. "Do you have the instructions that came with the set?"

I shook my head. "Sam tore into the box as soon as he found it. I threw it out. Sorry."

"I think there's a part missing."

My mother was still talking. "Military kids trick-or-treat too. Fort Myer can't be nearly as crowded. And your father has some friends on post there."

"Sounds like a great idea. Maybe we can do it next year."

My father stood up. "I'm going to take this set back to Hoffman's. There's something missing."

"But, Grandpa!"

He put his hand on Sam's head. "Don't worry, buddy. I'll bring it all back."

"Hey—Dad."

He turned.

"I wanted to talk to you about something." I was hoping to take him aside and confront him. They'd wired me. If I could get him to admit to what he'd been doing, then they'd have the proof we needed.

But he glanced at his watch. "Can it wait? We've got to get back downtown. We're meeting someone." He didn't wait for an answer. He handed my mother her purse and they left.

Chris came by Jim and June's midmorning on Saturday. "You were right. We picked up Hoffman. He was in possession of classified information."

"Has he told you anything yet?"

"No."

"Did you get my father?"

He shook his head. "Have you heard from him?"

"Not today."

"We have agents waiting. They can take him in when he shows up."

"So what do I do?"

"You do what you planned. Wear the wire just in case. Go out trick-or-treating. I'll follow you and I'll get someone else assigned to you too."

"What if you lose me?"

"We won't lose you. Just take your phone with you. Keep it on. We'll track it."

"I don't know. Is this really a good idea?"

"There's no reason to skip going out. We have Hoffman. We'll bring in your father when he gets back to the hotel. And then it will all be over."

"But there's got to be more of them than just Hoffman. They knocked Sam down at the rink. They ransacked the house. And then they blew it up. Hoffman didn't do all of that. I don't think he did any of it." But the fact that he might have ordered it done? That chilled me. A man whom I'd considered a dear, sweet person—a friend even—had placed my family in danger.

"He's in custody now. We think we've identified the operatives. At this point they wouldn't dare do anything that might connect themselves to him."

If I had thought it would help to tell Sam we were skipping Halloween, I would have, but what Chris said made sense. I chalked up my reluctance to residual uneasiness from being constantly on edge for the past few weeks. I tried to talk myself into being excited about Gilman. It was almost working until June dug up some costumes for Alice and me.

"We had these way back in the day." She beamed as she held them up.

Jim walked past.

She turned toward him. "Remember these?"

"Hey. Yeah. Sure! Underdog. Geez. How long ago was that on TV?"

"Wasn't *that* long ago. And look: Wonder Woman." She said it with a smile.

"Would you look at that! *That* one, I remember." He said it with a gleam in his eye.

Sam thought the costumes were terrific. He knelt and coaxed Alice into the red sweater with its blue cape.

"We used to have a Doberman." Jim winked in my direction as he helped Sam.

"So what do you think?" June asked the question with a raised brow as she held up the costume for me.

I was thinking that there was no way my wire wouldn't show

if I wore that costume. It was a Wonder Woman outfit from the Lynda Carter era. The blue hot pants had white stars on them. The top was a plastic breastplate piece that looked like it was molded to fit a Barbie doll. There were even gold-colored wristbands. "I don't think it will fit. But that's okay. I was just planning to go as I am."

June turned the costume around with a flourish. "It's adjustable. Look!" She pointed out the ties at the back of the breastplate.

"I have no idea what I'd wear underneath."

"But if you wear it you can do the pose!" She put her hands to her hips. "Remember?"

"I really don't think it will fit."

"But, Mo-om!" Sam wailed the word. "I'm Super Sam. You *have* to be Wonder Woman. You're my mom."

If he only knew how wonderful I'd turned out *not* to be. "I can't be Wonder Woman. I have to be Super Sam's Mom. I'll wear a sign that says SSM. You can help me make it." I held my breath, hoping that would sound like a good idea.

His face went stormy for a moment and then it cleared. "And you can walk Underdog just like you walk Alice!"

"Yes. Right!" Thank goodness he'd bought it.

73

It didn't take long that evening to visit our immediate neighbors. Sam, holding on to the plastic handle of the pumpkin June had bought for him, ran back and forth so that his Super Sam cape flew out behind him. I could tell he'd been practicing. A lot.

The blackened shell of our house was a blot on an otherwise picture-perfect block. The street past ours was mostly dark and the one after that too. I hurried us past them. It was only after we crossed the neighborhood's main artery that the party really started.

We heard a pulsing bass from three blocks away and could see flashes of light now and then above roofs as we walked. We hit the couple of houses that had lights on, then headed toward the end of the block where police had been posted. Joining the flow of people, we entered the throngs. I'd never been to Gilman Street on Halloween, but I'd heard about it.

Gilman Street was legendary.

If you lived there, you had to decorate. And not with cornstalks and harvest-colored ribbons. One of the houses turned its front lawn into a cemetery, complete with a vintage hearse and a skeleton on a motorcycle. Another house put up a false front shaped like the prow of a ship and outfitted it with pirate-themed decorations. The owners of a third house carved several dozen pumpkins and made a candle-lit, glowing arch out of them.

In a region populated by type A personalities, if you couldn't keep up with hearses and skeletons, then it was just better to buy somewhere else.

It was to Gilman that Sam insisted he wanted to go. Breathing a prayer that Chris was right, that we weren't in any danger, I grabbed hold of Sam's hand with my superglue grip.

At least I knew the FBI was following me. And my phone was stashed away at the bottom of Sam's pumpkin. If anything happened, it was more important that Sam stay safe than me.

As we joined the line of kids and parents moving at a snail's pace down the sidewalk, an unearthly shriek echoed through the night.

Sam's eyes widened. "Look!"

He was pointing to the roof of a house. A woman with long, stringy hair and a gown made of ghostly rags was wailing. Her eyes were ringed with dark circles. Her teeth had been blacked out.

"That's so cool." Sam breathed the words.

It was hideous.

"Do you think I can stand on the roof when I get big?"

"No."

Disappointment dimmed the glow in his eyes. "Why not?"

"There's a law."

He seemed satisfied with that answer. And as far as he knew, there were also laws about riding skateboards, staying up past nine p.m. on a school night, and stepping on worms that had stranded themselves on sidewalks.

Gilman Street probably was one of the safest places we could have been that night. We were surrounded by people. There were policemen posted at every block. And I'd brought Alice too. But still, anxious to return to Jim and June's, I tried to keep Sam moving down the sidewalk.

One of the houses on the block had set up a haunted house in their front yard.

"I want to do it!" Sam was hopping with excitement and there was a manic gleam in his eyes. I shouldn't have let him start sampling the treats he'd been collecting.

I tightened my grip on his hand. "No."

It seemed fairly innocuous. It had been set up in one of those long, narrow tents used at outdoor markets. There were multiple windows on both sides, which gave tantalizing glimpses of purple lights and bloody handprints. Eerie music wafted from the tent, and somewhere a fog machine was billowing vast amounts of creepiness.

"Can I go alone?"

"Absolutely not." I tried to keep walking.

He dug his heels into the sidewalk. "Please, Mom!"

"No." There was no way I was letting go of him.

"Everyone is going by themselves."

He had a point. But it was a flimsy one: nobody else had me as their mother.

"Please, Mom! I promise I won't be scared."

"I already said no."

We watched a pair of dinosaurs come out. Several Disney princesses. A pirate and a mummy ran past. A father in a Dracula cape strolled by.

Alice yanked on the leash.

I yanked right back.

A miniature Michelin Man, encased in rings of long white balloons, tottered along beside his mother.

Sam tugged on my hand. When I looked down at him, he was waving at someone.

I followed his gaze.

"Look, Mom! Granddad!"

74

What! Where?

Sam was jumping up and down, hand extended toward the Dracula that had passed us earlier.

He bent down toward Sam with a flourish of his cape and—

"No! Sam!" I tried to pull him away, tried to hide him behind me, but my father already had a grip on his other hand.

He looked at me over Sam's head. "You're hard to find, Peach." He wasn't smiling. Beneath his stage makeup taut lines stretched between his brow. His eyes swept the street ahead as he pulled us away toward a house on the other side of the street.

I tried to calm my fear. "We were just headed home. Do you want to come back with us? June said she'd have cupcakes waiting." Chris was out there somewhere. He said he would be following me. If we turned around, then it might bring us closer to him. Once he saw my father, he could arrest him and it would all be over.

He gestured with his chin toward the driveway. "How would you like to visit a secret hideout, Sam?"

He glanced up at me. "Can Mom and Alice come too?"

I gripped his hand even tighter. "You're not going anywhere without me, sweetie." Where was Chris? "But I really think we should go home, Dad. Sam's getting tired."

"No, I'm not!"

My father put his arm around my shoulders, enveloping me with his cape, as we skirted a candy line and blended with the shadows. He maneuvered us down the driveway and into the backyard. "There's a secret path to get there too. This way."

I didn't want to go anywhere with him. But the FBI was tracking my phone and they had me wired. Chris was on my tail. Only a minute more? Or maybe two?

At the oakleaf hydrangeas that seemed to delineate the property line, my father paused. "No need for a phone where we're going, Peach."

"I don't know what you're—"

"Give me your phone."

Considering the way he'd co-opted me into his spy network without asking, I decided not to press him. I dug it out from underneath Sam's candy and handed it to him.

He tossed it into one of the bushes.

We skulked across the next backyard, then down another driveway, leaving Halloween behind us.

The FBI had lost the ability to geo-track my phone, but I was still wired. "Where are you taking us?"

He shot a look at me over his shoulder and then reached back to grab me by the elbow. "Just keep up." Shedding the noise and the crowds, we stepped into relative peace. We were on one of the streets that didn't have sidewalks. It didn't even appear to have very many streetlights. It was narrower, less polished than the streets around it.

"Granddad?"

He grunted.

"I'm scared."

I squeezed Sam's hand. So was I.

My father led us to an old bungalow, built well back on the property. A dead willow oak leaned toward it, the moonlight filtering downward through its bare branches. The lawn was a battleground of insurgent kudzu and brambles; the shutters had tilted. At some point in the recent past, a hefty branch had splintered off from the tree and fallen through the top of a screened porch.

I pulled Alice with us down a front walkway made of paving stones that were sinking into the yard. We filed past parallel rows of boxwoods that had grown way beyond the bounds of clipped propriety.

In front of us, a storm door hung permanently open, providing easy access to the front door. My father put a hand to it. Pushed.

It swung halfway open and refused to budge any more.

He pushed Sam through and went in behind him.

As I began to slip through the door, Alice sat down on the top step, unwilling to go inside.

I tugged at her.

She wasn't having it.

I couldn't wait for her, so I dropped the leash and went inside. As I disappeared into the gloom, she must have thought better of staying out there alone. She scrambled in after me. The clicking of her toenails on the scarred hardwood floors echoed through the dark.

Where was Sam?

I'd entered a living room that had a gaping fireplace surrounded by built-in bookshelves. Walking farther into the house, I passed a pair of waist-high shelves marking off what must have once been a dining room.

"Mommy?"

Sam!

The dining room, in contrast to the living room, was bathed in pale, ethereal moonlight. It streamed in through a big bay window that took up the long side of the wall. And there, beneath it, sat Sam. I knelt beside my son, drawing him into my arms.

Alice padded over to lick his face.

"Are you okay?" Not waiting for him to answer, I held him away from me so I could see him. I positioned him in a splash of moonlight and smoothed an unruly lock of hair back across his forehead. "Are you all right?" I cupped his thin shoulders and drew him toward me in a hug. I wanted to fold him up and fit him back into my womb where nobody could ever harm him or steal him away again.

Ahead of us, somewhere, the floor creaked.

Alice barked, ears drawn back.

I straightened and placed myself in front of Sam.

My father emerged from a darkened doorway. He'd shed his cape.

I stood my ground. "Why are we here, in this falling-down house?" There weren't that many abandoned houses in the neighborhood. Hopefully that would give the FBI a clue.

My mother, dressed as Elvira, joined him. "We need Sean. We know he's alive. Where is he?"

We need? *We* know? Was my mother involved in all of this too?

"Grandma?" Sam grabbed my hand as his small, high voice pierced the gloom. "My daddy's dead." He stepped out from behind me. "He died. He's in the wormhole."

My mother's brow furrowed, marring her smooth, perfect complexion. "What?"

Sam eyed me. Glanced toward the ground. "He's in the wormhole."

I took over for him, bluffing for our lives. "I don't understand what you're asking. You think Sean is alive?"

They said nothing.

"Dad? You're the one who identified the body. You're the one who had him cremated. You both stood beside me at the funeral." If I could convince them that I thought Sean was dead, then maybe they would leave Sam and me alone.

How long had it been? Five minutes? Ten? Had Chris not seen us leave Gilman Street? I had to proceed as if he hadn't. As far as I knew, we were on our own.

Somewhere in the house, beneath us, something squeaked.

Beside me, Alice's ears lifted.

"Things weren't what they seemed. There was no body. Sean's alive. I know he is."

I said nothing.

"I need you to get him to come here. Tonight. Now."

"Sean's dead. He died in a car accident. I don't know what's going on, but I do know I can't speak to someone who's dead."

My mother and father exchanged a glance. I hoped that meant their certainty was wavering.

Alice got to her feet with a whine. Then she started digging at the floor.

I moved to grab her collar.

75

"Why is she doing that?" My father was not amused.

"I don't know." Not for certain. But the last time Alice did that, it turned out Sean had been in our crawl space.

"Get her to stop."

"Alice!"

Alice lifted her head, tail wagging, ears cocked.

I motioned for her to sit.

"Sean might be dead, but he left some notes behind, Dad. He wrote everything down. All of it." Rage—hot and violent—burned in my gut. "I know what happened in the desert." The FBI might not know where I was, but I was wired and they were still listening. They needed to hear my father admit to what he'd done.

His glance was colored by surprise. But he recovered. "What happened back then doesn't concern you."

"That's what they tried to tell Sean, isn't it? Why, Dad?"

"Everything I did, I did for the love of my country. Period. No matter what anyone told you, they'll never be able to say that I wasn't an honorable man."

"But, Dad, you—"

"Listen. Out there that night in the desert? I was just obeying orders. I was supposed to scout in front of the lines, report back any resistance, and keep going. We didn't encounter any resistance, so I kept going. Later that night, an order came to pause and regroup, but the message was garbled and it completely contradicted everything we'd been told at the start of the mission. So I can forgive myself for being suspicious."

"You disobeyed an order."

He licked his bottom lip. "There was a storm. We were in the desert. The comms weren't good, so I can cut myself some slack for that. My men were counting on me. Only I drove us straight into a minefield." He paused, eyes gazing out through the window. And then he refocused back on me. "When I saw those Russians surround us, I thought for sure we were done. I assumed they were Republican Guard. That's why I went out there by myself. Figured they might shoot me. But if they did, at least it would give the rest of the men some warning. Maybe some of them would be able to get away."

"Dad, why didn't you just—"

But he wasn't listening to me anymore. "Of course the Russian's offer was completely unexpected, and how could I not take it? It's not like people didn't know they armed the Iraqis. Not like we didn't know they advised them. Were they supposed to be actively fighting us? No. Would my battalion commander have liked to have known they were? Sure. It might have turned the whole thing into World War III. But that Russian swore up and down they were the only unit there. And he told me he'd show us their position so long as we destroyed it and they could get out without anyone knowing they'd been there. We were rolling over everybody; Iraq was collapsing. It was clear that we would win, so there was no point in fighting them. Why create an international incident for nothing?"

Beside me in the dark, Sam wrapped his arms around my leg.

"So think about it. In exchange for letting them go, I'd get safe passage through the minefield. I'd get the location of their position, and I'd be able to destroy it as well as get credit for creating that breach. And I knew that would make everyone forget that we hadn't fallen back like we were supposed to." He blinked. Looked at me. "You would have agreed to it too." He shrugged. "I figured it was pretty fair. They were on the losing side. He knew it, I knew it. Just a matter of time. He got the better end of the bargain. I thought so then, still think so now. And after Desert Sabre wrapped up, the war in Bosnia started. I think I was home for three months? Six? Something like that. Talked everything out with Mary Grace."

So my mother did know.

"She's the smart one. We figured I'd made the best of a bad situation. Then I ran into that Russian again in Bosnia. The Russians were all over the place. And they had all the intel. He shared some with me. I figured it was his way of paying me back for that favor I'd done him in the desert. He owed me one. Think he even said that. I said thanks, put it to work for me. But then I ran into him again."

I closed my eyes. I knew everything he was going to say.

"And he had some more information. And another favor to ask." He eyed my mother. "That's the one that made Mary Grace crazy. She swore up and down that I'd live to regret it. But by the time I talked to her, the deed was already done."

My mother's lips tightened.

He sighed. "That's the point when things started to change. Before that, the Russian gave me information like it was a gift. Know what I mean? After that, it was more transactional. And eventually, once I got to the Pentagon, the Russians assigned me to Hoffman. But it never involved life and death. It never involved the men."

My mother linked her arm through his.

"I promised your mother, swore to her, that I'd get out just as soon as I hit twenty years and retire. I would have, but they made me a general at year nineteen. So what could I do?" He looked straight at me. "I really need you to understand I'm not a traitor."

"But, Dad—"

"Sometimes the people at the Pentagon or the Kremlin just don't understand the way things look on the ground."

"But Bosnia, Dad. You gave the Russians details on convoy movements, didn't you?"

"We all did. So they could hand them off to the Serbs."

"You must have figured out that the Serbs were using them to target people and not to allow them safe passage."

"After the first few times that thought did cross my mind. But what could I do about it? I wasn't responsible for the Serbs' actions."

"But people died. Allies died."

"Sometimes in war, people get hurt."

"They didn't just get hurt. They got killed. And what about us? What about Sam and me? You almost got us killed. The Russians blew up our house."

"That wasn't me. That was Hoffman's doing. He arranged it. And it wasn't supposed to happen like that. It didn't seem like anyone was there. It was just that we wanted Sean to come out of hiding. He was the only one who knew about everything. Hoffman thought if he saw how serious we were, he'd contact us. It wasn't meant to hurt you." His gaze dropped toward the floor.

"All these years. How did you get away with it?"

"It was always a little tricky when I had to renew my security clearance. They ask a question about collusion, see my heart rate skyrocket. I explain about how many times I worked with Russians over the years. Just remind people of what they already know. I say, 'It just makes me nervous because someone looking at this could think I was a spy or something.' They laugh. I laugh." He stared out the window into the night. "In this business, you tell the truth as much as you can."

76

In the empty shell of that old, abandoned house, his words loomed large. But I couldn't let them stand unchallenged.

"You could have gotten out. You could have told them no."

"I did get out. But then defense companies put me on their boards of directors. And I started consulting. The companies kept my security clearance active. People wanted me to talk to them at their conferences and they wanted me to talk on their news shows, and all of a sudden I had this whole other career. But Hoffman was always there, asking for things." He glanced over at my mother.

"So when I found out that your Sean was uncovering my trail, who else could I talk to about it but Hoffman? I knew what kind of man Sean was. If the DoD hadn't given him a different job, he would have discovered everything. Then he would have told someone about it."

"So you're the one who got him transferred out?"

"That was me. Wasn't difficult to do. I still have some clout at the Pentagon." One side of his mouth lifted in a smile. "None of it's ever really been hard." He squared his shoulders, looked me straight in the eye. "Truth is, everyone wanted a hero, Peach." He shrugged. "I just gave them what they were looking for, that's all."

My mother stepped toward me, arm outstretched. "Your daddy never did any of it for the money."

They really didn't get it. Maybe it came from years of justifying their behavior. "Do you remember Sergeant Ornofo?"

"Ornofo?"

"Or Sergeant Abbott? Sergeant Wallace?"

"Yeah. Sure. E Company. They were with me in Desert Sabre."

"Now they're all dead."

"Oh. Well, I'm sorry to hear that."

"They're dead because they talked to me. About you. They were all murdered in the past two weeks."

"No." He shook his head. "No. I never—" He held up a hand. "I never—I never ordered anything like that. It wasn't me."

"You know what they said about you? They said you were good people. They said you knew how to take care of your troops."

"I didn't think . . . I mean . . . who would have known that . . ."

"Is that how you take care of your troops? You get them killed?"

My mother grabbed my arm. "Don't talk to your father that way!"

I pulled it from her. "Don't you get it? Let me explain it to you. Your husband betrayed our country. He raised me to tell the truth and be nice to people and keep my integrity, but you know what? He never did any of those things himself!"

My father began to bluster. "Now, that's not—"

My mother gasped. "Georgia Ann!" Her brows shot up.

"It's hard to do the right thing, you know? It takes sacrifice. And self-denial. And a whole lot of *not* having fun along with everyone else because you told me people expected more from us."

Mother's jaw dropped and then it snapped back. "Don't you sass me, young lady! It's not like—"

I held up a hand. "I believed everything he said. I believed it all. So guess what, Dad? I'm your worst nightmare. You'd better be careful when you start telling other people how to live. They just might take you seriously."

My mother's eyes were snapping. "Don't you even start, Georgia Ann. You are not the innocent in all of this. You are just as involved in this as we are."

"But *I didn't know!*" A sob burst out before I could stop it. I didn't know; I never knew.

My mother smiled her beauty-pageant smile, as if she were sharing an extraordinary talent. She gathered me into her arms as if I were a child. "Of course you didn't." Moonlight glinted off her teeth. "That was the genius of the thing." She pressed a kiss to my forehead and held me away. Her gaze had gone cold. "We're all in this together. So quit being so naïve. They already came for Hoffman. Your father got suspicious when he went to pick up some information this morning. Then Hoffman waved him off. So we don't have much time left."

My father offered me a hand. "We just need to fall in now and march along. Understand? We all live or die together."

My mother gestured toward the wall where two suitcases were waiting. "And don't worry. I've brought everything you need. So let's get moving!"

77

My father bent to pick up one of the suitcases. "We still need Sean, Peach."

"Don't call me that!"

He held up a hand as if to fend off my words. "I don't want him to get killed. I really don't. It's not worth it—not when we can all leave together. You must know where he is. Give him a call. Get him to come with us." He almost sounded like he cared.

Sam had hooked his fingers to one of my belt loops and was holding on tight.

"Sean's dead, Dad." I hadn't yet admitted to them that he was alive. And I wouldn't, as long as it kept giving them a question mark where they wanted a period. "So you're really doing this? You're running away from everything you've ever known? Why? You can't actually think the Russians are going to welcome you with open arms. You haven't succeeded. You were supposed to be the new secretary of defense. You've failed."

My mother took the suitcase from my father with her free hand, walked over, and pushed it into my arms. "We're going. Now."

My father put a hand to my mother's arm. "Mary Grace, maybe she's right. This is giving everything away. Everything we've worked for; everything we have. Maybe we should stay. Maybe we could—"

She shook his hand off and then her composure crumbled. Her eyes narrowed; her lips tightened. "Don't you even start! If you would have just listened to me in the first place! If you would have just listened to me, then we wouldn't be here now—"

I reached around and put a hand on Sam's back, pressing him to me. As unobtrusively as possible, I tried to back away from them. I needed to get us out of the moonlight.

We ran into Alice.

I stumbled.

They didn't even notice.

I took another step backward.

Alice retreated with us.

My father was trying again. "But I can get past this. We've done it before. We'll just frame it as international cooperation. Say the events have been misinterpreted. Pull out the battle-fog excuse. It'll work just like—"

"JB, you're *not listening*!"

I bent to the side, pulled Sam around, and quickly undid the strings of his cape. Then I spoke directly into his ear. "The bad guys are here. Understand?"

His eyes locked onto mine.

"You need to go hide."

Tying Sam's cape around Alice's neck, I positioned myself in front of Sam, praying they wouldn't notice him melting away into the shadows. And if they did look in our direction, maybe they'd mistake Alice for him.

My father kept talking. "I'll tell them. I'll just tell them everything. I'll explain. What I did, I did for the good of—"

"Save it." My mother turned to me.

I lifted my chin and squared my shoulders, trying to make myself as big as I possibly could. I didn't know what they'd do if they discovered Sam was gone.

"If you ever want to see Sean again, then he's going to have to come with us. And we're leaving. Now."

"He's dead. I'm his wife. Don't you think I'd know if he was alive?"

My father dismissed my words with a frown. "We just need you to do what we're asking, Peach. Your mother's right. We have to leave. We've got a car. And there's a boat waiting on the Eastern Shore. Once we make it to Cuba—"

The man speaking to me was not my father. The man in front of me was panicked, vacillating, and weak. Or maybe the man standing in front of me always had been my father. It's just that I had never truly seen him. I stood there looking at him through tear-glazed eyes. "Turn yourself in."

"What?" My parents spoke in unison.

"Turn yourself in. You said they already have Hoffman. If you turn yourself in, if you agree to testify against him, maybe they'll give you immunity."

"Do you really think . . ." My father looked at me as if he were hearing me for the first time. He walked toward me, in and out of the pools of moonlight.

My mother was already shaking her head. She grabbed my father with her free hand and spun him around. "No! Don't you even think of it."

"But—" My father stood there in the dark space between moonbeams, gaze fixed on her, eyes pleading. "But maybe it would work. Because it wasn't treason. It wasn't like that. Don't you remember, Mary Grace? That night I met that Russian in the desert, I was just doing him a favor. It didn't mean anything."

"Pardon me?"

"It was just—"

She stepped forward, reached into the shadow, and grabbed him by the collar. "What I need for you to do is keep the story straight." She dragged him into a pool of light.

"I didn't—I never— It's not like I ever gave them any information that was vital."

"JB."

My father tried to laugh. Moonlight reflected off his teeth. But the sound didn't make it out of his throat. "It's not like they ever asked me to kill the president or anything."

Their shadows, entwined and distorted, were projected onto the opposite wall.

"The story."

"It's not like—"

My mother put an arm around him. It looked like she was embracing him, but when she stepped back, I saw her pull a gun from his waistband. As my mother stepped back and raised her arm, a shadow sliced through the moonlight.

"—not like I was really a spy or—"

"Mom—" I lunged toward her.

She didn't even stop. She didn't flinch. I don't think she even blinked.

"—no!"

She pulled the trigger.

By the time I reached her it was too late.

Alice had sprung ahead of me, bolting from her haunches to her feet. She had planted herself between my father and my mother. I saw her barking, but I couldn't hear anything. The report of the gun had muted everything else.

He rocked back onto his heels as if someone had shoved him. Stood erect for a moment, straightening as if he were drawing himself up for a salute. Then his knees folded and he crumpled to the floor.

"Daddy!" I knelt by his side.

He sat there holding a hand to his chest. But he couldn't contain the blood that seeped out beneath it. He drew in great noisy gulps of air.

Beyond him, in the darkened doorway, I saw Sean emerge from the shadows. He stepped forward toward us.

I shook my head and inclined it toward the living room, where I suspected Sam must be hiding.

My mother stood over us, shaking her head. "He can't even die without making a mess of it."

He convulsed, folding into himself. Closed his eyes for a moment and then opened them. "Mary . . ." Blood burbled from his mouth.

"We're all in this together." My mother said the words to herself.

Then she turned her hollow-eyed gaze on me and swung the gun up in my direction. "We can't just leave you behind."

I raised my hands.

She shifted her gaze to my father.

"Grace . . ." His hand reached out toward her.

She frowned and focused her attention on me. "In a situation like this, you have to be able to keep the story straight." She dropped her arm, bringing the gun down to her side. "Now we don't have to worry about his side of it. So I just need *you* to focus on keeping the story straight, Georgia Ann. Get up." She brought her hand up and gestured toward the living room with the gun.

I stood and stepped away from my father.

She blinked.

My father moaned. "Help me . . ."

"I was not going to go back to Mobile and tell all those Sinclairs that they were right after all. That JB Slater would never amount to anything." Her gaze flicked to him. "All our lives, I've been trying to turn *you* into a hero. Well, that was my mistake. Now *I* can be the hero."

". . . you can't . . ."

"You're the one who can't." She raised the pistol and shot him again. In the head.

I closed my eyes. I never wanted to open them again.

But Alice whimpered, nudging my hip with her head.

My fingers closed around her collar. I didn't want her giving away Sam's absence or Sean's presence.

"Georgia Ann?" Her voice was testy.

I opened my eyes. Carefully, slowly, I put my other hand up.

"We need to go!"

"Yes. Okay. We need to go."

"So *move it*!"

I ordered Alice to sit. Then I extended my hand to my mother. "Better give me the gun."

"What?" She looked down at the gun in her hand. "Yes." Her gaze ricocheted over to me. "Yes. I suppose I should." But she made no effort to hand it to me. "We had it all planned. All we had to do was take care of Sean. In the beginning it was easy; no one listened to him anyway. Why should they? Then it turned out we didn't have to do anything at all. That car took care of everything. It was perfect until your father went to the morgue. No body? That was just too suspicious. Shame, though. It really would have been better if he'd died. He was the only one who knew."

"*I* knew."

She laughed. "Oh, sugar pie! We weren't worried about you." She reached out and patted my cheek.

I flinched.

"You've always done whatever we've told you to. That's what I told your father to tell Hoffman. And you and Sam had your own use. We figured Sean would come out of hiding if the two of you were in danger. And in the meantime, you gave us information. You led us to the people who could prove the story if they thought about it hard enough."

"How? How did you find all those people and kill them? You never had Sean's notes."

She shrugged. "You googled the names, though. Before you clipped the cable."

Realization hit me like a punch in the gut. I thought I'd been so careful.

She laughed. It was a laugh of surprised delight. A laugh that wouldn't have sounded out of place in a ballroom or at a charity fundraiser. "Hoffman took an impression of your house keys once when he visited. That's how they got inside that weekend we went to the beach. They wanted to add some audio and video feeds. That's what they were doing with the gas meter, but you didn't let them stay. The plan would have worked. I'm still not sure, though . . ."

Her gaze wandered over to my father. Then it swung back to me. "I don't know why it didn't."

"Mother?" I stretched out my hand. "The gun."

She straightened, pulling her shoulders back as she lifted her chin. "You and I did the right thing, Georgia Ann." She gestured toward him. "We discovered your father was a spy. Hoffman was the spymaster. Once we found out, there was nothing else we could do. We had to stop him, didn't we? That's the story. Don't forget it. What I need for you to do now is back me up on it. If we both say the same thing, then it's their fault, not ours. Do you understand me, Georgia Ann?"

I nodded.

She flashed her beauty-pageant smile again. "There's no reason for anyone to say anything now. It's finished; no harm done. We let it end with them. We'll just say that when confronted with espionage, we did the right thing." She handed the gun to me.

I took it. Cocked the hammer and pointed it at her. "One of us did, Mother. When confronted with treachery and treason, *I* did the right thing."

78

My parents were spies. Both of them.

And I was too.

It used to be, as I looked back on life with my parents, that I could explain them away with multiple excuses. My father was military. My mother was a Southern belle. I was an only child. They were helicopter parents. They hadn't been willing to let me go. I hadn't been willing to leave.

Used to be I could see every possibility but one.

But at that moment, I couldn't see anything else.

As a physicist, I'd always known that the answers to the big questions were staring at us. They were right in front of our eyes. We just couldn't see them because they'd camouflaged themselves in our reality. The key to unlocking the mysteries had to be things we'd seen a million times and always managed to overlook. They had to be assumptions we didn't realize we had made.

The assumption I'd taken for granted? The one I hadn't even known I was making?

It was me.

I was the assumption. I'd assumed that I was an interested but uninvolved bystander.

My mother smiled that beauty-pageant smile again. She reached out toward me with both hands. I didn't budge.

She held those hands up, palms out. "You don't want to do this, sugar pie. You know you don't."

"Sean?" I hoped he was still somewhere in the house. I needed him to call the police. My hand was starting to shake. I put my other hand up to reinforce it. I blinked. In that play of moonlight and shadow, my eyes had started playing tricks on me. I didn't know how long I could stand there like that, next to my father's body. It felt like I was just one "sugar pie" away from pulling the trigger.

But it was Chris who walked into the dining room at my call. "You're doing just fine, Georgie."

My mother's eyes widened when she saw him. "Thank goodness! I'm afraid my daughter's been under a lot of stress lately."

Chris positioned himself between me and my mother, but he was talking to me. "I have two other agents with me. You can put the gun down. They've got her covered."

I didn't move; they didn't know my mother like I did. They didn't know what she was capable of.

"I'm just going to take out a pair of handcuffs." He grabbed one of my mother's arms and cuffed it.

My mother was still talking. "I hope you're just doing this for my safety. The one you really should be worrying about is Georgia Ann."

Chris eyed me. "Just give me another couple of seconds and this will all be over. You okay?"

"I'm fine." I wasn't. I didn't know if I would ever be fine again.

My mother was full-on babbling by that point. "She's normally not like this. She wasn't raised like this. Not by me, anyway."

He turned my mother around, took her other arm, and cuffed it too. Another agent came forward and took my mother by the forearm.

Chris turned to face me. "Want to put that gun down now?"

My mother tried again. "If you're looking for the whole story, you'll want to hear it from me. It's best not to listen to anything *she* says." As she was led away, she sent a glance back in my direction. "I'm sorry, Georgia Ann, but this is *not* how I raised you!"

I followed her out to a waiting car.

Chris came along too.

I just wanted to make sure that she didn't smile her way out of anything.

As we stood there, Sean walked into the yard. He was carrying

Sam, cupping our son's head so he wouldn't see his grandmother's disgrace.

There was a bigger show unfolding in front of us than there had been over on Gilman. The county police had barricaded the street at both ends. EMTs, FBI, and DoD—anyone with a badge and anything to do with foreign intelligence, domestic crimes, or emergency medicine showed up, lights flashing, sirens shrieking.

The police took a statement from me. They took one from Chris too. He'd lost sight of me in the crowds. Once he realized we were gone, he tracked the phone. When he saw that I'd dumped it, he had to scramble. He'd arrived just after my mother killed my father.

When they were done with Chris, he joined me on the periphery as I stood there—shadows behind me, lights before me—waiting. We were there together when my father's body was carried out and my mother was taken away.

As the car drove off, Chris shifted and began to speak. "You know, you did the right thing."

"Sean did the right thing first. He tried to tell people what he found out. But no one wanted to hear it."

He glanced at me, blue and red lights reflecting off the planes of his face. "How about this time I make sure it gets heard. By the right people in the right places."

I nodded. "Turns out Sean isn't dead."

"Yeah. I saw him." He tugged at the leather brim of his baseball cap.

"And you aren't the father of a fifth grader."

"No." He slanted another glance at me. "I was always on your side, though, Georgie."

"How did you know? About Sean?"

"We didn't. We suspected. And it seemed like if he was alive, eventually he'd let you know."

"You made a good shadow. You were always there."

"In real life I'm just a normal guy who made a deal with his elderly neighbor. I take her dog for a walk every morning, and in exchange she lets me take out her trash every week and play handy-man around her house once in a while."

I couldn't help smiling. "You're a nice man, Chris. If that's your real name."

"I can't really say."

Finally, the police and ambulances had gone. All the other agencies had followed and even Chris had ambled away. At the end, there was just Sean and Sam.

And me.

Sean stooped to let Sam down. As his feet touched the ground, he slipped his hand into Sean's and stretched the other one out toward me. And suddenly Sam and I were both caught up in Sean's arms, locked together in his tight embrace. "It's going to be all right now. Everything's going to be all right."

I broke down, sobbing.

Sam put a gentle hand to my cheek and patted it. "It's okay, Mommy." He slipped an arm around my neck in a hug and then laid his head on my shoulder. "It's like I said the whole time. Daddy was just in the wormhole."

79

Sean's resurrection was a seven-day wonder. We decided to tell everyone that he'd been on a confidential mission and that I'd been given misinformation about his death; it was just a big interagency screwup. It was a testament to how many people in Washington had spent time either doing secret stuff or pulling their hair out communicating between agencies that people accepted it as true.

Jim couldn't seem to stop slapping Sean on the back. June couldn't bear to see him with an empty plate. We spent several nights, the three of us, sleeping in their guest room bed before moving into a furnished apartment. There, we waited for the insurance company to settle the claim on the house while we tried to get used to the new universe in which we were living.

As I was emptying the dishwasher one night, my phone rang. The old one.

I fished it out of my pocket. "Georgia Brennan speaking."

"Georgie? Hey. It's Ted."

"Ted." Ted? It took me a moment to place him. Ted. My boss. From work. "Hi."

"Hey. Yeah. Well, we've got it all figured out."

"All what figured out?"

"How to cover you. We straightened it out. We can put you on another contract for a while. Yeah. So I was hoping you could come back in next Monday. Start up again."

Come back? Start up again? "No."

"What?"

"No. I said no. I can't." In that former lifetime, when I used to work for Ted, I would have added, "Sorry." But I wasn't, so I didn't. I hung up instead.

I'd been putting out some feelers in the world of quantum science. It was a small community, so it didn't take long for word to get out that I was looking for a job. I wanted to work with people who were willing to look at things with clear eyes and challenge their assumptions. I needed to be with people who pursued truth with the same passion that Washington pursued power.

As the story hit the news, Russia insisted that Hoffman was a rogue operative and that he was not, and never had been at any time ever, acting as a government agent. To their credit, cable TV news analysts were nearly unanimous in decrying that statement as false.

Hoffman started to talk. He was a longtime Russian plant. They'd created an East German cover story for him, allowing him to "escape" through the Berlin Wall in order to set him up as a sleeper agent in the West. He'd run my father for years.

He revealed the locations of the dead drops my father used to pass information back to him and the part my mother had played in passing those messages. I had been the bridge between them, but she had provided the signal. Key words in her Instagram posts let Hoffman know when my father had a message for him. Key words in the comments Hoffman left, under a false name, on her blog let them know when he had information for them.

The gray cars I'd been noticing had been both FBI tails and objects of my paranoia. It turns out 20 percent of cars in the US are silver or gray. The fact that the car the Russians drove, the one that had killed Edgars, and the one I had seen on the way to Mr. Wallace's were also gray? Pure coincidence.

My mother's relations in Mobile quietly began to put it around that what my mother had done just proved her ancestry. Why else would she have killed her own husband? Everyone knew her branch of the family was slightly odd. It went back to the beginning, to the family's colonial roots. The French had been there way back when, so was it really any wonder? Everybody knew you could never trust the French.

She would have hated knowing they were saying that.

I had told the FBI to look into deaths associated with the veterans of my father's old units. Eventually the news got out that there had been a purge of personnel who had served under him, and a web-based conspiracy began to gather steam. The claim was that a third party had been bumping people off in order to smear my father's reputation. The false-flag theory became a rallying cry for crazies and crackpots across the nation that winter. They thought it incomprehensible that my father would have done all those things people were whispering about. And on top of that, it just didn't make any sense to them. He was General JB Slater, for goodness' sake!

In spite of everything, I wanted to feel bad for my mom and dad. I thought I *should* feel bad for them. They were my parents, after all. And the only grandparents Sam had ever known. But I was never really their daughter. I'd been a prop, a useful tool in their espionage toolkit. And they'd stood by while the Russians tried to kill my husband, hurt my son, and silence me.

I settled instead on pity. And disgust.

I rebuffed all requests for interviews. A few extra-zealous reporters tracked me down, but I stopped answering my cell phone and refused to open the door to anyone. And after a while, people went back to the familiar comfort of believing what they wanted and left me alone.

The army offered Sean his old job, but he declined. He'd decided to write a book on my parents instead. He wrangled with the government over his security clearance, but considering that he wasn't really dead and that his clearance hadn't yet expired, he was allowed to keep it. That meant he could include much of what we'd discovered, although the book would have to be vetted by the appropriate authorities. Though the finer details of my parents' actions hadn't yet been released, enough clickbait was circulating—"Beauty Queen Killer!" "Hometown Boy Gone Bad!"—that it was generating buzz. Though the book wouldn't be published until summer, it was already breaking records for advance sales.

At one point he asked me what I thought had happened. How a four-star general, the quintessential boy next door from Arkansas, could have become one of the worst spies our nation had ever known. I told him that my father had gotten lost one dark and stormy night in Iraq and he'd never managed to find his way home.

Chris must have been good for his word, because in January the Senate Intelligence Committee asked me to testify, offering immunity in return. Several lawyers with high-powered Washington reputations reached out to offer their services. I interviewed them all and chose the one who laughed when I made a joke about the theory of relativity.

As I got dressed the morning of the first day of the hearing, I chose my clothes with care. I needed to dress in order to elicit the response I hoped for. If I wanted to be taken seriously, I needed to look like I took myself seriously.

My mother had taught me that.

For all intents and purposes, I was the sole survivor of the JB Slater family. I was the one entrusted with my father's legacy. In some respects, he'd been a good father. In all respects, he'd been a bad patriot. He used to tell me that you only offer an excuse if you've failed at your duty. That's how I looked on his justifications for collaborating with Hoffman: they were all excuses.

I'd only visited Jenn at work once or twice during all the years she'd spent on the Hill, so the maze of corridors in the Senate building was incomprehensible. As I walked deeper into the building, the bursts of camera flashes and the number of microphones shoved toward my face increased. My lawyer and her assistant played defense, clearing a path for me.

The hearing room was rife with cameras. As I sat behind a table at the front, most of them turned toward me. Though we'd asked for a closed hearing, the committee had denied the request.

Jenn's senator held a seat on the committee. His prematurely silver hair and those intensely blue eyes were instantly recognizable from the years he'd spent in government. As the chairwoman pulled the microphone toward her chest and began speaking, he looked at me.

I met Senator Rydel's eyes. Smiled.

A look of confusion marred his famously rugged features for a moment, as if he was wondering whether he knew me.

I was remembering the conversation I'd had with Jenn the night she was killed. After Rydel had read the information I'd provided, her father and mine had been in the same situation. The Russians had been able to blackmail them from one side and Jenn's senator from the other. But one thing had never been clear: Who was going to play that role, apply that pressure, to the senator? I hadn't yet mentioned his name to the FBI. With Jenn gone, he must have been thinking he was free and clear.

The chairwoman called the room to order and then introduced me to the committee.

As I scanned the senators sitting before me, incredibly, Jenn's senator winked at me.

"Ms. Brennan." The chairwoman smiled. "Don't worry. We don't plan to keep you long. Please rise and raise your right hand."

I stood.

"Do you affirm that the testimony you're about to give this committee is the truth, the whole truth, and nothing but the truth, so help you God?"

Did I ever.

AUTHOR NOTE

Several years ago I was listening to George Musser talk about his book *Spooky Action at a Distance: The Phenomenon That Reimagines Space and Time—and What It Means for Black Holes, the Big Bang, and Theories of Everything* on NPR. Something deep inside told me I *needed* to read this book. It's an instinct I've come to rely on. Long before I know what I'm going to write next, my subconscious is already at work on the story idea. So what else could I do but obey? Confession time: I am *not* a quantum physicist. I never even had the chance to take physics in high school. But I've never been able to choose my characters; they choose me. I did a lot of catch-up reading in order to weave physics into this book. It's no one's fault but my own if I didn't get it right.

Another subject that required research was the first Gulf War of the modern era. It took place from August 1990–February 1991. In response to Iraq's August 2 invasion of Kuwait, President George H. W. Bush authorized Operation Desert Shield on August 7. The United Nations Security Council gave Iraq's president a deadline of midnight on January 16, 1991, to withdraw from Kuwait. In the early hours of January 17, once the deadline lapsed, President Bush gave the order for the air offensive, Operation Desert Storm, to begin. Over 88,000 tons of bombs were dropped by coalition forces in over 100,000 sorties during a five-week period. The ground campaign, Desert Sabre (originally called Desert Sword), began on February 24. The ground war lasted only 100 hours before Iraqi resistance was destroyed and President Bush called for a cease-fire on February 28.

As mentioned in the story, General Franks, commander of the US Army's VII Corps, originally stressed that his troops should keep moving during the opening phase of the ground campaign and should not become decisively engaged with the enemy. Everyone was supposed to keep to the plan. When the order went out that evening to pause, it was puzzling; pausing was the one thing no one was supposed to do. But Franks was worried about the possibility of friendly fire that night.

The Soviets were indeed present in Iraq, prior to and during the war, as long-time Iraqi allies. They had trained and equipped the Iraqi army. Under Soviet President Gorbachev's leadership, the Soviet military had been obliged to retreat from Eastern Europe, and the defense budget had declined. The prestige the military had maintained during the decades of Soviet power was gone. Is it any wonder that they attempted to carve out a place of power for themselves behind the scenes as they worked to broker a peace treaty? But were the Soviets actually present in the desert to fight alongside the Iraqis as I depicted? Not that I could find. And not that anyone ever reported. That was purely a product of my imagination.

The Gulf War left Soviet credibility badly damaged. The Soviet weapons Iraqis used were no match for the coalition's technologically advanced arsenals. The military training the Soviets provided the Iraqis had only led to their defeat. There was an attempted coup in the USSR on August 18, 1991, led by the KGB. It weakened President Gorbachev's hold on power. By December 8, the USSR was officially dismantled. On December 25, Gorbachev was "demoted," becoming only president of Russia.

As I was developing this story, I knew JB Slater's betrayal had to do with something that happened in the desert during the ground war. I didn't spend too much time early on trying to figure it out because unexpected things always happen during wars. I trusted that during my research I would come across something, some incident, I could work into my plot. Imagine my dismay toward the end of my first draft when I was reminded that the war was an undisputed triumph, meticulously planned and executed, using the most technologically-advanced weapons. And it lasted a mere 100 hours from start to finish. Yikes! I was ready to shred the whole manuscript.

All my fears were allayed, however, when I read about the poor weather conditions that first day of battle. I have never been more delighted to see the words, "It was a dark and stormy night."

The underlying theme of this story is, of course, the search for truth. I've spent a lot of time the past three years thinking about the topic. It's been alarming to watch as truth has lost ground to opinion. As a culture we have decided to base our beliefs not on the meticulously crafted scaffolding of verifiable fact, but on the flimsy foundation of things we wish were true. Worse, we've decided that everyone can have their own truth. But if your truth isn't true for someone else, then by definition, it's not actually true.

We are all more than entitled to our own experiences, which in turn can shape our world views, but truth is something that cannot be modified by any of us. Truth exists in the wild; no one owns it. It just *is*—whether we like it or not, whether we want it or not. And it doesn't depend on any of us for its survival.

As a person to whom words matter very much, the devaluation of truth scares me. It should scare you too. But I also believe that a longing for truth is embedded in the human heart. And if truth really does exist independent of you and me, I have faith that our search must eventually lead us toward each other.

ACKNOWLEDGMENTS

Writing a novel is a group project. I am incredibly thankful that when I proposed the idea of a contemporary suspense novel to my agent, Natasha Kern, she didn't even blink. She encouraged me. I am even more incredibly grateful that when I sent her my best first attempt at this novel, she didn't cry. Instead, she told me how to make it better and then referred me to Jennifer Fisher of JSF Editing. I will always be grateful that this story found its way into her capable hands.

Jocelyn Bailey deserves more praise than I can possibly give her. This story was above my abilities in many ways, and there were multiple points at which I could have fallen down during the editing process, but she kept believing I could pull it off. Jocelyn's enthusiasm and encouragement for the story made me do my best not to let her down. And then Erin Healy helped take everything to the next level and showed me how to be a stronger, cleaner writer. I am also thankful to Jodi Hughes who shepherded this book through the final stages of the publishing process.

And that's just the start.

Ryan Carpenter graciously talked to me about being a military historian and took me on a tour of the Pentagon. Mike Phillips shared with me his personal experience of coming across a land mine during Desert Sabre. Any discrepancies between my words and their reality are my fault, not theirs.

I could not have completed this book without the friends and neighbors who never failed to ask me how things were progressing and who were unfailingly patient in listening to me tell this story again. And again. Ginger Garrett, Maureen Lang, and Anne Mateer, author friends and fellow travelers on this writing journey—all cheered and commiserated as they reminded me that I was not alone. Or going crazy.

Crucial to this process were the readers who kept asking when my next book was coming out. And if I was ever planning to write more contemporaries. At long last, I can tell you that I am!

And finally, and forever, my family must be thanked. My husband, Tony, answered my questions about everything having to do with technology, computers, the federal budget, and government contracts. And my own sweet girl patiently put up with me during the weeks when I wasn't quite tuned in to all that was going on around me because I was listening to the voices in my head.

DISCUSSION QUESTIONS

1. What sound, scent, or image never fails to take you back in time to a memory of a particular person, place, or experience?
2. How have you lived your life: with curiosity, in hot pursuit of the truth? Ambivalent toward the truth? Afraid of what you might discover if you found out the truth?
3. You may have heard the saying "all truth is God's truth." Do you agree?
4. Is truth good or bad? Moral or immoral?
5. How far will you go to pursue truth? At what point does the pursuit become too costly?
6. In Chapter 52, Georgie is grappling with whether she can trust Sean. "Everyone trusted someone until they realized they couldn't. Everyone thought they knew what love was until they discovered they didn't. Everyone thought they knew the truth until they found out it was a lie. But how do you let go of one to take hold of the other?" Have you ever clung to a person who wasn't trustworthy, a love that wasn't true, or an idea that wasn't honest? Why? What role do the head and the heart play in those calculations?
7. Have you ever had an experience that led you to question everything? How did you distinguish the truth from the lies?
8. One of the most difficult challenges we can face is to change a long-held belief to fit a newly acquired set of facts. It's less difficult to alter that new set of facts to fit the long-held belief. In other words, it's much easier to lie to ourselves than admit that we were wrong about something. Why do you think that is? Can you think of a time when this tension played out in your life? Which choice did you make?
9. How do you define the word *heroic*?

Photo by Tim Coburn

ABOUT THE AUTHOR

Siri Mitchell is the author of fourteen novels. She has also written two novels under the pseudonym of Iris Anthony. She graduated from the University of Washington with a business degree and has worked in various levels of government. As a military spouse, she lived all over the world, including Paris and Tokyo. Siri is a big fan of the semicolon but thinks the Oxford comma is irritatingly redundant.

SiriMitchell.com
Facebook: SiriMitchell
Twitter: @SiriMitchell